Discover the series you can't put down . . .

'A high level of realism . . . the action scenes come thick and fast. Like the father of the modern thriller, Frederick Forsyth, Mariani has a knack for embedding his plots in the fears and preoccupations of their time'

Shots Magazine

'The plot was thrilling . . . but what is all the more thrilling is the fantastic way Mariani moulds historical events into his story'

Guardian

'Scott Mariani is an ebook powerhouse'

The Bookseller

'Hums with energy and pace . . . If you like your conspiracies twisty, your action bone-jarring, and your heroes impossibly dashing, then look no further. The Ben Hope series is exactly what you need'

Mark Dawson

'Slick, serpentine, sharp, and very very entertaining. If you've got a pulse, you'll love Scott Mariani; if you haven't, then maybe you crossed Ben Hope'

Simon Toyne

'Hits thrilling, suspenseful notes . . . a rollickingly good way to spend some time in an easy chair'

A Today

THE CRUSADER'S CROSS

Scott Mariani is the author of the worldwide-acclaimed action-adventure thriller series featuring ex-SAS hero Ben Hope, which has sold millions of copies in Scott's native UK alone. His books have been described as 'James Bond meets Jason Bourne, with a historical twist'. The first Ben Hope book, *The Alchemist's Secret*, spent six straight weeks at #1 on Amazon's Kindle chart, and all the others have been *Sunday Times* bestsellers.

Scott was born in Scotland, studied in Oxford and now lives and writes in a remote setting in rural west Wales. You can find out more about Scott and his work on his official website: www.scottmariani.com

By the same author:

Ben Hope series
The Alchemist's Secret
The Mozart Conspiracy
The Doomsday Prophecy
The Heretic's Treasure
The Shadow Project
The Lost Relic
The Sacred Sword
The Armada Legacy
The Nemesis Program
The Forgotten Holocaust
The Martyr's Curse
The Cassandra Sanction
Star of Africa
The Devil's Kingdom
The Babylon Idol
The Bach Manuscript
The Moscow Cipher
The Rebel's Revenge
Valley of Death
House of War
The Pretender's Gold
The Demon Club
The Pandemic Plot

To find out more visit **www.scottmariani.com**

SCOTT MARIANI

THE
CRUSADER'S
CROSS

avon.

Published by AVON
A division of HarperCollins*Publishers*
1 London Bridge Street
London SE1 9GF

www.harpercollins.co.uk

HarperCollins*Publishers*
1st Floor, Watermarque Building, Ringsend Road
Dublin 4, Ireland

A Paperback Original 2021
1
First published in Great Britain by HarperCollins*Publishers* 2021

Typeset in Minion by Palimpsest Book Production Limited, Falkirk, Stirlingshire
Printed and Bound in the UK using 100% Renewable Electricity
at CPI Group (UK) Ltd

MIX
Paper from
responsible sources
FSC™ C007454

THE CRUSADER'S CROSS

PROLOGUE

Normandy,
Christmas Eve

After weeks of unusually low temperatures, even for the colder regions of the north of France, the anticipated snow-fall that had got everyone laying bets on whether or not there would be a white Christmas had finally hit with a vengeance earlier that day. Hour after hour it had been coming down thick and steady, blanketing the rural land-scape, in some places already drifting knee-deep and more. As evening came and a biting wind from the north-east chilled the temperature down still further, those sections of minor road that the local authorities had managed to keep clear became treacherously icy in places.

All in all, it wasn't the most ideal of nights for anyone to venture out in a car, let alone on a motor scooter. But it seemed that someone had been foolish enough to take that chance.

The three men who heard the sound of the crash were called Serge Fournier, Richard Desmarais and Michel St

Martin, members of the security team whose job it was to man the gates and, weather permitting, patrol the perimeter of the fenced compound. Their duties really existed only to satisfy the requirements of the training facility's insurers and the local police, given the activities that went on within the compound and the nature of some of the equipment stored there. Tucked away as the place was in this quiet and uneventful corner of rural Normandy, the need for a security guard team was little more than nominal.

The trio were all looking forward to spending a little time with their families over the festive season, but the nature of their employment was going to keep them duty-bound throughout most of it. They were used to such things, all three of them coming from a military background in which they'd spent more Christmases cooped up on army bases or hunkered down in hostile territory in a variety of war zones around the world than celebrating at home with their loved ones. By contrast, this was luxury. Despite the snow drifted up against its walls and layered thickly on the roof, the gatehouse's interior was as warm and cosy as any prefabricated security building was ever going to be. The men had a gas bottle heater roaring merrily in one corner, a stove with a pot of coffee permanently bubbling away in another, a snug little berth in the back for one of them to nap on during the night shift rotations, and they were comfortably insulated from the freezing conditions outside.

The crash happened at almost exactly 10.30 p.m., when all three men were awake and drinking coffee. Richard Desmarais was in the middle of sharing an amusing anecdote with his companions when the ominous and unmistakable crunch, followed by the clattering and grinding of something heavy and metallic sliding down the road, interrupted him mid-stream. It sounded as though it had happened not far from the gates.

'Shit! Did you hear that?' Serge said.

Richard put down his coffee mug and ran to the window, but there was nothing much to see out of it except the falling snow. 'Sounds like someone's in trouble.'

They were trained to respond fast to any emergency, and they wasted no time. Grabbing heavy coats, woollen hats and powerful torches from the hooks by the hut door, they raced outside. Jesus, it was turning into a bloody blizzard out here. They pulled up their collars and kept their heads down as the freezing wind drove the snowflakes into their eyes. The compound's gateway adjoined a narrow, twisty country road that went on for kilometres with hardly another property in sight. Its surface was neglected, potholed and fairly challenging even at the best of times but tonight it had become treacherous in the extreme, with a sheet of black ice that had formed right across from one verge to the other. Michel slipped and almost fell, windmilling his arms to keep his balance. 'Whoa. Watch your step, boys.'

'There!' Richard shouted, shielding his eyes from the snowflakes and shining his torch. The motor scooter had gone careening across the icy road and was jammed half in the far-side ditch at an angle with its rear wheel sticking up and still spinning. Serge's and Michel's bright torch beams sliced through the streaming flakes and quickly found the rider. He was sprawled flat on his belly in the middle of the road, his face turned away from them so all they could see was the back of his black helmet. His upper body appeared well padded by a heavy winter motorcycle jacket that was already becoming sprinkled with snow as he lay there, not moving. He couldn't have been travelling very fast, but an unlucky tumble even at low speeds still could be dangerous, even fatal.

Fearing the worst, slipping and sliding on the ice, the three security men ran towards him. Richard crouched down next to the inert body. 'Mate, are you okay? Can you hear me?'

To their relief, they saw that the rider was still alive. 'We need to get him inside the hut,' Michel said urgently. 'He's going to freeze to death out here!'

But Richard shook his head. 'No, you can't move him. Worst thing you can do. He could have a spinal injury and you end up paralysing the poor bastard.'

'We can't just leave him there!'

'I'll call an ambulance.' Richard stood up and was unzipping his parka to get at his phone when the three men and the body on the ground were suddenly washed with the glow of approaching headlights. The security team turned to face the lights, blinking, shading their eyes from the glare. The minivan rolled to a gentle halt, controlled and skilled. This driver knew what he was doing on ice. The poor guy on the scooter hadn't stood a chance of staying upright.

'What happened?' asked the driver, stepping out of the van and walking towards them. He was a tall man. He seemed quite sure-footed on the slippery surface.

Michel noticed that the driver spoke French with an accent. Italian, he thought, maybe. 'There's been an accident.

Guy came off his scooter. He's alive but we don't know how badly he might be hurt.'

As the driver stood silhouetted against the headlights it was hard to make out his features, except that he had dark hair and a long, thin face. Condensation billowed like smoke from his lips. It must have been warm in the vehicle but he was wearing a heavy winter coat and gloves. He looked over at the fallen rider. 'I hope he's all right, but he must be crazy. Who rides a scooter in this weather?' His passenger joined him and stood at the driver's shoulder, but said nothing. He, too, was wearing a thick parka, with his hands in his hip pockets.

'Do you folks carry a breakdown triangle or a road cone in your van?' asked Serge, thinking about ways they could warn any more approaching vehicles of the accident scene up ahead. Though it was unlikely they'd see any, in such conditions, at this time of night and on this night in particular, when everybody would be at home enjoying Christmas Eve. Two passing vehicles in the space of as many minutes was already an unusually high volume of traffic for the lonely stretch of road that passed the compound.

'I'm not sure,' said the driver. He turned to the passenger. 'Jacques, do we have anything like that?'

'I don't think so, Jean,' said the passenger. He spoke French with the same accent as the driver. 'I'll go and take a look in the back.'

While Serge was talking to them, Richard had got out his phone and was getting ready to dial 18 for Emergency Services.

That was when the scooter rider scrambled to his feet, with astonishing speed and miraculous agility for someone who, the instant before, had been supposed critically injured.

He reached into a pocket of his padded jacket and came out with a small CS gas spray gun that he aimed in Richard's face and fired. Richard dropped his phone and let out a yell of shock and pain as the pressurised stream of liquid tear gas spattered all over his face and into his eyes.

For half a second, Serge and Michel were too stunned to react. But the driver of the van and his passenger didn't appear in any way fazed by what had just happened. That was because they were involved. Before Serge or Michel could do a thing to stop it, the pair from the van pulled identical CS sprays from their own pockets and let rip.

CS gas is technically a powder. Aerosolised on release it makes contact with the skin and instantly becomes a potent acidic liquid that causes extreme burning pain, temporary blindness, respiratory difficulty and disorientation. The coordinated attack on the three security men rendered them completely helpless to defend themselves as, next, the van passenger and the scooter rider produced blackjacks from their jackets and stepped in quickly to club each of them over the head. Michel, doing all he could to fight back but quite incapacitated by the gas, was the first to hit the snowy road unconscious. He was followed a second later by Serge, and then Richard.

'Good job,' said the driver of the van, reverting now from French to their native language. The van's sliding side door had opened and the remaining three members of the gang stepped down onto the icy road carrying holdalls and gathered close to the driver. His name wasn't Jean, but César, César Casta. He was the leader of the gang and the planner of tonight's attack.

'We weren't expecting more than three on the gate,' Casta said. 'If there are any others inside, we'll deal with them.'

'There's the one in the farmhouse,' said the front seat passenger, whose real name was Pasquale di Borgo. 'The crippled guy.'

Casta smiled. 'Oh, that one. He won't be a problem. Ángel, not too banged up?'

Ángel Leoni was the member of the gang who'd been elected to ride the scooter the short distance from where the van had been waiting to the compound's entrance, where the staged accident was to take place. He was an expert motorcyclist, but even he couldn't have got much further than he had on the slippery road. The snow and ice were the one part of their plan that hadn't been anticipated, though it had added an extra element of realism. 'I'm fine,' he replied, taking off his helmet. He was wearing an extra layer of protective clothing under the thick bike jacket, and had suffered no more than a couple of bruises.

'All right,' Casta said. 'Masks on and let's get to work.'

They put on the black three-hole balaclavas that would hide their faces from the cameras inside the compound. The motor scooter was kicked and shoved all the way into the roadside ditch, where it wouldn't be seen. It was untraceable to them in any case, having been stolen days earlier. Then two men each grabbed a hold of Michel, Richard and Serge and dragged the unconscious bodies to the gatehouse, where they were laid side by side in a corner out of sight of the windows and securely bound up with thick plastic ties around their wrists and ankles, tight gags over their mouths for when they woke up.

While that was being attended to, Leoni and di Borgo opened one of the holdalls and took out the weapons. There was a loaded semi-automatic pistol for each member of the team, fitted with a long silencer. Casta had made it very clear what the guns were to be used for. This place was guarded by more than just men, and the gang were expecting to encounter that obstacle before long as they made their way into the compound.

'Not bad,' said one of the men, the new recruit, admiring his weapon with a fascinated glitter in his eyes. He racked its slide, chambering a round, and aimed the cocked weapon at the unconscious security guards. 'Let's see how well they work, shall we?'

'Put it away, Petru,' Casta snapped at him fiercely. 'That's not what we're here for.'

'I say we plug all three of them right now,' said the man called Petru. 'It's called operational security.'

'I said put it away,' Casta repeated. 'You know the rules. Break them, and you'll regret it.'

Petru met his leader's glare with a look of calm defiance. He didn't lower the gun right away. Then he shrugged and said, 'Whatever. You're the boss.' He stuck the weapon in his belt.

Casta kept the hard glare on the new guy for a moment longer, not much liking the cocky expression in his eyes. 'And I give the orders. You remember that.'

'Yeah. Right.'

Casta pulled the glare off Petru and turned to the others. 'Look for keys,' he ordered.

'I thought only the crippled guy had the keys,' said di Borgo.

8

'Check them anyway, just in case.' Which they did, but their search of the three unconscious guards and around the hut yielded nothing.

'Fine, then we'll make the crippled guy hand them over to us,' Casta said.

'What if he refuses?'

'Then we persuade him,' Casta said.

The compound's gates, as tall and strong as the wire mesh fence that circled the whole perimeter, were operated from a console near the security hut door. At the press of a button they whirred open. Di Borgo ran back to the van, drove it through the open gates and left it parked by the gatehouse where they would return for it later, with the key in the ignition as Casta had told him to. Inside the van were several more holdalls, empty and waiting to be filled with the loot the men had come here to plunder. While di Borgo was moving the vehicle, the team member called Carlo Cipriani was shinnying up the pole next to the gatehouse to snip the phone landline wire with a pair of long-handled cutters. Once that was all taken care of, the first phase of the invasion plan was complete. The second would be carried out on foot.

'Of all the shitty nights we could have picked,' di Borgo complained, brushing snow off himself.

'Stop your bitching,' Casta told him. 'We couldn't have asked for luckier weather. The whole damn place is cut off. And with this little device,' he added, reaching inside his backpack and taking out a box that looked like a radio transmitter, with multiple stubby antennas, 'it's even more cut off.' The device was a portable signal jammer that would kill all mobile phone reception inside a two-hundred-metre radius. 'Once we're inside, even if the crippled guy gets wind of us and tries to raise the alarm, he won't be able to.' Casta activated the jammer and tossed it back in the pack. 'Carlo, how are we doing with that landline wire?'

'Done and dusted,' replied Cipriani, showing him the wire cutters he'd used to cut the line.

'Good. Are we ready?'

'We're ready, boss.'

'Then let's do it.'

Casta turned off the lights and the gatehouse fell into darkness. Then, with him in the lead, the six men set off down the track that wound into the heart of the compound. Moving away from the gates they passed without a glance under the weathered metal sign that stood high overhead on two tall posts. In itself, the gate sign gave no indication of what this place was, or what purpose it served, though the intruders knew it precisely. The sign bore only the name. Two words.

It read: LE VAL.

10.46 p.m., Christmas Eve. The attack had begun.

Chapter 1

Jeff Dekker had been vowing and declaring for the last two days that he could smell snow coming, and eagerly challenging anyone who expressed doubt to put their money where their mouth was. Nobody would take his bet, however: in general Jeff's authoritative nose deserved its reputation for accuracy in those kinds of matters, as he'd successfully predicted the majority of white Christmases all through the time they'd lived here at Le Val. His friend and business partner, Ben Hope, had often joked that it was Jeff's former career as a naval commando with the Special Boat Service that had developed his uncanny olfactory powers by training him to sniff out icebergs and growlers from miles away across polar seas. Those days of active service were well behind him now, just like Ben's own years in 22 SAS – though the two men's current occupation was hardly an idle one by comparison.

Anyhow, if snow was coming, Ben was damned if he could tell. For the moment the sky was still blue, the birds were chirping in the bare trees, and the winter sun was shining palely down over the quiet, peaceful part of rural northern France that had been his and Jeff's home and workplace for the last several years. It had been just the two of them, to begin with, working with a variety of assistants and helpers who came and went. Later they'd been joined by a former British Army sniper called Tuesday Fletcher, a cheerful yet highly capable younger man of Jamaican origin, who was now as much a part of the core team at Le Val as its two founders.

The tactical training centre was a curious kind of business enterprise to have come to exist in an agricultural area mostly devoted to dairy farming, apple growing and the resulting production of delicious Normandy cheeses and cider. Strangers to the area might have wondered at the tall security fence that bordered a long, long stretch of the lonely little road, and the secure entrance with the gatehouse manned around the clock by security guards. The place could have been taken for a military camp, or some kind of training centre for the local gendarmerie – an impression easily confirmed by the sounds of gunfire that were frequently to be heard coming from deep inside the fenced compound. Locals were quite used to it by now, and any curiosity they might once have felt concerning the presence of the facility within their midst had long since faded. Meanwhile Le Val's directors and staff had been fully accepted into the community. People in these parts were especially warm, generous and welcoming, once they got to know you – and even if you *were* a Brit – and Ben, Jeff, Tuesday and the rest of the team were all well liked by the residents of Saint-Jean and Valognes, which were the local village and the nearest town.

All the more reason, then, for Ben to receive so much genuine concern and sympathy as he hobbled through the streets of Valognes that cold, sunny morning. Almost everywhere he went he was accosted by familiar faces, all wanting to know what had happened to him. There were only so many times he could repeat the story of how he'd come to be limping around with a crutch and a foot in plaster. The whole business was getting a bit tiresome and it couldn't be over soon enough for him.

He'd suffered far worse injuries in his time, though none so foolish and annoying as the accidental fracture he'd suffered in late November. At least the automatic gearbox on his new car, a blue BMW Alpina D3 that was a replacement for the one he'd utterly destroyed earlier that year (not an unusual event in Ben's life), allowed him some freedom as he could drive around with just one foot. He had to be grateful for the fact that it was the left ankle that had been broken.

Ben's constant companion during his convalescence from the accident had been Storm, his long-time favourite of the German shepherd dogs who, technically, were required to earn their keep patrolling the Le Val compound. Storm had allocated himself a break from his guard duties in order to take care of his beloved master, shadowing Ben's every limping step. The dog was used to lounging about in the back of a big Land Rover Defender and didn't quite so much appreciate the confines of the Alpina's rear seat, but it seemed that nothing could tear him from Ben's side.

Ben's purpose for coming into town that morning was to collect a prescription for more painkillers, fairly heavy-calibre stuff that the little village pharmacy in Saint-Jean didn't stock. He disliked taking them, but they helped. All the years he'd let the army pump all manner of drugs and vaccines into him without a word of complaint; why worry about a few little pills? It was only liver damage, after all.

After his visit to the pharmacy, a place where he wasn't as well known and therefore hadn't had to tell the story of his injury, he set off down the busy street to another place where he *was* known, and likely *would* have to. The place in question was a small bar and brasserie belonging to his old pal Marcel Boisrond, who not only served an excellent croque monsieur toasted sandwich but also had no problem letting dogs into his establishment. That made him one of the good guys, in Ben's book.

As it happened, when Ben hobbled into the brasserie he discovered that Marcel wasn't around. Working the bar in his place was a slim, dark-haired woman who was maybe a dozen or fifteen years younger than Ben. He hadn't seen her before and thought she must be a recent hire. He limped up to the bar, rested his crutch against the polished wooden top, and gestured for Storm to sit. At the wordless command the dog instantly went down on his rump.

It was a fairly rare thing for Ben Hope to walk into a bar and not order his habitual single malt scotch – Marcel actually kept a bottle of ten-year-old Laphroaig in stock especially in case Ben might pay a visit. But it was a little early in the day for the hard stuff, so Ben ordered a black coffee and a glass of water to wash his pills down with. His French was extremely fluent and his accent so faint that he often managed to pass for a native. The barmaid said she'd bring them over to him. He thanked her, picked up his crutch, released the dog from his sit and made his way over to their usual table as she attended to the coffee machine. She wasn't being particularly talkative, and Ben thought he understood the reason why.

He had always been a highly perceptive man, and his natural observational skills were honed by his Special Forces training and subsequent experience. In the few short moments he'd spent standing at the bar, he'd made three particular observations: the first of them of no real consequence at all, the second only slightly more so, and the third more so again, which was related to the second in a way that made him aware of an uncomfortable dynamic going on in the bar.

All of which told Ben that trouble was about to kick off.

Chapter 2

Ben's first and most innocent observation was the little sprig of mistletoe hanging above the counter, a pleasing Christmassy touch seldom seen much nowadays. The second was the group of young English guys, seven of them, tourists he assumed, occupying a table at the side of the bar room and making a good deal of noise. They'd no scruples about drinking beer before lunchtime, and had evidently knocked down quite a bit of it. Ben often found the behaviour of a certain type of British traveller abroad to be as embarrassing to him personally as it was obnoxious to the locals. That in itself wouldn't have concerned him so much, if it hadn't been for his third observation, namely the frown on the barmaid's face and the way she kept glancing nervously in the direction of the group.

Ben reached his usual table in the corner, propped up his crutch once more and lowered himself into a chair. It was his usual table because it gave him a view of the whole room, the door and the street outside. Ben always liked to have a vantage point like that, wherever he went. Force of habit, pretty much instinctive after half a lifetime spent watching your back in the likely event of very real extreme danger. The dog laid himself down flat on the floor by the table. Ben found a piece of training treat in his pocket and chucked it down for him.

A few moments later, the barmaid came over carrying the tray with Ben's coffee and a small carafe of water with a glass. She offered him a smile as she set it down, and he thanked her again. He noticed the way her smile disappeared as she turned to walk back to the bar, passing the British guys' table. He also noticed the way they all stared as she went by, craning their necks to ogle her and exchanging stupid, wolfish grins and knowing looks.

Idiots. But they weren't his concern. He opened a pack of painkillers, tapped out two pills, knocked them back with some water and then reached for his coffee. Black and strong and rich. Best coffee in town. He leaned back and savoured it slowly, one sip at a time, waiting for the meds to relieve the ache in his foot and ankle.

Outside the brasserie window, the traffic rumbled by on the slushy road and the townsfolk of Valognes went back and forth doing their Christmas shopping. But Ben wasn't watching any of that happening. There were other things going on inside to draw his attention. As he sat there with the dog at his side, he observed one of the Brits at the other table get up and go over to the bar, where the barmaid was polishing glasses. Every group of young men has to have an alpha male; and the lower the general IQ level and the higher the lad factor in that group, the more of a moron that alpha male is likely to be. This guy was a prime example. His face was redder than his hair and his arse was hanging out of

17

his pants as he rose from their table with a 'Watch this' kind of look and went swaggering up to the bar and leaned his fleshy bulk on the counter top. 'Miss? Oy, Miss? *Pardonnay moi*, Mademoiselle.'

'I speak English,' she replied, if only to save him from his terrible French.

'Come here, darling,' he said with a grin. After a moment's hesitation and another frown she reluctantly put down the glass she'd been polishing and stepped closer to the counter. The guy's friends were all watching intently and suppressing guffaws as their alpha male beckoned to her and said, 'Come closer.'

She stiffened and came a step closer, the way a person would step closer to a rotting corpse.

'Me and the boys would like another drink. But seeing as we've been spending so much cash in this place, I'd like a favour from you as well.'

'What is that?' she asked him.

He pointed a chubby finger up at the sprig of mistletoe that hung above the bar. 'Know what that is?'

She nodded, said nothing.

'See, in my country, at Christmas a guy can ask a pretty young lady for a kiss under the mistletoe and it's bad luck if she refuses. That's, like, tradition, yeah?'

The barmaid eyed him suspiciously. 'So?'

'So it's Christmas,' he said. A loud snigger came from his table. 'I'm asking for a kiss. You have to say yes.'

'This is not the tradition in France,' she replied. Standing her ground, arms folded.

'But you know how to give a guy a kiss, yeah? Bet you've

given plenty of nice French kisses before. Come on, darling. It's my birthday. Me and the boys are here to enjoy ourselves and I'm asking for a kiss to make me happy.'

'You want another drink?' she asked, reaching for a clean glass and sticking it under a beer tap. 'Birthday boy will get a special drink, but no kiss. I already have a boyfriend. Kisses are only for him.'

'Come on, bitch,' he said, grabbing for her arm. 'All I'm asking for is—'

And then the half-poured beer was in his face. He recoiled from the bar, spluttering and gasping. 'Oh, you fucking slut!'

Ben hadn't been the only one in the room watching this moron's behaviour with growing annoyance. Storm was picking up on the building tension, and had sat up on his haunches, frozen absolutely still and rigid, all his senses fixed on the source of the trouble. Ben hadn't officially put him in a *down*, or else the dog wouldn't have moved at all. At this point, a small hand signal was enough to command him to remain sitting.

The moron stood dripping with beer and seething at the barmaid. His friends were in an uproar over the unfair treatment this ungrateful French chick had dished out to their mate, and he wasn't about to lose face in front of them. This was how things escalated. Ben had seen it so many times. And so he broke the sequence, the best way he knew how.

He called out, 'Hey, you.'

The moron turned away from the bar and stared across the room. 'Are you talking to me?'

'Yes, I am,' Ben said. 'And I strongly suggest you go and sit down before you get more trouble than you can handle.'

But of course, the moron didn't do that. He did what all morons do, and have been doing since the beginning of recorded history. He bunched his fists by his sides and screwed his face into an angry scowl and began walking across the floor towards Ben. He eyed the plaster on Ben's foot and the crutch propped against the wall. The scowl on his face spread into a smirk and he suddenly had more of a swing to his step.

Which, considering the fact that Ben wasn't alone, and especially considering the kind of companion he had with him, was a serious error of judgement.

'What're you going to do, gimp? Hit me with your crutch?'

Ben said, 'The argument's not between you and me. It's between you and him.' He pointed at Storm.

The guy's eyes darted to the dog, then back to Ben. 'You can't bring dogs in here.'

'He's a guide dog,' Ben replied.

A fresh snigger appeared on the guy's face. 'What, are you blind as well as crippled?'

'He's a different kind of guide dog,' Ben said. 'One whose job it is to guide you and your friends on a better path through life.'

'Oh, yeah? What better path?'

'The path to freedom and enlightenment,' Ben said. 'In your case, it leads straight out of that door and back out into the street. You still have time to follow it. That is, if you want to walk out of here intact.'

But some people really were beyond educating. 'I'm not going anywhere, dickhead. You want some of this?' The moron darted back towards the bar and snatched up the empty glass whose contents the young woman had flung into his face. 'I'll be having words with you later,' he promised. 'After I'm done with this bastard here.' He cracked the rim of the glass against the back of a chair, splintering it into a jagged spike.

Ben didn't move from his chair. His voice was calm. 'That was provocative. We don't like provocation, do we, Storm?'

The dog made no reply, but it was clear to all what he was thinking.

'That dog comes near me, I'll slash its stupid throat.'

'You want to find out what'll happen if he comes near?' Ben said. 'I only have to say two words. Here's the first.' He spoke to the dog. 'Storm; *ready*.'

At the sound of the command, Storm was instantly up on his feet. Ninety-five pounds of lean muscle, fur and teeth, ears pricked and tail carriage high, eyeing the moron with unblinking focus. The moron stopped in his tracks.

'Don't think of it as a dog,' Ben said. 'Think of it as an advanced weapons system. One that's completely safe and harmless until I pull the trigger. But if I do, it can run three times as fast as you can, and you can say goodbye to the road to enlightenment. It'll be the road to the hospital to get your balls sewn back on. That is, if my friend here hasn't already eaten them. There's no training command for "spit them out". Even if there were, they wouldn't be much use to you half chewed up.'

'I'm not scared of no fucking hound dog,' said the guy, but without the least shred of conviction.

'One more word from me,' Ben told him, 'and you're a eunuch. Or else you and your pals are gone in the time it takes me to finish this last bit of coffee. Your choice, fella.'

There wasn't much left in Ben's cup and it took him less than a minute to drain it. Twenty seconds before the cup was empty, there were seven fewer people in the bar room. The alpha-male moron was first to hurry out of the door, tripping over himself in his haste to preserve what little dignity he had left and swiftly followed by his friends. Ben watched through the window until the group had slunk sullenly off down the street and disappeared.

'Thank you for what you did,' said the barmaid, coming over with a little brush and a scoop to clear up the broken glass.

'I didn't do anything.'

'Then I should be thanking him,' she said. She laid down the cleaning things and crouched down to pet the dog, who'd suddenly become as malleable as a puppy and loved the attention he was getting from her. 'He's beautiful.' Looking back up at Ben with a smile. 'My name's Nathalie.'

'He's Storm. I'm Ben.'

'No, please. Don't get up. Your poor foot. What happened to it?'

'Just a knock. I'll live.'

'I hope it gets better soon.' She added, 'When you came in here, I didn't know you were English.'

'Half Irish,' he replied. 'But this is home now.'

'Here in Valognes?'

'No, out in the sticks, near Saint-Jean.'

'I moved to Valognes recently,' she said, flicking her long dark hair. 'Living with my mother and two cats. It's only temporary.'

'Until you and your boyfriend find a place?'

She shook her head and smiled. 'I don't have a boyfriend. That's just what I tell certain kinds of dicks who come in here. Would you like a drink? It's on the house.'

'Thanks, but I'll be on my way. I don't think those gentlemen will bother you any longer.' The painkillers had relieved the ache in his ankle about as much as they were going to. He hauled himself out of his chair, silently cursing that bloody plaster, and grabbed his crutch.

'*Joyeux Noël*,' Nathalie said with a smile as he was leaving.

Ben was heading out of the door when his friend Marcel, the proprietor, suddenly appeared carrying a box of catering supplies. They greeted one another, and then Marcel noticed the plaster and said, 'What the hell happened to you?'

And Ben had to tell the whole damn story all over again.

Chapter 3

The sorry tale of how Ben had broken his ankle all began with the excavation project at Le Val that had been planned for several months, and finally got started late that autumn.

The original plot of land that Ben had purchased together with the farmhouse years ago, when he was first setting up his new tactical training facility, covered an area of thirty or so acres which had since expanded considerably as the business grew. Within the grounds lay a patch of ancient forest, dating back to pre-Roman times when this whole region would have been covered in deep, thick woodland filled with wild boar, roving packs of wolves and perhaps even the occasional European brown bear. More recently than that, somewhere around the time when William the Conqueror was marshalling his invasion force to set sail for England, a church had been built at the heart of the woodland.

Over the centuries that followed, the growth of the population and the resulting clearing of the land to make way for agriculture had decimated all but a tiny fraction of the vast tracts of forest. But Ben's patch had survived, and within it the ruins of the church still stood. Various sections of wall remained, some of them only knee-high, others intact enough to show where the original roof beams had rested. Stained glass, slates and stones had all been heavily pillaged through time and some of that stolen material had probably found its way into the construction of the older parts of the nearby village of Saint-Jean. The most impressive remaining feature of the ancient church was the surviving section of its round tower. At one time the tower might have stood forty or fifty feet in height, overlooking the trees and topped by a castellated belfry with arched windows all around. The circular walls had partly crumbled away long, long ago, but it didn't take too much imagination to picture it in its glory days.

Ben had always been a runner, a climber and a hiker, as well as being a man who loved and sought out the quieter, wilder places in the world, and from the earliest days at Le Val he'd formed the habit of running at least five miles a day through the fields and woods surrounding his home. As the beaten path through the trees was part of his habitual cross-country circuit, he'd very often pause to sit among the church's crumbled remains and bask in the peacefulness of the place while indulging his habit of smoking a Gauloise or two. More often than not, these quiet, reflective moments were shared by Ben's running-mate, Storm, who would be curled up at his feet or else sniffing for rabbits in the undergrowth.

Aside from just enjoying its presence Ben had always been fascinated by the history of the ruined old church. And in recent years he'd become increasingly concerned that the ingress of creeping ivy, tree roots and other invasive vegetation was eventually going to claw away all that was left of the ancient mortar, prise apart stone from stone and level its remaining walls and the round tower into featureless rubble. The forest had a life of its own that way, patiently and inexorably reclaiming the ground that man had taken from it. Millions of years from now, it might well be that every last trace of human civilisation, here and all across the planet, would have been consumed and erased by the forces of nature. There was little even Ben Hope could do to prevent that from happening; but while he was still here, while it was still within his power to do something about it, he hated to stand by and watch such a precious piece of history be slowly destroyed.

And so, after consulting with a specialist archaeological restoration firm based outside Paris that September, it had been decided that the old church should be rescued before it was too late, and sympathetically restored to at least some semblance of its former splendour. After two months of wading through all the necessary red tape, working out costs, conducting initial surveys and obtaining permissions, in early November the team from Paris, led by an amiable Dutch-Belgian archaeologist called Jacques de Klerk, had rolled in and set up a base of operations in one of the prefabricated huts used for running classes at Le Val.

The excavation project had to be extremely delicate and careful – Ben had no intention of letting anyone rip his beloved ancient woodland to pieces. He'd become deeply involved not only in the historical research process but in the physical task at hand, and when his busy working schedule allowed for it he was often to be found on site with the team members, whom he'd got to know well.

The detective work of de Klerk's restoration experts soon revealed that this wouldn't be the first time the old church had been rebuilt. While its most venerable parts could be confirmed to date back at least a couple of centuries longer, to the time of the Norman Conquest, other areas of stonework had been added sometime during the twelfth century, around the period of Christendom's second and third crusades against Saracen-held territories in the Holy Land. The heyday of the Knights Templar. The sieges of Jerusalem and Damascus. Just to touch the stonework and imagine oneself being transported back to those epic times of history was enough to make Ben's head spin.

But that was nothing compared to the mind-blowing revelation that was to come.

It began innocently enough, with the discovery by de Klerk's team of a mysterious hole in the ground within the footprint of the church. It was roughly circular and about two feet in diameter, covered with a large boulder that had obviously been there for centuries, completely overgrown by a thick mass of thorns. After they'd rolled the boulder away to expose the mouth of the hole, Ben and the team had been scratching their heads wondering what it was – a well or drain of some kind, had been their first idea.

They were about to find out that it was much more than that.

To help them in their geophysical survey the archaeology team had brought along a GPR or ground-penetrating radar device. Gone were the days when delicate and irreplaceable archaeological sites couldn't be properly investigated without resorting to the time-honoured but potentially horribly destructive use of shovel and pick. The hi-tech wizardry of the device now allowed time detectives to gain a pretty accurate idea of what lay hidden under their feet without disturbing so much as a blade of grass. On one previous excavation project the team had used it to locate lost burial chambers dating back to the time of Charlemagne. It had its limitations, de Klerk warned Ben – it wasn't great at detecting anything made of wood, and it also worked better with some soil types than others.

But they were lucky. And they were astounded, as the radar showed them what was buried under Ben's church ruins. Masked by dirt and layers of old vegetation the mysterious hole was, in fact, a stone-lined shaft that descended diagonally to a depth of about ten feet, levelled out and continued underground away from the building.

'This is no drain,' de Klerk said. 'And it's not a cellar either. This is a tunnel.'

Chapter 4

It soon turned out that de Klerk was right. As they'd carefully dug out the mouth of the shaft, easily wide enough for a person to fit into, they'd found stone steps leading downwards. Ben was the first to venture down there, despite de Klerk's warnings about the possibility of sudden collapse and getting buried under tons of dirt.

But Ben was too intrigued not to take the risk. He was accompanied by Storm, who refused to stay put as his master descended the steps. When he reached the bottom the mouth of the shaft was several feet above his head. Nobody had been down here in some thirty generations, maybe even longer.

As the floor levelled out beneath him Ben brushed away centuries of cobwebs, shone his torch and found himself in a dark, damp horizontal sort of mine-shaft. Underfoot were the type of cobblestones that had been used to pave medieval streets. The walls were rounded and lined with some kind of rough mortar, crumbling in places where it was pierced with tree roots and damaged by moisture, but otherwise surprisingly well preserved. Ben was reminded of the secret tunnels he'd known beneath an Alpine monastery where he'd once spent several months. Never in his wildest imaginings could he have thought something like this could have existed here at Le Val, right under his feet all this time, on his own land. Breathless with excitement at their discovery, he'd followed the course of the tunnel for nearly thirty yards until his torch beam hit a solid wall of earth and stone where the roof had caved in up ahead, and he was forced to turn back.

Undeterred, the team reverted to the magic of the GPR underground scanner to determine the path the tunnel took beyond that point. Back at the Le Val classroom that had been turned into the project's command centre, the data from its readings was collated on a digital map grid that allowed them to chart its exact route. To everyone's amazement, even the normally unflappable de Klerk's, the reconstructed image showed it leading right under the woods. It cut an almost perfectly straight line, diverting at one point to avoid a subterranean stream that nobody had ever known was there until now, and from there all the way to the farmhouse itself.

Ben couldn't believe that he had a secret passage attached to his house. More investigation using the now-indispensable GPR device pinpointed its entry point in the vaulted stone wine cellar at the rear of the building. Thinking it might be possible to enter the tunnel from that side, Ben, Jeff and Tuesday Fletcher had spent hours hunting for its mouth and digging and scraping at the stone wall. To their disappointment they found that the wine cellar end of the tunnel had partially subsided, too, leaving only a narrow crawl-space almost too small for an adult human to get through. To widen it would have meant attacking the house foundations, and Ben reluctantly gave up on the idea.

'It's an escape tunnel,' de Klerk said. 'That's the only possible explanation for why anyone would have built such a thing. During troubled times in history – and God knows there have been enough of those – priests could have taken refuge from attackers, and fled from the church to the house.' Correcting himself, he added, 'Or, I should say, to whatever kind of building originally existed on its site, given that the farmhouse is only a couple of hundred years old. Tunnels like this were a common enough feature of medieval architecture. For those who knew their secret, they were literally a life-saver. And this is one of the best-preserved examples I've ever come across. It's like finding hidden treasure.'

Before too long, de Klerk's words would come to assume a whole new meaning.

Around this time a new player had become involved in the intrigue. Ben had first met Victor Vermont the previous year, quite by chance in the village post office in Saint-Jean, and after a couple more social encounters had been invited back to Victor's home for a glass of his home-made apricot brandy: particularly fine stuff, as it happened. Victor was in his eighties, just about old enough to be Ben's grandfather, but despite the age gap between them, a lasting friendship had developed.

Victor was originally from these parts, having been born right here in Saint-Jean on the very day that World War II broke out, but had moved away as a young man to pursue a career as a museum curator. In that capacity he'd worked for many years in some of France's most historic towns, including Rouen and Amiens, as well as abroad. On his retirement, he'd returned to his birthplace and bought a rambling old house half a mile outside the village, which he'd set about turning into a veritable Aladdin's cave of art and antiquities, books and musical instruments collected over a lifetime. Ben had never known anyone so expert on history, especially medieval history, of which Victor possessed an encyclopaedic knowledge. He was also a lover of good wine and whisky, the owner of a collection of rare single malts that Ben especially appreciated. Age had only sharpened his wits: he was virtually unbeatable at chess, and he could play both volumes of Bach's *Well-Tempered Clavier* entirely from memory on the antique Kriegelstein grand piano that took pride of place in his salon. But for all his scholarly ways Victor loved nothing more than laughter and companionship. As fit as a fiddle, he walked or cycled the half-mile into Saint-Jean each day to do his shopping, share jokes with old friends he'd known since the 1950s, and chat up Madame Charpentier, the elderly widow who ran the village post office. She was four years his junior and they'd been childhood sweethearts; still besotted with her, Victor had confided to Ben that his long-term aim was to persuade the old girl to marry him. Ben wished his friend all the luck in the world.

Ben had always passively intended to find out more about the history of his home. Now that his curiosity had been sparked by the excavation project, it was to Victor that he'd turned in the hopes of learning more. The old curator was only too happy to offer his help. He was as intrigued by the archaeologists' discoveries as Ben was, and enthusiastically dived into piecing together other aspects of Le Val's past.

While Victor was burying himself deep in the kinds of obscure archives that only a wily old history buff like himself would even know existed, Ben had been getting more and more involved with the archaeological restoration project. By mid-November, de Klerk's team had carefully cleared away enough debris and tree roots from around the site to begin work on the church walls. The projected costs were spiralling, but Ben didn't care. The heap of reward money he'd been gifted by an Omani billionaire, Tarik Al Bu Said, in return for recovering a magnificent stolen diamond called the Star of Africa, had been sitting unused and half-forgotten in an account for years, waiting for the day he had something worthwhile to spend it on. That day had now arrived.

Progress had been slow, though. Everyone knew that sooner or later the winter weather might close in and force them to call a break to the project. In the meantime, Ben was determined to crack on both with rebuilding the church walls, and with reopening the tunnel. On a cold but sunny Tuesday in late November the first shipment of specialist building materials finally arrived. As the crane and the JCB roared and rattled in the background Ben was at work digging out the collapsed section of tunnel that had prevented him from being able to explore any deeper. Every shovelful of dirt had had to be removed by hand, because the structure was just too delicate to risk bringing in the heavy machinery. It was back-breaking work – but at last, on the afternoon of November 27th, a day Ben would remember for more than one reason, he was able to clamber back down into the newly opened section of tunnel and resume exploring.

And that was where he'd found the secret crypt.

More importantly, what was inside it.

Chapter 5

The crypt was a small stone chamber that had shown up on the GPR readings without anyone being able to figure out exactly what it was. De Klerk's best preliminary guess had been that it might be an anteroom used by the tunnel's builders for storing tools or materials like cobblestones and mortar, to avoid having to go all the way back to the mouth of the tunnel each time for resupplies. Or maybe as a nook for one exhausted team of workers to rest in for a few hours, out of the way, while another took their place.

And either of those might indeed have been its original purpose – but later, once the tunnel was finished, it had been put to another use. As a hiding place for something that someone in the past had valued so highly that they wanted nobody to find it. It had worked. For nearly nine hundred years, that precious item had remained perfectly concealed from the world.

He found the oblong casket raised off the floor on a block of stone, placed there presumably to protect it from the worst of the dampness. It was about three feet in length, two in width and one high, made of ancient oak now so decayed with age that it was almost falling apart as Ben carried it back up the steps to the mouth of the tunnel. It was far heavier than it should be for its size. What the hell was inside?

Seeing Ben emerge from the shaft with the mysterious object in his hands, de Klerk and Dupeyron, who was operating the JCB a few yards away at the top of a ramped incline of earth and rocks, instantly stopped what they were doing and came running over.

Ben laid the heavy casket on the ground, his arms straining with the weight. As they crouched there examining it, the rotted oak box completely fell apart to reveal the sealed lead compartment inside.

'We shouldn't open it here,' de Klerk said. 'Whatever's inside could be extremely sensitive to air and humidity. Twelfth-century scrolls, or some religious relic—'

But even as de Klerk said it, Ben had found, and accidentally pressed, the ingenious spring-loaded release mechanism. The heavy lid fell away, along with fragments of sealing wax dried and brittle with age. The box seemed to give a reluctant hiss as its contents breathed the air and saw the daylight for the first time after having lain hidden in the dark for so many centuries.

'Holy crap, will you look at that?' said Dupeyron, staring bug-eyed.

Inside the casket, the leather bag that had contained it all eaten away, was a large cross. It wasn't just any old wooden crucifix, because that wouldn't have survived the ravages of time either. As Ben lifted it out, feeling the hefty weight of it in his hand, the glitter of gold flashed brightly in the sunlight and the rubies and emeralds inset into the crosspiece sparkled vivid red and green along with other precious stones Ben couldn't put a name to. The lettering cut into the solid gold was medieval Latin script, still as crisp and sharp as the day it had been engraved.

Ben had seen nothing quite like it before, still less held anything like it in his hand. It was beautiful.

And in that moment, its beauty was Ben's undoing as he crouched there in the dirt gazing at the magnificent object in his hands. He was so transfixed that the sudden yell of 'Look out!' seemed to echo from some faraway place, not part of his current reality. He was peripherally aware of de Klerk and Dupeyron scattering in opposite directions, and as he looked up in alarm a fraction of a second later, of something huge rumbling towards him: the massive front end of the JCB with its dirt-clogged steel shovel raised up just high enough to see the screen of the driverless cab behind it, coming straight for him like a runaway locomotive.

He scrambled out of the way, clutching the cross, and narrowly managed to avoid getting crushed by the edge of the shovel and the clattering caterpillar tracks by flinging himself into the dirt with his legs outflung. The JCB came rolling by, inches from his feet, and collided with a grinding crash into a stack of big, square grey stone blocks, each too heavy for one man to lift, left there ready for the rebuilding of the wall.

That was enough to stop the vehicle's freewheeling momentum, but the force of the impact dislodged a large stone from the top of the stack. Ben watched, as though in slow motion, as the stone spun off its perch and toppled down, hit another and bounced, tumbling end over end in space. Seeing it coming right at him he writhed out of its path, but he wasn't quick enough to get his whole body out of the way in time. The heavy stone landed on his left ankle, rolled off and came to a rest in the dirt.

Ben simultaneously felt the crunch and heard the snap. The pain didn't come right away. When it did, it was excruciating.

'I'm so sorry!' Dupeyron was babbling over and over again. 'I mustn't have pulled the handbrake on properly!'

The Le Val team used walkie-talkies to communicate with one another across the compound. De Klerk got on Ben's and radioed Jeff Dekker, who promptly came roaring and bouncing over the rough ground in his Ford Ranger pickup. 'It's busted clean, mate,' was his instant diagnosis when he carefully inspected the injured ankle.

'Don't be stupid,' Ben protested through gritted teeth. 'It's just a bit of a sprain. Let me get up. I can manage.'

Jeff had seen this routine before, and he wasn't having any of it. With a steely eye he warned, 'You try walking on that foot, me old mucker, and you'll wish you hadn't. Now stay the fuck still and behave yourself while I call for an ambulance.'

If there was one man in this world with whom Ben knew better than to argue, it was Jeff Dekker. Relenting, he pointed over at the cross, which de Klerk had picked up and was examining it with something like awe in his eyes. 'Look what we found, Jeff,' Ben said.

'Yeah, very nice,' Jeff replied with barely a glance at it. He took out his phone.

There wasn't much that Ben could do but sit there on the ground and wait for help. Storm stayed by his side the whole time, whining and licking his face, the big golden eyes peering down at him full of anxiety. Ben patted his shaggy head. 'Don't you worry about me, boy,' he reassured the dog, holding his voice steady against the pain. Dupeyron had retreated to the sidelines, looking drawn and wringing his hands with guilt, but Ben had forgiven him already. Jeff, maybe not so much.

Thirty minutes later, Jeff had lost patience waiting for the ambulance. 'Fuck this for a laugh,' he grumbled. 'I'm taking you to the hospital myself. And not to those local bloody quacks, either.'

'Not Cherbourg,' Ben tried to protest.

'Yes Cherbourg, and don't be an awkward sod about it either.'

Grabbing some lengths of construction timber and a roll of duct tape from the back of the pickup, Jeff quickly fell back on his Special Forces medic training and made an emergency field splint for Ben's ankle. They loaded him carefully into the pickup with the passenger seat inclined back. 'I suppose that bloody hound of yours wants to come too,' Jeff grumbled. By way of a reply, Storm jumped into the rear of the crew-cab.

Jeff made the drive to Cherbourg in just over twenty minutes, pushing hard through the traffic and honking his horn aggressively at anything in his path. The emergency room nurses were already waiting when he screeched up outside the Louis Pasteur hospital. Moments later, much against his will, Ben was being whisked inside on a gurney.

The doctor who'd attended to Ben was Dr Sandrine Lacombe, and she was as much part of his reason for not wanting to be taken to this particular hospital as she was Jeff's reason for insisting on it. The first, because she happened to be an old flame of Ben's. The second, because it had been thanks to her surgical skills that Jeff himself, not too many years earlier, had survived being shot with a sniper's bullet that had been meant for Ben. It was at this same hospital, while hanging around in desperate anxiety for Jeff, that Ben had first met Sandrine. The relationship had flowered for a while, but for no more than a few months before they'd ended it by amicable mutual consent.

There was nothing too amicable about Ben when it was his turn to be the patient, however. Sandrine was all too aware how stubborn he could be at times and took a firm hand with him, but even she had difficulty quelling his absolute insistence that he was perfectly fine, and that there was nothing wrong with the swollen and agonisingly painful ankle that a day or two's rest couldn't put right. It almost took a gun to his head to get him into the X-ray booth, where of course Jeff's diagnosis was proved right, as indeed Sandrine had expected it to be. In the end, fuming and sullen, Ben had to relent as she personally dressed and plastered his left foot. Two hours later he hobbled out of the hospital with the crutch that he'd now have to depend on for the next six to eight weeks.

Jeff had been waiting for him outside with Storm, who welcomed his master's return with tail-thumping and a happy bark. 'Here he is,' Jeff said, grinning from ear to ear as Ben came limping out of the hospital entrance. 'Come on, Cap'n Ahab, let's get you home.'

Chapter 6

Ben's mishap had taken place three weeks ago now, with another three to five weeks to go before the detested plaster could be removed. Until that blessed day came, life seemed to have ground to a halt and his frustration made the time seem to go by even more torturously slowly.

To add to Ben's frustration, while he'd been out of action de Klerk's team had been making more discoveries, such as the existence of what had first appeared to be a second escape tunnel branching off from the first, about three-quarters of the way from the church to the farmhouse. On closer investigation with the GPR, they'd discovered that the medieval diggers had actually abandoned the main tunnel, possibly due to hitting too much rocky ground, and that the secondary branch was the section that reached the house. Part of the abandoned original tunnel had long ago collapsed; when the team cleared away bushes and undergrowth in a wooded thicket some distance from the rear of the farmhouse, they found the cave-in like a deep pothole in the ground, uncovered for the first time in centuries.

More recently, earlier that week de Klerk's team had called

a break to the church restoration project and gone back to Paris for the festive season, which at least helped to alleviate Ben's annoyance at not being able to help out. In the meantime, Le Val was still busy on the approach to Christmas, with the last training course of the season scheduled to begin tomorrow, December 18th.

To Ben's relief, once that class was done and dusted, it would all be over for a while and their teaching schedule wouldn't restart until mid-January, by which time, or soon afterwards, he hoped to have the plaster off. He'd been unhappy about being restricted to classroom teaching only, and having to let Jeff and Tuesday temporarily take over the more physical parts of his job, the parts he enjoyed the most by far. Those included running groups of trainees through live-fire exercises in what they called the Killing House. Modelled on the same design and construction as the one the SAS used at their training ground at Pontrilas near Hereford, the specially reinforced building could be configured to mimic the interior of an actual house, for hostage rescue simulations, or even used as a mock-up of an airliner, when teaching the finer points of dealing with a terrorist hijacking. A typical two-day training course involved several hundred rounds of ammunition expended, a lot of holes and some very badly shot-up bad-guy targets.

Sometimes it wasn't easy, explaining to normal people what you did for a living. When asked, Ben usually just replied, 'I'm in education.'

Many of Le Val's trainees were specialist police or military operatives, sent by their unit commanders to hone their craft with the instruction team that had rightly gained a

42

reputation for being one of the best in Europe, if not the world. The group of delegates due to arrive tomorrow for an intensive bodyguard and defensive driving refresher course weren't cops or soldiers, but a five-man private VIP close protection outfit based in Dijon and run by an ex-GIGN counter-terrorist task force commander called Pepe Jaeckin, whom Ben knew well and respected. The course had been booked months in advance and he'd been looking forward to it.

To hell with this bloody plastered foot, he thought morosely for the ten thousandth time as he drove home from Valognes. The prospect of having to sit on the sidelines yet again and let Jeff and Tuesday have all the fun for the next couple of days didn't help his mood in the least. Although, he had to admit, that morning's encounter with the morons in the bar had livened things up a bit for him. And he couldn't say that meeting Marcel's new barmaid, Nathalie, had been an entirely unpleasant experience either.

'You liked her, didn't you?' he said to Storm.

Storm licked his chops in reply.

'I'll take that as a yes.'

Ben was halfway towards Le Val when his phone rang. Switching the call to his in-car speaker, he saw with pleasure that it was from Victor Vermont. The last time they'd been in contact was nearly three weeks ago, shortly after the accident. Ben had been laid up at home when Victor had driven over in his old Nissan Terrano to visit and commiserate over his friend's broken bones.

Ben had had a surprise for him that day. Victor's eyes had almost popped out of his head at the sight of the gold cross.

He was astonished at Ben's account of finding it, and even more so at the proposal that followed.

'I want you to take it,' Ben had said. 'You're the only person I know who can help me find out about its past.'

'No, I can't possibly accept,' Victor had protested. 'You mustn't trust me with something like this, my young friend. I'd be terrified to keep it in my house for a single minute, in case anything happened.'

'There isn't a man alive I'd trust with it more than you, Victor,' Ben said warmly. 'Besides, what can happen, around here? We're hardly living in a crime zone.'

After a great deal of persuading, Victor had agreed to look after it, strictly for no longer than needed to examine it more closely. He already had a contact in mind who might possibly be able to help: the same person who'd already been instrumental in finding out more about the history of Le Val's old church. Of which, more soon, Victor had promised, saying he'd call the moment he had some news.

And so now here he was, calling.

'Benedict!' came the old man's cheerful voice through the in-car speaker. He'd always insisted on calling Ben by his full name. 'How's that poor old ankle of yours coming along?'

'Never better, thanks. I'll be climbing mountains before you know it.'

Victor sounded particularly animated today, as though there was something he was itching to share. 'I have no doubt of it, none at all. Do you have a moment to talk? I've made a discovery that might be of interest to you.'

'I'm on the road, just a few minutes from Saint-Jean. Why don't I come over?'

Soon after, Ben pulled into the driveway of the fine, if slightly decayed, old house. Storm hopped out of the back and pranced happily around as Ben grabbed his crutch and hobbled up to the front door. It opened before he could knock, Victor standing there beaming at him and almost dancing on the spot with excitement.

'Come in, come in. Have you eaten lunch? I'm planning on cooking up some mushrooms and garlic bread, and I have the nicest little Sauvignon Blanc to accompany them. I'd love to hear your thoughts on it.'

'I'm tempted, Victor, but I shouldn't.' Ben was being polite, but the truth was that he wasn't really a white wine person. Wine for him was hearty and red, or it wasn't worth having at all. And if someone offered him a proper drink it would be a good single malt – though even he would decline such an offer before midday, on an empty stomach that was already dosed up with painkillers. Apart from anything else, lunch with Victor was liable to drag on for much of the day, and Ben had preparations to make that afternoon for the new class arriving tomorrow.

'Never mind. Here, come into the salon and rest that foot.'

'You said you had a bit of news,' Ben said when he was ensconced in one of Victor's comfortable antique armchairs.

The old man's eyes sparkled. 'Oh, yes. And I don't think you'll be disappointed.'

Chapter 7

'As a matter of fact,' Victor said, 'I happen to have three pieces of news to share with you, Benedict. The first, which ideally I would have liked to announce over a glass of wine, or better still a flute or two of champagne, but it's still morning and one should always exercise moderation, especially at my age, don't you think—?'

'What's the news?' Ben asked. The old man's joy was so infectious that he couldn't help but smile, too.

'—is that after years of successfully resisting every fresh onslaught of charm that I could possibly unleash on her, my beloved Célestine – that is to say, Madame Charpentier – has at last consented to becoming my wife!'

No wonder the old rascal's eyes were sparkling and he was grinning like a schoolboy, Ben thought. Genuinely happy for Victor he said, 'That's absolutely fantastic. Many, many congratulations. I wish you both all the happiness in the world.' He got unsteadily up from his chair to shake Victor's hand.

'Neither of us is as young as we used to be, of course,' Victor said. 'But then again, we're not as old as we're going to be. *Carpe diem*, I say.'

'A wise philosophy.'

'And as long as I, being the elder, manage to live as long as my dear old friend Jules, we should at least have a few good years together.'

'Who's Jules?'

'I was just coming to that, as his name brings me to my second piece of news,' Victor said, still just as excited as before. 'Jules Dampierre was the director of the antiquities museum in Rouen where I had my first job as a junior curator back in . . . oh, it was so many years ago. After that he relocated to Paris, but we have always stayed in touch. He became a great mentor to me as a young man, though he was only some fifteen years my senior. He's in his nineties now, but still as astute as ever, and is someone whose infinitely expert advice I have sought many, many times in the past when faced with a challenge that exceeded my own meagre abilities . . .'

Ben smiled. You couldn't force Victor; you had to let him come to the point naturally.

'. . . as indeed I have done more recently, regarding the matter of this remarkable artefact that you've had the good fortune to discover buried under your very feet at Le Val. What a stroke that was!' Victor shook his head in amazement. 'Are you sure you won't have a glass of wine?'

'Quite sure, Victor, thank you. You were saying?'

'About my dear friend Jules. Yes. But by way of background information, let me first tell you what my own research has taught me about the history of your house and land.'

'I'm all ears.'

Victor settled in the armchair opposite Ben's and stretched

out comfortably with his fingers knitted in front of his chest. It was the posture he always adopted when he was about to launch into his favourite subject. Ben knew he was in for a lecture, but he was genuinely curious to find out what the old man might have discovered.

Victor asked, 'Have you, by any chance, ever heard of a man called Gaspard de la Roche?'

'I can't say I have,' Ben replied after a moment's reflection. 'Who is he?'

'He *was*, once upon a time, the lord of much of the land around these parts, as well as the proprietor of the manor house on top of whose ruins the farmhouse at Le Val was built in 1809,' Victor said. 'The original property dates back to seven centuries earlier.'

A quick mental calculation oriented Ben to the twelfth century. The same period to which de Klerk's archaeological research had dated the later parts of the church ruins. 'There was a medieval manor house at Le Val?'

'Indeed there was. The earliest reference I could find in the historic archives was from 1132, though the year of its construction seems to have been lost in the mists of time.' Victor smiled. 'What we do know, however, is that the lord of the manor, Gaspard, was an important knight in the service of Eleanor, Duchess of Aquitaine. I'm sure you're familiar with that name.'

Ben was no historian, and he had to dig deep into his memory. 'If I remember rightly, Eleanor of Aquitaine was the Queen of France.'

'Queen Consort, to be precise, having been the wife of King Louis VII without ever actually ruling. But you're quite correct, in essence. She later also became Queen Consort of England, on her marriage to Henry II. And mother to two future English kings: Richard the Lionheart and the notorious John Lackland, the author and signatory of *Magna Carta*.'

'So what's the connection to Gaspard de la Roche?' Ben asked. He could already feel himself getting reeled into this historical intrigue.

'It's quite a fascinating story,' Victor said. 'Not least because Eleanor led such a colourful and often highly adventurous life, especially for a woman in those days. Having married Louis at the tender age of only fifteen, she was still a young queen when, ten years later in June 1147, she took up the cross and set off for the Holy Land to join the Second Crusade. The First Crusade, you will recall, had taken place some fifty years earlier and ended with the recapture of the Holy City from the Saracens in 1099 and the establishing of the Kingdom of Jerusalem for Christendom. However, the Muslim forces continued to pose a great military and political threat during the intervening years. In 1144 Western Europe received the shocking news that Edessa, a key bastion of the Christian kingdom in the Holy Land, had been overrun and taken by the army of a powerful warlord and ruler of Aleppo and Mosul. His name was Imad al-Din Zengi.'

Chapter 8

'Zengi first emerged, as a force to be reckoned with, in the late 1130s,' Victor said. 'Even contemporary Muslim writers, who are generally quite united in their enmity towards Christendom, told of his brutality and the terrifyingly rigid discipline he maintained among his troops. If any of his soldiers so much as trampled on local crops without permission, he would have them crucified. But this was no common bloodthirsty maniac. Zengi had a brilliant sense of siege warfare and an engineering corps to implement his ideas.

'In late 1144, Zengi turned his attention to Edessa, the fortified crusader city in the upper Mesopotamian valley – in modern times it lies within south-eastern Turkey on the border of Iraq. Edessa was the eastern outpost of the crusader states, and the most vulnerable. The Christians had always been certain of their fortifications and the military prowess of their knights, but Zengi changed all that. He besieged the city and ordered his men to dig deep into the foundations of one of the walls. When they entered the city, they began to slaughter the citizens. In the words of an Armenian Christian who witnessed the scene, "Like wolves among a

flock of lambs, they fell. They slaughtered indiscriminately
. . . they had no mercy on the grey hairs of the elderly or
with the tender age of a child."'

How little things changed through time, Ben thought. As
a commander leading SAS missions into both Aleppo and
Mosul, and many other locations within that eternal theatre
of war, he'd witnessed enough brutal carnage for their names
to become forever synonymous in his mind with death and
destruction. One day there might be an end to these ever-
lasting conflicts. But mankind's historical track record made
that prospect seem pretty damned unlikely.

Victor continued, 'In response to the massacre at Edessa,
Pope Eugenius decreed that a second crusade must be
launched to quell the threat. Eleanor's husband, King Louis
of France, resolved to go, while armies set off from all over
Europe to take part. Of the hundred thousand or so
combatants who departed from France, a small number
were influential women, mostly the wives of wealthy noble
crusaders, who are said to have worn armour and ridden
astride horses alongside the men. Eleanor decided she, too,
should join them, with the intention of supporting her
husband Louis as well as her uncle Raymond, Prince of
Antioch, with whom she corresponded, and who was locked
in an eternal struggle with the Saracens. Raymond's territories were vulnerable to attack and it was hoped that
Eleanor's army would provide much-needed relief. She was
also eager to see Antioch. Some historians have suggested
that she had grown disenchanted with life at the stultifying
French court, chained to a husband who by all accounts
was a joyless religious fanatic even by twelfth-century

standards. Rumour told that Antioch was very similar to her beloved Aquitaine – lively, lush and fun, the latter being a quality that Eleanor was acutely missing from her life. And so off she went on crusade, this feisty young queen. She brought with her a retinue of some three hundred knights, lords and barons from all across France. Despite her youth and inexperience, she insisted on assuming personal military command over them.'

'And one of those knights was Gaspard de la Roche?'

Victor nodded. 'The contemporary accounts of the time make several references to his having accompanied the queen on the long, dangerous journey east. Finally the expedition arrived in the Holy Land, where Eleanor would remain for the next two years, often marching with her troops and personally witnessing the horror and slaughter of war. While her husband Louis proved himself to be a lacklustre and inefficient leader, Eleanor's braveness and hardiness in the face of terrible adversity inspired devotion among her band of knights, Gaspard de la Roche among them. According to one historical source I was able to dig up, Gaspard was at his queen's side on the weary march across the Phrygian mountains to Antioch, where the army hoped to reinforce the beleaguered Raymond. To their dismay, while en route they came across the ghastly remains of the army led by their ally King Conrad III of Germany, slaughtered to a man by the Saracens on a battlefield that ranged as far as the eye could see. It's almost impossible for us to imagine such terrible sights in the modern age.'

Ben didn't have too much difficulty in imagining it quite clearly, but he stayed quiet. He'd told Victor almost nothing of his own military experience, and he intended to keep it that way.

'Even worse was to follow some time later,' Victor went on, 'with the news that Eleanor's beloved uncle had been defeated and beheaded by the Muslim forces. Her husband Louis could offer her little solace during those difficult times. Their marriage had never been a close one and by this time it had become very shaky indeed – in fact it wasn't long afterwards that she called for its annulment on the grounds of consanguinity, he being her cousin. Instead it was Gaspard, among others in her close-knit inner circle of supporters and confidants, who comforted the queen in those moments of despair. There are indications that Gaspard may also have been aboard the queen's ship when it came under attack in May 1149, this time from Byzantine forces sent to kidnap her. Narrowly surviving that attempt, the ship was then caught up in a huge storm that drove it so far off course that for two months, until they finally reached port in Sicily, it was feared to have gone down with all hands.'

'I can see what you mean about Eleanor having led a colourful life,' Ben said.

'But as the grip of the Christian forces over the Holy Land became harder and harder to maintain in the face of superior enemy numbers, infighting and betrayal, poor communication, hostile terrain and broken supply routes, it became increasingly clear to even its most ardent champions that the Second Crusade was doomed to failure. Admitting defeat, Eleanor and what remained of her followers made the dispiriting journey back to France. With the annulment of her marriage to Louis she soon found herself being whisked off to England as the new bride of King Henry. She still had a long, sometimes difficult, life ahead of her, going on to live into her eighties. Almost as old as I am,' Victor said with a smile.

'And Gaspard?' Ben asked. 'What happened to him afterwards?'

Victor's smile wavered a little. 'Unfortunately that is where the historical record becomes somewhat vague, as far as he's concerned.' He explained that for all his efforts, he'd been unable to trace much of what had become of Eleanor's devoted knightly companion in the wake of the failed crusade. There was a suggestion that he'd returned to his home in Normandy, disillusioned by defeat, though no records existed of his activities after about 1152. Likewise, Victor had been unable to dig up any shred of a mention of the church on his lands.

'As for the fate of the medieval manor house in which Gaspard once lived,' Victor said, brightening, 'there it was possible to learn just a little more. A source from 1570 records the house as having been destroyed in the early 1560s, during the Wars of Religion that were raging across our country at that time. The property appears to have stood empty and abandoned for many years afterwards and been used as grazing land, until it was acquired by a well-to-do landowner in the late eighteenth or early nineteenth century. This was the gentleman who built your house, atop whatever foundations remained of the original building.'

'What about the tunnels?' Ben asked. 'They lead from the church all the way into the old wine cellar under the farmhouse. Do we know who used them, when they did, and why?'

'I'm sorry, Benedict. The lot of the historical researcher can be a cruel one, at times, when the records simply aren't there to examine. Just like the crusaders who were forced to withdraw from the Holy Land, we now and then have to accept defeat.'

Ben considered what he'd learned. As fascinating as it was, it offered little information about the cross. Disappointing. But then he remembered the remaining piece of news that Victor had promised.

'You were going to tell me more about your friend Monsieur Dampierre.'

'Indeed I was, after filling in the necessary background to the story. Now, as you recall, I was somewhat reluctant at first to accept such an artefact into my care, a great honour but also a grave responsibility of which I felt quite unworthy. Then the thought occurred to me that if anyone could help me to unearth the cross's past, it would be him. Did I mention that after his time in Rouen, Jules relocated to Paris?'

'You did.'

'His reason for doing so was to accept a post as senior curator at the Musée du Louvre, where he spent the last ten years of his career overseeing the care of many of the world's most prestigious and priceless collections before he retired at the tender age of eighty-five. Believe me, such expertise as I might have gained through my lifelong passion for antiquities pales by comparison to Jules's.'

'You're too modest, Victor.'

Victor shrugged. 'And so, on returning home that day with your precious artefact in my hands, after first photographing it and then locking it away as safely as could be, my next action was to contact him. I was soon able to persuade my old friend to lend his considerable skills to our cause. With typical zest and enthusiasm, he immediately set about the task. And I'm delighted to report that his efforts have not been in vain.'

Ben leaned forward, looking intently at Victor. 'He found out its past?'

'Of one thing, Jules is as convinced as I am: that your cross is an authentic medieval artefact, beautifully preserved, and a find of very considerable historical worth and interest even as it stands. But following our discussions and on close examination of the photographs I sent him, he has formed a hypothesis which, if proved right, he believes would multiply the cross's value, both historical and actual, a hundredfold. Perhaps even more. It would elevate your discovery from being a merely fascinating relic of the medieval period to a treasure of immense and unique significance.'

Ben shook his head, dangling on tenterhooks and impatient for more. 'Tell me about his hypothesis.'

Victor smiled and raised a finger in gentle warning. 'Now, now, Benedict. One step at a time. These things are not to be taken lightly. And you must understand that a scholar of such absolute integrity as Jules would never fully commit himself until there was no doubt whatever in his mind. At this stage it wouldn't do to go off half-cocked, so to speak. Besides which,' Victor added sadly, 'at this stage I simply don't know what Jules has come up with.'

'You don't know?'

Victor shook his head. 'He won't tell me until he has seen the cross for himself, in person. I'm extremely reluctant to ask him to travel out to Normandy. With your permission, I plan on making the trip to Paris, carrying the valuable object inside a locked case that will be securely attached to my wrist in such a way that to steal it, a thief would have to chop off my arm. I would spend a few days at Jules's country residence outside Neuilly, where he would be able to inspect it at his leisure and, I hope, reveal his thoughts more fully.'

'I really didn't mean for you to go to such trouble, Victor,' Ben said. 'All the way to Paris, just for me?'

'Not at all. Not at all. It's my pleasure. And it was high time that I paid a visit to my old friend, anyhow.' Victor paused, looking pensive. 'There is one consideration. Two days from now, December nineteenth, is the anniversary of the death of Jules's wife Jeanne, a dear lady who passed many years ago and is buried in her family plot in Limoges. He always goes to visit her grave this time of year, and is away for a few days. But he will be home again on the evening of the twenty-second. I will be in Paris to meet him the next day, and hope to have more news for you soon afterwards.'

Chapter 9

Six days before the attack

Early next morning, a chilly but as yet snow-free December 18th, the delegates for the last training course of the season rolled up at Le Val in a black Audi SUV with the tough-looking logo of Pepe Jaeckin's security company emblazoned on the doors. The five men had set off from Dijon the previous afternoon, spent the night in a hotel in Valognes, and were rested, psyched up and ready for two hard days of instruction. The team leader's name was Alain Garnier, and he'd been working with Pepe for some years now. The company was gaining a solid reputation and Pepe had high ambitions. The time had come to take the team's skills to the next level.

They'd come to the right place for that, and they were looking forward to working with the best in the business: as Le Val went from strength to strength the names Jeff Dekker and Ben Hope had attained near-legendary status in the small, self-contained and somewhat closeted world of tactical training. If Garnier was disappointed when Ben greeted the team with his crutch and plaster, he did his best to hide it. 'What happened?'

'Jumped out of a plane at ten thousand feet without a chute,' Jeff explained cheerfully. 'He will do stuff like that. Guy's a maniac.'

'Awesome,' one of the others said, before Ben had a chance to speak up for himself. One of Jeff's talents was for marketing. If it helped the business for people to think one of its directors was a maniac, then so what?

After a light breakfast and a brief introductory getting-to-know-you session, the delegates and instructors repaired to the classroom next door to the one that was being used for the archaeological restoration project. Jeff, Tuesday and the other two trainers, Bruno and Zed, both of them veterans of the elite French army unit COM FST, which was short for Commandement des Forces Spéciales Terre, took a back seat as Ben stood next to the big screen and briefed the team on their schedule for the next two days. The course was split into two phases, morning and afternoon of each day.

Ben said, 'The exercises we'll be covering in Phase One are designed to test a close protection team's ability to extract a VIP client from a building under attack, as may become necessary during a terrorist incident or a kidnap attempt. For this purpose we'll be using what we call the killing house, which replicates the training facility used by my old regiment, only with a few improvements.' He tapped a key on the laptop in front of him, and a floor plan drawing of the killing house's current incarnation appeared on the big screen. He tapped again, launching a slideshow of interior images of the killing house's makeshift plywood rooms and corridors.

'As you can see, for our scenario it's been set up to emulate the rear section and back exit of a hotel or private residence that is the target of the attackers. Your job is to extract your asset safely from a room inside the building, to that exit, and then outside, as fast and efficiently as possible. We'll be running through the exercise multiple times, allowing you to take turns playing the role of the VIP while the other four try to prevent Jeff, Tuesday, Bruno and Zed here from killing or abducting him.'

'*Try* being the operative term,' Jeff interjected with a shark-like grin.

'Though obviously, for this phase of the exercise we'll be using paintball weapons that simulate the real thing as closely as possible,' Ben explained. 'We do have a policy of not actually killing our clients. Only the really awkward ones.' This brought a laugh from several of the trainees.

'Phase Two, which we'll cover during the afternoons, is where the real fun begins,' Ben continued. He tapped another laptop key and the onscreen image switched to an exterior shot of the killing house that featured one of Le Val's latest innovations: a rectangular concrete skid pan that extended more than a hundred yards from the rear of the building, like a large car park with grassy run-offs to the right and left. It was laid out with arrangements of plastic traffic cones, and the concrete was heavily streaked with black tyre marks. At the opposite end from the killing house, the skid pan joined a concrete track that looped around in an oval two hundred yards across, like a miniature race circuit, except painted with white lines to emulate a normal two-lane road. The layout offered plenty of space for the

Le Val trainers to simulate all kinds of real-life situations.

'We kick off Phase Two with the assumption that the close protection team have got as far as extracting the VIP intact and alive from the building,' Ben told them. 'Hopefully, we'll have run through Phase One enough times that we can achieve that goal. From there, the team's job is to transfer the asset into a waiting vehicle and remove him to a secure location.'

That wasn't going to be made easy for them either, as Ben explained:

'The attackers will then proceed to give chase and attempt to intercept the escaping vehicle by whatever means possible. You all know that the majority of VIP abductions and assas-sinations take place during transit, and especially in vulnerable locations where a vehicle can be stopped, blocked in and surrounded by hostile players. There may be a kidnap vehicle, into which the intercepted VIP is loaded while the protection team are taken out. Or the aim may simply be to wipe out everyone inside the car, the asset included. The attackers may launch incendiary devices or pepper the car with gunfire.'

In short, as Ben made clear, anything could happen. The course would cover a vast range of possible scenarios, teaching drills and simulations, including ones that weren't taught in most military and police training exercises. They had their anti-ambush techniques down to a fine art. One of the most popular drills was practising ramming skills, when a pursuit vehicle attempting to block off the escape route had to be knocked out of the way without losing too much speed or endangering the passengers.

Ben and Jeff had both experienced these situations for

real during their Special Forces careers – in Ben's case he'd been through them plenty of times since, as well, working as a freelance operative – and they'd sought to inject as much realism into their training as possible. Before his injury, Ben had relished his role as the kind of hands-on teacher who'd actually been there and done it. Now, severely hampered by his plaster and crutch, he was relegated to the role of observer and bench coach while his colleagues got to play with all the big boys' toys.

'Any questions?' he asked when the briefing was over. There were none. 'Okay, let's head over to the armoury and get kitted up.'

Le Val's armoury was the holy of holies, where an extensive stock of weaponry, ammunition and related equipment was kept stored under the most stringent security regulations. It was built to be as impenetrable as a bank vault, encased within reinforced concrete eight feet below ground and protected by a series of no fewer than three steel doors to which only Ben and Jeff had the keys. Jeff wore his around his neck, like dog tags. Ben kept his set in a secret safe in his quarters, and changed the combination religiously once a month.

The equipment was all laid out ready and waiting on a long table. Everyone had to be securely togged up with bulletproof vests, face masks and goggles, because the high-powered paintball guns they'd be using could hit hard enough to cause minor injuries or even take out an eye. The bodyguard team would be firing with yellow paint, the instructors with red. As the trainees were getting dressed up and being issued their kit, Ben noticed more than a few lingering, envious glances were being directed at the steel racks that stored the rows and rows of real hardware, like kids in a sweet shop.

'Let's rock,' Jeff said.

Chapter 10

The ten men drove across to the killing house in three all-terrain buggies, and soon afterwards the fun got underway. The rest of the morning was predictably frantic, hot and noisy as the trainees were put through their paces, over and over again. The 'attackers' struck from various positions and in various formations, sometimes mounting their assault from outside the building, sometimes infiltrating the inside. Just like in real life, the bodyguards never quite knew where the next threat was coming from, and after three hours of this they were thoroughly exhausted and bamboozled, as well as liberally splattered with red paint. Out of the first five run-throughs of Phase One, their VIP asset got 'killed' twice and was abducted twice, with the last run being their one successful extraction, highlighting some significant areas of weakness to be addressed on the second day.

After a break for sandwiches and coffee and a welcome half-hour breather it was time to don crash helmets and get ready for the high-speed thrills and spills of Phase Two. The vehicle in which the protection team had to whisk their VIP client from the building was a fast Vauxhall saloon fitted with a special roll cage, rally-style seat harnesses and re-inforced windows, while the attackers would be using a van and two other cars in their attempts to cut off their escape. On the first attempt, the battered panel van driven by Jeff blocked the team's path, forcing the Vauxhall to an emergency stop. As Ben watched from the sidelines, the four attackers leaped from the van clutching high-capacity soft air assault weapons, surrounded the Vauxhall and proceeded to pepper it mercilessly with gunfire.

'You're all dead,' Ben told Garnier. 'Let's do it again.'

And they did, over and over, virtually every imaginable form of vehicle-on-vehicle assault barring tanks and aircraft, until the sun had sunk behind the trees and the afternoon light was beginning to fade. Engines yowled, tyres squealed, vehicles collided, rubber and wreckage were strewn all over the skid pan and track, fire and smoke filled the cold air. Voices yelling, whistles blowing, thunderflashes exploding. It was just another routine afternoon at Le Val.

But a day at Le Val wouldn't have been a day at Le Val without some live firearms work. Needless to say, no trainee would have been allowed to get within a mile of a loaded gun unless they'd first been through all the necessary advanced weapons training and been certified safe, which all of Pepe Jaeckin's guys were. For this last phase of their day's instruction the delegates swapped their paintball guns for the hardware they'd been eyeing so enviously in the armoury earlier. Ben and Jeff favoured the time-tested and extremely effective Heckler & Koch MP-5 submachine gun that been pretty much the mainstay of both men's personal armament during their days in Special Forces. It might be a dated design going back fifty years, but it was the yardstick by which all of the fancier, buttons-and-bells modern variants were measured. It was light, handy and eminently portable; it functioned when it was full of dirt, and even underwater. It spat out nine-millimetre rounds at an astronomical rate of fire, would happily cycle the crappiest, cruddiest ammo, and even when it ran dry its solid construction allowed it to be used as an effective contact weapon. You could knock the hell out of it and it would still work afterwards. It was a doddle to fit a silencer and it would accommodate all manner of tactical lights, lasers, extended magazines, whatever was desired, as though it had been born for the job. Most importantly of all, it had never let them down. There was just nothing quite like the old MP-5.

No wonder, then, that it was such a favoured piece of hardware among crooks, assassins and terrorists, who would do almost anything to get their hands on one.

For the last phase of the afternoon's training, with the whole area lit up by floodlamps on tall masts, the close protection team were required to negotiate a shoot/no shoot ambush evasion drill that involved driving at speed through a simulated underpass where realistic bad guy targets popped up at random, mixed equally at random with innocent bystanders, and had to be engaged with speed and accuracy from the moving vehicle. For every ten points gained from taking out a bad guy you stood to lose a hundred for harming a member of the public. The crackle of automatic gunfire could certainly be heard from some of the farms and smallholdings between Le Val and Saint-Jean, but the locals were well used to it. For the oldest of the old boys, it kindled nostalgic memories of the war.

By six in the afternoon, the day was done. The trainees had significantly increased their chances of being able to steer their valuable asset out of just about as much trouble and danger as anyone, short of a full enemy regiment, was likely to throw at them. The high degree of realism was necessarily destructive, and expensive. But when you came here to learn, you were getting exactly what you paid for, and something you wouldn't find anywhere else.

The trainees retreated to their quarters to nurse their bruised egos and revise what they'd learned. Ben and company spent the next busy hour clearing up the mess of the killing house and the skid pan and track. Then it was time for dinner, when everyone congregated around the big oak table in the farmhouse kitchen, an opportunity for relaxation and laughter as well as serious discussion of tomorrow's activities. By eleven o'clock the delegates were usually so exhausted they would creep off to bed.

All in all, it had been a good day. But as Ben clambered into his own bed that night he kept thinking about the peculiar behaviour of one of the trainees. His name was Robert Blondel and he was a new member on the team: early forties, ex-French Army, switched tracks to work in private security a couple of years ago. Pepe Jaeckin had told Ben on the phone that he'd recently taken Blondel on and expected good things of him. There was certainly nothing wrong with the guy, in terms of his skill level. In fact he seemed pretty promising.

But despite that, Ben had noticed a few things about

Blondel that stuck in his mind afterwards. He gave the general impression of being nervous and preoccupied, as though something was eating him. During breaks in the hectic action of the day, while the others were full of chatter and animation Ben had observed Blondel going strangely quiet and staring into space, apparently deep in thoughts that seemed to be troubling him.

Maybe that was just the guy's way, being naturally less outgoing and boisterous than the others, Ben had thought. Or maybe Blondel had worries at home that were on his mind. Money matters, relationship problems – who knew? Ben had soon put it out of his own mind. It wasn't until later, after they'd finished for the day, when Ben was stumping about helping as best he could to tidy up, that he'd had the chance to observe Blondel's odd behaviour more closely.

While parking one of the all-terrain buggies in the storage barn near the armoury where much of the equipment was kept, Ben had spotted Blondel wandering about among the buildings in the darkness. Ben was surprised, because he'd assumed the trainees had all gone off to grab some R&R before dinner – yet here was this one apparently exploring on his own. Blondel was clutching a mobile phone, as though he was in the middle of texting someone while on his walkabout.

Blondel appeared to be so focused on what he was doing that he didn't know he wasn't alone until Ben was right behind him. At the sound of Ben's voice, Blondel tensed up and turned suddenly around.

'Lost?' Ben said. His tone was perfectly pleasant. There was no reason for it to be otherwise. But Blondel reacted nervously as though he'd been challenged, or caught out somehow.

'No . . . I, uh . . . I was just having a walk around. Admiring the place. I mean, I've heard so much about it. Quite a set-up you have here, isn't it?'

'I'm glad you approve,' Ben said, in the same friendly tone. 'It's certainly taken us a lot of work to develop it to where it is now. And we still have a lot of plans for the future. I hope you found the day worthwhile?'

'Great,' Blondel said, with a nervous laugh. 'Everything I'd thought it would be, and more.'

'I'm pleased,' Ben replied. 'It'll be time for dinner soon. You should go and rejoin the others, and I'll see you up at the house in a few minutes.'

Blondel had gone off, and Ben had watched him, wondering what exactly was making him act so edgy. Blondel had been rather quiet at dinner, too, eating little, drinking maybe a little too much of the wine that Jeff kept pouring out for anyone whose glass was less than half full, exchanging no more than a few words.

Ben's impression of Blondel continued into the second day. In all other respects Day Two went off much like the first, except that the trainees had obviously absorbed some of the lessons of yesterday's failures, and put on a far better showing this time around. As before, Blondel fulfilled his part perfectly competently and showed plenty of ability. But as before, too, over lunch and in the quieter moments in-between exercises, he was visibly distracted and anxious. Most of all, Ben thought, when they were in the armoury getting togged up and issuing out the equipment. Blondel kept glancing around him with a peculiarly furtive expression in his eyes. Ben actually took him aside, smiling and asking, 'Everything all right, Robert?'

'Everything's fine, thank you.' The same nervous tone in his voice.

'If you're not feeling well, you can always take a break or sit this one out. Your team-mates will cover for you.'

'No, I'm fine.'

Which was about as much as Ben could say to the guy.

That evening saw all ten of them gathered around the farmhouse table once again, for another hearty meal and lots of laughter and bonhomie. The only one clearly not enjoying himself was Blondel, whom Ben had decided just to ignore if the guy wanted to be taciturn and antisocial. Alain Garnier was sitting to Ben's right at the top of the table, and over dinner he expressed his thanks for such a valuable two days that had taught the team so many lessons, not least by exposing so much of what they'd been doing wrong before.

'That's what we're here for,' Ben said. 'You're welcome to come back for more any time.'

'Fine by me, as long as Pepe's footing the bill,' Garnier replied with a laugh. 'But I think we should let some of our bruises heal first.'

Further down the table, Jeff was telling the other delegates about the Le Val team's plans for Christmas. Both Tuesday and he were jetting off to warmer climes: Tuesday to Jamaica in two days' time, to spend the festive season with family in Kingston, while the day after that, December 22nd, Jeff would be jumping on a long-haul flight to Australia. His mother had emigrated there a few years back and was remarried to a rugged outbacker by the name of Kip Malloy, who owned a hundred-acre ranch and farmed crocodiles for a living. Jeff liked to joke that he planned on bringing Tuesday back a crocodile-tooth necklace. Meanwhile, Bruno and Zed were headed south to Cannes, for a birthday bash with one of their former COM FST comrades.

Joining in the conversation, Alain Garnier asked, 'So Ben, what are your plans for the holiday season?'

'We asked him if he wanted to come down to Cannes with us,' Zed interjected. 'But he'd rather stay home like a sad fart and listen to his Bing Crosby Christmas album.'

'Better that than having to witness you lot making drunken arses of yourselves,' Ben said. He knew all too well the kind of raucous, riotous partying that took place when these guys let their hair down. Personally, he'd been there, done that.

'In any case,' he added more seriously, 'someone has to stay here to keep an eye on things, besides the three guys we have watching the gate.' Which was true enough, since Le Val's strict security policy demanded that at least one senior member of staff and armoury keyholder had to be on the premises at any given time. It was a rule that had only ever been broken in the direst emergency, such as when Ben, Jeff and Tuesday had all had to travel to Africa to rescue Jude, Ben's son, from pirates; and more recently, when Ben's then girlfriend Grace Kirk had found herself in deadly trouble at the hands of a cabal of intelligence operatives who also happened to be Satanists.

Thankfully those kinds of emergencies didn't happen every day – not quite, not even in the life of Ben Hope.

'I've no problem with taking it easy here on my own,' Ben said. 'Things will be nice and quiet for a change. Richard, Serge and Michel will be up at the gatehouse if I need anything, and I'll have the whole rest of the place to myself, with Storm and the pack. If it wasn't for this damned bloody ankle of mine, I'd actually be looking forward to it.'

'Wow. Ben Hope looking forward to taking things easy,' laughed Garnier. 'What's the world coming to?'

Jeff was in a merry mood that evening and had been joking and laughing all through dinner, but now he looked at Ben with an earnest expression in his eyes. 'I've told you, mate. The Land of Oz ain't going anywhere, and I've left it this long to pay Mum a visit. If you want me to cancel my trip and stay here to help you take care of things, just say the word.'

'Me too,' Tuesday chipped in. 'Doesn't seem right, us going off and leaving you like that, limping around on crutches.'

Ben knew that his friends meant every word of it, and he was touched by their generosity. 'No, I won't have you cancel your plans on my account. You guys go and enjoy yourselves. You deserve it. And everything will be perfectly under control here. It's Christmas time, after all. What could possibly go wrong?'

Chapter 11

One day before the attack

True to his word, on the afternoon of December 23rd Victor travelled up to an icy cold and windy Paris by train, carrying with him the precious gold cross in a briefcase securely handcuffed to his wrist. As the train rumbled into the Gare Saint Lazare he spotted the familiar tall, lean shape of his dear old friend Jules waiting for him on the crowded platform, and hurried out to meet him. The two men warmly embraced one another à la Française, with kisses on the cheek.

'It's so good to see you again, *cher* Victor. It seems so long since we last met, but you haven't aged a day.'

'I might say the same,' Victor replied, gazing fondly up at the deeply wrinkled face of the nonagenarian, who towered over him by several inches. Just three years short of reaching triple figures Jules might be, but he was as straight and fit as a healthy sixty-year-old – as befitted a man who walked four miles every day and tended fanatically to his two-acre garden, rain or shine.

'How was your trip to Limoges?' Victor asked.

'Very good, thank you. Jeanne sends her regards.' Jules had never accepted her passing and for twenty-five years had gone on talking about her as though she were still alive. It was just one of his little idiosyncrasies. 'But never mind me,' he added, smiling down at the case in Victor's hand and taking his arm. 'Come, let's waste no time getting back to the house.'

Jules drove an immaculate Citroen DS that he'd bought new in 1965. With a hiss of hydropneumatic suspension they glided off into Paris and didn't stop chatting away like a couple of schoolboys until they'd arrived at Jules's beautiful home in the suburbs of Neuilly. Inside, once Victor had finally managed to find the key to unlock himself from the case, they celebrated their reunion with a little glass of something. 'And now, you must show me what you've brought,' Jules said with a glitter of excitement.

Victor ceremonially opened the case, and Jules's wrinkly old eyes lit up with joy at the sight of the cross nestling in its blue velvet lining.

'Ah, ah, *mon vieux*, it's even more magnificent than your photographs would have had me believe. Look at these rubies and sapphires, and these patterns of tiny pearls so delicately set between them. May I?'

'Please, be my guest.'

Jules carefully slipped on a pair of white cotton curator's gloves to handle the precious artefact. Holding the heavy cross up to the light, he turned it over and over from all angles and savoured every detail with intense pleasure.

'I did happen to make one discovery that may interest you,' Victor said. 'Only late yesterday evening, in fact. Its owner as yet has no idea.'

'Do tell.'

'I draw your attention to the ruby that adorns the shaft at its junction with the crosspiece,' Victor said, pointing. 'Observe that it's slightly larger than the two either side of it. And do you notice the slight difference in the way it's been inset into the gold?'

'I do,' Jules said, peering very closely. 'I wonder why.'

'For the reason that it has another function, beyond the merely ornamental. Press it.'

'Like this?'

'Just so.'

Jules pressed the ruby with his thumb. There was a soft click from the shaft of the cross, and to his amazement it detached itself from the crosspiece, sliding away to reveal a shiny and perfectly preserved blade.

'A cross that doubles as a hidden dagger,' Jules observed with a chuckle. 'The longer section of the shaft doubling as a scabbard, while the crosspiece acts as a handguard. Well, well. How very ingenious.' He touched his gloved thumb to the edge of the blade. 'Still sharp, too. See how it offers to slice the fibres of the cotton.'

'I had already found that out,' Victor said, holding up a finger with a band-aid on it.

'Dear me, *mon cher*, you should be more careful.' Marvelling at the cleverness of its design, Jules slipped the shaft back over the blade and it latched into place with another click. 'Now, tell me again about the secret passageway where your friend make his remarkable find.'

Victor retold the story of its discovery while Jules went on examining every millimetre of the historic object. At last

Jules said, 'There can be little doubt of its connection to Gaspard de la Roche. But what I really wanted to get a closer look at is this. It's so minute as to be barely visible in the photographs, sharply focused as they are. You see?' Jules's bony finger indicated a tiny inscription on the shaft of the cross, smoothed and worn with age.

'I had seen it too,' Victor said, peering. 'I thought it was a hallmark of some form.'

'A natural conclusion to draw,' Jules agreed after they'd each taken turns studying the tiny mark through a jeweller's glass. 'After all, as any historian worth his salt knows very well, the use of hallmarks on gold and silver objects dates back considerably further, to as early as the fourth century. But now that I see it with my own eyes, I must beg to differ. In fact, I believe that the appearance of the marking supports my own personal theory, which after this afternoon has become far less of a mere hypothesis in my mind.'

'I'm excited to hear it,' Victor replied. 'But Jules, might I ask you to share your theory with me at this stage? Or are you determined to keep your old friend in a state of suspense that could prove fatal, if maintained even just a little too long?'

'Tomorrow, Victor,' Jules promised. 'A little suspense is good for the heart, you know. Now, let us return this splendid item to its case and lock it safely away while we attend to our evening meal. Roast lamb; I know it's one of your favourites. I've taken the liberty of opening a rather good bottle of Haut Brion for the occasion.'

* * *

The following morning they headed back into the heart of the city. Despite the bitter cold and possible threat of snow, the streets were bustling with Parisians doing their last-minute shopping before Christmas. Jules was being as secretive about their destination, and whom they might be going to meet, as he was about his mysterious hypothesis regarding the gold cross – which was securely bundled up in the case on Victor's lap as they travelled across Paris.

To Victor's surprise, it became apparent that they were headed for the Louvre Museum, Jules's old workplace, home to some of the world's richest collections of priceless historic artefacts. 'But it's Christmas Eve, Jules. Surely it will be shut.'

'I do still have some influence there, as it happens. My successor, the current senior curator of the antiquities section, has agreed to meet with us.'

'But why the Louvre, Jules?'

Jules just smiled. 'You'll see.'

They parked in a staff parking area and went in by a private entrance. Victor was introduced to Henri Carbonneau, now himself approaching retirement age. Carbonneau welcomed his former boss with all the polite respect due to a renowned ex-curator who was almost as ancient as some of the exhibits there. But it was clear he was put out to have been made to return to work in the middle of the holiday. 'Your visit was somewhat at short notice, Jules. Christmas is the only time I get off all year, and our grandchildren are staying with us.'

'I'm extremely grateful, Henri. And I sincerely apologise once again for the inconvenience. I believe you will agree it was worth it, however.'

Carbonneau took them into a private room where the

museum's treasures were cleaned, restored and examined. Before entering, the three of them had to don overalls and white cotton gloves. Victor still had no clear idea what they were doing here.

He was about to find out.

Chapter 12

The brightly lit room was empty apart from a table on which stood a wooden transit crate of the kind used for transporting valuables. Carbonneau approached the table and, with extreme delicacy, lifted the lid off the crate. The glittering object inside, nestled in the packing material that was required to protect it even for travelling short distances from one section of the museum to another, was one that Victor had only ever seen in photos, never in person. He blinked in amazement.

What they were looking at was a pear-shaped rock crystal vase, possibly the most famous example of its kind in existence and certainly the rarest. The light glittered off its cut surface and seemed to reflect a thousand colours. Its mount and base were made of gold, encrusted with precious stones.

'Well, here it is, Jules,' Carbonneau said. 'The piece you specifically wanted to examine. Believe me, it's not every day that we would grant such a request, not even for a former curator of your eminence. I had a hard time persuading the director.'

'Is this what I think it is?' Victor asked. 'The Eleanor Vase?'

Carbonneau nodded. 'As it's commonly known. The only surviving artefact known to have belonged to Eleanor of Aquitaine. Presented by her to King Louis VII as a wedding gift, on their marriage in 1137, although the crystal itself is believed to date back much further, to the sixth or seventh century, and may be of Moorish origin. Eleanor inherited it from her grandfather, William IX, Duke of Aquitaine, who had himself received it from a Muslim ally during a military campaign in Spain in the early 1120s.'

Victor said, 'This would have been when William joined forces with the Kingdom of Castille in an effort to liberate Córdoba from the Berber Almoravids.' History was coming to life in front of Victor's eyes, as it always had when he found himself in the presence of such entrancing relics of the past. But why had Jules requested a private viewing of the Eleanor Vase, in particular?

'Indeed,' replied Carbonneau. 'It would have been considered a magnificent gift, as such crystal vases were highly prized. But the filigree gold mount and jewelled circular base are a later addition, and of uncertain origin. They were probably fashioned here in France, sometime after Eleanor inherited the vase from her grandfather, though their style bears the influence of earlier Byzantine pieces. It may be that Eleanor herself had these components made specially by a master goldsmith. Certainly, there's no evidence to the contrary. Either way, her husband Louis VII seems not to have appreciated the gift. As you can see, the inscription on the base shows that he later gave it to Suger, the Abbot of Saint-Denis, who added it to his collection as part of the treasury of the abbey.'

Jules said, 'It's those twelfth-century gold additions that we're interested in, Henri. Now, Victor, show him the cross.'

Still not quite following Jules's train of thought but happy to be led along by his old mentor, Victor laid the case on the table a cautious distance away from the vase in its crate, and opened the lid for Carbonneau to view its contents.

'It's not brass, Henri,' Jules said.

'I can see that.' Carbonneau's eyes were popping.

'As far as we can ascertain, the cross dates back to roughly the same period as the vase,' Jules explained. 'Or, should I say, to the period of the gold mount and base into which the crystal was set during Queen Eleanor's time. Its extremely fine construction conceals a hidden blade. But more importantly, we also have compelling reason to believe that this cross belonged to Gaspard de la Roche.'

Carbonneau's eyebrows shot up, accentuating his already astonished expression. 'The crusader?'

'None other, Henri. And you don't need me to explain the connection between Gaspard and Queen Eleanor, I'm sure.'

Managing to tear his gaze away from the cross long enough to turn towards Victor, Carbonneau said, 'Forgive me for speaking so frankly, Monsieur, but you must be insane, walking around the streets of Paris with this in your possession. What if something happened to it?'

'My task is to ensure nothing does,' Victor replied. 'It's the property of a very good friend of mine, who discovered it only weeks ago.'

'Now, Victor,' Jules said with a smile. 'Allow me to enlighten you as to this theory of mine, whose mystery I know has been driving you to distraction. I can only pray that I was right. Henri, may I beg your permission to remove the vase from its crate, just for one moment?'

'Please do be careful, Jules. The president will bring back the guillotine especially for us, if anything happens to that vase.'

'It has survived my handling it in the past,' Jules told Carbonneau with just a hint of coldness in his tone. 'I doubt I shall drop it now. If anything, my dexterity has only improved with age.' As delicately as though it had been a baby bird, Jules lifted the vase just enough to expose the underside of its circular base. The gold was rougher-hewn under there. But clearly visible, stamped into the metal, was the same tiny mark that Victor had seen on the cross and thought to be a hallmark.

'I recalled having noticed this mark many, many years ago, during my time as curator here,' Jules said. 'I had always wondered as to its origin and significance, which had remained unknown to even the most astute historians. And now that I'm able to refresh my memory of it, the answer finally presents itself. Just as I thought, there can be little doubt that the identical and hitherto unidentified inscriptions on both the vase and the cross were put there by one and the same craftsman. They're a maker's mark.'

Carbonneau leaned over the cross to scrutinise it more closely, and breathed, '*Mon Dieu*, Jules, you're quite right. What a thing to have noticed!'

'I'm sorry I was secretive,' Jules said to Victor. 'I had to be sure.'

For Victor, the sudden realisation was like a bolt of lightning flashing through his head. He turned to Jules, wide-eyed.

'If Eleanor had employed a master goldsmith to create the mount for her—'

Jules nodded. 'Yes, and if that same master goldsmith were to have fashioned the cross, commissioned to do so at her behest—'

'—Knowing as we do the connection between Eleanor and the cross's presumed former owner, Gaspard de la Roche—'

'—Just as she gave the vase to Louis as a wedding present—'

'—She could have made a similar gift to Gaspard, to reward him for his loyalty and protection on crusade!' Victor cried out. 'A hidden dagger within a gold cross. What a fitting and splendid offering for a noble warrior.' For just an instant, doubts flooded him and he looked anxious. 'But how could we ever prove any of this was true?'

'My dear Victor, I would gladly challenge anyone to *disprove* it.'

The two old friends stared at one another, Victor dizzy with excitement, Jules flushed with triumph. It was Carbonneau, barely able to contain his own amazement, who concluded for them: 'Then that would suggest that the crystal vase may no longer be the only artefact of Eleanor's known to exist today. Which would be . . .'

'An unbelievably important find,' Jules said. 'I would consider that to be an understatement, even. Gentlemen, we may very well be looking at one of the most significant historical discoveries an antiquarian scholar could dream of.'

It took Carbonneau a few moments to regain his composure. 'If it should turn out that you're correct, and that this cross is indeed an artefact directly associated with Eleanor of Aquitaine, then it should be kept safely here in the museum,' he said, starting to bluster as the enormity of it sank in. 'Its value would be inestimable. And Monsieur here is walking around in public with it inside a briefcase! Now come, you simply cannot go on taking such an unconscionable risk. I must respectfully advise you to leave it in our hands while its authenticity is being verified by experts.'

'What experts?' Jules asked, ruffled. 'Do you not find the present company expert enough for you, young sir?'

'Don't misunderstand me,' Carbonneau protested. 'It's just that . . . I mean, can you imagine if someone were to steal it? It doesn't even bear thinking about.'

'Might I remind you that these decisions aren't ours to make,' Victor said. 'The cross rightfully belongs to the man who discovered it on his own property.'

'This friend of yours. Who is he, anyway?'

'His name is Hope, Benedict Hope. Only he can decide what should be done with it, whether he wishes to hang it on his wall as a curio—'

'God forbid!' Carbonneau gasped, appalled.

'Or sell it to a private buyer for an absolute fortune.'

'That would be tragic! Tragic!'

'Or, to pass it to the museum for safekeeping.'

'Do you think he would agree to that?' Carbonneau asked, his expression brightening, but only cautiously.

'I know this man,' Victor replied. 'I don't believe for one moment that he would be inclined to keep it for himself, or be seduced into parting with it for mere money. He's a person of great integrity, who I'm certain will do the right thing. But in return for the trust he has placed in me, I have to abide by his wishes, whatever they might be.'

'Very well,' Carbonneau said, pulling an unhappy face. 'Then what do you propose to do?'

'To return to Normandy as soon as possible, taking the cross with me,' Victor said, 'and to reveal to Monsieur Hope what we believe we've uncovered about its history.'

'You still have time to catch the eleven-thirty train,' Jules said, 'if we hurry.'

'But all this travelling to and fro only creates more unnecessary risk,' Carbonneau pointed out. 'Why can you not simply phone him from Paris and explain the situation? Then the cross remains safely here.'

'Because something as important as this has to be done face to face,' Victor said firmly. 'I will not risk giving my friend the impression that we three old men are somehow conspiring to cling onto his precious discovery for ourselves. He has to be completely free to make his choice, with all the facts and all the evidence in front of him. Whereupon, I've every confidence that I will be heading straight back here to Paris immediately after Christmas, to proudly donate the cross to the museum with his blessing.'

'Very well. You must do what you think is right,' Carbonneau said reluctantly. 'But the director would skin me alive if he knew the chance we were taking.'

'I've known the director for forty-five years,' Jules said. 'He was an idiot then, and he's still an idiot now.'

'Have no fear,' Victor assured Carbonneau with a smile. 'You'll be seeing it again, and soon.'

Chapter 13

As the snow came spiralling and flurrying down even harder, César Casta and his five associates, Pasquale di Borgo, Ángel Leoni, Raul Ramolino, Carlo Cipriani and Petru Navarro, passed under the overhead LE VAL sign and made their way along the long, curving track towards the heart of the compound. Though they'd had so little time to prepare for the job at hand, Casta was fully confident in his men's ability to carry it through – or almost fully. While the rest of them had worked together before on several occasions, the new recruit, Petru, was still an unknown quantity. He came highly recommended, but from his behaviour back at the guard hut and his general attitude, Casta privately suspected the guy might be a bit of a loose cannon. It wasn't Casta's place to complain, however. The boss had made his choice, and Petru had certain significant family connections that made it a diplomatic move to accept him: so Petru it was.

Casta paused for a moment to check his phone, firstly to

verify that the mobile reception jammer device in his back-pack was doing its business. Yup, the phone was functioning fine but there was no trace of reception. The closer they got to their target, the more effectively the jammer's range would block anyone within the compound from being able to raise the alarm. A handy piece of kit, indispensable nowadays. Mobiles were a monumental pain in the ass. In the olden days, back when Casta was a young thug learning the ropes of his trade, you just sent a guy up a pole to snip the phone wire and you were away. But a crook's skills had to keep pace with technology.

The second reason for checking the phone was to take a last look at the plan of the place, provided to Casta courtesy of the inside man the boss had planted at the tactical training facility just days earlier. The series of images he'd been emailed provided a detailed layout of the facility – the main house, the perimeter and gatehouse, the classrooms and other outbuildings, the two firing ranges, both long and short, and the killing house. But the main focus for the attack team tonight would be the armoury, whose invaluable contents were as attractive to men in their specialised line of work as a vault filled with gold bullion would be to a professional bank heist artist. Their inside man had been unable to provide actual images of the inside of the armoury, but he had given them enough detailed information about the loot stored there to make the boss happy.

All they needed to do now was get inside.

It had been agreed from the start that there were two basic ways of achieving that goal: the hard way and the easy way. The hard way would involve using hi-spec military shape charges to blast their way in through the series of three armoured steel doors – forget trying to penetrate the several feet of reinforced concrete that made the underground room as impregnable as a nuclear bunker. But as organised and well-funded as they were, Casta's gang lacked the luxury of such toys. Indeed, if they'd had access to those kinds of items, they wouldn't have needed to resort to extreme measures to obtain a few crateloads of fully-automatic weapons and other assorted goodies. They weren't quite in the same league as the big-boy terrorists who had the contacts and finances to get anything they wanted, from small arms to SAM missiles to chemical weapons, at the drop of a hat.

Unless you were prepared to spend twenty hours going at it with a cutting torch, that left the easy way: getting hold of the keys. Also thanks to their inside man, who'd been perfectly placed to eavesdrop on some very interesting conversations at Le Val just days earlier, the gang happened to know that one of the armoury keyholders, who'd stayed behind to take care of the place along with the skeleton security crew, was half-crippled and walking around with a plaster and a crutch. The gang knew all about the crippled guy. They had a whole profile on him: name, photo, and some notion of his military past and training. They even knew what kind of car he drove, a souped-up blue Beemer. As far as all that Special Forces stuff was concerned, Casta thought it was a load of hype. He didn't care how good the guy was. No way could he compete with six hardened professionals, fit, fully mobile, determined and armed.

The boss had been wanting to get his hands on a tasty

haul of military small arms like this for quite some time. Using several inside men similarly recruited to help them, they'd been remotely checking out similar locations for the last several months: one in Spain, one in Italy, one in Germany, one in the UK. The Italian one was the least organised and easiest to get into, but at the same time it was the least well stocked. All bets had been on the German option, until the report had come back that, by a fluke, Le Val and its treasure trove would be left deliciously vulnerable for several days over Christmas.

They couldn't have asked for a better stroke of luck. The boss had jumped at it straight away. Which hadn't left much time for planning and logistics. With all the rushing and last-minute crew changes it had meant accepting the insertion of a new team member about whom they knew relatively little. It was a compromise. But here they were. And it was happening.

Casta was convinced that the job could come off like a charm. Once the merchandise was safely delivered, he'd collect his cash and party for a while, before the next job came in. It had been a good year for him.

The snow was deep underfoot, and deepening every minute as fresh layers of fluffy flakes kept drifting down thick and hard. As the six men made their way down the long, sweeping curve of the track towards the heart of the compound the first of the facility's buildings came into view through the trees, the glow of floodlights casting beams in which the cascading flakes seemed to dance and swirl like swarms of moths.

'You ask me, instead of all this stealth crap we should've

just driven in and stormed the place,' muttered Petru Navarro in their native language as they trudged through the snow.

'Is that a fact?' Casta snapped back at the new guy, instantly regretting it. Strong commanders didn't get into a debate with men like this. The likes of Petru needed a firm hand, not pandering to.

'That's right,' Petru said. 'And I'll tell you something else, too. These masks you're making us wear are bullshit. Only assholes and wannabe warriors wear shit like this on their head.'

'You'd rather get your face on camera, man?' Raul Ramolino asked him.

'I'd rather be able to breathe,' Petru said.

'Keep it on,' Casta warned him, 'or you'll have me to deal with. If you can't breathe, then why don't you save your breath and shut the fuck up?'

'Yeah, man,' Leoni muttered. 'We don't need your bitching.'

'You shouldn't talk to me like that,' Petru said in a quieter voice.

They ignored him. 'So remember the plan, boys,' Casta told them. 'The crippled guy's bound to have a weapon or two stashed away in the house, so what we have to do is surprise him so he can't get to them. When we reach the house we go in hard and fast, all at once. By the time he knows what's happening, it'll be all over. Okay?'

'He'd better not be armed,' Petru muttered. 'Anyone pulls a gun on me is a dead man.'

'Which is nothing compared to what you'll be if you fuck about,' Casta warned him. He was about to add, 'I don't give a shit who your uncle is,' but chose to keep that part to himself. He was beginning to strongly regret bringing this troublemaker along.

Now they were getting closer, they could hear the sound of dogs barking from the direction of the buildings. Again, thanks to the inside man, the gang knew the exact number of guard dogs that patrolled the compound. They even knew their names: Storm, Blitz, Sabre, Diablo and Bomber. Though they doubted the brutes would respond to a pat on the head and a biscuit. Casta wasn't taking any chances.

'Here they come, right on cue,' Casta said. 'They know we're here, all right.'

'Don't miss a trick, do they?' said di Borgo.

The barking was growing rapidly closer, though nothing was yet visible. All six men tensed, waiting. 'Get ready, boys,' Casta said. 'These fuckers will tear you up, you let 'em.'

Instants later the first guard dog appeared, a racing black wolflike shape silhouetted against the glow of the illuminated buildings, sending up a spray of white powdery snow as it came streaking towards them with long, powerful strides. The German shepherd spotted the six strangers on the track and halted twenty-five metres away, eyes fixed unwavering on them, big ears pricked up in full alert mode. A deep bark erupted from its chest and became a warning growl. The lights glimmered off its fangs. It wasn't trained to be an attack dog, because attack dogs don't give warnings. The message was clear: *turn around and leave now.*

Casta drew out the long silenced pistol, took a couple of steps closer to the dog, raised the weapon and took aim. The dog sensed the threat and charged, snarling and snapping its teeth. Casta stood his ground and squeezed the trigger.

The shot was like a muffled handclap, muted even more by the denseness of the falling snow. The dog was fifteen metres away and closing fast when it squealed and fell, then picked itself up and tried valiantly to keep coming. Casta shot it twice more, and now the dog was down and staying down, lying still on its side and turning the snow pink.

'Incoming,' di Borgo said, whipping out his own gun as another black shape came tearing out of the trees towards them. The report of the pistol was followed by a sharp crack and a whining ricochet as his bullet missed its fast-moving target and glanced off a tree trunk. The dog kept coming straight for them, locked on its target like a missile. Di Borgo went to take another shot, but before he could get it off Petru had nailed the animal in his sights and rattled off a stream of bullets, chasing it. The dog veered off course as the shots kicked up little explosions of snow at its feet. Then his sixth round caught it in the flank, and it howled and went writhing down into the snow, mortally injured.

'Gotcha,' Petru said. He thrust his weapon back in its belt.

'Now go and finish it off,' Casta told him.

Petru shrugged. 'What for? It's only a stupid mutt. Why waste the bullets?'

'You can't leave it like that,' Casta said. 'Go over there and finish it.'

'I thought you said you hated dogs, man.'

'I do,' Casta said. 'That's why I prefer a dead one. If it's still alive it might make noise.'

'Fine, fine, suit yourself,' Petru grumbled. He drew the pistol back out and went trudging off through the deep snow to where the dog lay dying. He stood over it, pointed the pistol downwards and let off two more shots.

'There,' he muttered, trudging back to rejoin them. 'Finished. Happy now?'

'You're a real asshole, Petru, you know that?' said Cipriani. Petru flipped him off with a scowl. 'Eat me.'

Casta held a finger to his lips. 'Shhh.'

The six men fell silent, listening hard and scanning for more dogs. Two down, still three to go, but there was no sign of life. 'Maybe they're locked up in the kennels,' Leoni said. 'Or in the house with the crippled guy.'

'Keep your ears and eyes open,' Casta said. 'You see something with four legs and teeth, kill it.'

They moved on.

Chapter 14

So it looked like Jeff's nose had been right after all. As Ben stood at the window of the farmhouse kitchen, watching the picture-postcard winter scene outside, he was thinking he was glad he hadn't taken that bet. The snow had been coming down relentlessly for hours and he was pretty sure it'd continue throughout the night. By morning parts of the compound would be three feet deep, while the thermometer was still dropping steadily. By contrast the farmhouse was toasty warm, the antiquated but still perfectly serviceable central heating system kept running at a luxurious temperature by the red-hot coals of the kitchen range, stoked day and night this time of year.

Ben felt sorry for the three guys in the gatehouse, and although they had a decent heater and could brew up enough hot coffee to melt a glacier, he'd thought a couple of times that evening about radioing them to come over and warm themselves up indoors. Maybe he'd call them in a little while. It was Christmas Eve, after all.

His thoughts turned to Jeff in the scorching heat of Australia and Tuesday basking in the tropical sunshine of

Jamaica. He hoped they were having a good time. They deserved it. It had been a hard-working year for everyone.

Ben's glass had run dry. He picked up his crutch from where it was leaning against the sill next to him, turned away from the window and hobbled over to pour himself another modest measure of Laphroaig. Only the third that evening, or was it the fourth? Either way, enough to let the comforting warmth spread all through him and almost – almost – soothe away the irritation of being stuck indoors when he could be getting on with something useful. Though in truth, over the last couple of days, since the others had gone off and left him alone in the house, he'd been slowly beginning to relax into the routine of having nothing to do except potter around and take it easy. At this moment, he felt it would be quite pleasant to flop in an armchair, listen to some music and go on with the book he was reading, a dense and detailed history of the crusades that he'd borrowed from Victor. If he went on like this, it would soon be the pipe and carpet slippers for him.

'Coming?' he said to Storm, who was curled up in his bed next to the warmth of the range. The dog followed him happily into the living room. Ben didn't use it very often – it was more Jeff's domain, with the big-screen television that he was in love with but which Ben had never once turned on. He wasn't much of a movie person and the TV news was all a pack of lies anyway. Ben fed an Art Blakey and the Jazz Messengers disc into the stereo, grabbed the book and made himself comfortable in an armchair by the lamp. It felt good to get off his feet. His ankle was hurting a little, but he'd resolved not to take any more painkillers that day.

Before opening his book Ben sat for a while, sipped his drink and enjoyed the peace of the moment. In the corner nearby stood the Christmas tree that Tuesday had insisted on dragging into the house, to create some festive spirit in the place while Ben was on his own. Tuesday was thoughtful like that. He'd fussed over hanging decorations (something Jeff Dekker was far too tough and manly to stoop to doing, of course) and even arranged presents around the foot of the tree. One of the wrapped gifts, distinctively shaped, Ben suspected was a bottle of Laphroaig for him, strictly not to be opened until Jeff and Tuesday's return after Christmas. The rest were mostly from clients: Auguste Kaprisky, their eccentric billionaire friend from Le Mans and one of Le Val's most ardent fans, always sent a case of champagne.

Tuesday had likewise gone to the trouble of setting all their seasonal greetings cards on the mantelpiece. Among the teeming collection was one from Ben's younger sister Ruth, once despaired of as lost, then found, who had been living for years in Switzerland. Another was from Roberta Ryder in Ottawa, who'd been a flame of Ben's at one time. Then there was one from Commander Darcey Kane, who hadn't, though not for want of trying; and still another from Madison Cahill, someone else Ben hadn't heard from in a while. She'd used to be Special Agent Madison Cahill of the United States National Fugitive Recovery Agency: in essence, a bounty hunter. Quitting that rough-and-tumble life she'd taken up the reins from her father, Rigby Cahill, now deceased, who'd made his famous name (and not a small fortune) hunting not people, but treasures. A brief note with Madison's card said that she'd relocated her father's old company to San Diego, with a new phone number and a note telling Ben to call soon. The two of them had never got together, but close.

Funny how Christmas time can make a man go all sentimental and nostalgic, Ben reflected as he cast his mind back to all those loves or near-loves he'd known. Sinking deeper into comfort and soaking up the rolling thunder of Art's drums and the mellow tones of Wayne Shorter's saxophone, he took another sip of his drink, heaved a sigh of something approaching contentment and then reopened Victor's book across his lap to go on reading about the Siege of Damascus in 1148.

He'd been deep in the narrative for a few minutes when Storm, stretched out like a long hairy carpet at his feet, raised his head with an inquisitive ear cocked towards the window and let out a low growl, followed by a soft 'Wuff.'

'What's up, boy?' Ben asked him, reaching out absently to pat his head. Storm's ultra-sharp hearing had probably picked up the hoot of a distant owl. He had a particular aversion towards owls, for some reason Ben had never been able to understand.

Storm normally would relax and lie back down at the touch of Ben's hand, but he didn't. He got up on all fours and paced across to the window, looking out, and gave another growl, deeper, longer and louder this time. Looking up from the book, Ben saw that the dog had drawn his lips into a snarl. That was odd. Storm had to be sensing something more than an owl out there. Maybe a fox was on the prowl. Well, it wouldn't get very far, with Le Val's guard pack roaming free.

'Do you mind?' Ben said to him, in a gentle but firm tone. 'I'm trying to read.'

Storm stayed fixed at the window, his body language tense. He let out a deep-chested bark. Then another, rearing up slightly on his hind paws. His hackles were raised, a ridge of bristles all down his back standing up like spikes. What was up with him?

Ben had raised the dog from a pup, and knew his ways intimately. As highly trained as he was, Storm wasn't above the occasional display of German shepherd trickery, with his own clever and various ways of distracting the two-leggeds from whatever activities the dog believed were less important than paying attention to him. The unwitting human could all too easily find themselves in the position where it was the dog training *them*, and not the other way around. But, putting down his book and watching Storm at the window, Ben knew that this wasn't one of those times. Something out there was bothering him. And it was something much more pressing than the local wildlife.

'Storm, what is it?' Ben said in a more serious voice, and the urgency in his tone brought an explosive flurry of barking from the dog. Then, suddenly, he wheeled away from the window and ran towards the door. The barking amplified into a continuous roaring and baying. He was going wild, rearing up full height on his powerful hindquarters so that he was nearly as tall as Ben, furiously raking the door with his claws.

Something was wrong. Something was very wrong. The book spilled from Ben's lap as he reached for his crutch and heaved himself out of his chair, hobbling across to turn off the music. A hundred possibilities were flashing through his mind. Was the house on fire? Had a fight broken out among the other dogs? Had Serge, Michel or Richard come running down from the gatehouse to report some crisis happening?

Ben had no idea. What came next was totally unexpected.

It was the sound of the front door crashing open and the farmhouse being invaded by multiple attackers.

Chapter 15

Ben Hope was someone who was used to encountering sudden, random outbreaks of violence. Experience had taught him it could come from anywhere, anytime, and had honed his responses so finely that almost nothing could shock or surprise him. Even walking down the street, part of him was always watching for suspicious movement – a carload of men pulling up at the kerb; someone stepping suddenly from a hidden entrance; the sound of running feet coming up behind. When he sat in a bar or restaurant he always took the corner table with a view of both window and door. It wasn't paranoia. It was just a careful, practical level of constant awareness of his surroundings. But in the cosy comfort of his own home, on a snowy Christmas Eve, surrounded by a secure, guarded perimeter – that took the unexpected to a whole new level.

For once in his life, Ben had been caught unawares.

The living room at Le Val was at the end of a long flagstone hallway that ran past the kitchen on the left and the staircase on the right, to the front door. Ben could hear a tumult of running footsteps in the hall. Maybe four, maybe five men, maybe more. He heard the kitchen door crash open. Heard a voice issue a hoarse and indistinct command in a foreign language that sounded familiar and yet unfamiliar. It wasn't quite Italian, and it wasn't Sicilian, but it was something close to both. And now there was a thundering of boots on the stairs, and more approaching the living room.

Ben's right hand instinctively went to the hollow behind his right hip where a pistol would be. That was, if he'd been carrying a pistol. If he hadn't been at home, where he wasn't in the habit of going around armed at all times. If his personal defence weapons, the faithful old Browning Hi-Power among them, hadn't been locked away in the security cabinet by his bedside, two floors up, totally out of reach.

Not ideal.

At Ben's signal, Storm fell silent. The dog stood planted in front of the doorway, as rigid as a statue, teeth bared. Ben hobbled towards the door. It was solid oak, three inches thick. As old as the rest of the house, dating back to a time when interior room doors had all had iron locks fitted to them. Ben was aiming to get the key turned before the running steps reached the other side of the door, but he wasn't fast enough. He was still five limping strides from the lock when he saw the handle turn; and in the next instant the door burst inwards and a man crashed into the room, less than two yards from where Ben was standing.

The man was all in black, except for the white sprinkling of snow that dusted his clothes. Black mask, black tactical vest, black handgun with a long black sound suppressor. The man's eyes fixed on Ben through the holes in his mask and the muzzle of the pistol swung around to point at its unarmed target.

Unarmed, but not quite. Ben did have one weapon with him in the living room.

The attacker didn't see the dog coming for him until it was too late to retreat back through the door or turn the gun on him. Storm was already in mid-air, all teeth and bristling fur, as the guy staggered back in terror, shouldering the door half-shut behind him and letting off an accidental shot that passed through empty air and punched a crater in the far wall. Then Storm's fangs were sunk into his gun arm and he was being dragged down and shaken like a straw mannequin.

Another intruder was coming up right behind the first. Same mask, same clothes, same snowy sprinkling, same weapon. He was shoving his way in through the half-closed door when the aluminium shaft of Ben's crutch whooshed towards his face and struck hard. Ben felt the guy's nose break with the impact, and heard the yowl of pain over the panic-stricken cries of his associate being savaged by Storm on the floor. The second guy fell back through the doorway, spouting blood through his mask. Without the support of his crutch the momentum of the blow sent Ben off balance, and he fell, too. But even as he hit the floor he kicked out with his good leg and slammed the door shut before managing to scrabble up to his knees and twist the key home.

Ben crawled away from the door, reaching for his crutch, but the shaft was bent and crumpled from being used as a club. The masked intruder was still completely helpless in Storm's teeth. He'd dropped his gun in his panic. Ben commanded, 'Storm, leave!' and the dog let go. The guy was out of trouble, but only for an instant. Ben snatched up the fallen pistol. At the briefest glance he knew it was an old-model SIG Sauer 9mm with a Mod-X9 silencer fitted, and he could tell by the weight that it was fully loaded.

But there was more than one way to use a gun. Especially when you wanted to keep the enemy alive in order to find out who the hell he was and what in the world he was doing here. Those questions would have to wait for now. Ben hammered the butt into the guy's head, fast and brutal, three, four, five times, until he wasn't struggling any more.

Footsteps thundered down the stairs as the attackers who'd gone up there rejoined those in the passage. There was a heavy pounding against the door. The lock was strong, and nobody made hinges and frames like that nowadays. They could resist any amount of pounding, for a while at least. Gunfire, maybe not so much. Ben heard the percussive thuds as bullets from a suppressed pistol hammered into the other side of the wood. It would take a higher-powered firearm, like a rifle or a slug-loaded shotgun, to punch straight through the thick oak with a single shot. But chew away with enough rounds of 9mm handgun ammo and, sooner or later, they'd be able to blast out enough wood to take out the lock. Ben staggered to his feet, grabbed Storm's collar and hauled him bodily away from the door, scared that a bullet might find a way through.

After several shots the firing paused. Ben heard raised, angry voices in the passage. It sounded like an argument was going on. Then a hoarse voice yelled in accented English through the door, 'We don't want to hurt anyone. We know you have the vault key. Slide it under the door and we'll take what we came for and leave you alone. Or else we're gonna burn this fucking house down with you inside it.'

So this was what it was about. They'd come here to rip off

the armoury. Which was already triggering an avalanche of unanswerable questions in Ben's mind. How did they know of its existence, what it contained, and that he was the keyholder?

And how had these bastards managed to get past the gatehouse guards?

Ben said nothing. Moments counted, before they got back to work taking down the door or decided to work their way around the side of the house and try to smash in through the window. The attackers must know that Ben was armed now, and they'd be deterred by the presence of the dog. But if enough of them came piling in at once, breaching his defences from the door and window simultaneously, there was little chance of repelling them.

Ben's mind was speeding as he tried to work out some kind of plan. The farmhouse was a rambling maze of inter-connected rooms. Beyond the living room was an old box room that Ben had long meant to tidy out, filled with all kinds of junk: dead computers, books that would never be read and DVDs that would never be watched, a bunch of broken chairs. Beyond that room lay a dusty unlit passage that led to a seldom-used backstair down to the wine cellar. And because it was traditional in France to take the protec-tion of one's precious wine stocks extremely seriously, the cellar's iron door was almost as impenetrable as the armoury.

'All right, then, you asked for it,' yelled the voice. Bullets began hammering at the living room door. Ben knew that their threat to burn the house if he didn't give them the key was a bluff. Once they had it, though, there was no telling what they might do.

He had no intention of letting either of those things happen.

Chapter 16

Ben grabbed his unconscious prisoner by the collar and started dragging him towards the box room door. The guy was heavy and Ben was unsteady on his feet. His ankle was hurting worse from so much strenuous movement. 'Help me,' he said to Storm, and seeing what Ben was trying to do, the dog fastened his teeth into the fabric of the man's jacket. Between them they dragged the dead weight into the box room. Ben could hear banging at the window now. He dumped the invader's limp body on the box room floor and hobbled back to lock the door behind them. There were now two barriers between him and the invaders, though that wouldn't remain so for long. Moreover, the box room door was much flimsier than that of the living room. If Ben was going to survive this, he needed to get further ahead of the curve, and fast.

The loud thumps from outside were suddenly followed by the crash and tinkle of breaking glass. An instant later, Ben heard the living room door burst open and the sound of thudding footsteps and loud voices spilling through into the room. They were in.

With Storm's help, Ben hurriedly manhandled his prisoner across the box room floor and out into the dusty passage beyond, locking that door behind them too. The passage was smoothly tiled, making it easier to drag a body in a hurry. The passage had no windows and no other doors, nowhere to go except dead ahead towards the wine cellar steps. Behind them, Ben could hear the attackers already hammering at the door into the box room. It wouldn't hold them up for long, and nor would the next. He was managing to stay ahead of the curve, but only just.

At the end of the dark passage they reached the top of the rough stone steps leading down to the arch of the wine cellar doorway. Ben's ankle was on fire and it was all he could do to stay on his feet, with no crutch. He bumped the unconscious prisoner down the steps, unworried about inflicting a few extra bruises on the guy in the process. The lock on the cellar door was a prehistoric thing covered with centuries' worth of black paint. He opened it with a grinding turn of the ancient great iron key, and managed to swing the heavy door open without falling over. The dank, musty cellar smell wafted out to meet them as Storm bounded into the dark doorway and then turned around to help Ben bundle and drag the prisoner inside. Ben jerked the key from the lock, shouldered the door closed with a resonating *clang* and relocked it from inside.

They were safe in here. If the intruders couldn't break into the armoury unaided they had little chance of getting inside the cellar, either. Though tactically an underground crypt wasn't a great choice of refuge, unless you were planning on remaining hunkered down there for the duration. Ben had other plans.

With the heavy iron door secured, what little light had shone from the passageway outside was now completely shut out. Ben and Jeff had never quite got around to installing any electric wiring down in the wine cellar; on his quite frequent trips to bring up more bottles, Ben had always relied on an electric lantern that he left here for that purpose. He groped around in the darkness, found it and turned it on, and suddenly the stone arches of the vaulted ceiling created looming, flickering curved shadows across the uneven floor and the many ancient oak barrels and wine racks that lined the rough, cobwebbed walls. Ben limped over to where he'd dumped the prisoner propped up in a corner by the doorway. Kneeling beside him and holding the lantern close, he stripped off the black ski mask to reveal the bloody, lean and unshaven face of a man around thirty years of age. The guy had long, thinning, greasy black hair slicked back over his skull, and an olive complexion that went with the accented English and the unidentified foreign language the others had been speaking in. Not locals, for sure. This crew had evidently travelled some distance to launch their attack on Le Val. A quick frisk of the man's pockets turned up no kind of ID, though Ben hadn't been expecting any. No phone, either.

That planted a thought in Ben's mind. It was far from his natural instinct to call the police in a crisis. Though in his estimation they might be about as much use as a three-legged stool much of the time, right now he needed all the help he could get. But when he took out his phone and went to start punching in the emergency call number, he realised that down here in the wine cellar he'd get zero reception. The joys of modern wireless technology. He put the phone back in his pocket.

The prisoner was slowly coming to, eyes rolling and unfocused, still stunned. It was time to wake him up. Ben jammed the muzzle of the silenced pistol in his face. Speaking French, he said, 'Welcome back to the land of the living, pal. It's just you and me now. Your friends aren't going to save you down here, so you'd better talk to me. What's your name?'

The prisoner hesitated, then eyed the muzzle of the pistol that was inches from the tip of his nose and blurted, 'Raul.'

'Raul what?'

'Ramolino.'

'You're not French, and you're not Italian. Where are you from?'

'Sò di Corsica,' the guy replied, in that language. Which explained why it had sounded so similar, and yet so subtly different, from Italian. So now Ben knew where the gang had travelled from. That still didn't explain what a bunch of Corsican thugs were doing trying to rip off an arsenal of weapons in the north of France.

Ben asked him, 'Who do you work for?'

At that moment he heard a loud, heavy thumping and pounding from the other side of the wine cellar door. It seemed that Raul's friends had broken through the box room and come to join them. *Good luck with that*, Ben thought, as the thumping went on. He said to Raul, 'Forget about them. They can't help you. I asked you, who do you work for?'

Raul Ramolino seemed about to say more, but then a look of defiance came into his eyes. Ben had seen that look plenty of times before, all the way back to his military days.

The prisoner decides to be uncooperative. You almost had to admire his spirit. Raul's face twisted into an ugly leer in the dim lantern light and he spat, 'Fuck you, Inglese.'

Ben shoved the pistol hard under his chin, the round end of the silencer digging into his unshaven jaw. 'Not the answer I was hoping for, Raul. If you'd really done your homework you'd know that I'm not English, I'm half Irish. Which makes me the kind of wild, crazy person who's perfectly likely to blow your damn head off if you don't play ball with me.'

Raul's pupils shrank to pinheads and he snarled in Corsican, 'So shoot me, asshole. I'm not telling you a goddamn thing.'

Ben got the gist of his meaning pretty well. He fixed Raul with a hard look for several seconds, and decided that the guy meant it. *Fine. Have it your way.* There wasn't time to waste on dragging it out of him. So Ben reached out with his left hand, grabbed a fistful of Raul's lank, greasy black hair and dashed his head mercilessly against the stone wall. Two, three, four hard knocks later he let go of the hank of hair and Raul's head lolled sideways onto his shoulder.

Ben wiped his greasy hand on his trousers and muttered, 'To be resumed.'

In the meantime, he needed to make sure Raul didn't get up to any tricks once he came to again. The cellar was full of all kinds of useful bric-a-brac that had lain around for centuries just waiting for such an opportunity. Ben found a length of rope hanging from a hook, probably once used for lowering wine casks down here, old but still strong. He used it to hogtie the unconscious Raul with his ankles and wrists bound together. The Corsican wasn't going anywhere, but just to be sure Ben used the last length of rope to fasten him to a sturdy iron ring in the wall.

Once that was done, Ben set about his main purpose in taking refuge down here. He wouldn't have let himself be cornered in an underground trap if he hadn't had a plan for getting out, unseen and unsuspected by the enemy. A long time ago, a much younger, greener Ben had received the words of wisdom from a gruff, grizzled SAS sergeant, one Boonzie McCulloch, his trainer, his mentor, later his friend: 'Always gie yersel' a back door, Laddie.'

And a back door was what Ben had – or so he had to hope. Holding up the lantern, he let its wobbling pool of light shine into the corner of the cellar where the rubble of the newly-rediscovered tunnel entrance lay strewn over the flagstones. 'You want to come with me, or you want to stay and look after this idiot?' he asked Storm. The dog looked at him with a cocked head as though the answer were obvious.

'Okay, let's go.'

Ben had already known that it wasn't much of a tunnel, at this end. The partially subsided mouth of the horizontal shaft was a tightly restrictive space for an adult human male to squeeze into, especially one badly compromised by a cumbersome plaster cast. But for a dog, even a large dog, it was easy. Storm could wriggle through the narrowest of gaps and even limbo his way under a farm gate. He planted both forepaws on the edge of the shaft, gave it an exploratory sniff or two and then scrambled eagerly inside, paws digging at the dirt and his shaggy tail disappearing into the darkness ahead of Ben.

Here goes, Ben thought. With the Corsican's pistol stuck crossways through his belt he gritted his teeth, shoved the lantern into the hole to light his way, and then clambered in after Storm. He had to worm inch by inch through the tight gap, and for a worrying moment it seemed he was stuck. His plastered foot caught against the rough stonework and a shiver of pain jolted up his shin. But then he found a purchase, and with some heaving and straining he forced himself through and found the tunnel mouth opening up enough for him to keep going. He thought *Fuck it* and started crawling.

Chapter 17

Ben had been in more claustrophobic spaces during his lifetime. He'd once escaped from a subterranean Scottish castle dungeon by crawling out of a sewer pipe, and in Africa he'd dug his way out of an earth pit in which he'd been buried with a pile of stinking corpses. But the oppressively constricted shaft, and the constant fear of being encased in a tomb beneath countless tons of rock and dirt should the whole thing suddenly cave in on top of him, didn't make for a pleasant experience this time around either. If there was one thing he'd vowed and declared he'd never do in his life, it was pot-holing. And here he was.

After just a few yards, he was deeper into the hole than anyone had been in the best part of a thousand years. Foot by foot, yard by yard he made his way, the rasp of his breath echoing back at him off the stone walls, the rough floor scraping against his knees and elbows, trying not to jar his bad ankle against the tunnel side and ceiling. He could hear Storm's panting from somewhere up ahead and called out for him to stay close, but the dog had disappeared into the darkness beyond the reach of the lantern's feeble glow. If not for the dog scouting the way ahead, Ben would have had no way of telling if it was even open.

After about twenty metres or so, just as it seemed as though the narrow shaft would go on forever like this, Ben nudged the lantern and felt it suddenly tilt as it toppled over the lip of a rocky ledge just an arm's length in front of him. He heard it go clattering down a stony slope and hit something hard. The light went out, and now Ben was in total darkness. He could feel the beginnings of panic rising up, and had to make a concerted effort to control it. Managing to reach an arm back down his side, he found his Zippo lighter in his jeans pocket and brought it up in front of him, flipped it open one-handed and thumbed the flint. The flame cast a soft, flickering orange light into the crevices of carved-out rock. Holding it out a little further he could make out the slope ahead, down which the lantern had tumbled to a stone floor that had been excavated a good three and a half feet deeper.

Ben wriggled to the edge of the slope and went slithering down it on his belly. Hobbling to his feet, holding the flame out in front and supporting himself against the craggy tunnel wall, he found himself suddenly able to straighten up to about three-quarters of his full height. The lantern was broken. He'd just have to pray he had enough fuel in his lighter to illuminate the way out of here.

Padding steps and the sound of panting from up ahead; the flicker of the flame was suddenly dancing in the pair of amber eyes that were peering worriedly at him out of the darkness. Storm had doubled back to find him, and licked Ben's hand as he stroked his fur.

'Lead on, boy.'

The raised headroom of the tunnel now made it possible to move a little more quickly. It was a popular myth that medieval humans were stunted and weedy by modern standards. As Ben had been reading in Victor's book, the massive size and sheer poundage of the average military longbow alone were proof enough that many of their original owners must have been brawny great giants of men. But whoever had dug out this tunnel obviously hadn't designed it to be used by anyone much above five feet tall. Ben had to shuffle along in a kind of duck walk, head bowed, knees bent. Storm kept darting off ahead and running back to nudge him along.

The steel lighter was getting uncomfortably hot in Ben's fingers and his ankle was aching. He was too concerned about Serge, Richard and Michel to notice the pain. What was going on up there at the gatehouse? Had anyone been able to raise the alarm? That was assuming they even knew what was happening. If not, it meant the intruders had managed to find another way inside the compound, which Ben doubted, because a lot of effort had been invested into making the perimeter fence secure. But if so, it raised the possibility that some kind of harm had come to the three.

And what about the remaining guard dogs, Blitz, Sabre, Diablo and Bomber? Were they alive? Were they dead?

Ben's anger, anxiety and frustration spurred him on faster. Soon afterwards he found that he'd reached the point where the tunnel branched off, one fork continuing up towards the church and the other leading into the original, abandoned section that the archaeology team had detected with their GPR magic eye.

He had no intention of following the tunnel all the way to the old church, because that would take him too far from the house to be able to retrace his steps, in his condition. Remembering the layout that de Klerk had mapped out, he turned into the abandoned section instead. Within less than a minute, he was beginning to worry that he'd made a mistake. It was suddenly much harder going as the tunnel became narrower and lower again, where the medieval diggers had struggled to carve through the rock before giving up. The airlessness down here in this dank, dark prison was threatening to make his flame gutter, and twice more he thought he was going to get jammed as he had to scramble over rocks and heaps of earth and stone that even Storm had difficulty getting past. His nagging doubts became so intense that he was on the verge of turning back, until he realised that his flame was suddenly burning more brightly again; a moment later the sudden sensation of cold, fresh air on his face told him that he'd reached the point of the tunnel that he'd been praying he'd find.

This was where the impossible ground conditions had forced the medieval diggers to get too close to the surface, with the result that the thin crust of ceiling had inevitably collapsed under its own weight. The cave-in uncovered by de Klerk's team was now half filled with snow, except for a narrow aperture, like a trapdoor overhead, through which flakes were drifting gently to layer the floor, glimmering in the flicker of Ben's flame.

The hole was easily big enough for Ben to clamber up out of – or it would have been, if he'd had two good legs to stand on in order to reach up and pull himself through. On his first attempt he fell back to the floor and was half-buried in the shower of dirt and snow that he brought down with him. Seeming to sense that his master needed him, Storm peered upwards to consider the mouth of their escape route, then he bunched his muscles like coiling springs and in one tremendous leap he sailed straight up in the air and made it through. For a moment he was gone – then the shaggy, pointy-eared head reappeared at the edge of the cave-in, peering worriedly down at Ben with the falling snow already dusting his mane white.

'Good boy, Storm – now help me up.'

Ben reached up and managed to grab a hold of Storm's collar with one hand, while clawing for grip at the edge of the hole with the other. The dog whimpered, the pull of Ben's weight hurting his neck. It took a lot to hurt a German shepherd. But he understood what he had to do and he didn't give up as he backed away from the hole, using all his power to haul his injured human up onto solid ground the way rescue dogs were taught to drag earthquake survivors out of the rubble. Several gasping, straining moments later, the two of them were sitting in the snow at the edge of the cave-in, back on the surface at last. 'If we get out of this,' Ben promised the dog, 'you'll get a pound of sirloin steak as a reward for that.' Thump, thump. Storm's tail beat the snow. A huge rough tongue slobbered all over Ben's face.

Ben scrabbled to his feet. A rising wind from the east was driving the snow hard into his eyes, sticking to his eyelashes, his hair. The underground tunnel had shielded him from the wind chill, and now he was exposed to the elements wearing only a denim shirt, his body heat was stripped away instantly and he began to shiver. The farmhouse lights glowed through the falling snow, some fifty yards away beyond the trees and bushes. He hunted around in the snowy undergrowth, found a fallen branch that wasn't too rotted to use as a walking staff and leaned on it for a moment as he took out his phone and tried again to call the police. His fingers were already getting numb from the cold.

No reception. That was odd. Every inch of the compound usually had good coverage. Ben wondered why that might be. But there was no time for guesswork right now, as he contemplated his next move. Should he try to reach the gatehouse in the hopes of finding the three guys there in any kind of good shape, or should he return to the farmhouse? He quickly weighed up the options, thinking that if Michel, Richard and Serge were all dead anyway, it would be a wasted exercise. Every moment counted and he'd lost too much time already. He decided there was really only one choice open to him, and that was to get back to the house and do whatever he could to thwart this attack. For all he knew, the raiders were already hard at work breaking into the armoury. Getting hold of the key might just have been their easiest, quickest option; they might have others as a fall-back, like explosives. The right kind of shape charge could make short work of all three armoury doors in succession.

The idea of the entire Le Val weapons arsenal falling into criminal hands was unthinkable. And it looked as though, for the moment at least, he was the only person standing in their way. *Trying to bloody stand*, he reflected bitterly as another twinge in his ankle made him lean more heavily on his makeshift staff.

One thing was for sure. Storm had done enough to help already, and Ben didn't want to expose him to more danger. 'Go,' he said to the dog. 'Get out of here. Find the others.' But it was useless. No amount of commands was going to persuade the dog to leave his master's side.

'You and me then, boy,' Ben said. 'Let's go and get them.'

Chapter 18

The wind was piling the snow deep against the east-facing side wall as Ben worked his way cautiously around towards the front. The makeshift staff helped him move along more easily, but not much. He was so bitterly cold that he hardly had any sensation in the fingers clutching the drawn pistol, and even his good foot felt like a useless block of ice. He was going to freeze to death out here if he didn't get a jacket on.

That was when he saw the dark shape lying in the snow a few yards ahead, obscured by the tall shadow that the house cast in the glow of the yard floodlights. He couldn't make out what it was until he advanced a few more shuffling, hobbling steps – and then a pulse of horror shot through him as he realised that it was the body of one of the dogs.

Storm was already running up to his fallen friend. He stood over the inert shape and nudged it with his nose, making a whining sound. There was no reaction, no movement. Ben stumbled up to the body. It was Sabre, Storm's pack-mate since they'd been little more than pups. Ben had raised him, trained him, cared for him when he'd been sick.

And now these bastards had shot him. Ben reached out and touched him. He hadn't been dead for long. The snow was just beginning to cover his body.

There was nothing to be done for poor Sabre now. Ben pushed his burning rage to the back of his mind. Anger doesn't help you in combat. Anger clouds your judgement. Anger gets you killed. Especially when the odds are so stacked against you. Forcing himself to stay calm and cool, he advanced to the corner of the house and peered around the edge of the stone wall. The house seemed quiet and there was nobody in sight. The only movement was the flurry of snowflakes in the beams of the floodlights. He strained hard to listen, but the only sound he could hear was the moan of the cold, cold wind gusting across the yard.

Where were the attackers? Ben couldn't afford to make any assumptions. They might still all be inside the house, trying to smash their way into the cellar in the hope of finding him and recovering their comrade. Or else they might have retreated back outside to focus on their principal target, the armoury. He had no way of telling how many there were, but he was guessing that a typical raid team would comprise five or six men: minus Raul, meant maybe four or five remaining. Ben had been up against greater odds many times, sometimes far greater, and lived to tell the tale. But this wasn't a normal situation and he was painfully aware of the handicap of his bad foot. Even armed as he was, going up against multiple combatants with his speed and agility effectively halved would be suicide.

There had to be a better way – and there was. Across the yard from the house was the stable block that had been converted into Jeff Dekker's quarters. Its windows were in darkness and it appeared the attackers were ignoring it – they seemed to know their way around the compound pretty well, which begged questions to be answered later. If Ben could get inside, it would offer temporary shelter, badly needed warmth, and something more besides. In the back was a small computer room where Jeff had set up a split-screen monitor showing the live feed from the various security cameras positioned around different parts of the compound. That would allow him to observe what the enemy was up to, and figure out the best plan to defeat them.

First he had to make it across the wide open space of the yard unseen. He was going to have to move fast. He peered left, peered right, saw nothing. Took a deep breath and launched himself out into the open. Hopping, limping, stumbling, determined not to go falling headlong into the snow. For those few seconds it took for him to get across he felt utterly naked and exposed. But he made it, without getting seen or shot.

More a lover of modern gadgets than Ben was, Jeff had installed a heavy-duty keypad lock on his door in lieu of anything more traditional. Ben's fingers were too numb with cold, so he used a knuckle to punch in the six-digit code, a number that only he, Jeff and Tuesday knew. Storm slipped through the door ahead of him, and Ben quickly closed them in and relocked it.

He kept the lights off, able to see by the glow of the floods overlooking the yard. The heating was on inside Jeff's quarters but Ben was shivering badly. A heavy winter jacket hung on a peg inside the doorway – an item Jeff hadn't needed to take with him to Australia – and Ben slipped it gratefully on and beat his hands together and slapped his sides and stamped his good foot until some kind of circulation was going again. He crept up to the window, peered out and saw nothing, but his gut told him the enemy were still out there somewhere.

Like Ben, Jeff Dekker used two or three different mobile phones. He had his personal phone that he'd taken with him on his travels, and he also had a battered old Nokia that was used around the compound as a walkie-talkie. The Nokia was lying on the coffee table next to Jeff's well-worn sofa. Ben scooped it up and turned it on, and quickly found that just like his own it was getting zero reception. Which confirmed the suspicion that had been in his mind before: the enemy were deploying some kind of mobile signal jammer to cut off all mobile communications. That in turn meant that they'd probably cut the phone landline, too. No way to check that from Jeff's quarters, because Jeff didn't have one – however Ben was willing to bet that the old rotary dial phone in the farmhouse and the one in the office weren't working, either.

One more point to the bad guys. But now Ben was ready to start fighting back. He made his way through the darkness of Jeff's quarters to the back room.

'Okay, you bastards, let's see if we can't figure out where you've gone.'

Keeping the light off, Ben drew the curtain to mask the glow of the screen. Then he activated the security monitor and it flashed into life, displaying a grid of little rectangular mini-screens that showed all the camera angles around the compound. It was a tech gimmick that Jeff had set up in a fit of security-minded efficiency some time back, and then seldom paid any attention to. 'There's nothing to watch,' he'd grumbled. 'Nothing ever happens.' As though that were something to complain about.

Well, something was happening now, for sure. And Jeff's monitor system was coming into its own at last, as Ben was able to observe the entire facility from his hiding place. The images from the hidden cameras were recorded on a hard drive, so that if he'd wished, Ben could have scrolled back to watch the raid unfold from the beginning. But there was no time for that right now, and it was the live video feed he wanted to see. It gave him multiple camera views of the range, the front of the killing house, three different angles of the farmhouse and yard, the vehicle sheds, the kennels, the east and west sides of the perimeter, the gatehouse and the armoury. By daylight the camera views were full-colour and pin-sharp. By night, they appeared like the image in infrared NV goggles, grainy and overexposed, the whites too bright and the darks too dark. But still plenty good enough.

It was the last two views Ben was most interested in. Each image could be expanded to full screen by a click. He clicked the gatehouse view, and instantly saw something was badly wrong there. The hut windows should all have been lit up bright, but instead the building was in darkness. The gate was open, and there was a strange minivan parked near the entrance. No sign of movement.

He scrolled back to a multi-view and then clicked on the armoury screen. The camera was picking up a lot of glare from the floodlights, and the image was grainy and hard to make out at first. Ben could see nothing but inert shadows. But then, as he peered harder at the screen, a sudden movement flashed across it. The unmistakable shape of a figure all in black. Ben could see him clearly now, hovering just on the edge of the frame. A moment later the figure was joined by another, and then a third, who was carrying something.

Ben tried zooming in closer to see more, but the image only lost definition and he discovered he had a clearer view by zooming all the way out to the multi-view. He saw now that what the third dark figure was carrying was a large holdall, like the military deployment bags Ben had used himself in the army, black nylon, all straps and fasteners. The third figure, clearly visible at the centre of the screen, laid down the bag and unzipped it open. Ben watched as the three men got to work taking out a selection of tools: hammers, crowbars, a big pair of cutters. The sight gave him a certain grim satisfaction. It would take ten men as many weeks to even make a dent in the armoury's defences with such primitive hand tools. The thieves probably knew it, too. They'd obviously been banking on being able to access the keys.

Where were the others? Three, plus Raul in the cellar, added up to at least one man fewer, more likely two fewer, than Ben's estimate of their numbers. He guessed that while the three were working on the armoury, whoever was left over might be trying to break into the cellar to rescue their trapped colleague.

'Not going so well for you boys, is it?' he murmured to himself.

It seemed to him that the odds were evening out very slightly. The raiders might have disabled Le Val's communications, taken out the security team and neutralised the dogs, and the weather conditions might be working in their favour insofar as the place was effectively cut off from the outside world. But without a key to the armoury they were just as trapped here as Ben was, because they couldn't leave until they had what they'd come for. And they had no way of knowing that he was on the loose. Half crippled he might be. But, fighting on his home ground and with the element of surprise on his side, still extremely dangerous.

As the enemy were about to find out.

Ben drew the silenced pistol from his belt and examined it. The weapon was scuffed from his crawl through the tunnel. But more than serviceable. Its magazine was fully loaded apart from the single round that Raul had let off in his panic before Storm took him down. The attackers were using subsonic hollow point ammunition. Pretty damned effective on a German shepherd dog, as they'd already proved. But even more so against humans. Ben knew that very well, because killing humans had been his occupation for thirteen years and he'd killed many more in the course of his freelance work since those days. He hated killing. Never wanted to do it again. Not if he had the choice. He might have no choice tonight.

You called it, he thought. *Now you'll face what's coming to you.*

He unscrewed the silencer from the barrel. He disliked using sound suppressors unless strictly necessary, because they made the weapon too long and unwieldy and affected its balance during rapid fire. And Ben was a fast, fast shooter.

He was slipping the pistol behind his right hip when

another movement drew his eye to the multi-screen monitor. Nothing new was happening on the cameras that weren't focused on the farmhouse. On the three that were, he could see the brightly flaring headlights of a vehicle appearing from the bottom of the track and approaching the house.

As he watched, the boxy four-wheel-drive vehicle pulled into the yard, its headlights carving through the falling snow and sweeping an arc across the buildings, its tyres scrabbling for grip in the deep snow.

Who the hell could be turning up at Le Val in the middle of a snowstorm, on a night like this – this night, of all nights?

At first Ben thought it might be the police. Or maybe Serge, Richard or Michel had managed to raise the alarm, after all. But no, this looked like a civilian vehicle. In which case maybe the raiders had called in reinforcements, a bunch of their buddies turning up with heavier equipment to attack the armoury doors with. But that didn't make sense either. Not if the raiders' mobile signal was as dead as his own. And not if they'd come all the way from Corsica.

So who was it?

Then Ben recognised the vehicle that was pulling up outside the farmhouse, and a chill went through his heart like a knife.

It was Victor Vermont's Nissan.

Chapter 19

Victor's return from Paris had been delayed by the sudden onset of snow that afternoon. The city itself had been spared the worst of the wintry weather but as the train clattered westwards it hit progressively harder, until finally a whole section of track from Lisieux all the way past Caen was so badly affected that they had to make frequent stops for maintenance crews to clear the way. By the time the train finally arrived at the Gare de Valognes, what should have been a three-hour journey had taken closer to six and it was getting dark.

'I've never seen it this bad, and it's going to get much worse before it gets any better,' grumbled the taxi driver who drove Victor the slithering, cautious twenty kilometres through the white-coated landscape home to Saint-Jean. Parts of the winding country lanes were already hard to distinguish from the surrounding fields, which themselves were beginning to resemble Siberian tundra. 'And I ask you, what do we pay our taxes for, if those *sales enculés* [a very rude expression indeed, though Victor didn't blink at its use] in the municipal council can't even be bothered to salt the roads for the safety of their citizens, eh? Mark my words, monsieur, someone's going to get themselves killed if this keeps up.'

Sitting in the back of the car with his precious briefcase clasped on his knees, Victor could have replied dismissively, 'This? This is nothing. Why, there's hardly a flake on the ground.' And he could have given the driver an account of the two years he'd spent in Québec as a young assistant museum curator, as well as his six winter months working at the Museum of Far Eastern Antiquities in Stockholm. In those parts of the world, if you couldn't drive in snow (*real* snow, that was to say, not this mere trivial dusting) then you might as well not even venture outside for half the year. Victor prided himself on his winter driving skills – skills which, he observed, his taxi driver sadly lacked – but he listened good-heartedly as the chap prattled on, and kept his opinions to himself.

Evening had fully fallen by the time Victor eventually got home, exhausted and famished after the long journey. He unlocked the case from his wrist, turned up the heating, prepared himself a quick snack and downed a welcome glass of Bordeaux. Feeling revitalised, he grabbed up the phone. Now where was the address book? He rummaged through a stack of textbooks and periodicals, found it, and dialled Benedict's landline number. He was full of enthusiasm to tell his friend all about what he and Jules had learned about Gaspard's gold cross.

The landline number rang and rang. When there was no reply, Victor tried the mobile. No reply there either. Which was odd, as Benedict usually answered his phone promptly.

Victor left a voicemail message: 'Benedict, it's Victor. I'm home again, and I have some important and quite sensational news to tell you, *mon ami*. Call me back as soon as you can.'

Time passed. Victor had plenty to occupy himself – four large, thick books on the go, an article he was writing for a scholarly journal, the unfinished chess game he'd been playing against himself before his departure for Paris – but he couldn't concentrate on any of them. He sat at his desk examining the cross under a magnifying hobby lamp, marvelling at the sheer mind-boggling wealth of history he was holding in his cotton-gloved hands. Every so often he would glance over at the phone, half-expecting it to ring at any moment – but its silence was deafening.

'Come on, Benedict, where are you?' he muttered, looking impatiently at his watch. It was getting late. He tried both numbers again, and got still no reply on either. He left another message, this time on the landline, in case the first had somehow got lost in the aether.

After another half-hour had gone by and still no call from Benedict, Victor decided he couldn't wait any longer to tell him the amazing news. Looking out of the window at the relentlessly falling snow, he had to admit to himself that it *was* getting fairly bad out there. But it was nothing he and his trusty Nissan four-wheel-drive couldn't handle. The old girl was as happy on slippery and treacherous terrain as she was on a sun-baked highway. Le Val was only a few kilometres away. Victor decided he would visit in person and tell Benedict the amazing news face to face.

With the cross safely bundled up in its case on the passenger seat next to him, Victor set off along the snowy roads. The taxi driver might not have been completely wrong, after all. Victor couldn't remember seeing such conditions since that last winter in Québec – but he pressed on, undeterred. As he drove, his mind was bubbling over with all the things he had to reveal to Benedict.

On the interminable train journey from Paris a new thought had come to him, suggesting that there could be even more to the story of Eleanor and Gaspard de la Roche than he, Jules or Henri Carbonneau had supposed. Any medieval historian worth their salt was aware of the various contemporary rumours that had existed about Eleanor's supposed affairs as a young queen, and persisted long after her death. One of the more scabrous of those rumours, dating back to the Second Crusade, had insinuated that her relationship with Raymond of Antioch was somewhat more intimate than might normally have been expected between an uncle and a niece. The medieval rumour-mongers had gone even further, claiming that Eleanor's plan had been to give up her crown and remain with him in Antioch.

To this day it was still unclear whether or not this had been mere malicious gossip – but certainly it had had enough effect on her husband Louis VII to persuade him to arrange for Eleanor to be kidnapped and taken by ship to Jerusalem, where the jealous king had kept his wife prisoner long enough for the course of time to prove that she wasn't expecting Raymond's child.

How much truth there might be to all these stories about her, Victor couldn't say – though if indeed Eleanor had been unfaithful to Louis it was hard not to sympathise with a lonely woman bound in a loveless marriage to a grim, humourless religious fanatic. Might the neglected, unhappy young queen have also had a romantic liaison with her loyal crusader knight, Gaspard de la Roche? The opportunity would certainly have presented itself, such as during their sea voyage to Sicily in 1149. Although nobody would ever know for sure, Victor found the possibility tantalising – not for any vulgar prurient reason, but because of its potential implications for the human background story behind the gold cross. These were the kinds of connections that brought history completely to life for him.

But other concerns of a more immediate nature were beginning to press in on his thoughts as he drove, forcing him to pay attention to the road conditions. Entering a bend in the icy road just a little too quickly, he made the cardinal error of toeing the brake, felt the tyres lose traction and the vehicle begin to slide – then his better judgement kicked in and he rescued the skid with some skilful steering. When he almost lost control a second time and narrowly escaped veering straight off the road and down a steep, tree-studded slope, he began to realise he might have been a little rash in coming out here on such a night. But there was no turning back now, with Le Val just minutes away. The last couple of kilometres he covered at a crawl, and was glad when he caught sight of the facility's perimeter fence.

Victor was only vaguely aware of what went on at Le Val. Benedict made no secret of it, of course, though they'd never really discussed the matter in any depth – but he knew enough to understand that the team were highly securi-ty-conscious. On the couple of occasions Victor had come here before, both of them pre-arranged visits, the fellows in the gatehouse had been notified to expect him, and had opened up the gates to wave him through with a cheery smile. But as Victor approached the gates now, he found them lying wide open with apparently nobody on duty and the gatehouse all in darkness. Which momentarily struck him as a little odd – but he quickly put it out of his head. It was Christmas Eve, after all, and the watchmen must have been given the night off.

As he turned into the snowy gateway Victor noticed the faint tyre tracks that crisscrossed the entrance, as well as the minivan parked to one side and the fast-vanishing footprints in the snow that led down towards the house. But he had no reason to think twice about these things. Now that he'd managed to make it here in one piece, his thoughts had returned to Gaspard's gold cross. He couldn't wait to see Benedict's astonished expression when he told him the news.

The lights of the compound twinkled brightly through the trees and made haloes in the falling snow. Victor pattered and slithered his way down to the bottom of the track and turned into the yard, pulling up in front of the farmhouse. The lights were on inside, warm and welcoming.

Victor delicately lifted the briefcase from the passenger seat and got out of the car, smiling with happy anticipation. He was closing the car door when he saw the figure of a man approaching across the yard, silhouetted darkly against the glow of the floodlights.

'Good evening,' he called out, shielding his eyes against the lights with one hand to better make out the man's face. 'Is that you, Benedict? I tried calling, but I couldn't get through.' Holding up the briefcase with his other hand he added excitedly, 'I have the gold cross here. There's some amazing news I must share with you.'

As the dark figure came closer, Victor realised that it couldn't be Benedict, as the man was striding quickly towards him through the snow without a limp, and not carrying a crutch or a stick. He was shorter and bulkier in build, too. Then it must be one of his associates, Victor thought. He was about to say 'Oh, I'm sorry. Is Benedict at home?' when the stranger came another stride closer and Victor saw the black ski mask over the man's face. 'W-who are you?' he gasped.

The masked man said nothing. Then he reached down to his belt and pulled out a long, black pistol.

Victor's mouth fell open in sudden terror. 'No! Please! Don't—'

Still aiming the gun at Victor, the man reached up and plucked the mask from his head. His face was brutish and unshaven, with a heavy jaw and an ugly curl to his lip. His eyes glinted in the lights.

He said in accented French, 'What gold cross?'

Chapter 20

Icy fingers curled around Ben's heart and gripped it tight as he watched the figure of his friend get out of the Nissan. He was just a murky, featureless silhouette on the monitor screen– but unmistakably Victor Vermont, wearing a thick winter coat and a wool cap and holding something that looked like a briefcase.

'Oh no,' Ben murmured out loud. What in hell's name was Victor doing here? He would never have just shown up without phoning first – but then Ben remembered that, of course, the phones weren't working.

Ben had to warn him. Get him inside the house out of danger, close him up in the wine cellar where he'd be safe. Or tell him to get back in the car and get out of here and call the police. Whatever he did, he was going to have to do it quickly.

But Ben never got the chance, because the events of the next few moments happened so fast that he barely had time to react. Suddenly, Victor was no longer alone out there. Ben saw the taller, darker shape of one of the raiders appear from the bottom left-hand corner of the screen and stride towards his friend in the swirling snow. For an instant Victor seemed to think he knew the man, greeting him and holding up the briefcase as though he wanted to show him what was inside. But then Victor must have seen the mask over the man's face and realised something was wrong, because he started backing away in fear. The man came on aggressively, the long black shape of a silenced pistol suddenly clearly visible on the monitor screen. Victor kept backing away, stumbling in the deep snow that was drifted up against the corner of the house. The man raised the gun in one black-gloved hand while the other pointed at the briefcase. He seemed to be saying something, but Victor didn't appear to understand, still backing away, shaking his head as though he was saying *No, no, please, I don't know what you want but don't hurt me.*

The man whipped off his mask. He had his back to the camera angle and Ben couldn't see his face. But Victor could see it. And in that horrifying moment, just a tiny fragment of time that seemed to last forever, Ben knew that the man didn't intend to let Victor live.

Ben wanted to rush to his friend's aid. The whole sequence flashed across his mind at the speed of a neural impulse: he saw himself bursting from Jeff's door and go sprinting across the yard, drawing his weapon as he ran, firing, taking down this bastard before anything bad could happen to an innocent old man who had just happened to wander into the wrong place at the wrong time. But in that same tiny fraction of an instant he knew he'd be way too slow. Three seconds to stumble to the door of the monitor room. Another five to make it across Jeff's living room and rip open the door to race outside. Another five to go limping and staggering across the wide open space of the yard, until he got close enough to square his sights on the enemy and open fire. Thirteen seconds. That was how long it would take for a half-crippled warrior to fly into action. At least ten seconds too slow.

And then, in the next half a heartbeat, the situation suddenly escalated so fast that nobody could have saved Victor. Not even an SAS fighter on two good legs, at the peak of his powers.

As Victor was backing away towards the corner of the house, he reached inside the briefcase with surprising speed and his hand came out clasping an object that flashed brightly in the overexposed glare of the floodlights. Ben only caught the tiniest indistinct glimpse of it, but enough to realise with a shock that it was the gold cross, glittering and gleaming in Victor's fist like a firebrand. What happened next was more shocking by far. The man saw the cross and moved fast towards Victor with an arm outstretched to snatch it from him. Then there was a sudden violent flurry of movement as Victor, letting go of the briefcase, gripped the cross in both hands. Before Ben could register what was happening, Victor appeared to rip the cross apart into two pieces and then lashed out at his attacker, taking a wild right-handed swing at the man's head. Ben saw something fly in the camera shot, and realised that it was a spray of blood catching the light.

What had just happened?

The attacker rocked on his feet, bent over with pain. His unheard howl of agony seemed all the more surreal for its silence. For a tiny, fleeting moment it seemed as if Victor might have gained the advantage and have a chance of getting away. But that was too much to hope for. As though in slow motion, Ben saw the man straighten up and raise his pistol to point again at Victor. The gun kicked in the attacker's fist and a blurry streak of light showed the trajectory of the ejected cartridge case. Victor staggered, still holding the separated sections of the cross. The man fired a second shot. Then a third, and now Victor was crumpling to his knees and dropping the pieces of the gold cross into the snow.

Ben screamed 'NOOO!' But there was nothing he could have done to save Victor in time. Nothing he could do but watch the nightmare unfold on the monitor screen. Victor collapsed on his face, rolled over and lay curled up on the ground as the man stood over him and fired another shot that Ben saw kick a spray of blood from Victor's chest.

The killer bent to pick up the pieces of the fallen cross, slotted them back together, and thrust the artefact into his belt. Then, as quickly as he'd appeared, he vanished into the shadows behind the house, pressing his hand to the side of his head and leaving a dark trail of blood spots over the snow.

By then, Ben was already crashing through the outer door of Jeff's quarters, grabbing his walking staff as he went and racing out as fast as he could into the driving snow. The attacker was nowhere to be seen. Ben stumbled and staggered across the yard with his gun in one hand and the staff in the other. But trying to move faster than his limping gait would allow, he put too much weight on the makeshift staff and the branch snapped with a crack. His bad foot skidded out from under him and he fell to one knee beside Victor's car. Heaving himself upright, he gritted his teeth and kept moving, but as he reached Victor's body he knew in his heart that it was far too late to save him. Ben fell into a crouch beside his dying friend, dropping the gun into the snow.

Victor was still alive, but only barely. The pink of the snow was turning darker and melting as the warm blood kept coming. The bullets had punched a ragged pattern of holes in his upper body. Ben gripped his shoulders and shook him. 'Victor!'

Victor's eyes were rolling, badly out of focus. His lips parted and a blood bubble swelled and then popped, staining his mouth and chin red. He only had seconds left to go. Ben held him tight.

'Benedict . . . I . . .' Victor managed to say in a wet croak.

'Victor, it's all right. Everything's going to be all right.' Ben had spoken those words to many a dying man, to comfort their last moments. An outright lie, as a medical prognosis; but for those who believed in the existence of heaven, the soothing prospect that in a few more moments they would be going to a better place could be no bad thing.

'The . . . cross . . .' Victor gasped. 'I . . . tried. . . to . . .'

'I know,' Ben said. The tears were hot and burning in his eyes. He felt the cold wetness on his cheeks. 'I know you did. Rest now.'

Victor was desperate to say more, but he'd used up his final reserves of energy and now his life force was ebbing away. His last words came out as a hissing gasp, his eyes glazed over, and then he was gone, hanging limp in Ben's arms, his expression frozen into a look of shock and fear. The snow was already gathering on his lashes.

'Victor!'

Ben gently closed Victor's eyes. He knelt there for a few moments, holding him, numb to the cold, oblivious of the armed men running around Le Val, not caring about anything at this moment except his poor dead friend. Victor didn't deserve this to happen to him. He had been about to get married. He'd been looking forward to the rest of his life. And now it had been snatched from him by a brutal, pitiless killer.

'I'll get him, Victor,' Ben vowed softly. 'Whatever it takes. I promise you, I'll get him.'

Ben gently laid the old man's body down, then picked up the fallen gun and struggled to his feet. Storm had come running across the yard to join him. He nuzzled the body the way he'd done with his pack-mate Sabre, then looked enquiringly up at Ben and let out a forlorn whimper.

Looking around him, Ben saw the trail of footprints and the blood spots on the snow where the killer had fled up the side of the house and around the back. There was no question of giving chase, not in his half-disabled state. Ben's best chance of catching up with the man was when he went back to rejoin his cronies trying to break into the armoury.

That was when Ben noticed something else lying a couple of steps away from Victor's body, and he bent down to pick it up. It was a severed human right ear, neatly detached by what must have been a sharp blade. It was still warm to the touch, and oozing blood. And Ben had a pretty good idea whose head it had been attached to, until moments ago.

He was bewildered by the blade, though. On the monitor it had looked as though Victor, in that last moment as he fought for his life, had pulled the cross apart with deliberate intent. Which had to mean that during his examination of the artefact he must have discovered a secret double purpose of its design, a long, sharp tongue of steel that was sheathed inside the cross's shaft like a sword in a scabbard. Ben was no historian but he knew that for centuries, makers of beautiful objects had been finding artful ways to conceal blades and other weapons inside walking canes, pens, belt buckles, jewellery . . . and now, a magnificently ornamented golden cross that also turned out to be a hidden dagger. One for which Victor Vermont had given his life to try to protect it from being stolen. At least the killer hadn't got away completely unscathed.

That was far too little consolation. But it would do for a start.

Ben was about to throw the bloody ear away in disgust when Storm came up close and pressed his nose against it, sniffing furiously and giving it an inquisitive lick. The big triangular ears were pricked forwards, a fierce light burning in his eyes. 'Are you thinking what I'm thinking?' Ben asked him. The dog made no reply, but he might as well have nodded in agreement. Instead of tossing the severed ear, Ben wrapped it up in a piece of tissue and slipped it into his pocket.

It was time to move on. Though Ben hated to leave Victor lying there like this, right now he had no choice. He took off Jeff's winter coat and laid it over his friend's face and upper body. He said a quick, silent goodbye. Then he touched Storm's head and whispered, 'Let's go, boy.'

The dog trotted at Ben's side as he hobbled away from

the house, heading back across the snowy yard. The raiders were still out there somewhere, and Ben expected he'd find Victor's killer among them.

This wasn't over yet.

Chapter 21

But Ben's expectation was dead wrong. Because, in fact, Victor's killer had no intention of rejoining his associates. At this moment, in possession of his trophy, Petru Navarro was in the process of getting the hell out of here just as fast as he could.

Fifty metres from the back of the farmhouse, in the deep shadows of the trees, the Corsican stopped running and leaned against a gnarly trunk to catch his breath and gasp in pain. The whole right side of his head felt like it was on fire, and the warm sticky blood was all down his neck, soaking through his clothes, rapidly cooling in the subzero chill. He touched his fingers to his ear, and felt only a ragged little nub of flesh and cartilage. The whole damn thing was gone! *Oh fuck I'm disfigured. I'm disfigured. No,* he said to himself in his panic. *It's not your face, it's just your ear. That doesn't count for as much. Not like losing your lips or your nose, or an eye.*

But whether it counted or not, the agony was shocking, nerve-shredding, pulsating all through him. Fuck that stupid old man, pulling a sneaky trick like that. How was anyone supposed to tell he was going to whip out a goddamn sword and slice their fucking ear off? Petru wanted to go back and shoot him a couple times more. And he would have, but he had other fish to fry right now.

Oh, Christ, the pain, the pain. He'd heard somewhere that cold would help take it away, so he reached down and scooped a handful of snow and clapped it to his ear. It hurt even worse. 'Mother*fucker*!' Petru yelled in his native Corsican. But not too loudly, because he didn't want to give it away to the rest of the gang where he was. He'd only left them to go and check out the arriving vehicle. That asshole Casta would be wanting to know what was going on, but by the time he dragged himself away from trying to break inside his precious vault and found the body of the old man, Petru would be long gone.

Casta wasn't the only asshole. They were all assholes. The moment Petru had joined up with the gang, he'd known that the job would be a waste of time. How could it not, when the people organising it were a bunch of idiots?

If he'd been the one in charge, Petru would have done it all quite differently. First off, he wouldn't have missed the opportunity to use the three morons guarding the gate as leverage. Instead of knocking them all out with gas – whose retarded idea had *that* been? – he'd have dragged them at gunpoint into their security hut still fully conscious, tied them up and made'm sit in a row on the floor. Who wants to go first, he'd've asked them, and then before anyone could answer he'd have popped one of them in both kneecaps right there in front of his two mates, to show that he wasn't screwing around.

Then, before cutting off the phones, he'd have got one of the remaining two to call the crippled guy inside the house and tell him that a real badass mofo was holding them hostage for the vault keys. Hearing the screams of agony in the background, the crippled guy would have known this was for real. But if that didn't persuade the crippled guy to surrender the keys, then Petru would've popped the wounded asshole in the brain. No silencer, so the gunshot would sound good and loud over the phone. Then if the crippled guy still refused to play ball, he'd have popped another. By the time two of them were lying there with their brains spattered all over the wall and the third was crying for mercy and pissing his pants in terror, most men would have relented and given up the contents of the armoury just to make it stop. That's how people were. You could use that. It was armed robbery 101, for Christ's sake!

But no, instead Casta and company had to go and do it the soft way, insisting that you couldn't kill anyone except a couple of worthless mutts. Killing mutts was okay, and Petru had quite enjoyed gunning down the one that had met them on the track, plus the two more they'd encountered as they moved deeper into the compound. But dropping the hammer on a poor dumb animal was hardly the same as the real thing, and what kind of self-respecting hardcore criminal was afraid of killing anyone? Either the job was worth doing, or it wasn't.

No wonder the whole thing had fallen apart and the crippled guy had already screwed this gang of dickless morons by not only depriving them of the armoury keys but capturing their buddy Raul into the bargain. Not that Petru gave a damn what happened to Raul. The crippled guy could set the asshole on fire, for all he cared. Petru didn't give a damn about any of them. You've got to look out for Number One.

Petru cut through the woods and got as far as the spot where he'd executed his first dog before he paused to take a look at his booty. His ear was hurting so badly he thought he was going to throw up, and his clothes were sticking to him with all the blood that was still leaking down his neck and shoulder. But the excitement of his trophy took some of the edge off the pain. What the stupid crazy old man had been doing, going around with something like that in a bag, Petru neither knew nor cared. The moment he'd heard the word 'gold' out of the old fool's mouth and realised he was talking about what he had inside his briefcase, Petru had seen the opportunity to rescue something from this fiasco.

And he hadn't been wrong. Petru pulled the cross from his belt and thrilled at the heft and feel of solid gold in his bloody fist. Taking out his mini-torch and risking a little light, he spent a few moments examining the cross. He soon found the little button that released the hidden blade, whose treacherous nastiness awed him even more for having been on the receiving end of it. 'Oh, you cunning piece of shit,' he muttered, managing a grim smile.

He ran the torch beam up and down the shaft and cross-piece, and marvelled at the way all those beautiful little gemstones sparkled in the light. Even if Petru might not be able to tell a ruby from an emerald, he knew value when he saw it and these looked real enough to him. Nor did he have any understanding or appreciation of antique artefacts, but you could see this cross was old, really old, despite its fine condition. And the older these things were, the more valuable they were. Even just the melt-down value of the gold alone must be worth a hundred times the shitty wages he'd consented to be paid for tonight's half-arsed robbery. But to the right buyer . . . you could take that figure and add as many zeros to it as you wanted.

Worth giving up an ear for, for sure. Hell, Petru would have given both his ears for this. With enough money, you could get a plastic surgeon to stick on a couple of artificial replacements anyway, and nobody would know the difference. He was rich! Visions of red Ferraris. White powerboats. Swanky hotels and high-class call girls. And a way to get back at his uncle, that piece of shit who wouldn't even give him a proper job working for the family firm and was not, in Petru's opinion, worthy of the surname Navarro. Ha, ha! Who's the useless good-for-nothing layabout now?

Petru thrust the cross back in his belt and moved on, still bleeding like a stuck pig but grinning through the pain as he relished his good fortune. In just a few minutes he'd be out of here, before Casta or any of the other assholes realised. *Fuck 'em.*

He looked cautiously about him as he stepped out of the shadows of the trees and started heading back up towards the gatehouse. The deep tracks of the old man's car were still quite fresh, not yet erased by the falling snow. There was no sign of anyone coming after him, but he needed to hurry. Petru jogged along one of the tyre ruts. He knew he was leaving a blood trail, but so what? By the time any of the assholes got wind of what was up, he'd be well on his way to freedom. He felt no compunction whatever about abandoning his associates. Served them right for speaking to him the way they had. And for being a bunch of losers.

In a couple of minutes, he'd reached the gates. The minivan was half covered with snow already. He'd remembered Casta telling di Borgo to leave the key in it. Which at the time, Petru had thought was a stupid idea, but he wasn't complaining now. As he walked up to the van, he paused to gaze at the dark windows of the gatehouse, and briefly contemplated whether perhaps he should step inside for a moment and pop the three security guys. Leaving witnesses was a fool's game, in general. But then it occurred to him that he only had three rounds left in his pistol after all the shooting he'd done tonight. Popping the security guys would leave him with an empty gun, and he disliked the idea of going around unarmed until he could obtain another weapon.

Could always strangle or beat the fuckers to death instead, he thought. And on any other night but this, he probably would have. But he was in such pain and so keen to get out of here that it seemed like too much trouble.

Petru decided to leave it. He quickly brushed away the worst of the snow from the windscreen, then clambered into the van, fired up the ignition and carefully reversed the van out of the open gate and out into the road. The snow was seriously deep now, making the tyres slither and spin for grip as he got turned around. The last thing Petru needed was to get stuck up here in the middle of the road where the others could find him, and for a few instants worry stabbed his heart. But then the tyres found some traction again, and he was away, grinning and thumping triumphantly on the steering wheel.

'*Addiu, amichi.*'

Chapter 22

Recrossing the yard, Ben threaded through the narrow aisle between Jeff's quarters and the classroom building next door with Storm passing silently along behind him. The armoury was situated in a walled-off area to the rear of that cluster of buildings, and as Ben got closer he could hear voices and loud clanging noises as the raiders went on trying to smash their way through the first of the three armoured doors into the vault.

Normally Ben would have been able to slip through the shadows like a ghost, unheard, unseen, his presence totally unsuspected until he'd have been right on the enemy and ready to spring a surprise counterattack of paralysing speed and aggression. But that was normally, and this was now. Rather than risk getting too close to the enemy he veered left, heading towards the larger of the two storage sheds where much of the Le Val facility's equipment was kept.

The last time he'd ventured into this part of the compound had been the day he'd happened upon their trainee Robert Blondel making his little exploratory wander of the buildings. The shed was a tall wooden barn, its oak slats turned silver with age. The main doors, which faced in the direction of the armoury area, were tall and wide enough to accommodate large equipment like the Le Val tractor and JCB. Another smaller door lay around the corner, and that was where Ben headed now, working his awkward way along the edge of the building where a strip of deep shadow kept him hidden. He reached the smaller door and managed to lift the latch and get inside without making a sound. Storm followed him through the darkness as he hunted for something he could use as a support. Without some kind of crutch to replace his broken walking staff he wasn't going to get far. It was asking to get himself killed.

Ben found what he was looking for among a load of old building materials propped up in a corner behind the tarp-covered JCB. There were some off-cuts of timber left over from the construction of the covered firing points of the short pistol range a couple of years earlier, cobwebbed and forgotten; among them, a five-foot length of four-by-two with a shorter piece attached to one end like a T-bar. He tested his weight on it by sticking the T-piece under his arm and leaning on it hard. It was built for strength if not for comfort, and he decided it would serve fine as a crutch.

Ben left the barn much faster than he'd entered it, now able to keep his bad leg off the ground and plant the bottom end of the crutch in the ground ahead of him, to propel himself along in elongated airborne strides, like a pole-vaulter. He made his way like that back in the direction of the armoury, where the dark-clad figures were still hard at work.

Clang-clang-clang. It sounded like a demented blacksmith

at his forge. They were determined bastards, he had to give them that. But their total focus on their job had an air of desperation about it, as though what motivated them more than anything else wasn't the reward of emptying the contents of the vault, so much as the fear of the consequences if they came away empty-handed. Outfits like this were usually put together by a higher-up who wouldn't risk going on the actual job. And those higher-ups generally weren't terribly tolerant of failure.

Thirty yards away; twenty-five. Keeping to the pools of shadow thrown by the strong floodlights over the yard. The snow seemed to be coming down harder than ever, now falling straight to the ground, now eddying and spiralling in the gusts of freezing wind that channelled between the buildings, a veil of white in constant motion, camouflaging Ben's approach. He was nearly at the low block wall that ringed three sides of the vault entrance. He turned to Storm, gently touched his snout and murmured 'Quiet' in a voice that was barely audible to human ears but was as clear as a yell to a German shepherd. He crept the last few yards to the wall and lowered himself into an uncomfortable crouch behind it, so that he could just peep over the top of the stone coping without being seen.

The dark figures were just twenty yards away. Four of them, hunched over their work with no idea they were being watched. None of them looked like a man who'd just had his ear slashed off. Which meant that Victor's killer hadn't come back to join them. The others were so intent on their task that they seemed not to have even noticed, and probably didn't even know what had just happened over by the house.

Even Raul, trapped in the wine cellar, was probably the last thing on their minds right now

Four men, plus the killer, plus Raul, made six. That tallied with Ben's estimate of the raid team's strength. Where had the killer gone? He was either still somewhere within the compound, or he'd cut and run with his spoils. That wouldn't have surprised Ben, but all the same he was bitterly disappointed if he'd lost him. For a few seconds he wondered whether he should leave the other four here and go looking for him.

No. If the killer was gone, then so be it. Ben still had these four. They wouldn't be getting away so easily.

One of them was grasping the shaft of a long wrecking bar that they had wedged in between the edge of the outer door and the massive reinforced concrete slab into which it was set, while another stood over him pounding away like a wild man with a large lump hammer, the ringing impacts echoing off the buildings behind them. Their obvious plan, to pound the chisel end of the bar deeper into the gap so they could then try to lever it open, was as unsubtle as it was doomed to total failure. Ben had helped to pour the concrete and install the door himself, and he knew exactly how crowbar-proof the thing was. Even if you could drive the wedge in, you'd need a lever a mile long to exert even a fraction of the force needed to rip open the door. And then you still had two more inner doors to go before you were inside.

While those two were wasting their time in one way, a third man was desperately trying to pick the lock with some kind of long, slim implement like a screwdriver. Another exercise in utter futility. That lock could resist anything up to and including a direct strike from a fifty-calibre anti-materiel rifle. Meanwhile the fourth man was crouched nearby, watching, the set of his body language showing that he was getting worried and impatient about the lack of progress. He was wearing a small backpack. Ben thought the fourth guy must be the boss of the operation, or more likely the team leader, answerable to the same higher-up who'd dish out abuse and punishment if they failed to deliver the goods.

Storm was tense and alert at Ben's side, his head raised to watch over the top of the wall. The dog's lips curled away from his long, curved fangs and a deep, low growl rumbled from his chest. Bristles stood up like spines on his neck and his tail was standing straight upward. He was getting geared up for action against the intruders, and for a moment Ben feared the dog might fly at them, ignoring all commands. He shushed Storm with another gentle touch.

Clang, clang, clang. The man with the lump hammer was getting tired and took a break. His comrade holding the wrecking bar must have been getting numb hands from all the vibration through the steel, because he used the pause to rub and clap his palms together. The team leader snapped some harsh words, and they quickly resumed. The other guy went on assiduously picking and scraping at the lock.

Very quietly, Ben leaned his crutch against the wall. He braced himself as best he could, ignoring the strain on his bad ankle and the muscles of that leg, and reached back and drew out the pistol. The SIG had a very non-reflective surface and he wasn't worried about the weapon glinting in the lights as he smoothly, discreetly brought it to bear over the top of the wall and held it in a two-hand grip with his wrists and forearms resting on the coping stones. A 9mm in the right hands makes a fine equaliser for the physically impaired. The SIG had no external safety catch. Simplicity itself to use, just aim and squeeze; and at this close distance taking the men down would be like blowing holes in a pumpkin on a stick at point-blank range.

Ben lined his sights up on the man on the left, the one wielding the hammer. Finger on the trigger. The first and foremost rule of shooting, relentlessly drummed into all students until their ears were bleeding, was never to point a gun at anything you do not intend to destroy. And Ben was all too happy to destroy all four of these men. He planned on mowing them down from left to right, so fast that the last target he engaged would be dead on his feet even before the first one hit the ground. His only regret was that he wouldn't be able to bring them back to life so that he could kill them again. They might not have been personally responsible for Victor's death, but they'd done for Sabre and probably the other dogs too. That was a capital offence in itself, as far as Ben was concerned. He'd loved those dogs.

But then he checked himself, and relaxed the pressure on the trigger as a sudden doubt came into his mind. After what had already happened here tonight, there was going to be police involvement. No way to keep the authorities out of this. And when the inevitable fleet of screaming patrol cars and armed response cowboys finally rolled up, only to be shown a pile of bullet-riddled dead crooks, they might naturally assume that Ben was the one who had done the riddling.

Another rule was: *Don't shit where you eat.* Which might equally be translated into: *Don't let yourself get roped into a potential murder charge for having taken out a bunch of goblins on your own doorstep*. The worst crimes these four would have been seen to have committed were attempted robbery, accessory to murder, and killing a few dogs, which legally amounted to no more than destruction of property. Thanks to the wisdom of the modern justice system, there were people who walked out of jail within a handful of years for committing worse offences. It was doubtful that a judge would consider that gunning these four down to be a proportionate response, especially when the court took Ben's military expertise into account. It was at such times that a man's level of training and skill could count against him, in a big way.

With a regretful sigh, Ben took his finger off the trigger and lowered the gun back down behind the wall. At that moment, the guy who was picking the vault lock suddenly turned to the team leader, and Ben heard him say, '*Induve hé Petru?*' Ben's ear was getting attuned to the language now he knew what to listen for. 'Where's Petru?'

Petru. So that was the name of Victor's killer.

'I don't know,' the guy holding the lump hammer said in Corsican. 'Want me to go check?' He seemed eager to get away from his relentless battering.

'We've got work to do,' the team leader replied impatiently. 'There's no time to worry about Petru. Or Raul either. Get on with it!'

'*Mi face mal u nasu,*' said the guy holding the wrecking bar. Complaining about his broken nose. He must have been the one on the receiving end of the aluminium crutch earlier, Ben realised. Painful, but not as painful as getting your ear slashed clean off. Certainly not as painful as what Ben would have liked to do to him.

'*À l'inferno cù u nasu,*' the team leader snapped back at him. 'To hell with your nose.'

They got back to work, and the feverish clanging resumed. They could be here all night; then again, they had all night. But Ben didn't intend to let things drag on any longer. An alternative plan was forming in his mind. If he couldn't kill them all where they stood, then he would have to take them prisoner like Raul. Which would entail splitting them up, because a lone semi-cripple couldn't easily capture four able-bodied, armed enemies without something going badly wrong.

Ben ducked low behind the wall, tucked the gun into his belt, grabbed his crutch and moved off, back towards the storage shed. The metallic hammering noises went on unabated behind him. Safely inside the building, he shivered and hugged himself and vigorously rubbed his frozen hands to try and get the blood going in them. The luminous green dial of his watch told him the time had just gone past midnight on December 25th.

'Happy Christmas,' he murmured to himself.

He set about putting his plan into action. Now the defence of Le Val was about to begin in earnest.

Chapter 23

Ben grabbed a corner of the tarpaulin that covered the JCB and dragged it down to the dusty concrete floor. Setting down his crutch for a moment he gave Storm a hand-signal command to sit and stay, to keep him at a safe distance. The dog watched with his head cocked to one side as Ben hauled himself awkwardly up into the machine's cab.

The JCB was more Jeff's baby than Ben's, but he had a pretty good idea of how to operate it. There were two joysticks instead of a steering wheel, like an aircraft, a whole panoply of switches and buttons, and a hand throttle lever rather than a pedal. The key was always in the ignition. He twisted it to the start position, waited for the warning lights to go out, jabbed a button to activate the hydraulics, then fired up the engine. The machine came to life with a clattering, rasping roar that sounded twice as loud inside the barn. He was pretty sure that must have grabbed the enemy's attention. But it was nothing in comparison to what was about to happen next, before they had time to react.

The great hydraulic arm with its toothed digger bucket jerked into motion and rose up into the air like the head and neck of a dinosaur woken from a deep sleep. Ben slammed the transmission into forward drive, gripped the twin joysticks and set the machine rolling. It wasn't unlike driving a tank. The caterpillar tracks clattered and spun for grip on the concrete floor, then bit down and the monster lurched aggressively forwards, belching out a choking cloud of diesel exhaust, as Ben jammed the throttle lever to max power. Its front end was pointing towards the tall double doors of the barn. Which was where Ben was going, but he wasn't going to open the doors first.

He waited for the last moment before the massive jarring impact, then threw himself out of the cab. Landed on the concrete with a lightning bolt of pain that knifed through his bad ankle, rolled like a parachutist and staggered back upright just in time to see the lumbering machine crash into the solid wooden planking of the doors. The great toothed shovel hit first with a rending, splintering crunch, followed by eleven tons of chassis and body that ripped through as though the barn were built out of balsa wood. Fragments of shattered planking burst outwards into the snow. One door was utterly destroyed and the other torn from its hinges and flattened to the ground as the JCB went rolling straight over it and out into the night, heading unstoppably in the direction of the armoury.

At which point the raiders, already alerted by the sudden and shocking engine roar from inside the barn, were thrown into total and complete panic. One yelled, *'Simu sott'à attaccu!'* 'We're under attack!' All four scattered in opposite directions as the lumbering machine came straight at them, drawing out their pistols and opening fire in a ragged series of muffled shots. Bullets sparked and pinged off its bodywork and tracks and punched holes through the glass of the cabin where the driver would have been, if there had been one.

But pistols against an eleven-ton metal dinosaur were as effective as going up against a Panzer tank armed with a kid's air rifle. The machine surged onward, ploughing over the frozen ground, its tracks leaving dirty ruts in the snow, roaring and clattering and totally out of control. It reached the low wall where Ben and Storm had been hiding moments earlier and went straight on through as though it hadn't been there, reduced it to instant rubble and kept on coming, dragging a large piece of broken wall from its steel shovel.

What happened next was something Ben couldn't have planned to happen in his craziest imaginings. As the runaway JCB reached the armoury the great piece of broken wall shook loose from the shovel and one side of the caterpillar track rode up over it, tilting the whole machine over at an angle. An operator would have stopped the machine, backed up and then gone forward again on a different tack or used the shovel to sweep the chunk of broken wall out of the way; but the unmanned monster had no such common sense and its angle of lean quickly increased until its entire mass, made top-heavy by the weight of the massive hydraulic arm, was dragged over sideways and capsized with a crash that shook the ground. The tracks went on spinning in empty air for a few moments until the engine stalled and the machine fell silent.

Eleven tons of heavy metal lying directly on top of the armoury trapdoor, immovable unless the raiders had brought an industrial crane with them. The four men could only stare in horror at the scene of total carnage, knowing their objective was now completely, irretrievably trashed beyond all hope of salvation. In a howl of fury and despair the team leader screamed '*CAZZU!*' Which needed no translation, as the universal expression of utter defeat.

Watching from the shattered entrance of the storage barn, Ben felt the glow of triumph and sensed that the tide had just turned badly against the enemy. Now he needed to maintain the offensive and press on with the rest of his plan. Staying hidden in the shadows he pulled out his pistol and let off two fast rounds. The reports from the unsilenced weapon cracked out sharply in the cold night air. He was aiming in the general direction of the raiders but deliberately pulling his shots wide so as not to hit them. The first bullet shattered a side window of the classroom building beyond the armoury area, and the second struck the caterpillar track of the overturned JCB and ricocheted off with a yowling screech. The shots were designed to draw attention, and they couldn't have failed to do so. He heard a hoarse cry of '*Hé u tippo infirmatu!*' 'It's him! The crippled guy!'

Ben didn't have a lot of time to think about the significance of that, but in the space of that split second it registered in his mind as being very strange. And interesting. The only glimpse any of the raiders had had of him until now was during that failed storming of the farmhouse's living room when two of them had managed to get in the door. The first had quickly become Ben's prisoner, and even if he'd noticed the crutch in Ben's hand, he'd scarcely had the opportunity to share that information with his colleagues while Storm's teeth were in his arm. As for the second guy, in the heat of the battle and retreating from the doorway with his nose smashed to a pulp it seemed unlikely that he'd even have known that it was the shaft of an aluminium crutch smacking into his face at high speed, as distinct from any other kind of improvised impact weapon.

So how did these men come to refer to Ben as 'the crippled guy'? Where had that information come from? And how did they know it was him? That implied they knew he was alone in the place, apart from the security team.

Those were questions he'd have to ponder later. Drawing back inside the barn he cut across from the smashed main doors to the smaller side door and made his way out into the night. Peering around the corner he saw the raiders splitting up to go hunting for him. They hadn't spotted his muzzle flash and didn't know where his shots had come from. As the other three went racing off in other directions, only one was heading directly his way. Which was exactly what Ben had wanted them to do.

Using his new speed crutch technique, Ben pole-vaulted his way from the corner of the barn in the direction of the skid pan and killing house. He'd have to cross a large area of open ground to get there. One slip and he was finished, and if his pursuer was a skilled shooter he risked taking a bullet in the back. But those were risks Ben had to take. He made it to the edge of the skid pan and paused to catch his breath, condensation billowing from his lips as he turned to see the black-clad figure of a man emerge at a run from behind the storage barns, some fifty yards behind him. Ben dug the end of his crutch into the snow and kept moving. In less than half a minute he'd reached the killing house.

Turning again, he saw that the man had spotted him and was giving chase.

That was when Ben suddenly realised that Storm was no longer with him. He'd thought the dog had followed from the barn, but now he was nowhere to be seen. Just then, the muted handclap of shots rang out, coming from somewhere beyond the farmhouse. Ben's stomach muscles clenched with worry. But at this moment there was little he could do about it. He yanked open the door of the killing house and hobbled inside. Peering from a window he saw that the raider was much closer now, tearing across the snowy open ground, pistol in hand. Ben could easily have gunned him down. But a different fate awaited the man inside the killing house.

The place was still set up the way they'd been using it for teaching Pepe Jaeckin's bodyguard team. Ben had personally designed the layout of the various rooms and corridors himself, and could have navigated his way around them blindfold. He'd also designed the clever power system of the killing house. To minimise the almost inevitable bullet damage with so much live firing going on, all the main electrical gubbins with the exception of the armoured wiring loom were housed in another outbuilding and remotely controlled by a handset. Ben took the remote down from its hook, activated the power but left the lights off. His pursuer would be following him into near-total darkness. A bad place to be. Like a hunter tracking a wounded lion right into the heart of his lair.

As Ben heard the door burst open and the footsteps of his pursuer on the hardboard floor, he was already slinking back into the recesses of the building. The crutch was too noisy to use. But it could have other uses. Without a sound, he limped through a makeshift door, then turned back on himself and through another. He paused in the darkness, listening intently. He could hear the tread of the man's boots as he came stalking down a passage, only a thin wooden partition separating them.

Ben reached out and gently tapped the partition with a knuckle. *Knock, knock.* A momentary silence as the man's steps froze to a halt; then the wheezing muffled cough of a silenced gunshot burst through the silence and a bullet tore through the partition, followed by three more. Ben had been expecting them and already moved on. From his new position he tapped again, more loudly. The man took his bait and let loose another five rounds, which again punched through the flimsy wooden wall and found nothing except empty air on the other side.

But the man didn't know that.

Ben cried out and hammered the end of his crutch hard against the floor, mimicking the sound of someone who'd been injured and collapsed. In the next instant the heavy footsteps on the other side of the partition resumed, faster now, as the man hurried towards the doorway of the room where he imagined his victim lay helpless, ready to finish him off. Before the man reached the doorway, Ben had already left the room by another exit. Knowing the layout of the maze-like passages as he did, he circled around in a loop. Within a few seconds he was back to the same room. His enemy was now inside, searching in the darkness for his quarry.

What Ben knew, which the man couldn't have known either, was that just days earlier this room was being used to practise shoot/no shoot drills with Pepe Jaeckin's team. And that the remote handset that controlled the lights also controlled the pop-up and turning targets that could appear as though from nowhere to surprise students of the art of tactical responsiveness. At the same instant that Ben activated the lights that filled the room with a sudden dazzling glare, he hit another button that made the life-size shape of a human figure come rearing up from behind a makeshift table. The target depicted a terrorist, all in black with a sinister balaclava masking his face and a pistol in his hand. Dazzled and startled and shockingly confronted with almost a mirror-image of himself, the man flew into a wild panic and fired a flurry of bullets into what his confused mind interpreted as some new opponent lying in wait for him. He was so spooked that he didn't notice the presence creeping up from behind.

And then it was too late.

Ben said, 'Coo-ee.'

The man half turned around, clutching his pistol, just in time to catch a blurred glimpse of the long piece of four-by-two timber whooshing towards his face. It caught him across his left temple and cheekbone with a resonant meaty *smack* and he went down hard without a sound. Ben kicked the pistol from his hand, beat him viciously about the head a couple of times more and then dropped the four-by-two and fell on top of his enemy with a knee pinning his throat. The man tried to struggle but Ben kept him pinned down tight, compressing both carotid arteries. In a few more moments he would become unconscious as the blood flow stopped to his brain. In a few more moments after that, anoxia would start to cause permanent brain damage, and ultimately death.

Ben kept his knee down. The guy went limp, but still Ben didn't take the pressure off. A wild, murderous passion of hate was welling up inside him and he wanted to see this man die for what he and his gang had done here tonight. But then the voice of reason inside his head said, *Don't do it*. Ben came to his senses and took his knee off the man's throat. He was still deeply unconscious, but at least he'd wake up. Which was more than could be said for Victor and the dogs.

Ben rose unsteadily to his feet, breathing hard. He checked the man's pistol and found three rounds left in the magazine, which he popped out and transferred into his own weapon. Next he had to decide what to do with the guy. The killing house was full of all kinds of useful materials. He found a coil of strong, thin paracord and in moments had his enemy trussed up tightly on his belly like Raul Ramolino, with his feet bent up behind his legs and lashed to his wrists. He wouldn't be going anywhere. Ben turned off the lights and left him in the darkness.

Back outside, the easterly wind had stepped up a notch and the snow was turning into a blizzard. If conditions grew any worse, they risked becoming a near-total whiteout. The cold was piercing, but Ben still felt warm from the fight. Scanning what he could make out of the landscape of the compound, he could see no sign of Storm. Where had he gone? The gunshots had stopped. Ben was deeply worried about what might have become of him. By now he was certain that Storm had been the last survivor of the dog pack. Which meant that not only had Blitz, Diablo and Bomber gone the same way as Sabre, but that Scruffy was most likely dead too. The brave-hearted little mixed-breed terrier belonged to Ben's son Jude, but had come to live here at Le Val and was as much one of the gang as any of them. *Or had been*, Ben told himself grimly. And now if Storm was dead too . . .

There was nothing to be done about it. The enemy were still on the loose out there somewhere, and this fight wasn't over yet. Ben dug his crutch into the snow and set back off towards the buildings.

Chapter 24

Storm had no detailed understanding of what was happening, and didn't need to. His atavistic wolf brain operated by a set of primal laws and rules that were far simpler and more functional than those of the tall two-legged creatures who co-existed in his world, concerning itself with only the bare pragmatic essentials. Such as the fact that the two-legged creatures were to be viewed as belonging to any one of just three types. There were the ones he liked or even loved, like his Master around whom his life revolved. Then there were the ones to whom Storm felt quite indifferent, who came and went and had no impact on his existence. And then there were the ones who were Bad, and constituted a threat to the stability of his pack and the sanctity of his territory.

Why that might be was of no concern. Storm simply understood that those sacred things were under attack from Bad people, and that the way to protect and preserve them was to make the Bad people go away. The threat was to be eliminated according to the ways of nature, the way things had been for millions of years. Once it was no longer there, life would simply return to normal. Stability would return.

The pack would be safe once more. That, as far as it could be said to exist, was the wolf's credo.

When Storm had seen the group of strangers split up in different directions, his first instinct was to go with his Master. But then his attention had been distracted by one of the Bad ones who ran between two of the buildings, taking a route that Storm had been taking all his life. Storm's predatory instinct, honed by a hundred thousand generations of his wild canid ancestors before him, locked on and he gave chase. Once engaged in the pursuit, he would not stop until either the quarry was caught or it got away. The wolf brain had determined that the Bad one would not get away.

To enter the domain of the wolf is to step into a savage, implacable and alien world for which few humans are physically or psychologically equipped. This man was in it now. He was deep in it.

Just how deep, he was about to find out.

Ángel Leoni's intention had been to skirt around the buildings in the hope of heading off the crippled guy, who he was certain would be trying to make his way back to the safety of the farmhouse after pulling that stunt with the JCB. Ángel thought he was a pretty smart operator, and he was looking forward to proving it by being the one who caught the crippled guy. If they could get the armoury keys from the bastard, there might still be a chance of rescuing the job from total disaster. But as Ángel ran up through the gap between the buildings and emerged in the snowy expanse of the yard, there was nobody there.

'*Cazzu*,' he muttered under his breath. The crippled guy

must have gone another way. Ángel was about to double back and rejoin Casta and the others when he saw the dark shape hurtling towards him through the alleyway and his blood froze colder than the snow.

Among other things, Ángel considered himself a tough character. He'd never backed down from a fight in his life and he prided himself that he feared no man. But the visceral terror of what was coming towards him made his guts churn and his legs turn to water. He snapped off a wild gunshot that went wide and ricocheted off the wall of the alley. Then he turned and ran, wild-eyed, gibbering in fear.

Ángel sprinted across the yard and went slipping and stumbling around the corner of the house. In his frenzied panic he made little of the presence of the four-wheel-drive Nissan, parked in front of the house, that hadn't been there before, nor did he pay much attention to the dead body of the old man who lay nearby, half-covered in snow. All he could think about was the dog. He threw a glance back over his shoulder and saw it catching up with him. Still running for all he was worth, he let off another shot and a small fountain of snow flew up by the beast's running paws, making it veer slightly off course. He fired off another, and another, but he was too terrified out of his wits to shoot straight and he missed, missed again, and again, until the gun's magazine had run empty and its slide locked back.

And now the dog was coming after him again. He let out a cry of dread as he saw it surging closer and closer, gaining on him with every racing heartbeat. Ángel went stumbling desperately on through the snow, still gripping his empty weapon. He was a certain distance from the house now, heading into the dense patch of woods to the rear. As he pushed into the trees, branches whipped in his face and brambles ripped at his legs. There was a cleared area ahead, like a pathway cut through the undergrowth. Ángel steered towards it, thinking it could help him run faster. His breath was coming in rasping gasps as the icy air seared his lungs.

He could hear the soft thunder of paws getting closer. He cried out, '*Mamaaaa!*'

And then it was on him.

The German shepherd closed on its prey with his jaws wide open, and Ángel let out a scream of pain and terror as the long curved fangs locked tight into the muscle of the back of his thigh. His leg buckled under the weight of ninety-five pounds of predator dragging him down. If Ángel had fallen then, it would have been the end of him. But lashing out blindly behind him with his empty pistol he landed a lucky blow that caught the dog hard on the snout. There was a yelp and Ángel felt the crushing jaws let go of his leg.

Suddenly free again, his heart hammering faster than it had ever done in his life, Ángel went staggering on while the dog paused in his chase, stunned from the blow and pawing its face. He'd managed to buy himself a few precious seconds and put some distance between himself and this evil mindless thing that wanted to tear him apart, but he knew that within seconds the creature would catch up with him again.

A glance back over his shoulder told him that he was right. It was coming! Ángel braced himself for the impact that he was convinced would bring him down this time, tumbling to the ground with the brute on top of him ripping out his throat. All that would be left of him by morning was a tattered skeleton.

But now that terror was replaced by another as, without warning, the ground suddenly gave way beneath him and Ángel felt himself dropping vertically downwards through it. His cry of shock and confusion was muffled as snow filled his mouth and nose. Then he was through the icy rime that partially covered the hole, and for a heart-stopping instant he was falling into empty space. Before he'd had time to realise what was happening, his body landed on something hard and solid and he felt the awful snap of his leg breaking. Then he was rolling on his back in the darkness with bits of snowy dirt and torn, frozen vegetation raining down on him from the rim of the hole. His leg was twisted away from his body at an unnatural angle. A moment later the agony hit him and the scream exploded from his lips.

Storm was momentarily stunned by the blow that the Bad two-legged had inflicted on him. He sensed the injury to his long, sensitive snout and could smell the warm blood that dripped from the end of his nose into the snow. At the same time he also could taste the man's blood on his lips, and his predatory drive quickly overcame the hurting feeling. His eyes, possessed of far superior night vision to that of any human, locked onto their stumbling, staggering target up ahead and he broke back into a run, his paws churning up the snow, the pain now fully erased from his memory, single-mindedly determined to run down his prey and finish it off.

Then suddenly the running two-legged was no longer there. Storm impassively observed the man disappear into the ground, no different from the rabbits, rats and other burrow-dwelling creatures that his wild forebears had been hunting since before the last great ice age, three million years ago. His simple wolf instinct directed him to dig out the burrow until the prey could be dragged up to the surface, killed and eaten, or until it was found to have escaped and the hunt was abandoned. Success or failure; the wolf brain accepted either outcome as a natural part of the process, and felt no emotion about it one way or the other.

Storm slowed his pace and cautiously padded up to the edge of the hole into which the man had fallen, sniffing and snuffling. The German shepherd's powerful sense of smell detected the scent of the man's blood and the fear that was releasing molecules of pheromone from his skin, telling Storm that his prey was nearby. As he crept closer to the edge and peered downward he could see him clearly, sprawled against snow-covered rocks at the bottom of the hole. Most of all, Storm could hear the high-pitched sounds of distress that the two-legged was making.

Storm had no understanding of why the man's leg was all twisted the way it was, nor any interest in why he was screaming in pain and clutching it with both hands. The wolf brain feels no empathy, let alone compassion. Its only consideration, in these changed circumstances, was whether or not it was still able to reach its prey. Storm's mind computed the logistics of jumping down into the hole after the man. Inching forward, at its very edge he could feel the ground unstable beneath his paws, and backed uncertainly away.

After stamina and endurance for the chase, the wild hunter's greatest attribute is patience. Storm was in no hurry to abandon his prey, which sooner or later might crawl out of its burrow of its own accord, to be duly caught. He lay down in the snow by the hole, waiting, listening, watching. The high-pitched keening sounds of the injured human diminished after a while, then stopped altogether. The German shepherd nose with its two hundred million olfactory cells could detect the tiny variations in scent that occurred shortly after death. Equipped with the same sensory perception as a trained cadaver dog that will not signal to its handler the presence of a living person or animal, Storm knew the man was still alive.

Time meant little, but he was aware of its having passed by before new sounds attracted his attention. The dog turned his head away from the hole and his ears swivelled forward, instantly pinpointing the exact direction and distance of the sounds. They were coming from the heart of his territory, the other side of the house. The sounds of gunfire were a habitual part of his daily routine – but now he sensed that they signified renewed danger. And his Master was not here with him, so that meant his Master was in danger.

The nearby presence of his trapped prey no longer held his interest. Storm rose to his feet, turned away from the hole and ran off in the direction of the new threat.

Chapter 25

The thickening snow helped to conceal Ben's return across the open ground between the killing house and the clustered buildings of the compound. He was getting his new crutch-walking technique perfected to an art, although the pain in his ankle was getting worse. Reaching better cover he stayed close into the shadows, stopping frequently to rest and take stock of his surroundings. It was during one of those stops that he saw the dark figure of another raider emerge from the shattered doorway of the big storage barn, just a few steps away.

The man had either been hunting for Ben inside the barn, or lying in wait for him to return, before deciding to look elsewhere. He paused in the open for a moment, scanning slowly left and right, gun in hand, snowflakes sticking to his clothes and face mask, before he moved on towards the smaller storage barn. It was clear from his behaviour that he was totally unaware of what had just happened to his crony inside the killing house, whose heavily insulated outer walls had dampened the sound of gunfire and fighting within. He was even more unaware of the unseen presence now lurking behind him.

The wind had pried the door of the small storage barn partly ajar and was making it flap open and shut. The man raised his pistol, peered into the darkness of the building and stalked cautiously in through the doorway. Ben gave him a moment longer to get inside, glanced around to make sure the man was alone, then waited for the wind to catch the door again and slipped through the gap in the man's wake, quickly darting into the deep bank of shadow along the inner wall. The building was wooden like its larger neighbour, and the gaps between the slats allowed in just enough light from the compound floods to see by, along with little flurries of powdery snow driven through by the gusting wind. Rock-still and silent in the darkness, Ben could see the silhouetted figure of the raider creeping among the various stores of target bosses and frames, stacks of road cones, crates and boxes and butane gas bottles and diesel jerrycans and other assorted equipment, hunting for any likely nook or cranny where the fugitive might be hiding.

But now the line between hunter and hunted was getting blurry, and it was just about to become even more so for this guy. Ben detached himself from the shadows of the wall and in two long strides of his crutch he was right up close. He whispered, 'Psst.'

As the man turned, startled, towards the source of the sound the blunt, wet end of Ben's length of four-by-two timber punched a straight brutal jab into his Adam's apple, closing off his trachea and driving the wind completely out of him. The man staggered, dropping his weapon and clutching at his throat, unable to utter a sound other than a guttural kind of choking croak. Ben swept his legs out from under him with a violent scything blow of the timber that almost made him lose his own balance as his enemy pitched sideways. The raider came down like a sack of bricks on the hard concrete floor and would probably not have got up again too quickly, even if Ben hadn't followed up with a couple of sharp cracks to the head.

A strike like that to the throat could easily kill a man. Ben knew exactly how hard you could go without inflicting fatal injury. Crouching beside his fallen enemy he quickly determined that the guy was still able to breathe. Pity it had to be that way. But he wouldn't be able to swallow solid food for a month, which was at least some consolation.

Ben stripped off the man's mask, to reveal an ugly face with a nasty, bloody and very recent broken nose. He guessed that made this guy the one he'd hit earlier, inside the house during the first wave of the attack. It also revealed that the guy wasn't the owner of the severed ear in Ben's pocket, because both of his were still attached. Ben hoisted himself back up to his feet, limped over to a shelf and found an old oily rag that Jeff had been using to clean his chainsaw. It made an excellent gag, and the bale of fencing wire propped against the wall nearby was just the thing to bind the guy up with from head to toe. He was just lucky it wasn't the barbed or razor variety.

When it was done, Ben surveyed his handiwork and did a quick head count. Two down, plus the missing killer, plus Raul in the cellar, left just two remaining. The enemy numbers were whittling down fast and the tide was turning in Ben's favour, although anything could still happen.

He slipped back outside. He was getting increasingly

worried about Storm's disappearance and wanted to call the dog's name, but feared giving himself away to the two enemies still lurking out there. He strained his eyes to peer through the relentless snowfall in the hope that the familiar pointy-eared silhouette would suddenly come bounding towards him out of the night. Not a trace. Something like bleak despair rose up inside him and his spirits plummeted. He felt suddenly so tired, too exhausted even to be angry, as his grief at Victor's death threatened to wash over him in full force. He willed himself to focus and stay tight. This was no time to let emotions get the better of him.

But it was too late, and Ben had just let his guard down for one second too long. By the time he heard the crisp crunch of a footstep behind him, the masked raider already had Ben in his gunsights.

Chapter 26

Ben whirled around and saw the tall dark shape of the man standing there not ten metres away behind a veil of driving snow, pistol raised and pointed right at his heart. Whirled around so fast that his plastered foot slipped out from under him and he staggered and fell, hitting his head a cracking blow against the slat wall of the barn at the exact same instant that the gunshot boomed out. A white flash of pain exploded through his skull, and for an instant he thought he'd been shot.

He hadn't. But if he hadn't slipped and gone down, Ben would have been dead. The raider's bullet had punched through the wooden wall right where his target had been standing an instant before.

The dark figure fired again, lowering his aim as Ben scrambled in the snow to recover his fallen pistol and get to his feet. The second gunshot grazed the top of Ben's left shoulder and kicked up a spray of white behind him. He felt the searing wound gouge his flesh and knew that if he didn't keep moving fast, the next gunshot would be the last one he'd ever hear. He rolled and tumbled and somehow made it around the corner of the storage shed as two more shots blasted out, one of them passing through the wall right next to him and tearing the skin on his cheek with flying splinters.

His crutch was gone. His gun was buried in the snow. He was wounded, unarmed and helpless again. There was no possibility of escape. To even try would be futile. He was going to die, right here and right now.

Ben had faced sudden violent death many, many times before, and by a combination of skill and luck had never quite fulfilled his appointment. But he'd always known it would catch up with him eventually, and he'd long promised himself that when the time came, he would sooner face it standing up with dignity than be shot in the back trying to save his bacon.

So he hauled himself upright as best he could and stood there, ready for it, as the man in black stepped towards him. The gun was pointed at Ben's chest. Looked like Ben wasn't the only one who preferred his pistols without the encumbrance of a silencer. He waited for the booming report that would signal the end of his time. It hadn't been a bad life, though he would be leaving it with too many regrets. Victor Vermont was one of them.

The man in black with the gun took a step closer. But he didn't shoot. Instead, he spoke. Not in Corsican this time, but in English. He spoke it with the same accent as the others.

'So you must be Ben Hope,' the man said.

Ben could feel the warm blood trickling from his wounded shoulder, quickly cooling against his skin. There was little pain. That would come later – if there had *been* a later. He replied, 'I am. But I don't believe we've been properly introduced.'

'The name is Casta,' the man said. 'César Casta.'

'This was your operation?'

'I was just doing my job,' Casta said.

'So sorry to have messed things up for you.'

'It's not over until it's over,' Casta said. 'Do you have the keys to the armoury?'

'Right here,' Ben lied. The keys were locked in the combination safe in his quarters. But he was thinking that if he could trick Casta into getting close enough, he might be able to disarm him.

'Then toss them over.'

'I can't. You shot me. You'll have to come and get them.'

Casta chuckled. 'Yeah, right. So you can pull one of your tricks on me. I know how sneaky your kind are.'

'Then I suppose you'll just have to kill me,' Ben said.

'Not my style, *u mo amicu*. I might shoot both your *palle* off—' motioning with the gun at Ben's crotch '—if you don't cooperate. Or maybe I'll blow out your good knee and make you even more crippled than you are already. But killing isn't what I do. I'm a thief, not a murderer.'

'Tell that to my friend who's lying over there with four bullets in him. The innocent man you shot here tonight.'

Casta shook his head. 'Bullshit. I shot nobody.'

'But your man Petru did,' Ben replied.

'Petru.' Casta spat the name out as though he couldn't stand the sound of it. 'He's not my man. I never wanted him in the first place.'

'You just can't get the staff these days,' Ben said. 'Question is, what are you going to do about it?'

'What do you want me to do?' Casta asked, waving the

gun. 'I don't know where the fuck Petru went. He's gone. And I can't bring your friend back.'

Which was about as close to an apology as Ben was ever going to get from César Casta. 'No, you can't. But you can help to make it right. You can help me to find this Petru. He went off in such a rush I never got the chance to say goodbye properly.'

'I see. So it's a deal you want to make, huh? So what were you thinking of trading me in return? How about the armoury keys, for a start?'

Ben said, 'No, but I would promise not to go too hard on you.'

Casta laughed. 'You've got a set of balls on you, all right. It's going to be a real shame to blow them off.'

'I take it that's a refusal?' Ben said.

'I might be a lot of things, but a snitch isn't one of them. We don't betray our own people. Not even a piece of shit like Petru.'

'Now noble of you,' Ben said.

'Enough talking. Hurry up and toss me the fucking keys.'

'I told you, you'll have to come and take them,' Ben said. 'Or else pull that trigger, if you have the metal to do it. Better make it quick, though.'

'Fine. You asked for it.' Casta aimed the gun at Ben's crotch. Then he changed his mind and altered his aim to line up the sights on Ben's right knee. 'This is going to hurt like a bitch.'

'How right you are,' Ben said. He smiled.

'Are you crazy? What the fuck are you smiling at?'

'Turn around,' Ben said. 'You'll see.'

It was hard for Ben not to smile. Because in the last five or six seconds, while they'd been talking, a familiar shape had appeared in the distance, outlined dark against the snow. Two pointed ears and four racing paws, running fast. Storm had returned from somewhere beyond the farmhouse, cut across the yard and come hurtling full pelt through the alley between the buildings. Now he was almost on them.

Casta heard the soft thunder of his approach and turned in alarm, but he was far too slow and too late to save himself. Storm leaped at him from six feet away, sailed through the air and hit like a fur missile, taking the man straight down with his teeth fastened tight around the arm holding the gun. Casta screamed and thrashed on the frozen ground as the dog shook him from side to side as easily as if he'd been a straw mannequin. The pistol flew out of his grasp and disappeared in the snow. 'Get it off me! Help! Please!'

'Hurts, doesn't it?' Ben said. He let Storm go on savaging Casta's arm for a couple of moments longer before he gave him the command to leave. Storm let go and backed off, bright-eyed with excitement and licking Casta's blood off his chops. Nothing in his world was as rewarding as taking down a threat to his pack.

Ben picked his fallen crutch up out of the snow. Hefted it in both hands, braced himself and swung it like a golfer teeing off the world's largest golf ball. The solid timber cracked against Casta's head with a sound that echoed off the compound buildings. One good solid strike, and Casta was out of the fight.

Three down, plus the missing killer, plus Raul in the cellar. By Ben's count, there was still one raider out there in the compound. He wondered where he was. Hiding somewhere? Ben would deal with that soon enough. 'I thought I'd lost you,' he said as he hugged Storm tight and the dog covered him with slobber. 'Where did you go, boy? What have you been doing?'

The dog made a whinge of pain as Ben touched his muzzle, and Ben saw the nasty gash and the dried blood there, realising that Storm had got into a fight. The cut looked like the result of a blow from a hard implement. 'Are you okay? What happened to you?'

If only they could talk. Ben quickly checked him over for more damage, but found none. Storm's coat was all matted with bits of dead leaf and twigs, as though he'd been running in the woods behind the house. As happy as he was to be with his master again, he seemed agitated, as though he wanted to tell him something. Ben was beginning to wonder if that something might explain where the sixth raider was.

'All right, all right. Just wait a minute. Let me deal with this one first, okay?'

A quick forage in the smaller barn produced a coil of stout rope and a roll of duct tape. Ben got to work trussing Casta into a helpless cocoon, then dragged his unconscious body out of the snow and laid him on the concrete floor next to his associate. The first guy was beginning to come round, so Ben knocked him out again. Next he yanked off Casta's ski mask. Casta looked to be in his late thirties or early forties, a little older than the others. There was nothing much remarkable about his face, but what Ben found in his backpack was much more interesting. The mobile signal jammer confirmed the reason why both of his and Jeff's phones had been cut off. Ben switched the device off and then checked his phone. Working fine again.

Then he turned back towards Storm, who'd been sitting dutifully nearby watching, and said, 'All right. Now show me.'

It took Ben several minutes of arduous crutch-work to reach the spot in the woods that Storm wanted to lead him to. To get there, they had to pass by Victor's body, now just a mound in the snow. Ben couldn't look at it. The dog was yelping and barking agitatedly, running rings around him as he followed, dashing on ahead and then doubling back to nip at Ben's sleeve, as though urging him to *come and look what I've got. Hurry, hurry!*

The snowfall had petered out to just the occasional drifting flake, and now the wind was driving away the clouds to uncover a bright moon that reflected on the white landscape and lit it up like daylight. As Storm led him towards the edge of the hole, Ben heard the low moan from below. And there was the sixth raider, lying at the bottom of the collapsed tunnel with the moonlight shining on his agonised face and a very obviously broken leg.

'*Aiuta mi!*' came the muffled voice from below. '*Aiuta mi per piacè!*' 'Help me, for pity's sake!' The injured man squinted up towards the mouth of the hole, unable to identify the figure standing above him. '*Hè tù, César?*' Thinking it was his leader come to rescue him. Then as Ben stepped a little closer to the edge the man saw who it was, and his pain-streaked face turned whiter with fear. 'Please. I hurting so bad.' His English wasn't as good as Casta's.

'What's your name?' Ben said down the hole.

'Ángel!'

'Ángel what?'

'Ángel Leoni! Please! Help!'

'That depends, Ángel,' Ben told him. 'Did you kill my dogs?'

'No! I swear I no kill no dogs!'

'Who did?'

'César, he shoot one. Pasquale, he shoot another. Petru, he kill two of them. Maybe more, I don't remember.'

'Petru?'

'Petru Navarro. He and César, both are hating dogs. Me, I like very much.'

'I'm sure you do,' Ben replied, thinking of the deep gash on Storm's face and pretty sure this guy had put it there.

'Please! Is so hurting! Get me out!'

'Maybe I'll come back for you later,' Ben said. 'If I don't, then I suppose you'll just freeze to death slowly. What a shame that would be.'

Ben turned away from the hole and started moving back towards the house with the dog trotting happily at his heels. The raid was over and the attackers had been beaten, but there was still a long night ahead.

Chapter 27

Ben's first move in the immediate aftermath of the attack had to be to attend to his three guys Michel, Richard and Serge at the gatehouse. If Casta had been telling the truth, they'd be still alive – or so Ben hoped. His ankle was hurting too badly to make the hike up the track and he couldn't bring himself to use Victor's Nissan, so he hobbled across to the vehicle shed, next to the empty kennel block. Parked between Jeff's Ford Ranger pickup and his own BMW Alpina was the beaten-up communal workhorse Land Rover. It was as Ben was clambering awkwardly into it that he heard the pitiful, frightened little bark coming from underneath his Alpina.

Storm had already gone rushing over to investigate, crying with excitement and sniffing like crazy. Getting down on his knees to peer under the car, Ben saw with a rush of joy that it was little Scruffy. He must have been hiding here the whole time. He was shaking and terrified, and Ben had to coax the little guy out. Storm was anxiously licking him, like a mother with a puppy. Ben put the two dogs in the back of the Land Rover, fired it up and managed to drive one-footed through the deep snow to the top of the track.

As he'd pretty much expected, he found the gatehouse all in darkness and the gates themselves lying wide open. There were a lot of tyre tracks at the entrance, but no vehicle. Ben guessed that Petru Navarro had taken it, perfectly happy to abandon his associates here when he made his escape.

Ben entered the dark gatehouse to find Serge, Michel and Richard all tied up and gagged on the floor. The heater had been turned off. The gang would have let them freeze in here. Flipping the lights back on, Ben saw that the three men were shivering with cold and in a bad way, with red puffy eyes and mottled faces that lit up with relief and happiness at seeing him. As he undid their gags and released their wrists and ankles, the questions started flying. 'It's over,' Ben told them. 'One's escaped. The other five aren't going anywhere except prison.'

'You're hurt,' Serge said, noticing the blood on Ben's clothes.

'It's just a graze,' Ben replied. The wound was beginning to hurt, and it would get worse. But he welcomed the pain. It helped to take his mind off the real agony of what had happened that night.

'The bastards faked a road accident and fucking gassed us,' Richard said. 'I'm so sorry, Ben.'

'Nothing you could have done,' Ben replied. 'Can you walk?'

'We're fine.'

'Good, because I could use some help down there.'

As the Land Rover worked its way back down the track, Ben filled them in with more detail. 'As far as I can tell, they belong to some kind of Corsican crime gang. They came to rip off the weapons and ammunition in our armoury. And they knew we were down to a skeleton crew, and that I was on crutches, and that I'm a keyholder to the vault. Which made them see us as a soft target. And which also means someone must have tipped them off with insider information.'

'Wasn't anyone who works here,' Serge said. 'That's for damn sure.'

'I know that.'

'Then who?' Michel asked.

'That's what I aim to find out,' Ben answered.

Richard said, 'You're on crutches and you took down five men on your own?'

'Only three. Storm helped out with the other two.' Hearing his name, Storm gave a bark from the back of the Land Rover.

'I saw the lights of a car go through the gate a while ago,' Serge said. 'I was conscious by then, but I couldn't tell who it was.'

'It was Monsieur Vermont,' Ben said quietly. 'He turned up in the middle of it.'

'The old fellow from the village?' Michel said. 'I remember him. Shit, that was bad timing. Is he okay?'

'He's dead,' Ben said. His voice sounded hollow. 'Shot four times. The one who did it is the one who got away.'

Serge spoke first after their shocked silence. 'Why? Why would anyone shoot a harmless old man?'

'Because he had something the killer wanted. Something very valuable. And he had it because I gave it to him to look after. I think he came here tonight for the same reason. He'd still be alive otherwise.' Ben's fists tightened on the steering wheel. He couldn't shut the image of Victor's dead face out of his head.

'We'll find the bastard,' Richard said, his voice hard and tight with rage. 'We'll get him.'

'He's long gone by now,' Ben replied. 'No point in going looking for him. We have a lot of work to do.'

Back at the house, Richard and Michel dragged the still unconscious bodies of César Casta and his associate from the storage shed and loaded them onto the flatbed of Jeff's pickup truck, then drove across the snowy grounds to the killing house to pick up the third, who by now was wide awake and struggling like a wild man against his unbreakable bonds. Meanwhile Ben returned to the house with Serge and they headed down to the wine cellar to retrieve the hapless Raul Ramolino, who'd been awake for quite some time but made no progress in freeing himself from the hogtie knots Ben had trussed him up with. Serge took some pleasure in dragging Raul unceremoniously up the cellar steps and dumping him none too gently onto the pickup truck flatbed with his associates.

Next it was Ángel Leoni's turn to be rescued from the collapsed tunnel, hauled up on the end of a rope. He was making so much noise because of his broken leg that Ben cracked him over the head and knocked him out, just to shut him up. Storm hovered nearby, perhaps hoping they would hand Ángel over to him.

Once all five captives were loaded aboard the truck, they were driven over to the empty dog kennel block. The block was built to house up to eight large hounds, each partitioned inside its own heavy-duty pen made of steel and wire mesh. With five banged-up humans locked up inside, the row soon looked like a jailhouse after a particularly rough Saturday night. Ben freed them from their bonds so that those without broken legs could move about a little, but kept their wrists tethered behind their backs with plastic cable ties.

'What are you going to do with us?' wailed Raul.

'Keep you as our slaves for the rest of your worthless lives,' Michel told him.

Ben said nothing. Grief and depression were weighing more heavily on him with every passing minute, now that the urgency of battle was behind him and he faced the grim prospect of what lay ahead. The next few hours would be bad, and the coming days would probably be even worse. He felt as though life at Le Val would never be the same again. He didn't even know if he could go on living here.

With the phones working again, Ben's immediate task was to report the attack to the police. He spoke briefly and matter-of-factly, stating the essential facts as they had happened. He identified Victor as the one human fatality of the incident, and explained that he had five of the six perpetrators locked up, one in particular needing medical attention and the others mostly unharmed. The police call handler seemed more concerned about the security of the weapons store than the fact that an innocent man had died here tonight.

Le Val being no ordinary training facility, Ben was pretty sure the cops would be anxious to reach the scene of the crime as fast as possible, though the weather conditions would delay them for at least several hours and possibly until morning. They'd warned him not to touch or move Victor's body, for fear of disturbing the evidence. But there was no way Ben was going to allow his friend to lie there on the ground all night, like a sack of rubbish that had been thrown out. Richard, Serge and Michel helped him with the awful task of moving the old man's body inside the house. They laid him gently down on the floor of the hallway, half frozen and pallid blue-white. Ben covered him with a blanket. He had lost many friends, comrades and loved ones in his life. Few of them had moved him so deeply.

Though the police would take little notice of them, Ben had lost other good friends besides Victor that night. Assisted by Michel, he spent the next two hours searching for and gathering up the bodies of the dogs from the various parts of the compound where they had died. The first was Sabre, whom they retrieved from the spot near the house where Ben had found him earlier. With death in his heart Ben placed Sabre's body in the barn, where he could be left until he and his pack-mates were buried together the next day. Then a distraught, whimpering Storm helped them to locate the bodies of Blitz, Diablo and Bomber. They'd all been shot in the same way, each with at least two bullet wounds in him.

When all the dogs were laid out side by side on the floor of the barn, Ben asked Michel if he'd give him a minute to be with them alone. He spoke a few words to his old friends, tenderly stroking their fur. They looked so still and peaceful. Ben wept quietly for a while. Then he wiped his tears and composed himself and left the barn.

Chapter 28

It was a few minutes later that Serge found him knocking back a glass of Laphroaig in the farmhouse kitchen. 'You should let me take a look at that shoulder,' Serge said, eyeing Ben's bloody shirt with concern. 'It might need a few stitches.' Serge had had medical training in the French military, and he'd already demonstrated he was a dab hand with a needle when Jeff had gashed himself while putting up razor wire.

'I'm fine,' Ben said, pouring more whisky and knocking that one back, too. He could have finished the whole bottle and it wouldn't have touched the way he was feeling. 'I'll see to it later.'

'Then get some rest, for Christ's sake. You look exhausted.'

Ben drained his drink and set down the empty glass. 'Something I have to do first. You want to come with me to the kennel block?'

'I'd be glad to, if it's to blow those five pieces of shit straight to hell with a shotgun.'

As much as they might have deserved that, Ben's intention was in fact to offer some humane relief to the worst injured of their captives. Ángel Leoni was in a bad state, alternating

191

between near-comatose fainting spells and fits of screaming agony. Ben didn't have Serge's medical expertise, but as an SAS trooper he'd been taught the essentials of effecting field repairs on broken soldiers. With bandages from the Le Val first-aid box and bits of wood from the barn, the pair of them splinted the fractured leg up good and tight, and then heavily dosed the suffering patient with the last of the pain-killers Ben had bought in Valognes for his ankle.

'You're a much better man than I am, Ben,' Serge said to him as they worked. 'After what they've done? That takes some kind of saintly virtue.'

'I'm no saint,' Ben said.

'Then I don't know what that makes me. I'd want to strangle this fucker with my bare hands.'

They closed Ángel Leoni in his cell, and Ben limped along the row of mesh cage doors to where César Casta lay bound up, now wide awake and glaring at him. Behind the cell door to Casta's right was Raul Ramolino, to his left the one with the broken nose, and at the end of the row was the one Ben had lured inside the killing house.

The only one of the gang who could speak English well enough was Casta, so Ben spoke to them in Italian. 'The police are on their way. What your associate Petru Navarro did here tonight puts a murder charge on all six of you. Which means you five will be going to jail for many, many more years than you would have just for stealing a bunch of guns.'

'We didn't kill anyone,' protested the broken-nosed one in an indistinct, nasally voice. 'Our job was just to get the gear and get out of here. Nobody was supposed to die!'

'Just my dogs,' Ben said.

'Dogs are filthy animals that don't have the right to live,' Casta muttered.

'Look who's talking,' Ben replied. 'The only reason you're alive now is that you chose to attack me here, in my home, where I live and work. Otherwise, I promise you that nobody would ever have seen any of you again, or found your bodies. You're a lucky bunch. And you can make yourselves even luckier by talking to me. Then maybe when the cops turn up, I'll make sure they understand it was Petru who took it on himself, acting alone, to kill my friend. In which case they might just let the rest of you off the hook for murder. Better make it snappy, though. They could be here any minute.'

'Nobody talks!' Casta yelled in Corsican, twisting his head to address his fellow gang members.

'Your man there already told me Petru's surname,' Ben said, pointing across the kennel at Ángel Leoni. 'All I want to know now is where I can find him. The address of whatever rat hole he lives in, who his lowlife buddies are, where he hangs out. Handy little titbits that the cops won't be able to tell me.'

'Don't tell him any more!' Casta screamed at them in Corsican. 'Not a word! You hear me, you pieces of shit? We don't snitch! You know what happens otherwise!'

'I have a wife and kids,' the broken-nosed one moaned. 'I have to protect them.'

'Yeah,' Raul sneered to Ben. 'Never snitch. That's the rule. I already told you that, man. Are you stupid?'

Behind all the honour-among-thieves solidarity bravado was a lot of fear. Ben could see it in their eyes. Casta's eyes, most of all. Ben was beginning to wonder what kind of gang it was they belonged to.

He said, 'Stupid is as stupid does, boys. Have it your way. You all want to take the fall for Petru, that's fine by me. But if you think you're helping anyone by sacrificing yourselves, think again. I'm going to find Petru. Because hunting people is what I used to do for a living and I'm good at it. And when I find him, this is what the rest of him will look like.'

Ben took the severed ear from his pocket and held up the tattered, gory little flap of flesh so they could all take a good, clear, appalled look at it. He smiled at them, the kind of smile that makes a man's blood turn cold.

Not understanding Italian, Serge hadn't been able to follow much of what was being said. But the sight of the severed ear dangling from Ben's fingers required no explanation. He stared at it in horror, stared at Ben, and swallowed hard. So much for the virtuous saint.

Ben said, 'That's all that will be left of him, nothing but scattered pieces his own mother wouldn't recognise, if he has one. And that's all that will be left of you, too. Because one day, many years from now when you're old and grey, they're going to let you out of prison. And make no mistake, I'll be there waiting for you. You won't even see me coming.'

There was a long silence in the kennel block. Then Serge moved towards the doorway and said, 'I hear something. Sounds like the cavalry have finally made it.'

Ben had heard it too: the distant wail of sirens, getting steadily louder as what sounded like a whole fleet of police approached Le Val. Serge opened the door to the icy blast from outside, and they saw the broad halo of flashing blue lighting up the horizon beyond the trees.

'Still got time to change your minds, boys,' Ben said. 'They'll be here in just a couple of minutes.'

Ángel Leoni had been listening in silence until now, his face ghastly pale and covered in a sheen of sweat despite the cold, still waiting for the painkillers to start kicking in. With the look of a man driven to the brink of desperation he suddenly blurted out, 'Bar Royale in Porto Vecchio! Petru hangs out there. It's a nightclub, one of his uncle's joints!'

'Quiet!' Casta yelled at him. 'What did I tell you?'

'Petru helps to run the place, with his cousin Salvadore!' Ángel babbled on, unable to stop himself. 'That's where you'll find him. Please! I don't want to spend the rest of my life in jail! I've got my family to think of!'

Casta screamed, 'Enough, Ángel! They find out you ratted on his nephew, it won't be just your family that gets hung upside down and skinned alive! It'll be all of us!'

'Keep talking, Ángel,' Ben said. 'You're doing the right thing. Who's Petru's uncle?'

'Titus Navarro!' Ángel groaned.

Casta's face was livid and his eyes bulged in fury. 'Oh, you asshole! You've done it now. You just fucking *buried* us!'

Now that Ángel Leoni's floodgates had opened, Ben wanted to keep pressing him for more. But at the same time the chorus of sirens was growing rapidly louder as the police made their long-awaited mass descent on Le Val. Through the open kennel block door, the swirl of blue lights was illuminating the compound.

They were here.

Chapter 29

As Ben stepped outside to meet the cavalry, it looked to him as though the whole local force had rolled out and then some. A procession of four-wheel-drives, all wearing snow chains, rolled into the yard with a couple of ambulances, a pathologist's van and a forensic unit at their tail. Along with the regular gendarmerie vehicles were what few of the black-clad tactical response boys the regional Commissariat de Police could muster up at short notice. They spilled out of their truck and strutted about the yard toting submachine guns as though expecting a war to break out. They were a little late for that.

Meanwhile, from the lead police car stepped a plainclothes detective, who stood for a moment surveying the compound, spotted Ben and marched across. Even from a distance Ben recognised the type who liked to play the hard-ass. Every police department in the world had to have at least one, and Ben was going to be saddled with this guy. Wonderful.

'Inspector René Auclair,' the detective barked over the tumult of radios and voices and engines and dying sirens behind him. 'Who's in charge here?'

'I am,' Ben replied.

'You called the police?'

'Apparently. I'm Ben Hope. I operate this facility, with my two business partners Monsieur Dekker and Monsieur Fletcher.'

'And where are they?' Auclair demanded.

'In Australia and Jamaica. I've already been through all this on the phone.'

Auclair nodded grimly. 'Where are the bodies?'

'There's only one,' Ben told him, and again repeated much of what he'd told the police switchboard operator. Auclair seemed a little underwhelmed by the small death toll. Maybe a mountain of corpses might have helped to get his name into the newspapers.

'All right,' he said curtly. 'Now show me the arsenal.' No congratulations for having single-handedly thwarted the dangerous criminals. No expressions of sympathy for the deceased. Auclair's disapproving tone made it quite clear that he considered that a civilian facility harbouring weapons and ammunition only had itself to blame for attracting criminal attention.

'It's not exactly an arsenal,' Ben said, bridling at the term. He could tell that he and Inspector Auclair were going to get on great. 'It's just a glorified walk-in gun safe with a collection of mostly outdated kit. You probably have three times as much gear at the police HQ in Cherbourg. In any case, they didn't get in. Everything's exactly where it should be.'

'Lead the way. I want to see. Then you'll accompany me to the Commissariat for a statement, and perhaps we can get to the bottom of just exactly what happened here tonight.'

'Am I under arrest?'

'Not yet, but I wouldn't rule it out too soon. This is an extremely serious situation, Monsieur Hope.'

'I think I gathered that much.'

Together with five gendarmes and two of the armed response officers Ben led Auclair across the compound and showed them the scene of carnage that was the site of the armoury. 'Where is it?' Auclair snapped.

Ben pointed at the eleven tons of overturned JCB and told him, 'Under there.'

'Looks like a damn tank battle was fought here,' the tactical team captain muttered, eyeing the wreckage and shaking his head with something like envy.

'I'm sorry you missed it,' Ben replied, but the guy seemed not to register his sarcasm.

'This was just you?'

'And my dog,' Ben said.

Auclair said officiously, 'Needless to say, once all this mess is cleared up, someone will have to verify the contents of the vault.'

'And check them against the detailed inventory that you already have on file,' Ben replied. 'Right down to the last pair of ear defenders and rifle sling. I know the drill, Inspector. Meanwhile, I've got some actual crooks for you to take away, if you're still interested.'

Back at the house, the police were swarming everywhere. Ben and Serge freed Casta and his men from the kennels, and the relatively uninjured gang members were arrested, cuffed and loaded into police vehicles while Ángel Leoni was stretchered across to a waiting ambulance. Meanwhile the paramedics were in the process of carrying Victor's body out of the house.

The cops magnanimously allowed Ben a couple of minutes to attend to Storm and Scruffy. Once the dogs were safely housed in the now-vacated kennels with plenty of food and water and a heater blowing warm air, Ben noticed that Auclair's back was turned and took advantage of the moment to sneak into Jeff's quarters, the one building the cops hadn't yet thoroughly examined. When he re-emerged moments later, the contents of the CCTV hard drive had been erased. Then he was escorted into the back of Auclair's car, and a line of vehicles set off with the two ambulances bringing up the rear.

As they neared Valognes the roads were clearer of snow. Not long after, they were speeding along the white-fringed Nationale-13 in the direction of Cherbourg, eighteen kilometres beyond. The ambulances turned off towards the Louis Pasteur hospital while Auclair's car led the way to the Commissariat Central, an unprepossessing modern building in Rue du Val de Saire that housed the regional headquarters of the Police Nationale.

Deep in the bowels of the police HQ Ben was led to one of those featureless, generic interview rooms that weren't unfamiliar to him, and left sitting alone in a plastic chair for a long time. The radiators were icy cold to the touch and nobody had offered so much as a cup of coffee. Elsewhere, Michel, Richard and Serge would be receiving the same treatment. It was nice to know that their efforts in preventing crime were appreciated.

Ben used the time to work through all the unanswered questions in his head. Why had the gang picked that night to attack? How had they known that most of the Le Val team were going to be absent? Where had they got the knowledge that the lone keyholder was on crutches with a foot in plaster? And if it was safe to assume that none of that privileged insider information had come from anyone within the small, tight-knit organisation of Le Val itself, then who the hell could have provided it?

Now that he had a quiet spell to reflect, Ben could think of only one possible source of that information. He was thinking about Robert Blondel, Pepe Jaeckin's trainee who'd been acting strangely during those two days at the facility. Blondel was one of only five outsiders who'd been privy to all the talk of their Christmas plans, over dinner that second night. Blondel knew that Ben was hurt, and that he was a keyholder to the armoury. Blondel also knew that Jeff and Tuesday were jetting off on holiday. He'd heard enough, seen enough, to know all of it.

Ben's thoughts refocused on that first evening, when he'd happened to find the guy wandering around the compound on his own while the rest of the trainees were in their quarters resting and getting ready for dinner. It had seemed a little odd at the time. But maybe it wasn't odd at all. Maybe, with hindsight, it all made absolute sense.

He remembered the way that Blondel had been bent over his phone, so intent on whatever he was doing that he hadn't sensed Ben coming up behind him. Ben had assumed the guy was looking at texts or emails, but what if in fact he'd been using the phone to snap photos or video of the layout of the buildings? The spot where Ben had found him had been near the storage barn, just a short distance away from the armoury area. Blondel could have been taking recon-naissance images and mapping out the whole place on behalf of someone who had targeted Le Val as a potential source of weaponry and ammunition. Sought-after merchandise that would be hard to obtain by any other channel, and which could command huge prices on the black market.

Ben guessed that that someone would most likely have started out with a list of all the likely candidates, the small number of similar tactical training facilities that were dotted around Europe. By a process of elimination they might have whittled their list down to just a handful. Le Val would certainly have remained a top choice, because few if any of its competitors had earned themselves as stellar a reputation. With the shortlist drawn up, the next stage would be to recruit spies to infiltrate each potential target and provide intelligence, on whose basis a final choice could be made. Which must have taken considerable manpower and plan-ning, but *organised* crime was called that for a good reason. There were a lot of shrewd and wily minds in that world. And a lot of money to be made from a successful operation.

At which point, whoever was behind this had struck lucky with the discovery that Le Val would be at its most vulner-able to attack on that particular night. And the more Ben thought about it, the more convinced he became that their source of information couldn't have been anyone other than Robert Blondel.

If his hypothesis was right, the next question to consider was whether Blondel was an active member of the gang. Ben remembered how nervous and uptight the guy had seemed for those two days. At the time, he'd naturally assumed that

Blondel was troubled by some kind of private personal problems back home. Now, it seemed that he might have been nervous because he was scared of being found out.

But what if that idea was mistaken, too? There were other possible reasons for a man to feel edgy, in those circumstances. Such as if he was being somehow coerced to obtain information that he knew was going to be used for illicit purposes. There were many ways that a crooked mastermind could leverage a useful insider to provide information. A man with a family to protect, for example, was an easy target for threats and intimidation. Or, a man anxious to preserve some dark and shameful secret might be blackmailed to do almost anything to keep it from being known.

Whatever the case, if someone had been working Blondel, then he could have told them all kinds of things about Le Val. He could have described the gatehouse and given them an idea of how many security guys they might expect to find there on duty. Having been inside it, he could have given them a detailed account of the armoury's contents. He could even have told them how many guard dogs lived at Le Val, and their names.

And if all that were true, then Robert Blondel was someone else Ben needed to speak to.

It was after four in the morning by the time Ben had finished working out his thoughts. He was cold and tired and worn out with emotion. There was no handle on the inside of the interview room door, and he resented being treated like a prisoner. He was about to start banging on the door when it suddenly opened, and in walked Inspector Auclair.

Chapter 30

Auclair wasn't alone. With him was a female plainclothes officer Ben hadn't seen before, who was introduced to him as Detective Sergeant Madeline Chausson. She was maybe five years younger than her colleague and more pleasant by far, but she said little as the two cops sat at the table opposite Ben.

'Am I under arrest yet?' Ben asked. 'Because if not, I'd like to be taken home.'

Auclair gave him an acerbic smile. 'I'm sure we would all like that, being that it's Christmas morning, But we're not done here yet. There's a lot we need to go through.'

'Then you'd better get started, instead of keeping people waiting all night.'

Ben thought he detected a certain look of sympathy from Madeline Chausson, but she remained silent as he gave his statement and she wrote it all down verbatim on a pad. Auclair kept interrupting, firing off question after question, frowning over Ben's replies and then asking them all over again. It was an age-old tactic, designed to wear down the interviewee and expose contradictions in their account.

There were none. Ben stuck to the facts and spoke plainly. What he told them was the truth.

But it wasn't the whole truth. He'd already decided what details to reveal to the cops, and what to hold back. That was the reason he'd erased the CCTV footage from the hard drive in Jeff's quarters.

'You've given the names of three of the alleged attackers as César Casta, Ángel Leoni and Raul Ramolino,' Auclair said, peering at the handwritten statement in front of him. 'How did you find out those names?'

Ben chose to ignore the 'alleged'. 'They told me,' he replied calmly.

'And what about the name of the man you claim to have witnessed killing Monsieur Vermont? Did they tell you that, too?'

Ben shook his head. 'They're not very forthcoming with information.'

'So you don't know his name?'

'No, I don't,' Ben replied. His first lie.

'And there's nothing you can tell us about him?'

Ben met Auclair's gaze with an equally cold and implacable one of his own and replied, 'Other than the fact that he murdered my friend, nothing. You'd have to ask them.'

'They're not talking.'

'That's what I thought,' Ben said.

Auclair drummed his fingers on the table. 'Your three associates don't seem to be able to tell us very much, either.'

'Maybe that's because they were tied up in a darkened room during most of what happened. If they're not able to give you information, it's because they don't have any to give.'

Which was the truth as well, as far as it went. The name 'Petru' had only been mentioned once in any of their presence, while Ben and Serge had been with the prisoners in the kennel block. That conversation had been in Italian, which Serge had no understanding of. Ben would have trusted Serge not to tell the cops anything in any case, but he couldn't reveal what he didn't know. The same went for the details of the man Ángel Leoni had claimed was Petru's uncle, this Titus Navarro individual of whom César Casta and his men seemed so terrified. More information that Ben had decided to keep to himself. In his experience, the less the police knew, the less they'd be able to go barging about in their usual clumsy way, like an inept hunter scaring away all the big game.

'It's regrettable that we have no CCTV footage of the incident to examine,' Auclair said. 'Do the terms of your company insurance policy not require you to monitor around the clock and keep video recordings?'

'It's not compulsory,' Ben said. 'We're out in the sticks, hardly in a high-crime zone. And I don't think we could be reasonably expected to keep video footage of a snowy Christmas Eve, do you?'

'All the same, that could have been extremely useful in helping us to determine exactly what happened and fill in some of the blanks. For example I'm still not quite clear as to what exactly the victim, Monsieur, ah—'

'His name was Victor Vermont,' Ben said icily.

'Yes. What was Monsieur Vermont doing there? It seems like an unusual time to pay a visit, especially given the weather conditions.'

'I've already explained that Monsieur Vermont came to

return an item that I had lent him,' Ben said, as patiently as he could. 'He was an expert on historical artefacts. I'd asked him to look at something for me.'

'Can you elaborate on the nature of this item?'

'It was an old cross that I dug up in the grounds of my property,' Ben said. 'About so large, decorated with engravings and gemstones.'

'An old cross? Do you mean like a crucifix?'

'A crucifix has a depiction of Christ on it,' Ben told him. 'This doesn't. That makes it a plain and simple cross.'

Auclair didn't appreciate being corrected. 'Cross, crucifix, whatever. Does it have any value, this object?'

'I hoped it might,' Ben said. 'But on examination Victor told me it was cast out of brass and probably not much more than fifty years old, if that. The gemstones are just coloured glass. Basically it's worthless.' His next lie.

'But the killer presumably was unaware of that fact.'

'I think he must have thought it was made of solid gold and studded with real rubies and emeralds,' Ben said.

'In which case, I imagine it would be immensely valuable.'

'Especially if it was really old,' Ben said. 'But then again, what do I know?'

'So it appears that Monsieur Vermont was murdered over a cheap trinket,' Auclair said. 'An unfortunate mistake.'

Ben looked hard at Auclair and replied, 'For Victor, I'd say it was a little more than unfortunate.' Madeline Chausson stirred in her chair and tried to hide her disapproval of her colleague's tactless words.

Auclair seemed not to notice, and moved on to another tack. 'I'm curious. What would make someone venture out late on Christmas Eve, in the worst weather conditions imaginable, to return a borrowed item of no value that its owner was in no hurry to get back? It seems strange to me.'

'He was conscientious like that,' Ben said.

'Fair enough. And so, given the object's lack of value, I assume that there would be no way to trace the killer through it? Meaning that if it were valuable, it might reappear if and when he attempted to pass the stolen goods along. Typically these kinds of items are handled through a specialist go-between that we call a fence.'

'I'd say that's unlikely,' Ben replied. 'I'm sure that when he discovers it's just a lump of brass, it'll end up in a ditch somewhere.'

'Then our only chance of finding this man is if one of his criminal associates gives him up,' Auclair said. 'Regrettably, they appear extremely reluctant to do so. At present they refuse to speak at all.'

'I'm going to run the three names you've given us through the INTERPOL criminal database,' said Madeline Chausson, speaking for the first time since Auclair had introduced her. 'And we'll be able to run a fingerprint check in case those names are false. If these men turn out to have records, which is highly possible, we might be able to identify the killer from a list of known associates.'

'Although with so little in the way of evidence, that's something of a long shot too,' Auclair commented. 'If you were able to provide any more detail, perhaps some identifying feature for us to go on, it would be immensely helpful and make our job much easier. As things stand . . .' He shrugged. 'Well, you know, we can only do so much.'

'I wish I could,' Ben said. 'I'd do anything to help the police catch Victor's killer. But I can't think of a single identifying feature. It all happened so fast.'

Petru Navarro's severed ear was safely hidden back at Le Val, discreetly stuffed into a crack in the wall of the kennel block as the first police cars had rolled into the compound. Somewhere out there was a one-eared man who would match up with it. All Ben had to do was bring those pieces together. And the plan for how he was going to do it was already forming in his mind.

He said, 'How much longer are we going to sit here, officers? I've been through the whole thing three times over and told you everything I know. There's nothing you can honestly charge me for, because I acted completely in self-defence and with reasonable force at all times, and the only real casualty among the attackers was accidental, when he fell and broke his leg. Likewise my three associates acted in a responsible and restrained manner, even helping to patch up the wounded man. We've done everything in our power to cooperate with you. So if we're finished here for the moment, then I've got a lot of things to attend to.'

The two detectives looked at one another. Madeline Chausson said, 'I have nothing more.' Auclair reluctantly agreed. He stood up and said, 'We'll be in touch, Monsieur Hope. And in the meantime, do please try to keep out of trouble for the remainder of the holidays.'

Chapter 31

Half an hour later, Ben was riding back towards Le Val in the same police car that had brought him to the station. He reached home to find that the police were long gone, the forensics people having gathered up all the evidence anyone was likely to find until the snow thawed.

Serge, Michel and Richard had been brought back from Cherbourg an hour ago and were gloomily assembled around the table in the warm farmhouse kitchen, where they'd already made some serious inroads into a fresh bottle of Ben's whisky. Little Scruffy was fast asleep and snoring like a chainsaw in Serge's lap, but Storm had refused to settle until his master came home, and greeted him with whimpers and frantic face-slobbering. Ben slumped in his chair with a brimming glass of scotch in front of him, lit a Gauloise, and for the first time in all the years he'd lived here at Le Val, felt no joy at being back home.

For a long while they sat comparing notes about their separate interviews with the cops. As Ben had expected, Serge, the only one of the three who'd heard anything at all, had revealed nothing to them. 'What a bunch of jerks,' complained Richard, who particularly bitterly objected to the police's handling of the situation. 'The way they grilled me, you'd think I was the criminal. And as for that smarmy sack of *merde*, Auclair . . .'

'What about the bastard who got away, Ben?' Michel asked in a low voice.

'He got away,' Ben said. 'That's all there is to it.'

As the frigid dawn slowly drew closer, the four men went on trying to drown their sorrows. But some kinds of sorrows are stronger swimmers than others. Conversation grew more and more sporadic until eventually everyone was just too depressed to speak, and they finished their bottle in leaden silence as Ben worked his way through his pack of Gauloises. When Richard, Serge and Michel finally crawled off to get what little sleep they might, the first glimmers of sunrise were lightening the eastern horizon.

By Ben's reckoning, Jeff's time zone in Australia was eight hours ahead, while Tuesday, on the other side of the world, was six hours behind. Like a man facing the gallows he reached for his phone and made the two long-distance calls he'd been dreading but couldn't put off any longer.

Jeff had been enjoying a sun-baked afternoon's horse riding across the sprawling acres of Kip Malloy's ranch. Tuesday had been fast asleep after a happy evening spent with family and friends. Each man's reaction to Ben's news was much as expected: stunned disbelief followed by horror and outrage, inconsolable sadness leading into a state of grim acceptance, each promising to catch the first available flight home to France. Jeff went silent for a long minute when Ben told him about the dogs; Tuesday burst into tears.

Deeply moved by a fresh surge of emotion, Ben very nearly joined him.

When those agonising calls were done with, Ben stepped out to meet the Christmas morning sunrise. By its first red-golden glow, the snow-covered Le Val looked almost normal. It wasn't until he ventured across to the barn and the armoury area and saw the scale of the devastation by daylight for the first time that reality truly began to bite hard. And so began the long, exhausting clean-up operation. Ben would have to wait until after the roads were clear to hire in someone with a machine big enough to move the overturned JCB. In the meantime, there was more than enough work clearing up the battlefield to keep a whole team of men busy. Despite all he could do to try to persuade them to go home to their families and let him take care of things, Serge, Michel and Richard strongly insisted that they weren't going anywhere, were damned if they would let Ben deal with this nightmare on his own, and many more colourful words to that effect. Serge also finally managed to convince a recalcitrant Ben to let him look at his shoulder injury, which he sewed up and dressed as neatly as only a trained medic could.

They worked all of that day, and all of the next. It took all four of them six hours alone to hack out a patch of frozen ground in the field by the side of the house. There Ben buried his dogs and saluted their memory with a raised glass. He didn't know if animals were capable of experiencing grief the way humans did. Maybe it was a coincidence. But when the last shovelful of dirt was added to the grave, Storm let out a long, ululating, wolflike howl whose sound haunted Ben for a long time afterwards.

The following morning, December 27th, brought a deluge of cold rain that washed much of the snow away and turned the remaining drifts to rimes of brownish, half-frozen slush. It also saw the arrival of a gaunt-looking Jeff Dekker, aged ten years and falling down with jetlag. 'I should have been here,' he kept repeating, shaking his head in sullen regret as Ben walked and talked him through the events of Christmas Eve.

Later that same day, Ben had to go through it all again with Tuesday, who had rushed back from Jamaica as quickly as he could and been picked up from the airport by Serge. Tuesday was still shattered and raw from the news but, true to his character, doing all he could to dredge up even the slightest glimmer of positivity. 'Bad things have happened before. We'll move on from this,' he insisted as they sat around the table the next morning, having stayed up for most of the night talking.

'Never this bad, mate. It'll never be the same,' Jeff replied morosely.

Ben couldn't remember having ever seen the normally resilient Jeff so miserably low in spirits. But he understood what Jeff was feeling. It was as though something sacred had been violated, something broken that could never be made whole again.

That afternoon, the mobile crane operator Ben had managed to drag from his festive holiday removed the overturned JCB from on top of the armoury. With the wreckage cleared away, they were able to demonstrate to the police that the thieves had failed entirely in their attempt to penetrate the vault, and that the integrity of Le Val's weapons store had remained intact. Detective Inspector Auclair seemed disappointed to be denied the chance of launching a full-blown process to shut down the facility on the grounds of poor security. While he strutted self-importantly about the scene, not greatly endearing himself to Jeff and Tuesday, his more sympathetic junior officer Madeline Chausson took Ben aside with the news that the imprisoned Corsicans were still refusing to say a word, even to their court-appointed lawyer.

Meanwhile, though, Madeline confided, the INTERPOL database had revealed that all five had extensive criminal backgrounds and underworld connections. It turned out, not surprisingly, that César Casta had been a career criminal since the age of fourteen. Still in his teens he'd been pulled in for racketeering, operating illegal slot machines, drug dealing and pimping. Later on he'd graduated to armed stick-ups, which earned him an eight-year stretch in prison. He had also been suspected, though never convicted, of involvement with Corsican organised crime outfits Brise de Mer and the Venzolasca gang, which operated in Marseille and across southern France as well as on their native island.

As for Victor's killer, however, there was still no trace or clue as to his identity. Detective Chausson admitted to Ben that this was one trail that seemed likely to go cold. 'It happens. I'm very sorry.'

Ben was polite and respectful, thanking her for her efforts. Madeline seemed to feel genuine pity for his sorrow.

What Madeline couldn't see, what Ben kept hidden from her as deliberately as Petru Navarro's severed ear (now kept in a sealed wrapper in the fridge) and the rest of what he'd withheld from the police, was the fury that burned inside

213

him. As the paralysing after-effects of shock and grief slowly began to recede, his rage came up like volcanic lava from the depths to take its place, filling every corner of his being, threatening to take him over completely.

Ben had seen men driven mad by the power of rage. He knew what terrible things people were capable of when all moral inhibitions were stripped away and the dark side of human nature was allowed to take hold. Too many times he'd witnessed its destructive force first-hand, and he should have been afraid of it, but instead he embraced it. He could feel it growing and building up inside him, blazing hotter and hotter until its flames would be whipped into an uncontrollable inferno that could destroy anything in its path.

A man like Ben Hope, driven by passions as violent and unrelenting as those, was the most dangerous creature on the planet.

The stage was set. And soon, very soon now, a reckoning was coming.

Chapter 32

On the cold, sleety morning of December 29th, a crowd gathered at the church to mourn the passing of Victor Vermont. A man who had lived his life in the service of art and beauty, who'd never hurt a living soul or made a single enemy, who'd been beloved by everyone who had known him, was now mourned in death by almost the entire village of Saint-Jean and many others who'd travelled a long way to pay their respects.

Among those who had gathered to attend the funeral service was poor Célestine Charpentier, Victor's elderly sweetheart who had recently become his fiancée only to lose him before they could even be married. She was surrounded by a crowd of friends, who held her hands and gave her all the comfort they could. Also present was an older man in his nineties, tall and lean and bent not with age but with grief as he hunched in a pew in the first row, openly weeping with sorrow. There were many other displays of heart-rending sadness visible throughout the packed church.

Wearing his one good dark suit and an old regimental tie, Ben had been one of the first to arrive, but he stayed at

215

a distance from the crowd and sat at the back. To one side of the pulpit lay Victor's open coffin, surrounded by vast quantities of flowers. The mournful tones of the church organ played in the background.

Like almost everyone above a certain age in Saint-Jean, the local priest Père Barthélemy had been a longstanding friend of the deceased, and from the pulpit he gave a deeply moving, touching eulogy that brought many fresh floods of tears. When the service was over, the group of men from Saint-Jean who were to act as Victor's pallbearers solemnly carried the casket on its final journey. Ben would have wanted to be one of them, if it hadn't been for the cast and the crutch. Instead he limped along at the tail of the long procession of mourners who made their way through the thin sleet to the churchyard. Père Barthélemy said a few more words. Madame Charpentier took a shuffling step up to the graveside, so distraught she still had to be supported by her friends, and laid a wreath over the casket with a wrenching, tearful final farewell to her beloved Victor before she had to be led away, overcome with grief.

Ben stood at the graveside with his head bowed and watched the casket slowly descend. When the ceremony was over, the mourners began to drift away and return to the long line of cars that choked the road to the church. The sleety rain was coming down thicker, tracing icy trickles through Ben's scalp and dripping like tears from his face. He remained there until the last of the earth had filled the grave, so deep in his thoughts that he didn't notice the tall, lean figure of the old man he'd noticed inside the church earlier come up to him.

'Monsieur Hope?'

'I'm Ben Hope,' Ben said in French. The old man was two or three inches taller than he was, with features as sharp as a hawk's, now deeply etched with pain and sorrow. His eyes were red.

'You don't know me. My name is Dampierre, Jules Dampierre. I travelled from Paris this morning. Victor was a dear friend and an esteemed colleague.'

They shook hands. 'He talked about you with great affection,' Ben said.

'I would like to think that I was one of his closest friends,' the old man replied. 'I am also one of only two people who happen to know what Victor had in his possession when he died. The other being my former associate, Henri Carbonneau of the Louvre Museum.'

'I know what Victor had,' Ben told him. 'The crusader's cross.'

Jules Dampierre gave a sorrowful smile and shook his head. 'I'm afraid you have little idea, Monsieur Hope. The truth is, it's a little more than that. The sheer abundance of Christian icons in circulation in those times means that any number of them have survived to the present day. There are many crusader crosses. But only one like yours.'

'That's what Victor came to tell me?' Ben asked.

The old man nodded. His pain-filled eyes seemed to bore into Ben like lasers. 'But as he is no longer with us, I will tell you myself. What you discovered is what I believe to be one of the richest treasures in our history. Its value incalculable, its loss irreplaceable. With little doubt, it is the last surviving relic ever likely to be found of Queen Eleanor of

217

Aquitaine's days during the Second Crusade. And now, thanks to this tragedy, it would appear it's in the hands of some murdering piece of trash.'

Ben said nothing.

The old man went on, 'I have devoted my whole life to historical objects, and I love them with a passion. But I loved Victor so very much more. Now he is gone.'

Ben could make no reply. He found it hard to meet the raw, tormented gaze that Jules Dampierre was fixing on him from those bloodshot eyes.

'God forgive me, but I had to talk to you today, and tell you these things. Because if it hadn't been for you, Monsieur Hope, Victor would have been spared from the burden of such a responsibility. If not for the respect and esteem he had for you, he would have left it safely in the museum where it belonged. But instead, he saw fit to bring it to you that night. He was determined to show it to you in person, to share our discoveries with you and ask for your personal permission to allow the cross to be entrusted to the care of Henri Carbonneau at the Louvre.'

Ben was still silent.

'If he hadn't done that,' said Jules Dampierre, 'my dearest, oldest friend, the sweetest man in the world, would still be alive now. I hope you can live with that knowledge, because I'm not sure that I could.'

Then, without another word, he walked away, leaving Ben alone by the cold and windy graveside.

Chapter 33

As Ben walked slowly back to the car he knew in his heart that the old man was right, and a renewed sense of guilt burned through his simmering rage. Nothing could change what had happened. But what he had to do next would be done nonetheless.

Sitting at the wheel with the engine off, he lit a cigarette and quietly smoked a few puffs to get his thoughts in order. Then he reached for his phone and dialled the number for the Louis Pasteur Hospital in Cherbourg. The receptionist sounded bright and cheery, and evidently hadn't just attended a funeral. Ben asked her, 'Could you tell me if Dr Sandrine Lacombe is on duty today?'

'I'll find out for you. Who's calling, please?'

'A friend.' Ben gave his name and waited, and after a few moments the cheery receptionist came back and said that Dr Lacombe was in for the rest of the morning. 'She's busy right now. Can I take a message?'

'Tell her that I'm on my way there now,' Ben said, and ended the call. He crushed out his cigarette and fired up the

219

car. The Alpina's powerful twin-turbo roared into life and he floored the gas and took off.

Less than thirty minutes later, Ben hobbled inside the hospital entrance and up to the desk. The receptionist was some po-faced creature who obviously wasn't the cheerful lady he'd spoken to earlier. He asked whether Dr Lacombe was free yet, and after much tapping and frowning at a keyboard was told that she was on a break. 'I'd like to see her,' Ben said.

'Do you have an appointment?'

'I'd like to see her,' Ben repeated slowly. Whatever it was that the receptionist could see in his expression made her look visibly unsettled. She hurried away from her desk, and two minutes later Sandrine appeared through the swinging double doors at the end of the reception foyer. She was wearing her blue medical smock and her hair was scraped back tight from her face. She smiled as she recognised Ben, and walked up to him. The atmosphere between them was warm and natural, as befitted two people who had been very close and intimate, and parted as friends.

'I wasn't expecting to see you again so soon,' she said.

'I'm sorry to butt in on your break.'

'Don't worry about it,' she replied with another smile. 'So what brings you into my world, Ben? Is this a social call?'

'Not exactly,' he replied. 'I want you to take this thing off me.' He pointed at his foot.

'Of course you do. You and everyone else who has to spend weeks in plaster. It's one of the most frustrating things imaginable. But hey, that's what happens when you get careless around heavy machinery.'

'No, I mean I want you to take it off me right now, this minute.'

Her smile dropped. 'Surely you can't be serious? But why?'

'Because there's something I have to do, and I can't do it hobbling around with this lump attached to the end of my leg. That's why.'

Sandrine shook her head. 'It's much too early to remove it, Ben. It would be like taking a cake out of the oven when it's only half baked. What do you think would happen?'

'I don't need a lecture, Sandrine.'

'You're going to get one anyway,' she said sternly. 'Removing a cast too early is a recipe for disaster. If the ends of the fractured bone haven't set properly, any excess strain on them could cause them to come loose. At best you'd likely end up with a malformed or crooked ankle joint. At worst, you could cause a refracture that might not be so easy to fix next time. In other words, you start running around on that leg unsupported and there's a chance that you could cripple yourself for life.'

'I'll take that chance. I've taken worse.'

She sighed. 'Look. I know it's driving you crazy. I can see that. But please, give it just another two or three weeks. Even then, the bone will still be healing and you'll need to take care for a further month or so. You might need a course of physiotherapy to help you recover muscle strength, joint mobility and balance.'

Ben said, 'I don't have two or three weeks. I'm asking you, Sandrine. Will you take this thing off me, or not?'

The same look in his eyes that had frightened the receptionist made her peer at him curiously, her head cocked to one side. 'I heard something had happened at Le Val, Ben. I tried calling you, but the phone was always busy. I hope this isn't about that, is it?'

Ben said nothing.

'Here's what I'll agree to,' she said. 'Let me take a quick X-ray of that ankle. If I think the fracture is looking okay, I'll remove the cast. But otherwise it stays on. Doctor's orders.'

'Then I'll hack it off myself with a hammer and chisel,' Ben said. 'I don't care.'

'You do that, you're even crazier than I thought.'

But forty minutes later, looking at the results of his X-ray, Sandrine had to reluctantly concede defeat. 'I must admit, I've hardly ever seen a fracture heal so fast. Especially in someone your age, who smokes and drinks far too much. You're a walking medical miracle.'

'Walking, that's the main thing,' Ben said. 'So get it off me.'

'If you think you're just going to waltz out of here as good as new, think again,' she warned him. 'You're going to be in pain, and you're going to be weak. I'd recommend using a stick or a cane. Strict rest for at least the next two weeks, then gentle exercise only for another two weeks after that. Or you'll have to answer to me. Get it?'

'We'll see.'

Sandrine took him into a consulting room where she got to work with a little circular saw. As the cast came off in two neat sections, Ben flexed his ankle and a sharp twang of pain shot up his leg. He was determined not to let anything show on his face.

'How does that feel?' she asked, watching him closely.

'Feels perfectly fine,' he said.

Minutes later, Ben walked out of the hospital a free man again, filled with a liberating fierce energy that made his heart beat faster. A little pain, he could deal with. Weakness, he could overcome. He was back in the game, functional once more, and that was all that mattered to him. He marched across to his car, leaped behind the wheel, and blasted off towards home.

Jeff was in the office at Le Val, looking weary as he came off the phone with the insurance company, who were refusing to foot the bill for repairing the shot-up JCB. 'Screw 'em. We don't need their money.' He glanced over at Ben, then did a double-take as he saw him standing there in the doorway with no plaster and no crutch. 'So soon?' he asked, raising his eyebrows in amazement.

'Jeff, there's somewhere I have to go. Can you manage without me for a few days?'

Jeff swivelled around in his chair to face him. The pair had known each other a long time, and had often been in tight situations together where they'd needed to communicate non-verbally, just by subtle looks and signals. Nobody was more attuned to Ben's body language. Jeff couldn't know exactly what was in Ben's mind. But he had a pretty damn good idea.

At times like this, Jeff Dekker wasn't a man to start getting into the whys and wherefores. He just asked, 'You want me along?'

And Ben didn't need to offer a longer explanation than 'I go alone. Better that way.'

Jeff nodded slowly. 'Then go and get it done, mate. Here if you need us.'

'I know.'

Ben headed across to the house, ignoring the ache in his ankle and the cramping muscle pain in the lower leg muscles that were suddenly being forced back into action. He ran up to his quarters and jumped into a hot shower, then spent a few minutes massaging his leg and ankle. He fished a length of support bandage out of his personal first-aid box and wrapped it tightly around the weakened joint. Changed into fresh black jeans and denim shirt, he opened up the little gun safe by his bedside, where he kept his personal pistols. He selected his old favourite 9mm Browning Hi-Power, along with two spare magazines and a box of cartridges. Next he grabbed his old green canvas bag. It existed in a state of ever-preparedness, because if life had taught him anything it was that he could be called away at a moment's notice. Once he'd dumped in the pistol and ammo, he was packed and almost ready. After gathering a few additional items that he was going to need, he headed back outside and slung the bag into the rear footwell of the Alpina, leaving the back door open.

Just as Ben was about to call for him, Storm appeared around the side of the house with Scruffy bounding along at his heels. Jeff Dekker wasn't the only one who could read Ben's thoughts. Storm trotted up to him with his tail wagging happily. He poked his head in the open back door of the Alpina and sniffed intently at the green bag. The bag meant his master was going off somewhere on his travels, and that generally meant that Storm was left behind. But the dog also understood that the open car door was an invitation to come along, and he looked expectantly up at Ben for the signal to jump in the back.

'You and I have a job to do,' Ben told him. 'Let's go.'

Chapter 34

The Alpina sped southwards from Le Val through the slushy, dismal Normandy countryside with Storm watching the road like a back-seat navigator. Ben's plan had been formed since before Victor's funeral. He was certain that by now, Petru Navarro would have made his way back home to Corsica. If the information Ángel Leoni had provided was trustworthy, then Ben might be able to find Petru at Bar Royale in Porto Vecchio, the nightclub allegedly belonging to his uncle, one Titus Navarro, who might also be behind the activities of César Casta's gang. Then again that information might turn out to be bullshit; or alternatively Petru might choose to lie low and not return to the nightclub for a while. Especially now he was suddenly missing an ear, which might invite a lot of questions.

Whatever the case, Porto Vecchio was now Ben's primary destination, more than sixteen hundred kilometres away across all of France, equating to some twenty or more hours' drive even in a four-wheeled rocket ship like the Alpina. But Ben could afford a few hours' leeway, and he'd decided that while he was still in France he would pay a surprise visit to the home of Robert Blondel.

Before he could do that, he first intended to swing by Pepe Jaeckin's place, just six hours away from Le Val. Pepe lived in a comfortable, fairly remote seventeenth-century country home outside Dijon that he shared with a bunch of cats and a temperamental ex-stripper girlfriend whose stage name had been Roxie. Ben and Jeff had spent a weekend there once, some years ago, mostly a hazy memory thanks to the lashings of Pepe's home-made booze that had been consumed: Ben's main recollections were waking up in the morning in a bed covered in yowling cats, and the way Roxie had rather brazenly tried to throw herself at Jeff. Thankfully Pepe wasn't the jealous type, or the weekend might not have gone so well.

It was motorway all the way to Dijon and Ben pushed the Alpina hard, stopping only for fuel and a bite to eat: a hunk of bread and camembert for himself, a can of dog food and some biscuits for Storm. Skirting Paris he continued south-eastwards, and was in Dijon by early evening. It had been dark for an hour by the time he drove through the archway of trees leading to Pepe's place. Thinking about the cats, he left Storm in the car and walked up towards the house. The night was breezy and starlit, not as cold this far south. Some lights were on in the shuttered downstairs windows and he could hear the muffled beat of rock music coming from somewhere around the back.

Pepe wasn't expecting visitors and at Ben's fourth knock he cracked the front door open an inch on its security chain, peering guardedly through the gap. 'Yeah? What do you want?' Not the jealous type perhaps, though definitely a careful guy, that Pepe. Ben knew there would be a home

226

defence shotgun somewhere close to hand. But then Pepe's suspicious expression changed to one of pleasant surprise when he recognised Ben standing there under the porch. 'Shit! Why didn't you call? Come in, come in.'

Pepe showed Ben through a mosaic-tiled hallway to a spacious living area with exposed beams of ancient cracked oak that clashed horribly with the modern furnishings. On one white leather sofa lounged about thirty cats of various colours and sizes, all staring at Ben with hostility. On the other was Roxie, nicely relaxed after probably six or seven refills of the vodka apéritif she was in danger of spilling over herself as she mumbled an incoherent greeting Ben's way. She must have got started early that evening.

'Never mind her,' Pepe said dismissively, turning the music down low. 'Take a seat, man. Hey, I thought Alain said you had a leg in plaster.'

'Made a miraculous recovery.'

'That's the best kind, huh? Here, let me get you something to drink,' Pepe said, opening up his enormous booze locker. 'How about some dinner? I was about to start grilling steaks. Local beef, ribeye cuts, the best you'll ever taste. I do 'em with butter, lotsa butter, that's the secret. Home-cut pommes frites and a nice green salad on the side. You staying the night?'

Ben wasn't hungry and said he was just passing, but he accepted a glass of scotch while Pepe poured himself a gin and tonic. With a glance at the recumbent Roxie Ben said, 'Can we have a word in private, Pepe?'

'Sure, Ben, no problem.' Pepe led him to a smaller room down the hall that was used as a home office, with a cluttered desk and a collection of certificates all over the walls, together with framed photos from Pepe's time as a GIGN commander, back in the day. He closed the door and ushered Ben to a small settee. No cats.

'I heard about what happened at Le Val. That was a fucked-up deal. I'm really sorry about your friend.' News of the incident had travelled especially fast through the tactical community, and Pepe was full of questions. The main one being, 'How the hell could something like that happen? How did they even think they could pull it off?'

'That's actually what I've come to talk to you about,' Ben replied. 'I need your help.'

Pepe smiled, but his smile was uncertain. 'I'm happy to see you, man. I'm just not sure what I can do.'

'It's simple enough,' Ben said. 'I need you to tell me where I can find Robert Blondel.'

Now Pepe's smile melted altogether and became a rumpled frown. 'Blondel? What the hell's he got to do with this?'

'That's exactly what I intend to find out,' Ben replied.

Pepe shook his head, confused. 'What are you trying to say?'

'You asked me how the hell could anyone have thought they could pull off a robbery at Le Val,' Ben said. 'The reason is because someone with inside knowledge was feeding information to César Casta's boss, who I believe is connected to some kind of criminal organisation in Corsica. I know it wasn't me. And it wasn't anyone else connected with the place. In fact there's hardly anyone it could have been. When you whittle it right down, there's just one standout name on the list, and that's your guy Blondel.'

Pepe rose from his chair, spilling some of his drink, and

held up a defensive hand. 'Whoa, whoa. Stop right there. No way, man. I mean, no fucking *way*. Who the hell do you think you are, coming to my home like this unannounced and accusing my people of being mixed up in some kind of criminal conspiracy shit? Are you out of your fucking mind?'

'Take it easy, Pepe. I don't like it any more than you do. And if it turns out I'm barking up the wrong tree and Blondel had nothing to do with it, then I'll be happy, believe me. I just want to talk to him, face to face. Then I'll know the truth.'

'The truth,' Pepe repeated, staring. 'And then what?'

Something about the way Pepe asked that made Ben wonder if there was something else behind his words.

'And then I'll deal with it,' Ben said.

Pepe slammed his drink down on his desk, spilling some more of it over the surface but appearing not to care. He started pacing up and down the small office, breathing loudly and clenching his fists.

'Something's bugging you, Pepe,' Ben said. 'Don't think you can hide it from me, because you can't.'

Pepe slumped back in his chair with a heavy sigh, grabbed his drink and downed the last of it in a gulp. And now the truth came flooding out. 'All right, there's something you maybe should know,' he admitted. 'Fact is, Robert Blondel no longer works for me. He quit the day after Christmas. He didn't come to tell me personally. Not even by phone. I just got an email saying he was resigning and won't be coming back. Just like that.'

'He didn't give a reason?'

'No, and when I tried to call him to ask why, he wouldn't

even take my call. Me, the guy he's been working for, who respected him, who's only ever treated him well.'

'So you've no idea why he did it?' Ben asked.

'None, really. But here's the thing. When he first came on board, I thought he was a great addition to the team. But lately he'd been acting kind of odd.'

'Odd how?'

'Just *odd*. Kind of nervous, like he was stressed out, or there was something worrying on his mind. He'd been fine until that, no problems at all. Then I noticed this change come over him, a few weeks ago. I couldn't say when exactly. Alain Garnier, he noticed it too. Said Robert was acting a bit weird those two days they were up at your place. We thought he might be having some troubles at home. Or money, something like that.'

'He's never talked about his personal issues?'

Pepe shook his head. 'I mean, from what I can gather he's been around the clock a couple of times, same as all of us. Been married and divorced, started up a new family and all that, younger wife, little boy. There's an older kid, a daughter, from his previous marriage. Nineteen or twenty, at university somewhere. I don't know about the ex-wife. But that's all pretty routine stuff, right? Nothing out of the ordinary. Nothing like you'd say this guy's got serious problems. I don't pry into my guys' personal lives, you know, unless it's having an impact on their ability to do their jobs. We are who we are, that's sacred ground. Same for you and your guys, no?'

'Absolutely, Pepe.'

'But then the guy goes and quits on me like that without giving me any reason. And now you turn up telling me he's

230

maybe mixed up in something bad. Shit. I mean, what if you were right? Think of the hit my rep's gonna get, it comes out that my people are casing my clients' joints for their crooked buddies to hit. I'd be sunk below the bottom of the sea.'

Ben said, 'I wouldn't let this touch you or your business. If it turns out to be true, then it's between him and me. It goes no further. That's a promise.'

Pepe studied Ben's face as though gauging whether he meant that or not. Then he gave a slow nod and said, 'Okay. So what do you want me to do, set up a meeting with the guy? Get him over here on some pretext, like I owe him some back pay or something, and then you can have it out with him?'

'Doesn't have to be that complicated,' Ben said. 'Just give me his address.'

Chapter 35

The address Pepe had on file for his former employee was a modest family home in the sleepy little commune and village of Urcy, a few kilometres to the other side of Dijon. It was after nine in the evening by the time Ben had located the property, in a quiet street lined with semi-rural homes spaced far apart. He parked the car on a grassy verge some distance away and let the dog out to relieve himself. The temperature had dropped a few degrees. No snow, but the grass glittered with night frost. The scent of woodsmoke hung in the air. As Storm hunted about for a discreet spot to do his business, Ben lit a Gauloise and stretched his aching leg and ankle while thinking about the best way to handle this situation.

His original plan for getting information out of Robert Blondel had been simple and straightforward. Surprise was always the most effective method in these cases. He would slip undetected into the man's home when he was least expecting it, corner him and squeeze the truth out of him with as much force as might be necessary. If it turned out he was blameless, then Ben would let him go. If not, then the punishment would have to fit the crime.

But when Pepe had told Ben that Blondel had a young wife and a little boy, the situation suddenly became much more complex. Ben had no scruples about bursting into a man's home, pressing him very hard indeed and maybe leaving him with a couple of well-deserved broken legs, but not where there were innocent women and children around. The original plan was quickly ditched in favour of a slightly more subtle approach.

There was a long garden to the rear of the house, encircled by a low wall and mostly shaded by evergreen trees. After he'd put Storm back in the car Ben skirted the length of the wall. The houses across the street had shuttered windows and he couldn't see too many signs of life. He soon found a convenient spot where he could hop unseen into Blondel's garden, screened from sight of the house by a large, spreading conifer. It was a liberation to be able to move properly again, and he didn't care about being in pain.

He slipped from one patch of shadow to another, working his way around the rear of the house. Like the neighbouring properties, the windows of the Blondel family home were shuttered, but here and there Ben was able to make out glimmers of light shining from within. The flickering blueish glow of a TV told him someone was definitely at home. Moments later, he heard the cry of a child coming from inside, followed by a woman's voice and the banging of a door. He checked more windows, hoping to find one unshuttered through which he might be able to spot Robert Blondel, but it wasn't to be.

The house had a rear-facing veranda with kiddie toys strewn about on it. Ben stepped quietly up to the back door.

It had peeling paint and a window of opaque glass through which he could see light shining from deeper inside. The door wasn't locked, and for a moment he was tempted to slip inside the house so he could catch Blondel unawares. Resisting the urge, he knocked three times on the door. Thirty seconds later a light came on and he saw movement through the frosted glass as an indistinct figure stepped up to answer the door.

If it was Blondel, Ben toyed with the idea of grabbing him and whisking him off into the shadows of the garden before he could make a sound to alert his wife. Even that could be too risky.

But it wasn't Blondel. The door swung inwards and a young blond-haired woman appeared in the doorway, wearing a baggy T-shirt and jogging pants and clutching an infant boy in her arms. The kid was maybe a year old, with fair hair like his mother's. His face was red and tear-streaked, and he was pouting as though he'd just been interrupted in the middle of a tantrum and was ready to resume at any moment. His mother looked to be in her early twenties, at least fifteen years younger than Blondel. Her hair was tousled and she appeared tired and careworn.

'Madame Blondel?'

She nodded sourly. 'I'm Jeannette Blondel, yeah. Who are you? I don't know you. Why'd you knock on the back door?'

'I tried the front but there was no answer,' Ben said. 'I'm a friend of your husband's. I'd like to see him, if he's around.'

'Get in line,' Jeannette Blondel said with a bitter laugh. 'I'd like to see him too. He's been gone since before Christmas. Meanwhile there's a leak in the bathroom pipes, the damn car's broken down again, the electricity's about to be cut off because the bill's not been paid, and I've got no money. He's got no right to walk off and leave me to look after a baby on my own. It's bad enough he's away working half the time. Now he's not even here for the other half.'

It seemed that the guess about Blondel having personal problems had been right, Ben thought. 'I'm so sorry to have disturbed you, Madame Blondel. I can see I called at a bad time. You've no idea where he is?'

'Oh, I know where he is, all right,' Jeannette Blondel replied, and tossed her head as if nodding towards the direction her husband had absconded in. 'He's gone to crash out at our holiday place. Said he needed his space, whatever *that* means.' She snorted derisively. 'But he won't answer his phone, and twice I've gone up there to look for him and he wasn't there. Now that my car won't start and I can't even pay a mechanic to fix it, I'm stuck here.' She peered more closely at Ben. 'What did you say your name was? I thought I knew all of Robert's delightful pals.'

'Paul,' Ben said. 'I'm not from around here. I live in the north. Just passing through, thought I'd drop in and say hello.'

Jeannette Blondel didn't smile. 'Well, Paul, seeing as you're a friend of his, then maybe you can persuade him to shift his arse back home and do the right thing by me. That's *if* you can find him. You might have better luck than me. Hold on, I'll get you the address.' She disappeared inside the house for a minute, then returned clutching a Post-it note with a name scrawled on it. 'It's a trailer park,' she explained. 'About forty-five minutes' drive from here. We used to go there a lot, before this one came along.' She jiggled the child in her arms. He looked ready to kick off another round of tantrums. 'But now all Robert wants to do is crash there on his own and get drunk, or play cards with his mates. I just don't know what's got into him lately.'

'Me neither,' Ben said. 'I'll talk to him.'

'You do that, Paul. And you can tell him from me that if he doesn't straighten himself out pretty damn fast, I'm out of here and going back to Pontoise to live with my mother. I won't be treated like this, you know?'

Ben extricated himself as politely as possible, and left her standing there on the porch with the child in her arms. She watched him go, then disappeared back inside the house. As he walked back to the car, Ben was wondering what could have happened in Blondel's life to make him crash off the rails like this. He seemed to have pretty good prospects. He was fairly skilled and well qualified in a specialised line of work that was always in demand. An employer with stand-ards as high as Pepe Jaeckin's wouldn't have looked at him twice if he'd been some kind of slacker or good-for-nothing. Something had obviously gone badly wrong somewhere.

Ben used his phone to look up the directions to the address Jeannette Blondel had given him. Forty minutes later, he was pulling up at the security barrier that closed the private residential trailer park off from the road. Signs warned of no public access and twenty-four-hour surveillance. A pass key was needed to work the barrier and the office was deserted at this hour of the evening, so Ben left the car and entered on foot, bringing Storm with him this time.

It was the typical kind of holiday park, with rows of static caravans each in its own little plot. Some of the prefabricated homes were better kept than others, with nicely maintained wooden balconies and neat garden areas and personalised touches. This time of the year, about the only creatures who seemed to be inhabiting the place were the hordes of rabbits that Storm kept wanting to chase as they scampered here and there over the frosty moonlit grass. After a few minutes of searching around, Ben finally found the Blondels' trailer. It was modest, like their house, but not the kind of shit-pit that the average worthless drunk of a husband would use as a bolthole to escape his domestic responsibilities.

There was no car parked outside, and no lights or signs of life inside. Ben rapped on the door a few times and wasn't surprised when there was no response. He glanced around him in case anyone might be around, but the only witness to what he was about to do was a small doe rabbit that crouched frozen among the long grass, watching from a safe distance. Ben fished in his bag for a couple of items he always carried, a powerful little compact flashlight and a set of lock picks. He wasn't a complete stranger to breaking and entering. In another life he could have made a pretty good career out of burglary. The lock on the trailer door was a flimsy affair, and it took him less than a minute's work to get inside.

Ben stepped into Blondel's trailer home, Storm trotting in after him, looking up at his master as if to ask, 'What is this place? Are we staying here?' Leaving the lights off, Ben cupped the beam of his torch with his fingers and began to explore. The trailer was littered with empty spirits bottles and showed some signs of fairly recent habitation – a carton of milk in the fridge still had a couple of days to go before its expiry date, and the remains of a takeout meal were stale but not yet mouldy or mouse-nibbled. Blondel, or someone at any rate, had been residing here not so long ago. But where was he now?

After searching the living area, Ben moved up a narrow passage. One door was a little bathroom, another was a tiny second bedroom, and the one at the end was a master bedroom. The bed was rumpled and the room smelled of unwashed clothes. A small dresser was covered in assorted junk: magazines, crumpled shop receipts, a comb, a crushed beer can, an ashtray with the stub of a roll-up cigarette, an empty pill bottle. Ben sniffed the roll-up and caught the unmistakable whiff of cannabis.

He thought, *Hmm*. Next he looked at the empty pill bottle label and saw that it was an SSRI antidepressant medication also used to treat anxiety and panic attacks. The meds were prescribed to R. Blondel and the date on the label was just a week before Christmas. It hadn't taken the guy long to empty the bottle. That was interesting too, though in itself it didn't tell Ben much. Nor did the contents of the dresser's two drawers, which were stuffed with socks and underwear. None of it was women's clothing, which tended to confirm that the Blondels had pretty much stopped using the place as a couple.

The only other furniture in the master bedroom was a bedside cabinet, and that was where Ben struck lucky. It wasn't the collection of antacid medication and the second half-empty antidepressant pill bottle that drew his interest, but the small lockable metal file box that had been pushed right to the back of the cupboard and hidden behind a couple of old jumpers.

He pulled it out and sat on the bed to examine the box. Whatever was inside, Blondel possibly wanted to keep hidden from his wife by stashing it here in his de facto bachelor pad rather than at home. Ben shook it. There wasn't much in there. Something lightweight that jiggled around and slid from end to end, like papers. It could be love letters from a secret girlfriend, dirty photographs, all kinds of sordid personal items that Ben wouldn't normally have given a damn about, but which might explain the kind of trouble Blondel was in.

Less than thirty seconds' work with the lock pick later, Ben opened the box and found out the answer.

Chapter 36

The two items the box contained were something that Ben instantly recognised, because he'd seen things like this before and knew exactly what they signified. Nothing good, that was for sure.

One was a photo print showing a prettyish young woman with long, curly, sandy hair, about nineteen or twenty years old, who bore a slight facial resemblance to Robert Blondel. Ben remembered what Pepe Jaeckin had told him about a grown-up daughter from his previous marriage. It wasn't a posed picture, but had instead been taken from a distance, probably using a long lens. She was walking out of what looked like a college entrance, surrounded by female students of similar age, bags on their shoulders and files under their arms. The group were in the middle of some animated conversation that had them all smiling and laughing. They clearly hadn't known they were being photographed.

What singled out the sandy-haired girl from her friends was the arrow someone had drawn on the photograph, using a thick red marker pen. The effect was ominous, much more so in light of the other item Ben found in the box. It was a kidnap threat note, made up out of mismatched letters cut from a newspaper and pasted to a sheet of foolscap. An old-school kind of methodology, a pretty crude way of doing things nowadays, but no less intimidating and menacing for it. The note was in English and said simply:

REMEMBER WE ARE WATCHING HER
YOU HAVE BEEN WARNED

Ben knew the kidnap business extremely well, because for several years after he'd quit the SAS, locating the abducted victims of that ruthless industry and returning them safely home to their families had been his personal mission. He'd saved a lot of lives, ended those of more than a few kidnappers, and he'd learned many things. One was that going through official law enforcement channels was all too often the same thing as signing the kidnap victim's death warrant. Another was that the mere threat of a loved one or child being taken and locked away in some dark and dingy cellar, perhaps never to be seen again, was the next most terrifying thing to it actually happening. Perhaps even more terrifying, in some ways. Ben had also learned that while actual kidnaps were nearly always done with the aim of netting a quick profit by screwing ransom money out of the families, by contrast the threat of kidnap was all about control. *Do what we tell you, or face the consequences.* If there were crueller forms of manipulation, Ben couldn't think of any.

And so this was how they'd got Robert Blondel by the balls.

Ben understood that this note wouldn't have been the first contact Blondel had received from them. The initial warning would have been made via an anonymous phone call, or an email from an encrypted and untraceable source, telling Blondel what they wanted from him and warning him of what they'd do to his daughter if he refused. The letter was simply a reminder that this was real and wouldn't go away.

It all began to fit now. Blondel's odd conduct and obvious state of anxiety during those two days at Le Val. The change in his behaviour that had been noticed by his wife and colleagues. The anxiety and heartburn medications. The drinking and cannabis use. Taken together in context, they were the classic hallmarks of the unbearable stress suffered by a man being coerced to do something against his will and living in daily terror of what would happen if he didn't cooperate. The criminals had left their victim with little choice but to play the game, act as their inside man and feed them the information they needed to target Le Val.

Ben remembered Pepe Jaeckin telling him that Blondel quit his job without explanation the day after Christmas. The timing was interesting. Maybe by then, Blondel had heard the news that an innocent man had been murdered, partly thanks to his actions. Perhaps the sense of guilt had been what had pushed the man over the edge, making him give up his career and abandon his wife and kid, retreating here to his refuge to drink himself silly, smoke dope and pop depression pills.

In which case, why wasn't he here now?

Ben put everything back where he'd found it, and sat thinking for a while. Which was what he was still doing a minute or two later, when he heard a thumping at the door of the trailer. Storm let out a soft growl. Ben shushed him, got up and moved quickly and lightly from the master bedroom to the net-curtained window nearest the door.

Clearly visible outside in the moonlight, Blondel's visitor was a guy of maybe thirty or thirty-five, scruffy, bearded, hands thrust deep in the pockets of his hoodie and hopping from foot to foot as though he was either cold or impatient to be let inside, or both. He didn't look particularly dangerous, although you could never be too sure. Ben stepped quickly to the door, yanked it open, and before the scruffy guy could react he was being jerked off his feet and hauled inside the trailer. Ben closed the door, dumped the guy face-down on the floor and put a knee in the back of his neck. Speaking close to the guy's ear he said in French, 'What's your name?'

'L-Lucien,' came the muffled reply.

'Why are you here, Lucien?'

'I came to see Robert! You're hurting! Ouch! Agh!'

Ben slackened the pressure on Lucien's neck, but only a little, and frisked him while keeping him face-down against the floor. He found a wallet containing credit cards, driving licence and about fifty euros in cash. The name on the cards and licence was Lucien Pichard.

'What the fuck, dude?' said the muffled voice. 'Who are you?'

'It doesn't matter who I am,' Ben said. 'What matters is that you answer my questions truthfully and without hesitation. Because if you don't I'll break both your arms and dump you in the nearest river. Do you understand?'

'Yes!' Some people became marvellously responsive under pressure.

'What are you doing here and why are you looking for Robert Blondel?'

The answer came back instantly, 'I come here sometimes, and we play poker. I sell him a bit of weed, too. Please don't kill me!'

'Do you have any on you right now?'

'In my – agh! – in my pocket!'

Ben found the little bag of skunk and fished it out. Looked as though Julien Pichard was telling the truth. The guy was a small-time drug dealer.

'Bad luck for you,' Ben said. 'I'm the police, and you're under arrest.'

Lucien groaned. 'Shit, man, come on. It's strictly for my own use. Nobody gets arrested for that any more. I have rights.'

'I'm looking for Blondel. Do you know where he is?'

'I might.'

'Details, Lucien. You help me find him and I'll let you go. Otherwise, you're going to jail.'

'Okay, okay,' Lucien gasped. 'H-he might be up at the shack. That's where I was going next if he wasn't here. I'm going there anyway.'

'What shack?'

'It's, like, just this old hut by the river. Some of the guys use it for fishing and stuff.'

And stuff, Ben thought. 'All right, Lucien. So here's what we're going to do. You can guide me up to your buddies' riverside hideaway. And if you behave yourself very nicely and do exactly what you're told, I'll let you have your dope back and forget I ever saw you here. Deal?'

'Whatever, dude. Deal.'

Ben closed up the trailer and with Storm pacing along behind, closely watching, he frogmarched Lucien all the way back to where he'd left the Alpina. Parked by the security barrier was a scrappy Fiat Punto that hadn't been there before. Lucien's car, Ben assumed. 'We're going in mine,' he said, blipping the locks. He bundled Lucien in the passenger seat. Storm hopped in the back and sat with his nose an inch from the back of Lucien's neck. 'Any tricks,' Ben said, 'and he'll bite your head off. Now lead the way.'

On the map, the Ouche river cut a meandering blue curve some ninety-five kilometres long through much of Burgundy's Côte-d'Or department. In some places the river was touristy and commercialised, while in others it flowed through quiet and sparsely populated areas where the big tourist barges didn't venture. The fishing shack was located in one such spot, tucked away almost completely out of sight on a bend in the river and accessible only by a potholed dirt road that was almost too rough for the Alpina to handle. Ben's guide the petty drug dealer behaved himself perfectly, and directed them straight to the place. It was getting on for midnight by the time Ben killed his lights and engine and rolled to a silent halt forty yards from the shack.

The moonlight shimmered on the surface of the river and gave enough illumination for him to make out the dilapidated wooden hut half-swallowed by foliage, close to the water's edge. There was a broken-down jetty on the water, with a rowing boat moored to it. Parked in the shadows at the end of the track were three cars. A wisp of smoke trickled from the flue-pipe chimney that jutted from the shack roof, and there was a glimmer of orange light in its windows.

'This is it,' Lucien said, pointing. 'And that's Robert's car over there, the black Citroen. The Toyota Land Cruiser with the flame paint job, that belongs to a dude called Bull. He's often here.'

'Bull?'

'What they call him,' Lucien said with a shrug. 'If you saw him, you'd know why. I don't know the dude's real name.'

'Another customer of yours?'

'Hey, if it's going around, he's always in the market. So, like, what now?'

Ben handed him back the little bag of skunk weed. 'Deal's a deal. But you won't be doing any business tonight. Off you go.' He turned off the interior light so that the car would stay dark when the doors opened.

'B-but dude, I'm expected.'

'Not tonight,' Ben said. 'You can conduct your business here another time.'

'How'm I supposed to get back to my car? We're in the middle of nowhere here.' No 'thank you so much for not arresting me, officer'. Some people were just plain ungrateful.

'Walk,' Ben said.

Lucien eyed him suspiciously. 'What kind of a cop are you anyway?'

'The kind who'll launch your arse into orbit if he claps eyes on you again. So get out of here.'

Lucien Pichard was about to protest more. But then he

saw the look in Ben's eye, and swallowed hard. Storm backed it up with a low, menacing growl, an inch from Lucien's ear.

As Lucien Pichard vanished into the night, never to be seen again, Ben walked up to the riverside fishing shack and pushed open the door.

Chapter 37

The first thing that hit Ben as he stepped inside the shack was the smell of cannabis and booze, mixed with the smoky fumes leaking out of the wood-burning stove. The second was the sight of three men in there, lounging around on junkyard furniture, clutching bottles of cheap whisky and rum and puffing joints by the dim flicker of candlelight and the glow of the fire.

One of the three men was possibly the most outsized human being Ben had ever seen, some kind of genetic throwback with a massive barrel chest, gangly great arms and a head the size of a pumpkin. His mass enveloped most of the two-seater sofa that looked ready to collapse under the weight. Tiny beetling eyes squinted out from under an overhanging slab of forehead. The second man, sitting to the giant's left, was an undernourished little scrap of a guy with a goatee and round glasses.

The third, prostrated on an old car seat by the opposite wall of the shack, was Robert Blondel. He was visibly the drunkest of the three, head lolling and the hand clutching the joint hanging to the floor.

The floorboards creaked as Ben took another step into the shack. Leaving the door open so that the cold night air came flooding in, he addressed the monster and the scrawny guy and said, 'Sorry to spoil your fun, gentlemen, but the party's over. I'd like to have a quiet word alone with my friend Robert.'

Blondel's head straightened up on his shoulders and he blinked several times, sobering up fast as his bleary-eyed look of recognition turned to one of shock, then of outright terror. He snapped rigid in his chair, spilling his bottle and dropping his joint. 'Oh no. Not you. W-what are you doing here?'

'Jeannette sent me,' Ben said. 'She's not too pleased with you. But it seems to me you've got bigger problems, Robert.'

The big guy heaved himself up out of the half-collapsed sofa. Rising all the way up to his feet he seemed to grow impossibly tall, and the shack ceiling made him bow his head slightly as he glowered down at Ben from a great height. The floorboards sagged and groaned as he stepped up to meet him. The two clenched fists were bigger than boxing gloves. 'I don't think Robert wants to talk to you,' he said in a slurry voice about ten octaves lower than was quite normal. 'Whoever the fuck you are,' he added.

Ben met the giant's gaze. 'You must be Bull, am I right? Listen, Bull, I don't want any trouble here. So I suggest you leave now, while you still have the legs to carry you.'

Bull took a couple of seconds to digest this and compute its meaning. Then he reacted by drawing back a massive arm and taking a swing at Ben. The punch could probably have propelled him crashing through the shack wall, if it had landed. But it came in so low and slow that, for Ben, it was like watching a Hercules troop transport plane coming in to land. In no particular rush, he stepped aside to let the enormous fist sail past him – and then in the next moment Bull was hurtling out of the shack door, his own momentum helped by a little aikido move Ben had been using on slow-witted hulks like him for years and never seen to fail. Bull catapulted down the steps, hit the dirt face-first and went sprawling down the riverbank.

Ben said, 'Storm, ready.' And by the time Bull was back on his feet, windmilling his giant fists and bellowing like a berserk Chianina ox, the German shepherd appeared as if from nowhere and bounded up to him with jaws wide open. Bull staggered back in alarm, missed his footing and fell into the dark river with a howl and a splash. Meanwhile, Blondel's drinking companion with the goatee and the glasses leaped from his seat, rushed past Ben and bolted from the shack, barely seeming to touch the ground as he made his escape to his car.

Ben signalled to Storm, and the dog backed off as Bull managed to clamber up the riverbank, pouring water and gasping hoarsely. Shooting a daunted look at Ben he staggered squelching to the parked Land Cruiser and took off up the track after his friend.

Now Ben was alone in the shack with the man he'd come to see. Blondel hadn't moved from the old car seat, blinking and gaping up at him in confusion. 'Your wife doesn't seem to think much of the social company you keep,' Ben told him. 'Frankly, I'd say she has a point.'

All of Pepe's men were trained in unarmed combat, but

there was no way Blondel was prepared to get into it with Ben, even if he hadn't been tanked up on cheap spirits and stoned half out of his brain on pot. He stayed where he was, opening his mouth to speak but unable to form any words.

Ben stood over him. 'You know why I'm here, Robert. Or you should. You heard what happened at Le Val?'

Finding his voice again Blondel burst out, 'I didn't know it would go down that way! It's not my fault. Those fuckers made me do it!'

'I know they did,' Ben replied. 'Or your two buddies there would already be carting you to hospital by now. What's your daughter's name?'

Blondel's eyes opened even wider. 'I . . . it's Karen . . . But . . . how . . .?'

'I saw the photo they sent you,' Ben told him. 'I read the letter. Is it the Corsicans?'

It was like watching a person physically dissolve. Blondel's face twisted with emotion and his whole body sagged as all the pent-up agony of tension seemed to come flooding out of him at once. His hands began to shake and tears dripped down his cheeks. 'I don't know anything about any Corsicans,' he mumbled through his sobs. 'All I know is what they threatened to do to her if I refused to help them.'

'First things first, Robert. Is Karen all right? Is she safe? Have they harmed her in any way?'

Blondel nodded and shook his head abjectly. 'She doesn't know a thing about it.'

'Let's keep it that way,' Ben said. 'There's been enough pain and suffering already.'

'I thought . . . I thought you must have come to kill me for what happened to your friend.'

'I wanted to,' Ben said. 'Believe me, I was full of ideas about how I was going to make you pay. But now I know that you did what you had to do to protect your family, Robert. I don't like it but I understand your reasons. That's why I'm not going to hurt you.'

'You're not?'

'No, I think perhaps we can help each other,' Ben said.

Blondel's shoulders sagged with relief. 'I need another drink.'

'You've had plenty enough already. Just tell me what happened.'

The fire was dying. Ben tossed another log on it from the stacked pile, then perched on the edge of the sofa where Bull had been. He gave Blondel a moment to compose himself, then sat and listened as the guy began to talk.

Chapter 38

It had all started months ago, Blondel explained. That summer, Pepe Jaeckin had sent some of his team on a close protection job in Marseille, to stand in as hired bodyguards for a visiting businessman from overseas while he attended a conference. It had been a pretty routine assignment, dull as ditchwater, but Blondel had only recently joined Pepe's outfit and he'd been filled with pride and enthusiasm for having been picked for the job. 'At the end of the four days, before flying back up to Dijon, a bunch of the lads hit the town, me included. We'd all had quite a bit to drink by the time we ended up in this rough joint down near the docks. That's where it happened. Or at least, I think it did. I've spent so many hours trying to work it out in my head that I just don't know any more.'

'Keep talking,' Ben said.

'Anyhow, just the week before, Pepe had told us the news that he'd got us booked on a course with you guys at Le Val, for later in the year. Everyone was stoked about getting to train there, the reputation you have, the kinds of drills you do, how you're famous for doing more live-fire training than anyone else in the business, and all that stuff. Anyhow, there I was, talking to these girls.'

Ben could already sense where Blondel's story was going. A macho lads' night out on the town, far away from the suspicious gaze of wives and girlfriends. The classic combination of a little too much booze, the attentive presence of some alluring younger females and the irrepressible male desire to paint themselves up as action heroes, and tongues soon began to wag.

'Yeah, I admit it,' Blondel said. 'I probably shot my mouth off a bit. I was still the new guy, still wanting to prove myself, and I was as excited as the rest of the boys about coming to Normandy in December, getting to train with machine guns and live ammo. And girls love to hear about all that kind of big boy stuff, shooters and fast cars and blowing shit up. Or these girls did, anyway. This one in particular; her name was Anna. Or maybe it was Annette. It's all hazy now. All I remember is how jam packed the place was, the noise, the music. Lots of tough guys hang out there, with God knows what kinds of connections to all kinds of crooked goings on. All I can imagine is that someone must have overheard. Then word must have got back to someone else. I can't believe I could have been so stupid, opening my big trap like that.'

Ben remembered what Detective Chausson had told him about the Corsican gangs operating in that city, less than four hundred kilometres from their island base. He'd had his own dealings in the seedier districts of Marseille, in the past. The criminal underworld there was as rough and nasty as it got, with a long history of violence. It was easy to imagine how loose talk could end up reaching the wrong ears. Sloppy work, he thought. First thing the SAS were taught: *loose lips sink ships.*

'It can't be helped now,' he said. 'Go on with the story.'

Blondel heaved a deep sigh. 'How they even got my number, I don't know. I might have got my phone out at some point during the night. Someone could easily have sneaked a look at it while it was lying on the table at my elbow. Anyway, not long after getting back to base in Dijon, I was contacted. The guy who called me spoke French, with a foreign accent. Sounded like an Italian to me, but I'd no idea who he was. It started out okay. He told me they wanted me to do a job for them. I laughed and said no thanks, I already have a job. You'd have to double my money. "We're not offering you any money to work for us," the guy said. "We're offering you the life of your daughter." Next thing he's telling me that they're watching Karen. She's a student at the Paul Sabatier University in Toulouse, taking a degree in Earth Sciences. I couldn't believe what I was hearing. I couldn't breathe. I can't even begin to describe the things he threatened against her if I refused to cooperate. They've got places where young girls get taken and end up as junkies and prostitutes. She's only twenty years old.'

More tears were streaming down Blondel's face as he talked. 'He made it very clear that if I tried to contact the cops or made any attempt to warn her, I'd never see her alive again. They said I had no choice. I had to do what I was told. Then he told me that I was to case your place and report back to them.'

'And that's what you were doing the night I found you wandering about,' Ben said. 'You were taking pictures of the buildings. Feeding back your reconnaissance intel. You told them what you'd learned about most of the team going away at Christmas. How I had to stay behind to look after things on my own, and that I had a foot in plaster.'

'I got the impression they were looking at other possible targets,' Blondel said. 'I guess that when they found out those things, it's what made them pick your place. I'm so sorry to have been a part of this, Ben. It was only supposed to be a robbery. They just wanted the guns. Said nobody was going to get hurt. And that was bad enough on its own, but I believed them. And now someone's died because of me.' He shook his head, looking as utterly wretched and miserable as anyone Ben had ever seen. 'Why'd it have to happen, Ben? Why?'

'Because they picked the wrong guy for the job,' Ben said. 'His name is Petru Navarro. Even by their standards, he's a psychopath. Bad luck for Victor. Worse luck for Petru himself. Because I *will* find him.'

'What a mess,' Blondel muttered. 'And all because of me. I can hardly live with myself any more. And I'm going crazy with worry about Karen. I'm so scared of what they'll do to her if they find out I talked to anyone.'

'Nobody's going to hurt your little girl,' Ben said. 'That's a promise.'

'How can you stop them? These people are killers.'

'All the more reason why you can help me to help you keep Karen safe,' Ben said. 'Anything you can tell me about the men who recruited you could be useful information.'

'I swear, Ben,' Blondel said with desperation in his eyes. 'If I knew anything, I'd tell you!'

'Does the name Titus Navarro mean anything to you?' Ben asked.

'Never heard of him. Who is he?'

'According to the men who did the hit on Le Val, you wouldn't want to know. He's some kind of big cheese on Corsica. Just the mention of his name has them pissing dust.'

'I wish I could help you. I don't know what to say. I didn't even know they were Corsicans until you mentioned it before.'

Ben had been hoping Blondel might be able to tell him something about the gang bosses behind César Casta's operation, or something that might verify what Ángel Leoni had said. But he'd already known that was a long shot. Any organised crime outfit worth the name would have several strata of hierarchy, and the men who'd dealt directly with Blondel would be somewhere near the bottom, mere foot soldiers. A pawn like Blondel wouldn't have had any idea who even they were, much less their superiors. Even the boss behind the raid on Le Val might not be any higher within their organisation than middle management, equivalent in rank to an army captain or a lieutenant. That was how it worked. Jobs got delegated, and the men at the top of the tree might not even know about them.

'What am I going to do?' Blondel groaned. 'I feel so powerless.'

'I'll tell you what you can't do,' Ben replied. 'You can't sit here drinking and drugging yourself slowly to death and feeling sorry for yourself. You've got a wife and kid at home who need you. Toe the line, Robert. Or you stand to lose a lot more than you've lost already.'

Blondel was silent for a long time, then sighed. 'I've been

weak and I've acted like a fool. I'm so sorry for all the pain and troubles that I've caused. Please find it in your heart to forgive me.'

Ben said no more. He left Blondel still sitting there with his head bowed in guilt and misery, a broken man, and walked back to the car.

As he drove away, the compass needle in his mind was pointing south-east to his next destination, far away across land and sea, nestling in the crook of southern France and Italy. And somewhere, lurking among the cities and villages and forests and mountains of that rugged Mediterranean island, Petru Navarro would be waiting for him.

Chapter 39

Ben spent the rest of the night driving downward through France, a 700-kilometre rush for the south coast. Stopping only for fuel, he learned from a quick internet search that the fastest, most direct and most frequent ferry crossing over to Corsica at this time of year was from Nice to the island's northern commune of L'Île Rousse.

And so, come early next morning, Ben was at the Port de Nice, grabbing a croissant and a coffee, purchasing his ticket and loading the Alpina aboard a car ferry for the five-hour voyage. Ben had booked a cabin for himself and Storm. He dumped his bag on the bunk, then headed back up on deck as the ferry departed from the port.

Corsica had been officially part of France since 1768, but 1200 kilometres south of home it felt to Ben like a far different country from the one he lived in. The temperature was a balmy ten degrees and the sky was a perfect powder blue. Low season, the ferry was half empty. He walked aft along the deck, leaned against the stern railing and smoked a couple of Gauloises while watching the ferry's churning white wake and the French mainland slowly sink below the sea horizon. Then he and Storm returned to the cabin, and the dog curled contentedly up on the floor while Ben stretched out on the bunk, letting his muscles relax and the soft motion of the boat gently rock him. He was too tired even to pay attention to his troubled thoughts or the constant ache in his bad ankle, and the moment he closed his eyes he was drifting down, down, into a dreamless, bottomless void where nothing could reach him.

Five hours later, as refreshed and restored as he could be, he was rolling the Alpina back down the loading ramp onto the dock of the L'Île Rousse ferry port. The midday sunshine cast a billion sparkling diamonds across the surface of the Tyrrhenian Sea, and the craggy mountains of the island loomed beyond the other side of the harbour. From here, his destination of Porto Vecchio lay a further two and a half hours' drive away, right down near the southernmost tip of the island.

This was a wilder place than most Mediterranean countries, with a population density only a third of mainland France's, and that isolated into scattered enclaves by the island's uncompromising topography. Two-thirds of the land was uninhabitably mountainous and more than a fifth was covered in dense forest. The roads were either straight and wide highways or narrow and twisty passes, with not much in between. Ben ploughed on hard and fast, focusing little on the scenery that seemed to veer from one extreme to another: glitzy azure bays that gave the impression of travelling through the French Riviera, suddenly giving way to jagged mountain landscapes even more breathtakingly rugged than the Scottish Highlands or the west of Ireland, where he had lived for some years.

He had always been a light and economical traveller, tending to stop little and eat less en route. But thinking of his hungry companion he pulled over at a little roadside bar-restaurant operated by a friendly elderly couple who took an immediate liking to Storm, fussing over him so much that Ben worried the dog was going to forget all his training. While Storm feasted happily on a heaped dish of rice and raw minced lamb, Ben drank a cold beer and ate a meal of civet de sanglier, a wild boar casserole lovingly prepared by his hostess. Then he was on his way again, finally reaching Porto Vecchio around three in the afternoon. His purpose for being here would have to wait until evening, which gave him several hours to set up his base, reconnoitre the place and work out his best plan of attack.

Porto Vecchio seemed to have about a million hotels. Ben wound around the narrow streets hunting for something suitable, and struck lucky with a small, simple establishment a short distance from Santa Giulia Beach. It was run by a corpulent and hugely talkative lady named Laetitia who was more than happy to accommodate four-legged guests, all the more since her hotel was all but empty at this time of the year. Once he was settled in, Ben drove back into the heart of the town and he and Storm went exploring in search of Bar Royale, the nightclub where Petru Navarro reportedly hung out. Ben had already worked through all the possible reasons why Victor's killer might not be found there, but right now it was his best and only lead.

He soon found the nightclub, a large and fairly flashy venue not too far from the winding streets of the old district and the famous sixteenth-century citadel that had once been the heart of the fortress town. Bar Royale was closed and wouldn't be reopening until evening. Ben wandered off, looking for all the world like just an ordinary guy out walking his dog, instead of a man bent on avenging his dead friend. The sides of the nightclub were laced with narrow alleys but to its rear it faced out towards the sea, with a view of a marina that, in high season, would be filled with yachts and pleasure boats.

Even midwinter in Porto Vecchio felt like early springtime in Normandy. Ben strolled on a while, slowly sipped on an espresso in an open-air café terrace in the Place de la République, then returned to the car and drove back in the direction of his hotel, detouring towards Santa Giulia Beach. His normal routine, before the accident, would have been to go for a run along the water's edge, accompanied by Storm who loved those outings and would gladly trot along with him for a hundred miles. But remembering the warning not to overdo it with his weak ankle, he limited himself to a brisk hike along the long, sweeping curve of white sands with the cool sea breeze in his hair.

The beach was almost deserted. To one side of him stood the ever-present mountains and forests of the island; to the other, the lapping tide and the sea, spectacularly blue for wintertime. Ben had always loved the ocean. For a while he could almost have forgotten where he was, if it hadn't been for the simmering darkness in his heart. The closer the time approached when he might meet Victor's killer, the more acutely Ben could feel the intensity of his rage. But he had to control it. Personal feelings could only cloud his judgement and make him less efficient in what he needed to do.

In the late afternoon, as the sunset glittered multi-hued across the water, he slowly walked back to the car and returned to the hotel. He fed Storm another meal, provided by loquacious Laetitia, who had generously offered to let the dog eat in her kitchen. Dogs were a great unifier of people, and Ben liked people who liked them. Just as much as he disliked people who tried to harm them.

'What would you like for dinner this evening, Monsieur Hope?' Laetitia wanted to know.

'I'll be going out tonight,' Ben told her. 'I might not be back until late.'

'You would like for me to look after him?' she asked, petting Storm. 'He is such a gentleman, like his master.'

'I'd appreciate that. Thank you.'

As he said it, the thought flashed into his mind that if something happened to him tonight and he never returned, at least the dog would have a good home with this kindly lady. Then he dismissed the thought, because thinking like that was bad luck. But it was too late. The seed had been planted, and it unsettled him.

Ben reckoned that Bar Royale wouldn't get into full swing until later in the evening, when the lure of the island's nightlife was more likely to draw the likes of Petru Navarro from whatever hole he might be hiding in. He rested up in his room until nine, biding his time.

'I know you want to come with me,' he told the dog. 'But where I'm going, you wouldn't like. And I'm not sure they'd appreciate you much either.'

Then it was time. Ben took his pistol from his bag, and for a moment he considered the possibility that he was going to need it tonight. But on reflection, he decided to leave it behind, safely hidden here in his room. He quietly left the hotel and retraced his steps back to Bar Royale. The night was colder now, but not so cold as to deter the jostling crowd of mostly young people that thronged in the street below the nightclub's huge neon sign. The steady *thump-thump-thump* of loud bass-heavy music boomed out from the entrance, which was guarded by a troop of burly bouncers who were all obviously veterans of the weights room at the local gym. None of them was quite in Bull's league for sheer overwhelming mass, but they were much more useful-looking and apparently in the mood to crack the skull of anyone who even dreamed of getting inside the club without paying.

Ben joined the crowd and let himself be swept along in the crush, paid his cash and received an ink stamp on the back of his hand by way of a ticket. He'd always felt there was something faintly concentration-camp-like about those stamps. Inside the club, the music was so loud that it made his ribs vibrate. Lights flashed and strobed like a jungle firefight at night-time. The floor was packed tight with three or four hundred people all dancing in that peculiar way with their arms raised above their heads, as though they'd all entered a competition for who had the loveliest pits.

Ben threaded his way through the morass and was glad to reach the relative haven of the bar, where six barmen were rushing to serve the tide of punters clamouring for drinks. When he'd pushed his way to the front, shouting over the deafening beat of the music Ben asked if Petru Navarro was in tonight. If what Ángel Leoni had said was right and Petru helped to run the place along with his cousin, then Ben figured that his name ought to be known to the bar staff. But all he got in response was a dead-eyed stare and a head shake, so in case he hadn't been heard, he repeated the question.

'I don't know anyone of that name,' the bar guy yelled back over the racket.

'No? What about his cousin Salvadore?'

To which the bar guy reacted with such a studious expression of complete blankness that Ben instantly knew he was lying.

Leaning right across the bar to be heard he said in the guy's ear, 'Maybe you know Petru's uncle Titus. I'm told that he owns this place. Is that right?'

That name, at least, seemed to get some traction. The bar guy frowned. 'Who wants to know?'

'Hope, Ben Hope. My friend César Casta recommended this place. Said I might be able to hook up with our mutual pal Petru.'

The barman said nothing. He made a gesture as though to say 'Wait there', and disappeared through a door into a back room. He left the door slightly ajar, and Ben could see him talking on a phone, head bent low and his hand cupped to his other ear to block out the din of the music, before he reached out and closed the door fully. A minute later the door opened and the guy reappeared, suddenly all smiles and beckoning for Ben to come closer. '*Petru*, right?' he yelled. 'Sure, sure, of course I know who you mean. Everybody around here knows Petru. So you're a friend of his?'

'We're like this,' Ben said, holding up crossed fingers.

The bar guy fished a bottle of beer from under the counter, uncapped it and slid it across the top. 'Please, it's on the house.'

Ben took the drink, playing along. 'So is Petru here tonight?' His voice was getting hoarse from all this yelling.

The bar guy shook his head and shouted back, 'Not tonight. But you asked about Uncle Titus, right? If you're a buddy of his nephew he'd love to meet you. They'll take you to him.'

He pointed. Ben had already seen the two guys approaching through the crowd of punters, and he understood that was who the bar guy had been talking to on the phone just now. He turned to look at them, feigning a look of pleasant innocence. One of them had a shaven head and the other still had a little hair, but apart from that they looked like twins, in matching silk suits that appeared silvery in the flashing coloured lights. Bulging bicep and deltoid muscles strained at their jackets. Ben couldn't see any telltale bulges that would show they were carrying concealed weapons, but it was hard to be sure. The silver suits stepped up closer to him, and broke out all friendly and smiling like the bar guy. Ben had seen more convincing smiles on alligators in Louisiana.

The bald one asked, 'What was your name again?'

Ben repeated it.

'You want to meet Uncle Titus? No problem. Come this way.'

Chapter 40

Ben set his unfinished bottle down on the bar and went along with the two silver suits. The bald one walked in front, leading the way towards a side door marked RÉSERVÉ AUX EMPLOYÉS, while his slightly hairier twin brought up the rear. Despite their smiles it felt like being discreetly arrested. Ben's manner was easy and his pace relaxed, but he was ready for the fact that his welcoming committee might not be as friendly as they appeared. Beyond the door lay a long, narrow corridor with carpet on the walls, where the thump-thump-thump of the music was muted like canned gunfire.

Now they were out of sight of the nightclub punters, the bald silver suit turned to Ben and said, 'I have to frisk you. Just a formality, okay?'

'No problem,' Ben said. He'd expected this to happen, and it was the reason he'd elected to leave his gun at the hotel. Though now he was starting to question whether that had been the right move. Damned if you do, damned if you don't. His instinct was telling him that he could very well be walking into a bad situation. But it was too late to worry about it now. He raised his arms and let the guy do his work.

He was pretty thorough and proficient at it. When it was done, the bald guy nodded to his companion. 'He's clean.'

'His office is just along here,' said the other silver suit, motioning towards a door up ahead. 'He's waiting for you.'

But when the door swung open, Ben saw that his instinct had been right. This wasn't any kind of office. The only furniture in the small, square, windowless room was a single wooden chair. The part about someone waiting for Ben had been true enough, but it wasn't Uncle Titus. Unless Uncle Titus did double duty as a bouncer in his own nightclub. There were two of them, and Ben recognised them from earlier: the bone-breakers who'd been working the entrance. One had long, dirty biker hair and a leather waistcoat that barely fitted over his massive shoulders. The other could have been Bull's little brother, if he hadn't more resembled an orang-utan. They were both about the same height, which was about a foot taller than Ben.

Ben hesitated, then stepped into the room. What the hell. The silver suits closed the door. The bald one took a small key from his pocket and locked it. The pair took up their positions on either side of the doorway, their hands clasped casually across their stomachs. Biker Boy and the orang remained mute, staring at Ben with bulging eyes as though just waiting for the command to wade in and take him apart.

'Now you'd better start talking to us,' said the bald suit. 'Starting with who you are and what you're doing in our place.'

'Do you always vet your customers this carefully?' Ben asked.

'Your name, asshole.'

'I already told your man back there my name. It's Hope. Ben Hope.'

'What do you want with Petru Navarro?'

'I heard he had a little mishap,' Ben replied, wiggling his earlobe. 'Just wanted to pay my condolences and check up on how he was.'

'What makes you think he'd be here?'

'You people need to brush up on your communication,' Ben said. 'I already gave your man at the bar that information. My friend César Casta told me I might find him here. Have to say I'd have expected a more cordial reception, based on what he said. Maybe I'm in the wrong place.'

The silver suits grinned at each other. 'Oh, you're in the wrong place all right,' the bald one said.

'There you go. I knew it. I'm new in town, see? Don't know where anything is. I haven't even checked to see if there's a good hospital nearby.'

'Hospital?'

Ben nodded. 'It'd be a shame if there wasn't. Not for me, I mean. For you. Because unless you decide to take a sensible approach here, that's where you'll be spending the next few days. Maybe longer, depending.'

The bald one gave a snort and said to his twin, 'You hear that, Marcu? Guy thinks we ought to be sensible.'

The one called Marcu scowled and replied, 'Maybe he thinks we ought to let him walk out of here.'

'I would advise it,' Ben said. 'But before you do that, I'd like you to tell me where I can find Petru. I have something of his that he might want back, before it gets too manky for a surgeon to sew back on. Last time I looked, it was starting to turn green.' The severed ear was currently in Laetitia's refrigerator, back at the hotel. She might not be too pleased if she discovered it while looking for her yogurt.

'Let me tell you what's going to happen, asshole,' said the one called Marcu. He nodded in the direction of the two silent, glaring bouncers. 'These gentlemen are going to teach you a lesson about not sticking your nose in where it's not wanted.' He signalled to the pair. 'Do your stuff, boys. Afterwards you can dump whatever's left of this piece of shit in the alley.'

On Marcu's command, Biker Boy and the orang went into action. They stepped fast towards Ben and made a lunge for him both at once, coming on shoulder to shoulder like a seven-foot wall of muscle falling on top of him. Ben had known exactly how they were going to play it. Which was with no finesse at all, but plenty of brute force. And he'd already worked out just how best to respond. In a situation like this, you didn't want to be caught in the middle of the twin attack, but instead move to the edge, controlling your position and giving yourself an exit route at all times: evade, strike, evade, and keep moving.

Except, in a street fight against multiple assailants, you would be moving to escape. In a closed room with only one door, there was nowhere to escape to. Whatever was about to start, Ben had to finish it.

Chapter 41

So as something in excess of five hundred pounds of bone-crushing power came straight at him, Ben skipped to one side faster than they could react, flashed out an even quicker hand and drove Biker Boy's head against the orang's. The meaty crack resounded satisfyingly in the small room. It might have dissuaded most opponents from fighting on, but its effect on these guys was only to annoy them.

It also taught them to adopt a slightly different tactic for their second wave of attack. This time they came at Ben from opposite sides. Throwing their big arms out wide to try to trap him in a circle and cut off his escape, but their tactic was clumsy. As they closed in, Biker Boy threw a powerful punch at a slightly downward angle, aiming for Ben's head. By the time his fist reached its intended target, Ben's head was already ducking out of its path. The momentum of the blow carried it straight through that empty patch of space until it found a new target, which was the orang-utan's left clavicle.

No amount of lifting weights can make the human collar bone any stronger than God designed it to be. Its inherent fragility is actually a built-in safety measure, acting like the crumple zone of a car to absorb damage and prevent injury to more important body parts, like the neck. But that was of little comfort to the orang as his clavicle gave way with a sound like a snapping pencil. He was out of action for a moment as he reeled backward, clutching at his shoulder and yowling in agony.

Which gave Ben time and space to focus his attention on Biker Boy, who still had all his weight on his left foot from the follow-through of the massive punch. Ben ducked down low to the guy's right side and came surging up, using the power in his legs to drive his uninjured shoulder into the guy's sternum. It doesn't matter how big and heavy they are when they're off balance. Biker Boy toppled over sideways, and in the confines of the small room his head cracked against the wall with considerable force.

With Biker Boy temporarily stunned, Ben skipped back to finish off the orang, whose pain and fury were fuelling him on for a charging assault. Ben let him come on, then sidestepped at the very last moment and caught him in the throat with a pincer web strike. Done wrong, you can break your own thumb. Done right, it can severely incapacitate or even kill. Ben had been trained to do it right, every time. The orang went slamming straight down on his back with a crash that shook the floor. A stamping kick to the face would ensure that he stayed there for a good long while.

Now the Biker Boy was roaring back in, streaming blood from the part of his head that had put a dent in the wall. Most of these kinds of fighters, who relied on their big brawny upper-body power to hammer opponents to the ground with the crudest tactics, didn't know how to use their legs. That was fine by Ben, because it also made them less watchful of what their opponent was doing with theirs. As Biker Boy came steaming towards him like a runaway express train his eyes were on Ben's whirling fists and he wasn't expecting the savage, cobra-fast low side-kick to the knee that drove the joint inwards far past the point of its resistance. The stale breadstick *crunch* was drowned by Biker Boy's scream.

Less than seven seconds into the fight, and both big guys were now seriously damaged. But Ben had known it was only a question of time before the two silver suits weighed in. They were lighter on their feet than the big guys, but strong and powerful and far more intelligent. The bald one launched himself away from the doorway, danced around Ben's left flank and came at him from behind, throwing a heavy punch. By the time Ben sensed the approach and was beginning to turn around to meet it, it was too late for him to dodge the blow entirely. A strike that could have broken Ben's jaw just grazed the left side of his face, but was still a jarring impact. White starbursts exploded in front of his eyes and he retreated a couple of steps, towards the corner of the room. That wasn't a place he wanted to be.

Meanwhile the other silver suit, the one called Marcu, had snatched up the wooden chair and was holding it with the legs jutting forward, trying to jab Ben further into the corner. Once he was pinned there, unable to move left or right, they would have him. Ben launched a higher kick that passed through the middle of the chair legs. The flat of his foot impacted against the underside of the seat and propelled the backrest viciously into Marcu's upper lip, right below the nose. Any teeth that weren't dislodged entirely would be badly loosened. Marcu let out a cry and charged forward again with the chair, but now Ben had sideslipped to the left, escaping the death-trap of the corner, and was dancing towards the door. The left side of his face was burning hot where the bald guy's punch had caught him. He knew he needed to finish these two fast, because if more came there would be far less chance of getting out of this.

Marcu hurled the chair; Ben dodged; the chair hit the wall with such force that it shattered into pieces. Ben snatched up a broken-off leg as it rolled across the floor in front of him, and held it in his fist like a short baton. For a few moments the silver suits circled him, watching him intently, waiting for the right opening to both come at him. There was dead silence in the room apart from their hoarse, ragged breathing. Then they charged, surging at him in a pincer movement. Ben skipped to the side and rammed the jagged end of the broken chair leg into Marcu's temple. It was a potentially killer blow, but at this point in the fight Ben didn't have the luxury of soft tactics.

Marcu went down without a sound, instantly unconscious and liable to remain that way for quite a while. The bald guy was more canny, more skilled, and by now he was getting a handle on Ben's fighting style. Ben struck at him with his improvised baton but missed. The bald guy managed to get a grip on Ben's arm and twisted the chair leg out of his grip. A sharp jolt of pain shot like electricity through Ben's wrist. Seeing his advantage, the bald guy followed up with a punch to the ribs. It landed hard, driving half the air out of Ben's lungs.

Ben staggered. Three men were on the ground but now he was beginning to tire. It felt like he'd cracked a rib. His face was throbbing and there was a nasty degree of pain in his bad ankle that was slowing him down more. He could lose this. While the bald guy was yet to have a blow landed on him, and he was fresh. A smile of triumph curled his lips.

But sometimes it's when you become convinced you're winning that things turn bad for you. That was when the bald guy made his fatal mistake. He rushed in to try to grab Ben by the throat with one hand while going for his eyes with the other. Ben caught him by the right thumb, twisted it and bent it and folded it across the back of his right hand, and felt it give with an appalling splintering snap.

The bald guy wailed in shock and agony. Ben kept hold of the useless thumb and used it to lever the bald guy's wrist right around, breaking that too. Then with all the savage energy left in him, Ben smashed a backhand hammer punch into the middle of the bald guy's face that spread his nose across his cheek like a burst ripe tomato. Then hit him twice more, feeling the fight going out of him now. He whirled the bald guy around so that his back was to the wall. Shoved the heel of his hand under the guy's bloody chin and drove the crown of his skull hard, *hard* against the wall. Then again. And then once more for good measure. That was enough. The bald guy's eyes rolled over white and he slid down the wall to the floor, leaving a red smear down the paintwork.

Winded and in pain, Ben staggered to the door and pressed his ear against it, listening hard and hearing nothing but the dull bassy boom of music from outside in the corridor. He turned back to the four unconscious bodies and quickly

275

frisked each one for identification. He came up with four wallets, four driving licences that appeared to be legit, and a bundle of cash which he pocketed as spoils of war. The silver suits were actually twins, with the same date of birth and the surname Agostini. The bald one's first name was Stefanu. Ben found the door key in his pocket.

But that was pretty much all he was going to get out of them, unless he waited around for one to wake up so he could ask him more nicely for information about the whereabouts of Petru Navarro. Waiting around wasn't a viable option. That meant Ben had risked getting the hell beaten out of him for nothing, and he was displeased with himself as he left the room.

The corridor was empty. If a whole gang of reinforcements were coming to aid their comrades, there was no sign of them yet. Locking the door, he toyed with the idea of going back to speak to the bar guy who'd set him up with the four lovelies. But that probably wasn't a good idea either. It seemed he was back to square one.

Ben found a push-bar fire escape door and stepped out into the night, finding himself in the same bare-brick alleyway where his charming hosts had no doubt intended to dump his bleeding, battered remains after they'd finished with him. To his right, the alley was a dead end littered with wheelie bins and stacks of drinks crates. To his left, he could see the lights of the street.

Then, as he emerged from the alleyway and started heading in the direction of the Alpina, a black Mercedes SUV suddenly came blasting up the street to meet him. It swerved and hammered up onto the kerb at an angle, blocking his path. All four doors flew open, and four men in dark coats stepped out. They weren't stopping to ask the time. Ben found himself looking down the barrels of three pistols and a Skorpion submachine gun.

The guy with the Skorpion wagged its muzzle towards the back of the car and said, 'Get in.'

Chapter 42

Some invitations are hard to refuse. And Ben had the feeling these guys might not take no for an answer, anyway. One of the back-seat passengers stepped aside to let him in. Then he was sandwiched between two armed men, doors were slamming shut and the Mercedes was barrelling off down the street.

'I don't suppose it would do any good to ask where we're going,' Ben said. There was no reply. He hadn't expected one. His ankle felt stiff and his ribs and face ached from the two punches he'd taken back there. The Mercedes was a big car, smooth and comfortable with a lot of legroom in the rear, so rather than try to overpower four more men and take his chances making his escape he stretched out, relaxed into the soft leather of the seat and closed his eyes.

Half an hour had gone by when Ben felt a prod and a voice said, 'Get out.' Get in. Get out. Not the most conversational of people, these guys. He expected there would be more talk in a minute. Unless they'd just brought him here to execute him.

Wherever here was. Stepping out of the car, Ben looked around him and saw plush, elegant gardens and an enormous ornamental fountain, illuminated like day by the light pouring from the windows of a magnificent white mansion.

'This way,' said the guy with the Skorpion. The gun was out of sight now, but escape still wasn't an option. Two more men had appeared by the thick stone columns of the mansion's entrance with unfriendly Dobermans on chain leashes. The dogs had clipped ears that stood up like devil horns, and made Ben think of the clipped ear wrapped in cellophane back at the hotel. He wondered if being brought here was bringing him any closer to being reunited with its owner.

Ben's escorts showed him inside the grand entrance. He found himself in a vast marble-floored hallway with a domed ceiling painted to look like Michelangelo. Great tropical plants with giant frond-like leaves stood in tall alabaster urns, either side of elegant Grecian statues. From somewhere in the background came the soft tinkle of music: Chopin, or maybe Liszt. The heavies withdrew, leaving Ben alone in the hallway as a man appeared at the head of a broad, winding marble staircase and came stepping unhurriedly down to greet him.

If this was the boss of the operation, he wasn't quite what Ben might have expected. He was somewhere between forty-five and fifty years of age, with thick dark hair swept back from a high brow and greying elegantly in streaks. Dressed in crisp designer jeans and a loose white silk shirt open at the neck he was slim, handsome and tall, exuding a natural kind of grace and a well-bred air. He reached the bottom of the staircase and smiled pleasantly as he crossed the hallway with an extended hand. When he spoke it was in perfect English, with a touch of transatlantic accent that hinted at an education at some Ivy League university like Yale or Harvard. Portrait of the thuggish organised crime kingpin, not.

'Major Hope, my name is Titus Navarro. It's a pleasure to make your acquaintance.'

Ben looked at the outstretched hand and kept his own by his side. He replied, 'Under the circumstances, I'm not sure the sentiment is mutual.'

Titus Navarro nodded thoughtfully, not the least offended. 'Of course. I understand perfectly. I sincerely hope that you can forgive me for the manner in which I was compelled to have you brought here. And it appears,' he added, eyeing the fresh bruise on Ben's cheek, 'that you may have received a less than civil reception from my employees at Bar Royale.'

'I'm sure they were just doing what they were told,' Ben said.

Navarro replied, 'Please accept my sincere apologies, and my absolute assurance that the order to treat you so roughly did not come from me. Their instructions were to entertain you until my men arrived, no more. Unfortunately the kind of people one has to employ for an operation of that kind are by necessity somewhat crass and prone to simple-minded overreactions. Clearly there has been a misunderstanding, and for that, certain individuals will be punished. You have my word.'

Ben handed Navarro the key to the room in which he'd locked the silver suits and the two bouncers. 'They've already had all the punishment they can stand for one night. You'll find them still in reasonable condition, but there are a few bone fractures that'll need medical attention.'

'Of course,' Navarro replied, taking the key. 'Thank you for your forbearance. I trust the matter is now settled, with no hard feelings?'

'I wouldn't go that far, Signor Navarro. There are still a few unresolved issues on my mind.'

Navarro smiled. 'I'm very much aware of that, Major. It's the reason I wished to invite you to my home and speak with you personally. Would you care to step this way?'

He led Ben from the hallway down a marbled passage lined with carved gilt Second Empire chairs and classical busts on pedestals, to a fine double doorway that opened into a large and tastefully furnished salon. A fire was crackling brightly in the high lapis lazuli fireplace, and a vast crystal chandelier hung from the ornate ceiling. 'Please do make yourself comfortable,' Navarro said, motioning to a suite of velvet-covered chairs and settees. Ben sat, if only just to take the weight off his ankle.

'You have a very nice home,' he told the Corsican. 'Breaking into people's houses and business premises and slaughtering their friends and animals must really pay. Because I'm assuming César Casta was working for you, and so far you're not denying it.'

'That's what I wish to discuss with you,' Navarro said. 'I'm happy we could talk like this. But first, can I offer you something to drink?'

Ben's first instinct was to refuse. He didn't drink with crooks, as a rule. But he needed something to take the edge off the pain of his various injuries. They were starting to mount up. He replied, 'Whisky. Single malt.'

'I believe I'll join you.' His host walked over to a handsome antique drinks cabinet and selected a bottle and a pair of cut-crystal tumblers, which he set down on its marble top to pour out two generous measures. 'Ice or water?'

'Just as it comes,' Ben said.

Navarro graciously handed Ben his drink and settled in an armchair opposite. 'You wanted to talk,' Ben said. 'So now you've got me here, I'm listening.'

Chapter 43

'I appreciate your candour, Major Hope,' Titus Navarro said. 'Now allow me to be candid with you. In addition to the apology for what happened at my business premises tonight, I feel that I also owe you an explanation with regard to certain other matters.'

'Before you get started, I'm not a major any more, Signor Navarro. I don't like to be called it.'

'Duly noted. Then what should I call you?'

'You can call me Ben.'

'And you must call me Titus. As a token of my sincerity and desire to be as frank with you as I possibly can. From what I know about your background, and now meeting you in person, you strike me as being someone with whom I can speak openly.'

'Is this your way of saying sorry for sending your hired thugs to my home to steal and kill?'

Navarro sipped his drink, pensively weighing what he was about to say. 'Let me tell you a little about my late father, Ghjaseppu Maria Navarro. I'm sure his name is unfamiliar to you, but I can assure you that it was one to strike fear into the hearts of many men. Not just his enemies, but also those who worked for him. My father was a hard and tough man, some might say ruthless. In the world he grew up in, rising from the worst poverty imaginable, he needed to be. He was someone who believed very much in traditions, in the old ways of doing things.'

'What was that?' Ben said. 'Concrete shoes, cut-throat razors, dissolving bodies in quicklime? We're talking about the Corsican mafia here, correct?'

'That isn't a term I choose to describe my family enterprise,' Navarro said. 'It may have been, back in my father's day. But since I inherited the business from him five years ago I've made every effort to bring it into the twenty-first century, with the resolute aim of becoming completely legitimate within another five.'

'Oh, I could tell that from the machine guns and the attack dogs,' Ben said. 'Snatching people off the street at gunpoint in a black Mercedes has "law-abiding citizen" stamped all over it.'

Navarro spread his hands. 'To make a transition of the kind I'm describing is a difficult undertaking. I won't pretend that it's without its challenges and setbacks. Certain revenue streams are hard to let go of. Old alliances, old scores, old customs; it takes a great deal of work and commitment to undo the legacy of the past.' He smiled. 'And in some respects, one often tends to find that those kinds of methods can still be very effective. Given the nature of some of the men who work for us, it really doesn't hurt to keep them in fear. Sometimes it's the only way to maintain their respect.'

Ben thought about the panic-stricken terror that the mere mention of the name Titus Navarro had instilled in César Casta and his gang. He said, 'You mean like letting someone like Robert Blondel believe that your men were intending to carve up his twenty-year-old daughter if he disobeyed orders?'

Navarro shrugged it off. 'What a man believes can have a powerful action on his behaviour. It's a game of bluff. When you have a certain reputation it takes only a whispered threat, however insincere, and they'll do anything. That's human nature.'

'So you're giving me your assurances that Karen Blondel is safe?' Ben asked. 'No harm comes to her? Because otherwise, you and I are going to have a serious problem here.'

'Do you know the girl?'

'I've never met her, and I don't expect I ever will,' Ben replied. 'It doesn't matter. If you know anything about my background, you know that I don't like kidnappers. If anything happens to her, you'll have to face the consequences for that.'

'You're a very frank man,' Navarro said, looking at him closely. 'And a very brave one, for speaking so directly. But yes, you may rest assured that the girl is perfectly safe. The man served his purpose. I have no further use for him.'

'Wrecking innocent lives as though they meant nothing,' Ben said. 'It's not the most obvious way to signal your intentions of going legit.'

'I'm fully aware of that fact. You may think me a hypocrite, and I confess it's not an unwarranted accusation. All the more reason why I'm determined, fully committed, to move the Navarro business operations into a whole new era, leaving the old days behind us.'

Ben was watching Navarro's eyes as he talked. The eyes always told you everything. And Ben could see no lie in them. He was being sincere.

'And that brings me to the main point,' Navarro said. 'The recent incident in Normandy.'

'This is the part where you explain yourself, and I'm supposed to act understanding.'

'I can't make excuses for what happened,' Navarro said. 'Nor can I expect you to lay aside your very understandable grievances. What happened, happened, and I must take responsibility for it. I only hope that you can hear me out, and understand how deeply unhappy I am with the situation.'

'I'm going to take some convincing.'

'I will be the first to admit that my efforts to decriminalise my operations have so far been less successful than I had hoped. For all my good intentions, the family business remains what my father made it, earning much of its revenue by a variety of illicit means.'

'You already have guns,' Ben said. 'Why did you need to steal more?'

'It's purely a matter of supply and demand,' Navarro said. 'The objective of obtaining the weaponry from your premises was intended to fulfil the needs of some of my fellow Corsicans, who require more in that line than I'm otherwise able to supply.'

'You were going to sell them to another crime gang?'

'Not exactly. I'm happy to explain. If you were to take a tour of my country, you might notice that many of the bilingual road signs are defaced to remove the non-Corsican French place names. That's just one small sign of the long-standing opposition to French domination of the island, which many still regard as colonialist tyranny. You may be aware of the various groups that have long been advocating Corsican independence from France, not all of them content to restrict themselves to peaceful political means.'

'So the guns were meant for separatist terrorists.'

'Or freedom fighters, as I'm sure they would rather be labelled. The armed struggle of the FLNC, that is the Front de Libération Nationale Corse, dates back to its first attacks in 1976, which saw bombings in several towns including Porto Vecchio. Over the years they attacked banks, municipal buildings, tourist destinations, police stations, military installations, anything they perceived as symbols of French occupation. Some years ago, the main body of the FLNC declared a cessation to its armed struggle against our colo-nial rulers. However, a number of radical splinter groups remain. One of these, cash-rich thanks to their secret spon-sors but poor in weaponry, approached us some time ago for help.'

'Which you were only too happy to offer, despite all your big talk about going legit.'

Navarro shrugged. 'I'm not a political animal. This was a business proposition, pure and simple. And my operation requires a vast amount of income from multiple sources to keep moving towards its eventual goals. So, yes, somewhat reluctantly I might add, I agreed to a deal with the freedom fighters. They were willing to pay the right price for military small arms that were compact, concealable and effective. Our conclusion, after months of research and intelligence gathering, was that your facility offered just what we needed. I needn't explain how we managed to infiltrate the security team of which Blondel was a member.'

'Then you hired César Casta to do the job.'

'Not the kind of individual I enjoy doing business with. The man is one of those deeply undesirable characters from which my organisation aims to disassociate itself, in the longer term, but presently cannot.' Navarro put his hand on his heart, as though swearing an oath. 'I personally adore dogs. Mitzi, my Pomeranian, sleeps at the foot of my bed every night and I would happily shoot the man who tried to hurt her. On my mother's life, if I had known Casta intended to harm animals, I would never have employed him. I give you my assurance, not only will he and his associates never work for me again, but that they will face consequences for their actions. Prison will not be the end of the story for them.'

'César Casta is one thing,' Ben said. 'Petru Navarro is another.'

Titus Navarro took another sip of his drink, then let out a long, regretful sigh. 'This is a very painful subject. You obviously know that Petru is a blood relation to me, as our shared surname would indicate.'

'Your nephew,' Ben said.

'I'm sorry to say that's correct. My elder brother Saveriu, Petru's father, is no longer with us. Though it breaks my heart to say it, some might regard that as a good thing. Even my own father used to worry about what would happen when Saveriu took over the family business. My brother was wild and unpredictable, prone to mindless violence and destined to self-destruct from a young age. It was his enthusiasm for cocaine that finally did for him. The fatal overdose happened the year before my father passed away, and was what enabled me to take over in his place.'

Navarro gave a resigned shrug. 'Unfortunately, it seems that many of my brother's less desirable traits were passed on to his only child. Petru has always been a problem. From his youth, if he wasn't abusing drugs and alcohol he was abusing women. His is a long and ugly history of violence and debauchery that has seen him land in trouble more times than I care to remember. But family – you know how it is. Time and again I've bailed him out. Fortunes have been spent bribing police officials to look the other way. I knew there was little point in trying to steer my wayward nephew towards any sort of legitimate occupation. He would only cause more trouble, and moreover he would do it out in the open where I could no longer protect him. And so I always found him small jobs to do within the confines of the family business, never anything too responsible. Even then he constantly embarrassed me by being undisciplined, clashing with his superiors, refusing to stick with the plan, going his own reckless way.'

Ben understood where this was leading. 'But despite all that, you gave him the job on Casta's crew.'

Navarro nodded. 'Every time he messed things up, he would beg me to give him one more chance to prove himself. And like a fool, I always relented. And so, yes, I confess that via my subordinates I exerted pressure on Casta to make him take Petru into his crew. I warned my nephew that this was his last chance. If he failed me this time, I would turn my back. Perhaps some part of me still believed he must have some good in him. Instead, to my dismay, in the aftermath of this disastrous operation I now learn that my degenerate nephew has killed an innocent man. It was one of Casta's people, Ángel Leoni, who informed us, calling from jail.'

'You must have been so upset,' Ben said. 'A man of your moral scruples.'

'I can't blame you for feeling hostile towards me. However, I implore you to accept that I'm being completely honest. These things I'm telling you, about my family and my business, I would never confess to anyone. Yes, I run a criminal enterprise, despite all my efforts to leave that world behind. We take things that don't belong to us. We exploit the weak and the innocent and deal in commodities like drugs and guns that do untold damage. We extort money and services from people using threats and intimidation. Sometimes we even have people physically beaten, when there's no alternative and they simply will not listen to reason. But my father's ways are not my ways. I took a personal vow many years ago that I would never take a person's life. I don't kill people.'

Ben said, 'Maybe you don't. But I do.'

There was a silence. Navarro paused for a sip of his drink, eyeing Ben with a thoughtful look. 'I'm aware of your extensive military record, or what little of it I was able to find in my investigations. And I know the look of a killer. I've seen it before and I can see it in you, now we've met face to face. But I also sense that you are a moral man, and a decent human being. Your love of your dogs, your deep loyalty to your friend, your concern even for the safety of a young woman you have never met, your compassion towards a man who betrayed you. I admire your strength, your courage and your integrity. It's the warrior code. I like you, Ben. I'd like to think that you and I have much in common, despite all our differences.'

'You can think what you like,' Ben said. 'It's of no consequence to me.'

'All the same, there's no reason why men like you and I should be in opposition. It seems to me there's a way to resolve this situation.'

Ben asked, 'Are you offering me a deal?'

'What I'm offering you is a token of my respect. I realise that I can never repay my debt to you, or amend the loss that you have suffered. But please tell me what I can do by way of reparation for my part in it.'

Ben said, 'Your nephew has to pay for what he did. You can stand aside and let me do what I came here to do.'

Navarro pursed his lips. 'That isn't quite what I had in mind. You're asking me for permission to kill my own kin. My brother's only son.'

'Either that, or get ready for a war,' Ben said. 'It's your choice. Petru is a dead man, either way.'

'You must surely realise that's a war that you could never win,' Navarro said. 'One man, alone, against all the power at my command? You wouldn't leave Corsica alive.'

'Maybe not,' Ben said. 'So be it. That changes nothing.'

'I see. That's unfortunate. I was hoping that I could prevail on you to agree to resolve this differently. Some financial arrangement, perhaps.'

'And Petru?'

'I would have said leave him to me, to devise some other way that he could be punished. I could have him exiled. Or I could keep him under house arrest, with my personal guarantee that he could never do anything like this again.'

Ben shook his head. 'I'm sorry, Titus. That won't wash. I don't want your payoff. And I don't trust guarantees.'

'I can see nothing I can say or do will deter you from your course.'

'Unless you kill me right now,' Ben said. 'Or try to. Call in the guys with the guns, and let's see how it goes down. I promise you one thing, though. If I don't come out of it alive, neither will you.'

'Neither of us wants that.'

'Not if there's another way,' Ben said.

Navarro sighed and looked downcast. 'It's a terrible business.'

'It is what it is,' Ben said.

'I don't even know where Petru has gone,' Navarro admitted. 'On his return home from France he briefly made contact with my elder son, Salvadore. But since then he's disappeared. He's not at his father's villa, where he normally resides. I doubt whether he has the money to rent another. In fact I happen to know that my nephew is quite broke. Meanwhile nobody at Bar Royale or any of my other places has seen him, and the team of men I have searching for him have found no trace.'

'You think he's avoiding you?'

'He must have realised that I would hardly approve of his actions. How long he thinks he can go on hiding from me, who can say?'

'What about other contacts?'

'There was a girlfriend, Maddalena. I have people watching her apartment but he hasn't gone there either. The only thing I know for certain is that he's still on the island. I have a contact within the police who would let me know instantly if he tried to leave. But Corsica is a big place. Petru is not just a creature of the city. He grew up running wild in the hills and forests, and knows the remoter parts of the island well. He could be anywhere.'

'If he's here, I'll track him down,' Ben said. 'It's what I used to do for a living.'

Navarro fell silent for a beat, staring down at the floor and looking suddenly exhausted. Ben saw a man who had been wrestling with an ethical dilemma that was tearing him apart. 'I warned Petru what would happen if he let me down again,' Navarro said. 'This was his last chance. Now, thanks to him, my own hands are stained with blood. He made me break my vow.'

'Then what's it to be, Titus?' Ben said. 'Do I get a free hand in this, or do you and I go to war?'

The Corsican looked up at Ben with haunted eyes. Nodded a slow nod of mournful acceptance. 'You say my nephew is a dead man. Of course I know you're right. He only has himself to blame. After what he's done, he's already dead to me now. We've crossed a line that can't ever be uncrossed.'

'So let me find him. No interference from you or your soldiers. When it's done, I'll leave Corsica and you'll never hear from me again. That's a promise.'

Navarro said nothing for a beat. He shook his head. Ben

thought he was going to reject the whole proposition. But what the Corsican said next surprised him.

'No. I want to know when it's done. My men will give you a number to call. I expect there will be a body to dispose of?'

'That's not an unreasonable expectation,' Ben said.

'I would much sooner that the authorities were not involved. It would be preferable to make private arrangements. To keep it within the family, so to speak.'

'As you wish,' Ben said.

Navarro reached out his hand, and this time Ben took it.

'He's all yours.'

Chapter 44

Titus Navarro's men drove Ben back to Porto Vecchio in the black Mercedes. This time, the guns were nowhere to be seen. It was heading towards midnight now, and Bar Royale was still in full swing. Light and music spilled out onto the street as a steady stream of punters kept arriving, keeping the bouncers on the door busy. They were going to be two short for a while.

The men in the Mercedes dropped him off where they'd picked him up, and drove away without a word. Ben walked back to the Alpina, a little stiffly. Before heading back to the hotel he drove around Porto Vecchio looking for a late-night drugstore, where he bought a bottle of scotch and some basic medical supplies. On his return to the dark, quiet hotel he retrieved Storm from Laetitia's kitchen and took him back up to his room. The dog was bursting with joy to see his master again. There had been moments back there when it had seemed fairly unlikely that would ever happen. Ben knelt on the floor and let himself be slobbered over, hugging him tightly.

Some things made it worth coming back home in one piece.

Ben went into his little ensuite bathroom, stripped off his shirt and examined the big florid bruise across his ribs in the mirror. Pretty much everything hurt, but there was little to be done about a cracked rib, except to bind it up as well as you could and just deal with the pain. After taking a long, hot shower, he unravelled the whole roll of bandage he'd bought and spent a few minutes carefully winding it around his chest, good and tight, in overlapping layers. Once that was taken care of, he checked the bullet graze in his shoulder. It was healing fine, another scar to add to his collection. Next, his face. It had been a good punch and he was damn glad he hadn't taken the full force of it. His cheekbone was going to show up some pretty colours, but there was no apparent structural damage, no loose teeth.

'You'll survive,' he muttered to himself as he padded bare-foot to the bedroom. He sat on the bed, slurped some whisky from the bottle, and thought about where he was at now. He'd both gained something tonight, and lost something. Thanks to his discussion with Titus Navarro he now had carte blanche to deal with his problem without having to worry about the intervention of the mob – but he'd also expended his one and only lead, such as it had been, for finding Petru Navarro. On balance, he was pretty much back where he'd started.

Remembering what Titus Navarro had said about Petru's girlfriend Maddalena he briefly toyed with the idea of staking out her place, before dismissing it as of little value. Knowing his uncle and as anxious to avoid him as he seemed to be, Petru would probably have figured out she was being watched, and wouldn't go near the place. He wouldn't try to meet up with her anywhere either, for the same reason. In short, there was little chance of the Maddalena connection going anywhere.

But that was when Ben suddenly realised that he might have a better one. He reached for his phone.

It was half past midnight, but Jeff Dekker was a night owl. He picked up Ben's call on the second ring, instantly recognising the caller ID. 'Where are you, mate?'

'Jeff, do we still have the Christmas cards that were on the living room mantelpiece?'

'What the hell do you want to know that for?'

'I haven't got time to explain. Do we still have them or not?'

Jeff sounded nonplussed but he replied, 'Tuesday's tidied up the place. You know what he's like. I'd imagine they're all in a recycling bag, waiting to be picked up next Wednesday.'

Tuesday was big on recycling. Jeff would just have dumped the lot in an incinerator. Ben said, 'Good. Can you do me a favour? I need you to dig out the one from Madison Cahill and call me back with her new number, okay? She wrote it inside.'

'Madison Cahill. The American bounty hunter chick?'

'That's the one.'

Long experience had taught Jeff there was little point in asking Ben too many questions. Fifteen minutes later, he called back with the number.

Quarter to one in the morning in Porto Vecchio was 3.45 in the afternoon in San Diego, California. Ben dialled the number, and moments later he was hearing the familiar voice of his old friend Madison. The last time they'd seen each other was in Hawaii, at the beach home of her elderly father. He hadn't been in contact since Rigby's death.

She sounded happy to hear from him. 'Wow. Ben Hope. The one who got away. To what do I owe this sensational surprise?'

'You said to give you a buzz sometime. So here I am.'

'I'm glad you did. It's been so long. What's happening in your life?' News of the attack on Le Val obviously hadn't reached as far as San Diego.

'Oh, this and that,' he replied off-handedly. 'Nothing very exciting. Pretty dull and boring, in fact.'

Their paths had originally crossed in Belgrade, where Ben had been on the trail of some bad people who'd stolen a precious old music manuscript. His very first encounter with the black-haired American fugitive recovery specialist (she'd always hated being called a bounty hunter) had been on the wrong end of the Beretta 98 she was pointing at him, just moments before the two of them had got caught up in a running shootout and a car chase along the banks of the Sava River. Not long after that, they'd almost both died in a vicious gun battle at the home of a sadistic Serbian gangster called Zarko Kožul. It was safe to say that their brief acquaintance had been a fairly intense experience.

Madison chuckled. 'Why is it I have a hard time believing that a day in the life of Ben Hope could ever be dull and boring?'

'Have to get older and wiser sometime,' he said.

'Bullshit. You don't change.'

She didn't sound as if she'd changed much, either. Ben

could visualise her: the black biker jacket, the raven gypsy ringlets, the ballsy attitude.

'What about you?' he asked. 'How's it going, chasing after the world's lost treasures?'

Madison gave him all her news. She was involved in some major new projects and her business was firing on all cylinders, picking up where her father had left off. An early high point of his career, long before she was born, had been the discovery of one of several Nazi treasure trains reputed to exist. It had been hidden underground in a collapsed tunnel deep in the heart of Poland, all eight of its carriages loaded to the roof with bullion, artwork and 1940s paper currency. The cargo's value had been in excess of $50 million, which in 1974 was worth considerably more than it was today. Rigby had netted a staggering thirty per cent of the cash and used it to found the little empire that Madison had now inherited. Now, a little bird had put her on the trail of what might turn out to be another of the legendary Nazi treasure trains. 'Imagine striking lucky a second time. Dad would have been proud.'

'Genius must run in the family,' Ben said.

She laughed. 'I had a good teacher.'

Madison had been closely involved in her father's adventures from childhood, often accompanying him on his trips all over the world, and so taking over the reins from him had been a natural progression. 'All the same, it's been a hell of a learning curve. But it beats tracking down scumbag bail fugitives and getting into firefights. I only wish that Dad could be here to help me. I still miss him every day. Keep expecting him to walk into the office, telling me all the things I'm doing wrong.'

'I was sorry that he passed away,' Ben said. 'You got my card?'

'Yeah. It was sweet. I was kind of hoping you might be in touch a little more often, though. But that's how it goes, I guess. Story of my life. Are you seeing anyone?'

'Not currently.'

'Then maybe there's hope for me yet. Planning a trip out west any time soon?'

'Perhaps one day,' he replied. 'Right now I'm in Corsica.'

'Doing what?'

'Looking for something,' he told her. 'Actually that's the reason I thought of you. It's kind of up your street.'

'Ah. I might have known it wasn't my fabulous charms you were thinking of. Well, sure, glad to help if I can. Shoot.'

The most convincing made-up stories were often half true. Ben told her about the medieval church they'd been excavating at Le Val. She was fascinated to hear about the discovery of the gold cross. 'That's awesome. Dad would have been thrilled.'

'So was the burglar who pinched it.' Leaving out the more dramatic details, he explained how a thief had broken into the house and made off with the artefact.

'What a piece of shit,' Madison said, getting hooked deeper into the story. 'So this guy's Corsican, I'm guessing?'

'I've managed to track him as far as Porto Vecchio,' Ben said, being deliberately vague. 'But now the trail's gone cold.'

'Bad deal. I'd like to kick his ass, too.'

'I'm only interested in getting the cross back, if I can,' Ben lied.

'Who is this light-fingered sonofabitch anyway, some kind

of antiquities specialist? How did he know you had it? Insurance company inside job? There's plenty of crooks out there who'll steal pieces to order, if they know what they're looking for.'

Ben replied, 'No, he's just an opportunist lowlife with no knowledge of what he's taken. Apart from the fact that it's made of gold.'

'Yeah, well, you don't have to be much of an expert to recognise that,' Madison said. 'Gold has a way of grabbing people's interest. And you say this happened just a few days ago?'

'He's not been back in Corsica long. Unless he managed to offload it on his way down through France, I'm betting he still has it with him.'

She sounded thoughtful. 'Hmm. In which case, seems to me like your guy is going to need to go to a local fence to get the best deal.'

'That's what I was thinking too,' Ben said. 'And it's the reason I called. Are you still in contact with your old pal Ulysses?'

Chapter 45

Rigby Cahill's treasure-hunting operation had depended on a global network of contacts, not all of them legal and above board. The most shadowy of the bunch, but the most reliable and profitable to Rigby, had been a highly specialised art and antiquities fence, a legend in the business known only by the name 'Ulysses'. He'd been based in Bucharest, though he'd handled business all over the world. He was rumoured to be Romanian but apart from that, nobody had seemed to know anything about him. Not even Rigby Cahill had known the secret of his real identity, though he'd trusted the man implicitly and they had enriched one another through the years. Back when Ben and Madison had been running around Serbia together, it had been the mysterious Ulysses who had provided the information that led to the recovery of the music manuscript.

'It's been a while since I last heard from him,' Madison said. 'But if anyone could help you track down this hot property of yours, it's him. He knows everyone in that world.'

Ben asked, 'Can you put me in touch with him?'

'Sure, I might still have his contact details somewhere. I'll get him to give you a call. But be careful what you wish for. He doesn't do this for pleasure. He's gonna want a cut of its value. Even if you're not selling.'

'That won't be a problem,' Ben said. If Ulysses could help Ben locate the fence to whom Petru took the cross, then maybe that connection could trace another connection back to Petru himself. In which case, then the Romanian could name his price. If the money wasn't in Ben's account to pay for it, then he'd remortgage Le Val. It didn't matter.

They talked for a short while longer, and then Madison left him with the promise that she'd try to locate the Romanian and pass on Ben's number. 'Guess I'll hear from you again sometime.'

'You never know,' he replied. 'Good luck finding your train.'

'Hey, if I run into any problems there, maybe I'll give you a call.'

'I owe you one. You know where to find me.'

When the call was finished, Ben reclined on the bed, stretched his aching muscles, closed his eyes and tried to sleep, but for the rest of that night he was haunted by jumbled and troubling images of death and pain. He couldn't tell if it was the death and pain that were already in his wake, or the death and pain that still lay in his path. By five in the morning he was up again, standing at the rail of his little balcony and smoking Gauloises as he gazed out across the rooftops sloping down towards the bay, at the moonlit sea beyond. Behind him inside the room, his phone lay silent on his bed. Every so often he glanced back to it, wondering whether Ulysses would ever call. Six a.m. in Bucharest. Romania was one hour ahead.

The phone remained silent.

The sunrise found him on the same lonely, deserted stretch of beach he'd walked along the previous day, throwing a piece of driftwood for Storm to chase, watching the dog run full pelt along the sands and splash in the sizzling surf, and wishing he could run with him. It was that feeling of being in limbo that made Ben feel so restless and agitated. Waiting was the worst, always had been; whether it was the anxious pursuit of critical information or the lull before the storm of battle. Ben had spent half his SAS career waiting, all psyched and kitted up, sometimes for days on end, only to have to endure the order to stand down.

If Ulysses didn't call, he didn't know what the next phase of his plan could be. Set up home in Porto Vecchio until Petru Navarro resurfaced somewhere. Scour every bar on the island, kick down the door of every scumbag who'd ever so much as spoken two words to the man. Risk damaging his pact with Titus Navarro by collaring his son Salvadore and find out if he knew more about Petru's whereabouts than he was letting on. Ben worked through a dozen possible strategies as he trudged the sand, Storm thundering excitedly back and forth along the beach, but nothing seemed to offer much promise of success. He walked slowly back to the hotel and ate a light breakfast in Laetitia's empty dining room with his phone on the table in front of him. Eight in the morning in Corsica was 9 a.m. in Bucharest.

Ulysses didn't call.

Ben returned to his room, smoked another cigarette, unwound his bandage, took another shower, towelled himself

304

dry and replaced the bandage. Another long hour dragged by. Nine in the morning was 10 a.m. in Bucharest.

Ulysses didn't call.

By eleven o'clock, Ben was walking through the winding medieval streets of the old town, not sure if he was killing time, wasting it, or implementing a clever plan to surprise Petru Navarro in the act of wandering incognito around Porto Vecchio, hiding in plain sight. Coincidences like that could happen, once every couple of million years or so. He returned to the café terrace he'd visited yesterday, sat at the same outdoor table in the warm winter sunshine and drank another cup of the same variety of espresso. He placed his phone in front of him, next to his cup, but the phone refused to ring. Midday came and went. Ben wasn't hungry. Twelve-thirty was half past one in the afternoon in Bucharest. Still no Ulysses.

Sometimes you have to genuinely give up on a thing before fate can intervene to make it happen after all. By ten to one, Ben was becoming more and more certain that Ulysses wasn't going to call, and turning his mind to other options.

And then, at precisely one o'clock, 2 p.m. sharp in Bucharest, the phone began to ring.

The man's voice on the other end of the line was crackly and deep, flavoured with a thick accent that was unmistakably Eastern European. 'This is Ulysses. I gather from our mutual friend that you require my help in a matter of business.'

Chapter 46

Soon afterwards, Ben was back on the road again. This time he was cutting westwards across to the opposite side of the island and further up-coast, a drive of nearly three hours. His destination was the port city of Ajaccio, which was Corsica's capital and largest population centre, as well as being home to a certain gentleman by the name of Rocco Vanucci, whom Ben had never heard of until today, and likely never would have if not for Madison's underworld connections.

According to the all-knowing Ulysses, Vanucci was the only fence in Corsica who would be even remotely capable of dealing with such a high-end item as Ben was trying to track down. He was well known to the criminal underworld for his magical way of converting certain kinds of hot property – pilfered jewellery, artwork and other ill-gotten articles that were often virtually impossible for the ordinary criminal to sell on the black market – into ready cash, for a percentage. It was rumoured in certain circles that he'd been peripherally involved in the 2011 theft of three priceless Renaissance paintings from Ajaccio's Musée des Beaux-Arts, which was thought to have been carried out by members of the Corsican Valinco, Brise de Mer and Venzolasca crime gangs.

Vanucci was fairly well known to the police as well. But despite multiple past arrests on suspicion of dealing in stolen goods, he had never been charged, let alone convicted. As Ulysses pointed out, the fact that he kept getting away with it wasn't necessarily down to any great brilliance on his part, since the crime detection rate in the lawless land of Corsica was more or less on a par with Mexico's.

In his heyday, Vanucci had been making a lot of money, which he'd enjoyed spending, and he was known for his tendency to be rapacious in clawing back as much commission as he could from his deals. The problem was that trends and fashions change, even in the world of crime. Having enjoyed a spate of lucrative art thefts over a period of a decade or so, in recent years there just hadn't been enough of that specialised kind of skulduggery going on in Corsica to keep Rocco in the manner to which he'd become accustomed. Murder was what the crooks on the island did best – Corsica had the highest rate of it in Western Europe, which dovetailed nicely with the relative inefficiency of their police force when it came to actually catching anyone. But the murder business didn't pay much to a man like Rocco. The combination of declining opportunity and a nasty gambling addiction had resulted in him falling on harder times. Nonetheless, rumour had it that he was still very much in the game, and his reputation among the underworld remained solid.

'There is no doubt in my mind,' Ulysses had informed Ben over the phone, 'that if your opportunist thief was in the market to pass along a valuable, historic piece such as you describe, Rocco Vanucci would be his top choice, if not his only choice.'

On the matter of payment in exchange for all this information, it had turned out that Madison was wrong. Ulysses had been happy to offer his services free of charge, seeing as Ben was a friend of the daughter of the late, great Rigby Cahill. The Romanian had even gone so far as to offer to reach out to Vanucci and set up a meeting between them, but Ben had gratefully declined. He didn't want Vanucci to know he was coming.

It was approaching five in the afternoon by the time Ben reached Ajaccio. As far as he could see, the city was almost a larger carbon copy of Porto Vecchio: the same red-roofed old buildings tightly clustered around the winding streets that rose steeply up from the port, the same broad vista of blue sea, amazingly vivid even in wintertime; the sweep of sandy beaches along the Gulf of Ajaccio, the harbour with its many piers dotted with boats of all shapes and sizes; the palm trees and the ever-present looming green mountains in the background. The address Ulysses had given him was in the downtown area of the city, which was mainly concentrated in a densely populated strip along the coast, the rest being mostly suburban sprawl. Ajaccio's most famous son, a certain Napoleon Buonaparte, had been responsible for many of the vast structural improvements to the old city, which was originally sited on marshland.

A veritable font of knowledge, that Ulysses.

Rocco Vanucci lived on the third floor of an unprepossessing apartment building on a hilly street with a narrow view of the port in the distance, sandwiched between an even dingier-looking brasserie and a store selling refrigeration and air conditioning equipment, across the street from a tobacconist's shop. Washing lines were strung from the apartment building's balconies, clothes flapping in the light sea breeze. It wasn't exactly the abode of a successful criminal mastermind. Ulysses hadn't been kidding when he'd said Vanucci had fallen on hard times.

Ben parked the car a distance away for discretion's sake, clipped Storm up on his leash, and they walked back to the apartment building. From the entrance foyer Ben could hear the blare of music and the crying of a baby drifting down the stairway. The residents' mail boxes in the foyer looked as though someone had tried to attack them with a screwdriver. A hand-scrawled sign sellotaped across the lift doors said ASCENCEUR HORS DE SERVICE, but Ben didn't think he'd have trusted it anyway. He and Storm climbed the stairs to the third floor. Ben hadn't known whether to expect trouble, but he had his pistol cocked and locked and tucked in the waistband of his jeans, out of sight below the hem of his leather jacket. Better to have it and not need it than to need it and not have it, a wise axiom that had been proven many times.

At the end of a dim, faintly musty-smelling corridor with a flickering light, they reached the door of Vanucci's apartment. Ben could hear a radio playing from within. Someone was home. Ulysses had said that the fence lived alone, as far as he knew. Ben was glad of that, because if Vanucci was unwilling to talk to him he might have to get rough. He checked his details one last time, then raised his fist to thump on the door. That was when he saw the door was hanging open a crack. The flimsy frame was splintered where the lock had been forced, and recently judging by the freshly exposed wood.

Things like that were never a good sign.

Getting a bad feeling, Ben gently nudged the door open wider and peered through into the apartment's narrow hallway. The sound of the radio was louder inside. He stood very still, listening for any other sounds, but could hear nothing.

He called out 'Rocco Vanucci? Hello? Anyone home?'

No response. Ben slipped the pistol from his jeans. He motioned for Storm to sit and stay, and the dog instantly dropped down to his haunches, waiting intently for the next command. Ben padded into the apartment with the gun pointing forward, his thumb riding the safety catch. The nude pin-ups on the walls of the hallway tended to confirm that the fence lived alone, unless he had a very tolerant spouse. There was a tiny, grubby kitchen to one side of the passage, a bathroom at the far end. To the right of the bathroom, another door led to a living room, and that was where Ben found Rocco Vanucci.

Chapter 47

There was no longer any point in calling out the man's name, because he wasn't in a fit state to hear a word. Vanucci's skinny, middle-aged form was lying sprawled out and inert on the living room floor next to the wreckage of a smashed coffee table and an overturned TV console unit.

Ben stepped quickly over to him. At first he thought that Vanucci was dead. There was blood all over his face and on the crown of his balding head, and more of it spattered down the front of the ripped T-shirt he was wearing. His eyes were shut and his tongue was hanging out of his badly split lips. He seemed not to be breathing. Ben felt for a pulse and found it, weak and erratic. Vanucci was alive, but he'd been savagely beaten up. And it hadn't happened long ago, because the blood on him was still fresh. Maybe less than an hour.

Ben quickly checked the rest of the apartment. There wasn't much else to it: just a single bedroom that smelled of unwashed sheets. Whoever had violently assaulted the man in his home was long gone. The apartment hadn't been ransacked, the way it would have if someone had been here looking for something of value. On the bedside table Ben found a stack of casino winnings receipts for various paltry amounts. It looked as if Vanucci was still up to his old habits, and probably losing far more than he won.

Ben returned to the unconscious body and crouched beside it, thinking hard about who had done this, and why. An avowed crook like Vanucci was always liable to get himself beaten up. It was an occupational hazard. Hence, the potential chances of just happening to find him all messed up like this at any time weren't completely remote, especially for someone with a gambling problem who might owe money to the wrong kind of folks. But something about the timing of the attack suggested to Ben that this could be more than a coincidence.

Only one person could decide the answer for sure. Ben reached into his bag for the small cellophane-wrapped package that until earlier that day had been hidden at the back of Laetitia's fridge. Being all cartilage and skin, Petru Navarro's ear hadn't decomposed as badly as another body part might have, but even so it had certainly seen better days, and wasn't very pleasant to handle. However there was still enough of its original owner's scent on it for a super-sharp German shepherd nose to pick up. Ben held the ear out for the dog to sniff and said, 'Find him, Storm. Find him.'

When he was two years old, Storm had undergone the basics of bomb detection training. No man-made gadgetry in the world could locate explosives and ordnance like a well-trained canine, and German shepherds were naturals at the job. Once he had the scent imprinted on his olfactory memory, he would track its source with uncanny accuracy and then alert his handler to it by lying down beside it and giving a bark. Ben had expanded his training to include human scents, and they often used him at Le Val to demonstrate the usefulness of dogs in fugitive tracking. Nobody ever evaded him.

The shepherd sucked the odour of the putrid ear deep into his nasal passages and went to work, sniffing all over the apartment with the focus and concentration of a fighter pilot. Tail wagging, nose to the ground, he minutely investigated every corner of every room, but kept coming back to Vanucci and tracing circles from the entrance and along the hallway to where the man was lying. It took him under a minute to map out the trail of the attacker and locate the source where the scent was strongest, on the victim himself. Storm dropped prone next to Vanucci's unconscious body and looked expectantly up at Ben with a bright, happy bark, exactly how he'd been taught. This was the most fun game in the world for him.

For Ben, it was ninety-five per cent proof that the ear's owner had been right here in this apartment within the last hour or so. The other five per cent could only be confirmed by Vanucci. Which wasn't going to happen, until the guy received urgent medical attention. And either way, Ben couldn't just leave him like this, or he might die.

He pulled out his phone, dialled 17 and called the attack in to the police, giving no name. His phone was a burner and the number couldn't be traced to him. When that was done, he used a piece of toilet tissue from the bathroom to carefully wipe down door handles and anything he might have touched, then slipped away from the apartment and left the building. Just a man casually walking his dog along the street, the most innocuous thing on earth. He crossed the road to buy some cigarettes at the tobacconist's shop, and chatted amicably for a few minutes with the proprietor. Once again Ben's false name for the occasion was Paul, and he was from out of town. The shopkeeper admired Storm and kept petting him. Dogs, the great unifier.

'Hey, what's up?' the shopkeeper said, interrupting himself as they heard the pee-paw of sirens coming down the street. They stepped out of the shop to watch the police car lurching to a halt outside the apartment building opposite, with an ambulance in tow. 'Someone must be in trouble,' Ben said. They watched as the two officers from the cop car and two paramedics from the ambulance hurried inside the building. A few minutes later, the injured man was being brought down on a gurney and the paramedics were loading him into the ambulance.

'Another heart attack, I'll bet,' the shopkeeper said. 'Everybody seems to be getting them these days.'

'You know the guy?' Ben asked. If the shopkeeper knew Vanucci, he might have seen his mystery visitor, too.

'Yeah, I've seen him around, but he keeps himself to himself and doesn't come in here,' the shopkeeper replied. 'They'll probably cart the poor sucker off to the Misericordia. God help him. My brother Patrice was there, came out worse than he went in.'

The Centre Hospitalier de Notre Dame de la Miséricorde was the general hospital in Ajaccio. By the time the ambulance set off with the battered Rocco Vanucci in the back, Ben had got to his car and followed at a discreet distance.

On arrival at the hospital, he watched the paramedics unload the patient and a team of medics wheel him inside. He reckoned it would be a while before Vanucci would be in a fit state to receive visitors. That meant more waiting, but Ben was here now and he had nothing better to do, nowhere else to go.

About an hour after the patient had been admitted, a police car rolled up outside the reception entrance. Ben watched from a distance as a couple of uniforms, not the same two who'd been at the apartment, went inside. Through the glass doors he saw them stroll up to the desk and speak to a receptionist. Someone in a white coat came up to speak to them, and then Ben lost sight of them. Just a few minutes later, the cops re-emerged, got back into their car and drove off. Ben waited another thirty minutes, decided the coast was clear, then ambled up to the entrance and pushed through the doors.

Posing as a concerned friend of Rocco's, he eventually managed to speak to a doctor who told him the patient was lucky to be alive, but now conscious and stable. 'Whoever did this really went to work on him. The police were here before, asking questions. Maybe you should be talking to them.'

'I don't know anything about it,' Ben said. 'I only just found out what happened. Can I see him?'

'He's in room 27, first floor. But absolutely no visitors for the moment. You'll have to come back tomorrow. That's what I told the police, too.'

'Of course. Thank you, doctor.'

Chapter 48

Getting past the medical staff was easy. Ben took the fire escape up to the first floor and wandered down an empty corridor. How he hated the smell of hospitals. He'd been spending far too much time in them lately. This particular one looked as though it hadn't been modernised much in the last fifty-odd years, and had been running on a shoestring budget for even longer. Everything was broken, doors closed with tape, linoleum cracked and peeling off the floor. A Third World feel about the place. Ben could understand why some people wanted to see Corsica liberated from being a second-rate province of France and get on its feet as an independent nation.

Finding a staff-only door, he slipped inside unseen and found what he was looking for in the storeroom the other side of it. He re-emerged a few moments later wearing a blue orderly's uniform and pushing a clattering trolley laden with bedpans, whistling a merry little tune as he nonchalantly followed the signs for the patient rooms. None of the other hospital staff paid him any notice, apart from a pretty nurse who smiled as he went by.

Ben watched from down the corridor as another nurse emerged from the door of patient room 27. When she was gone, he peeked cautiously through the door and saw to his satisfaction that the patient was in there on his own. Ben darted into the room and quietly closed the door.

Rocco Vanucci was lying on his back with his head and shoulders raised on the inclining bed. The parts of his face that weren't covered with dressings were mottled purple and puffy. His split lips bristled with stitches. The medics had put a splint over his broken nose and his nostrils were stuffed with cotton wool. One eye was swollen up like an Easter egg. The other one rolled sideways to peer at Ben as he entered the room.

Ben stepped up to the bedside and said, 'Hello, Rocco. Glad to see you doing better. You won't remember me, but I was in your apartment earlier. Fenced any tasty stolen antiques lately?'

Vanucci's one good eye stared at him in confusion, then opened wide with terror. He could hardly move from all his injuries, but tried to shrink away from Ben, reaching out in panic to press the bedside call button for distressed patients to ring for a nurse. In Corsica, gangsters must really send thugs into hospitals dressed as orderlies to finish off their victims.

Ben moved around the bed and gently blocked his arm. 'Relax, Rocco. I'm not here to hurt you. I just want to talk, okay?'

Breathing hard and staring at him wildly through his one open eye, Vanucci managed to croak, 'Who . . . are you?'

'I'm the owner of something that was taken,' Ben told

him. 'And I'm looking for the man who took it. You know what I'm talking about, don't you? You won't come across many pieces like it.'

Vanucci was rigid with anxiety. He mumbled something indistinct, the stitched, swollen lips making it hard for him to talk. Ben had to lean close to make out what he was saying.

'I don't . . . have it. I swear.'

If Ben had been ninety-five per cent certain before, now it was closer to ninety-seven. 'All right, let's say that you don't. The police are keen to know who worked you over like this. So am I. Can you identify your attacker?'

'Said . . . his name was Rossi,' Vanucci managed to say, slurring his words badly and wincing at the tug of the stitches. 'Lucca Rossi. Never . . . seen him before.'

'Did you get a good look at him?'

Vanucci tried to nod his head, groaned at the pain from his contused neck and shoulders. 'Kind of.'

Ben asked, 'Would you say he had any obvious defining features? Something you'd easily recognise?'

Vanucci nodded again, more carefully. 'He's . . . only got . . .'

'Only got what?'

'One ear,' Vanucci said.

And that was the clincher. Proving that Storm had been right on the money. The ninety-seven per cent had just gone up to 101.

'His real name is Petru Navarro,' Ben said. 'You might not have heard of him, but I'll bet you recognise that surname.'

Another slow, painful nod. Of course Vanucci recognised

it. Everyone even loosely associated with the Corsican criminal underworld would know it all too well.

'Let me tell you what I think happened here,' Ben said. 'I think our friend Petru came to you looking to make a deal. He's got a valuable antique gold cross that's burning a hole in his pocket because he doesn't have the contacts to sell it, and you've got a reputation for laundering those kinds of items into nice, clean cash, for a fee. So he got hold of your number, and called you to arrange a meeting at your place. Except I think that when you clapped eyes on the merchandise, being the grasping little crook that you are and business obviously not being too great these days, you fell back on your old ways and cranked up your commission fee a little too high. My guess is that Petru didn't appreciate that very much. He can get a little wild sometimes. Takes offence easily, flies off the handle and likes to hurt people. Tell me, Rocco, am I on the right track with any of this?'

Another slow, painful nod.

'So I think now Petru's decided to take his business elsewhere. Except the chances are he won't have much luck, because everyone knows that you're the top man in Corsica. In fact, when it comes to this kind of merchandise, you're the one and only. Correct?'

Somewhere under all the swelling and bruises, a tiny smirk of satisfaction flickered across the visible parts of Vanucci's face.

'And I'd also bet that you'd like to hurt him back, for what he did,' Ben said. 'So do I, for my own reasons. I'm not interested in the cross. I want him. And if you help me get what I want, I can help you get your own back on this bastard, in a way that he'll never be able to touch you or anyone else again. All I need from you is one thing. You'd better be up for it.'

The smirk of contentment on Vanucci's battered face hadn't lasted long. It quickly melted back into a look of pure terror. Ben knew what he was thinking, now that he knew who'd attacked him. He shook his head, the fear stronger than the pain. 'The Navarros—'

'Don't worry about comeback from them. Petru was never a major player in their organisation. Now he's out on his own. The Navarro gang have cut him loose, and they've got people looking for him because of something he did. That's the reason he gave you a fake name. Now—' Ben took out a phone, not his own. 'What you can do for me, you can do with just one call. I lifted this from your apartment, because I thought it might come in handy. I'm guessing that one of these incoming calls is Petru's number. You're going to call it back, and tell him that you're really sorry that things went the way they did. You're going to beg his forgiveness for being disrespectful, and tell him you've reconsidered his kind offer and you'll agree to act as his fence for a much-reduced commission. As a matter of fact, it's such an honour and a privilege to do business with a man of his calibre that you'll gladly do it for free. Then you're going to set up another meeting with him, just as soon as you get out of hospital.'

Vanucci was so frightened that even the liver-coloured bruises on his face had turned pale. 'No, no, I can't—'

Ben smiled. 'Oh, yes, you can, Rocco. And you will. Because

if you don't, then what I'll do to you will make what Petru did look like a gnat bite by comparison. You won't leave this hospital for six months.' He handed him the phone. 'Now get talking.'

Chapter 49

Rocco Vanucci was highly reluctant, but did as he was told. He dialled back one of the numbers on his phone, and Ben made him put the call on speaker so he could listen in. It rang and rang, and for a moment Ben was worried that Petru might have been using a one-off phone to make the call, and had since disposed of it. But then a man's voice answered. It sounded tinny and thin coming from the phone, but Ben's heart quickened knowing that he was hearing the voice of Victor's murderer for the first time.

Vanucci dutifully repeated everything Ben told him to say, humble and contrite, speaking slowly and awkwardly through his painful lips. Yes, Signor Navarro. No, Signor Navarro. While he talked, Ben stood close by with one eye on the door and his fingers crossed in case a nurse picked this moment to show up. If that happened, he might have to gag and bind her. He hoped it wouldn't.

'How did you figure out who I was?' Petru asked suspiciously. Ben had anticipated that question. This was the weakest part of his plan, because if Petru smelled a rat, even just a whiff of one, he could simply hang up the call and disappear forever. But then, the man had no way of knowing that Ben was looking for him. And why would any of the Navarro gang know to chase up the Rocco Vanucci connection? Ben was fairly confident that Petru would fall for the subterfuge.

'Your . . . ear, Signor Navarro,' Vanucci replied, looking anxiously at Ben. This was the line he'd been instructed to use, if asked. 'Word gets around. I heard that you had . . . an accident. That's how I realised Lucca Rossi was really you.' He was talking so much that the stitches in his lips were bleeding and tears of pain were streaming from his one open eye. But with a volatile short-tempered psychopath on the line and Ben watching over him with a steely eye and ready to carry out his own threats, poor Vanucci had no choice but to stumble on. 'If I'd . . . known sooner, I would never have asked . . . for more money, I swear. I hope . . . you can forgive me.'

'Huh,' Petru Navarro grunted dismissively. He seemed to be swallowing their deception. It was amazing what a little ego massaging could do. 'The ear, it's just a scratch. Nothing I can't handle. So you say you'll do the business for free, yeah?'

'Absolutely, Signor Navarro. It would . . . be an honour.'

'All right then, it's a deal. You're showing the proper respect, Rocco. That's good. But I never forgive anyone who tries to fuck with me, so you'd better be on the level. Fuck with me, I won't go easy on you like I did before. I'll gouge your fucking eyes out. Then I'll shove my fist down your throat and rip your fucking heart out through your mouth. Then I'll—'

'I'm a professional, Signor Navarro. Talk . . . to any of my former clients and they'll tell you the same thing. I can be . . . trusted.'

'You fucking better be,' the voice rasped.

There was a tense silence on the phone as Petru made his mind up.

'All right,' he said at last. 'I tell you what we're gonna do. I'll meet with you again. But not at your place. First, it's a scummy shithole and I don't hang out in scummy shitholes. Second, I never go to the same place twice. It's not good business. So I'll be by the steps of the Place d'Austerlitz at midnight tonight. You meet me there. I'll bring the merchandise. You get ready to get some real results, fast. This thing is worth a packet and I ain't waiting around to get what's coming to me, understand?'

Vanucci shot Ben a look of horror. 'Tonight? But I'm in . . . hospital, Signor Navarro. I'm all banged up. I can't just walk . . . out of here.'

'I don't give a flying fuck where you are, you worthless piece of garbage,' the voice yelled down the line. 'I say that's where I wanna meet, that's where you're gonna be. Or else you be ready to die, Rocco. Big time. Got it?'

'I'll . . . be there,' Vanucci replied mournfully. 'I promise. Signor Navarro, hello? Hello?' But the line had gone dead.

'He's going to kill me,' Vanucci said, slumping into his pillow. 'I know it. I can't hardly move, let alone be there at midnight.'

'Who said you were going anywhere?' Ben asked him.

Chapter 50

There were several public squares across France named after Napoleon's famous military victory in 1805 at Austerlitz. But only one that was situated right next to the coastal cave where the future emperor was said to have hung out as a boy, watching the ocean and perhaps dreaming of his immortal destiny.

Ajaccio's Place d'Austerlitz was a good choice for a clandestine nocturnal rendezvous. The square was flanked on all four sides by busy avenues and boulevards that made for a fast getaway in any direction, if needed. It was a wide open space where you could see anyone coming a long way off. At night the area was all brightly lit up with floodlights, focused on the statue of Napoleon that stood resplendent on his stone plinth, wearing his famous cocked hat, at the top of a long, broad flight of steps. The stairway cut up between steep rocky banks wooded with tall, bushy evergreen trees. A pair of imperial eagles perched atop stone columns flanked the foot of the steps, one column engraved with the date 1769 and the other 1821, marking the dates of the great dictator's birth and death.

It was at the base of the 1769 column that Petru Navarro stood waiting for his meeting with the fence. Petru had always been a great admirer of Napoleon, part of why he'd chosen this particular spot to meet. Now *there* was a man who didn't mess around getting what he wanted. This audacious motherfucker had conquered the world and would have gone on to even greater things if he hadn't been betrayed by a bunch of lousy traitors and cowards.

As a fellow Corsican and self-styled patriot, Petru had often thought about his own grand destiny and future conquest of the world. One that might have been slightly more modest in its scope than the great man's, but only slightly. With the blood of his illustrious grandfather Ghjaseppu Maria Navarro running in his veins, it seemed only right that one day he would take over the Navarro crime operation and turn it into a proper empire all of his own. Someone had to restore it to its former glory, before his namby-pamby uncle Titus wrecked the whole thing with his pathetic plans of going legit. What was wrong with the guy? If they went legit, then how the hell did they stand a chance of competing with the other crime gangs, like the Brise de Mer boys and the likes of the Valinco and Venzolasca families, who were otherwise being given a free hand to grab all the action for themselves? Uncle Titus's father and brother must be turning in their graves with shame.

Petru had long had his own ideas about exactly how he would run things. He felt strongly that his time had come. And now it was war. He was gonna take whatever cash Rocco Vanucci could get him for the gold cross, and he was gonna use it to hire enforcers to help him muscle his way back in, depose his uncle and take his rightful place at the head of the family. He still had a few loyal guys who supported his ambitions and would become his lieutenants in the reborn business operation.

One of the loyal was standing at the foot of the other eagle column. His name was Albertu Guerini, and Petru had brought him along tonight for a couple of reasons. First to watch his back, in case that sneaky piece of shit Vanucci tried anything in revenge for the well-deserved kicking he'd received earlier today. Then when Vanucci took charge of the precious merchandise that was nestling in Petru's back-pack, Albertu's strict orders were to stick to the little lowlife like glue until the cash was safely in their hands. He was a big, burly, intimidating sort of guy. Not too bright, obedient and unquestioning, completely trustworthy, happy to carry out acts of sadistic violence on command: the perfect henchman. Petru would have sent him in to beat Rocco up on his behalf, if it hadn't been that Petru enjoyed doing those things himself. So he'd made Albertu wait in the van while he kicked down Rocco's door and did the business.

Petru took particular pride in being the kind of leader who led from the front. When his time came, he would be a hands-on kind of crime lord, like his father would have been, like his granddaddy was.

It was a cold night. The winter days on Corsica could be warm, but the nights got chilly. There was a stiff breeze blowing in from the sea, making the trees around the monu-ment rustle. Petru and his henchman had been waiting here since ten to midnight. It was now ten past the hour, and still no sign of Rocco. Petru didn't like to be kept waiting like this. He was getting restless, pacing about the foot of the column and rubbing his hands to keep warm. His ear hurt like shit. He no longer wore a dressing on it, believing that exposure to the air would help it heal better. Besides, dressings were for women, children and *omosessuali*.

Twelve minutes past; and now Petru was getting seriously annoyed. He ripped out his phone and punched in Rocco's number. When the creep picked up he was going to say, 'Hey, you little turd. You're supposed to be here. Where the fuck are you?'

But instead the dial tone went on until the automated voice message kicked in to say there was nobody there to take the call. Unbelievable! Petru's blood began to boil at the thought that this little rat bastard would disrespect him like this. Another whispering rustle blew through the treetops as a stronger gust of wind came in off the sea. Petru turned towards Albertu to say, 'We give it five more minutes. If he's not here by then, we're going round to his place to kill this fucker. This time you can do it and I'll watch.'

But Albertu was no longer there.

Petru wondered where the hell he'd gone. The bright floodlights by the monument cut deep, dark shadows among the trees either side of the steps. He thought that maybe Albertu had wandered among the trees to take a piss. Which was not an acceptable reason to abandon your post like that.

'Albertu? Get your stupid big fat *culo* over here. We've got work to do. Albertu? Hey, I'm talking to you, man!'

No reply. Just the whistle of the wind and the rumble of late-night traffic in the background.

Petru stared angrily at the trees, but could see no movement. It was as if the shadows had just opened him up and swallowed him whole. Petru felt a tingle up the back of his neck. Something was wrong. Something was happening.

Petru was still carrying the pistol he'd used for the job with César Casta's bunch, the one he'd shot the dogs and the old man with. It was all topped up with fresh ammo now, a full mag plus one up the spout. He jerked the weapon from under his jacket and racked the slide.

That was when he heard the giggle coming from the top of the steps.

Chapter 51

Ben had turned up early, and he'd been watching the rendez-vous point from various angles for nearly an hour as he invisibly skirted around the edges of the Place d'Austerlitz. He was hidden behind the cover of a low wall a hundred yards away on the far side of the square when, a few minutes before midnight, the van turned up.

The vehicle was a plain white Fiat Ducato with only one working headlamp and a rattly exhaust. It pulled off Avenue Nicholas Pietri into the empty parking area at the eastern end of the square. As Ben watched, two men got out, slammed the doors shut and began to stride purposefully across the wide open space in the direction of the monument. One of them was tall, burly and broad, and either bald or shaven-headed, with the same kind of look about him as the bouncers at Bar Royale in Porto Vecchio. The other was shorter, with a baseball cap on his head, carrying a small rucksack that sagged from his shoulder as though it contained something heavy. He wore a lightweight black jacket. His body shape was squat and solid. Ben couldn't make out much detail at this distance, but he believed that he was looking at the same man he'd watched on a video surveillance monitor, killing Victor Vermont.

Rocco Vanucci's new business associates had arrived. The beaten-up old van they were driving didn't look like the conveyance of a big-time gangster. Ben remembered what Titus Navarro had said about his nephew being broke. The van tended to confirm that. It wasn't surprising that Petru appeared so anxious to milk every penny he could from what he'd stolen. Ben wasn't surprised, either, that he would bring a companion along for the rendezvous. If the heavy object in his rucksack was what Ben thought it was, Petru wasn't going to carry it around the streets without a henchman for protection. Nor was he about to hand his precious prize over to the likes of Rocco Vanucci, without a trustworthy aide to ensure the fence didn't abscond with it.

Things really weren't going too well for Petru. He might be worried about his precarious situation. Or maybe he wasn't, being a psychopath. Psychopaths had little sense of the consequences of their actions in the real world. Either way, he had no idea what was coming.

Ben went on watching as the pair took up their positions at the foot of the monument steps. The big guy went over to stand by the eagle column on the right, and the shorter one Ben believed to be Petru Navarro went over to the left. Petru unslung his rucksack and set it on the ground, but didn't venture more than a couple of steps away from it as he paced impatiently back and forth, frequently looking at his watch.

Ben skirted further along the side of the square, staying low behind the perimeter wall. When he was level with the foot of the monument steps, about forty yards to the right, he came to the break in the wall with the little path he'd scouted out earlier, leading up behind the right-hand eagle column with tree cover overhanging on both sides to form a dark tunnel of year-round foliage. The strong white light from the floodlights illuminating the Napoleon monument cast deep shadows that Ben could slip into, completely hidden, his presence utterly unsuspected.

This was his element. Enveloped in the shadows and the darkness he felt as comfortable as an ordinary citizen feels tucked up in a warm bed or lounging in a cosy armchair. He followed the path as far as the rear of the eagle column, then left it and padded stealthily among the trees, silent as a stalker, careful not to crack any small twigs underfoot. Moving the way only a trained man can move. The leaves overhead rustled softly in the breeze. Both of his opponents were certain to be armed. Ben had no intention of getting into a gun battle here tonight. His battle plan was to take the enemy out one at a time, quickly, quietly, discreetly. Neither of them would know what was happening until it was too late.

The big guy was first in line. As Ben crept through the shadows of the trees he could see him from the side now, just a few yards away. The big guy was still standing there with his arms folded, eyes front, gazing impassively out across the square. They were obviously expecting Rocco to come from that direction. Across to the other side of the steps, Ben could see Petru Navarro continuing to pace restlessly to and fro, increasingly agitated as the minutes crept past beyond the rendezvous hour.

Now Petru was getting out his phone to make a call, probably to Rocco, demanding where the hell he was and yelling at him for being late. Nobody would be answering. Rocco's phone was in pieces, somewhere in the sewers beneath Ajaccio.

Just then a stiffer gust of wind blew across from the sea and rustled through the trees overhead. With that sound diversion, Ben saw his chance to attack.

In two long strides he was up right behind the big guy, who was still completely unsuspecting of his presence. Ben's arms shot past either side of his head like a pair of striking cobras. With one hand clamped tight over the big guy's mouth to stifle his cry of shock and surprise, and the crook of the other arm wrapped vice-like around the guy's throat to cut off his airway, Ben jerked him backwards off his feet and dragged him into the trees the way a leopard drags a stricken gazelle into the long grass to finish off its kill. He was a large and heavy man and he struggled hard, but he stood no chance of resistance. Ben silenced him with three sharp blows to the head and then choked him off so that he fell quickly unconscious.

There was no time to secure him. And Ben wasn't inclined to show much mercy. He'd done that at Le Val, letting them all live. He'd had his own reasons for doing so, but those reasons no longer applied here on the enemy's home ground. Ben cupped his left hand under the big guy's stubbly chin, pressed the flat of his right palm against the back of his shaven head, and in one sharp angular twisting motion he snapped his neck. He let the limp body flop down dead among the shadows.

One down.

Next it was Petru's turn.

Victor's killer was off the phone. He'd turned round to say something to his crony, and realised that the big guy was no longer there. Ben heard him call out, 'Albertu? Get your stupid big fat *culo* over here. We've got work to do. Albertu? Hey, I'm talking to you, man!'

Ben stepped over Albertu's body and moved a little closer, to where he could see Petru more clearly through the trees without being spotted. In the glare of the monument flood-lights he could make out the red, ragged mess of the ruined ear below Petru's baseball cap. The injury looked badly inflamed and necrotic and infected. It must hurt like hell, but Petru's behaviour and body language showed little pain. Only a crazy person acted like that.

With no response coming from his buddy Albertu, now Petru was shifting from angry to jumpy, smelling danger and realising something was up. His right hand darted inside his jacket and came out holding a pistol. He pointed it towards the trees. He was closer now than Ben had ever been to him before. His shoulders were thick and bunched up under the glossy black material of his jacket. He had a wide neck, like a bullock, and a strong jutting jaw. His eyes darted left and right, scanning the shadows for movement but clearly not seeing any. Even so, a reckless crazy guy might easily start spraying bullets blindly into the darkness. And one of those bullets might easily find its mark, just by chance.

Ben drew his own pistol and lined the sights up square on Petru. He could have killed him then, so, so very easily. Revenge for Victor was just a flick of a finger away. One shot and it would be over, before Petru even knew what had hit him. Then Ben could return home to Le Val, be with his companions again and get back on with his life.

It wasn't that Ben didn't want those things. He did. But a quick, clean death with his boots on and a gun in his hand was far too easy, even glorious, an end to be granted to a man like Petru Navarro. Ben didn't want Petru to die like that. He wanted to take him away from here, somewhere quiet and private, so that they could talk. So that Petru understood precisely what was happening to him, and why. Ben wanted him to learn about the innocent old man that he'd murdered in cold blood. He wanted to tell Petru about the irreversible changes that Victor's senseless slaughter had brought upon the lives of the people who had loved him. About Célestine Charpentier, now grieving for the man she'd wanted to spend the rest of her life with. Jules Dampierre, mourning the loss of his best and oldest friend. So many happy future moments that had been dashed and destroyed forever. Then Ben wanted to tell Petru about the dogs that he'd raised from puppyhood and watched grow up into fine healthy animals, only to have to bury them with his own hands. He wanted Petru to know their names.

Ben wanted to explain all that to Petru, and he wanted to be able to watch his face and look deep into his eyes as he told him those things, searching for any tiny flicker of humanity or remorse in there. Only then would he kill him, with a single execution shot to the side of the head. It would be pitiless, surgical, colder and harder than glacier ice.

That was the death that Petru Navarro had coming.

Petru went on scanning the shadows of the trees, swaying

the muzzle of his gun left and right, hunting for any possible target. Ben moved a little closer again, barely breathing, still keeping the sights of his pistol lined up on his enemy's centre of mass.

Any moment now. Whichever way it went, it would be over quickly.

And then, everything suddenly changed.

Chapter 52

Petru suddenly froze rigid, as though a sound had caught his attention. His head snapped around to the side and he stared up the line of the flight of stone steps that led to the Napoleon monument.

In the next instant the sound happened again, and now Ben heard it too. It was the giggle of a young woman, coming from the direction Petru was looking. A pair of figures appeared at the top of the steps, next to the foot of the statue, clearly visible by the bright glare of the floodlights. It was a young couple, probably no more than teenagers, out for a midnight stroll in the park. Holding hands, messing around. The girl had long dark hair that caught the light as it waved in the breeze. She giggled again.

Petru burst into a run. Snatching up his rucksack he went flying up the steps two, three at a time, with explosive energy, gun in hand. Ben realised what his enemy's plan was, and tore out from the shadows of the trees to give chase. But Petru had a head start on him, and he was already more than halfway up the steps. He threw a look back over his shoulder and his eyes locked with Ben's, filled with recognition. They'd never met before, but Ben understood that Petru would have seen his photo from the Le Val website. Each member of César Casta's raid team would have needed to be able to identify the crippled guy they were targeting for the armoury keys. Now the crippled guy was here in Corsica gunning for him, and he wasn't crippled any longer.

Petru was nearly at the top of the steps, roaring at the teenagers like a lunatic and pointing his pistol. The kids were suddenly paralysed with terror. Enjoying a romantic night-time stroll one moment; now confronted with an armed madman rushing towards them. The girl screamed and clung to her boyfriend. Ben was chasing up the steps, but he was a long way behind. He pointed his gun for a shot at Petru, knowing even as he did it that at this upward angle the kids were right in his line of fire. He couldn't shoot. He kept running instead. A jolt of pain burned up his bad leg and he almost stumbled, but kept going, bounding up the steps at a sprint.

Petru had reached the top of the steps. The girl screamed again as the gun-toting maniac closed on them and clubbed her boyfriend viciously out of the way with the butt of his pistol. The young guy tumbled to the ground as Petru grabbed the girl and yanked her bodily around in front of him like a human shield as he turned to face the steps. His left arm clasping her tightly to his chest, he thrust the pistol over her shoulder to aim at Ben, who was three-quarters of the way up the steps and closing fast. The boom of the gun split the night, followed by the whine of the ricochet as Petru's wild shot cracked off the memorial steps. Ben gritted his teeth, ducked his head low and kept moving. He was afraid to shoot back in case he hit the girl.

Petru squeezed the trigger again, but he'd got a stovepipe blockage in his ejector port that stopped the gun from firing. He needed both hands to rack the slide and clear the jam, and momentarily had to let go of the girl, who twisted stumbling away from him. Ben saw his chance and fired once, but Petru's gun went off almost at the same instant. Ben flinched and his shot went wide, punching a small crater in the plinth of the Napoleon statue. Petru rattled off another stream of shots that forced Ben to dive down against the steps and press his head and body tightly against them as bullets whanged and whistled around him. Then the shots suddenly stopped coming. Ben surged back up to his feet and cleared the last few steps to the top. Now he was standing at the foot of the statue. The girl's boyfriend was on the ground, trying to get up, blood streaming from a bad gash to his head where Petru had pistol-whipped him.

Ben scanned left and right for Petru, his gun following the line of his eyes. He couldn't see him. Moving in the bent-knee crouching posture that combat operatives adopted to keep their head low, he darted around the back of the statue plinth ready to open fire. Petru wasn't there either, but the girl was.

She was lying curled up on the ground a few feet away from him. Her dark hair was spread out like a scarf, covering her face. She wasn't moving. Then in the bright illumination of the floodlights, Ben saw the shocking, vivid redness of the blood that was pooling fast under her prone body. His heart began to thud and for an instant he thought that the one shot he'd fired must have ricocheted off the plinth and hit her. But as he turned her over, he saw the wound pumping blood from her belly and realised she'd been knifed.

Petru was getting away, but Ben had no choice but to let him run. He crouched by the girl and tore at her clothing to expose the stab injury. It was only a small puncture, but the blade that made it had been long as well as thin, and it had gone deep. The blood was welling out fast. If he didn't do something quickly, she was going to bleed out and die. You couldn't tourniquet a stomach wound. All you could do was apply pressure, and hope that you could stem the flow. Ben pressed his fingers into the wound and felt the warm wetness of her blood all over his hands.

Petru was gone. It didn't matter. The girl was more important.

The girl's boyfriend was up on his feet now, staggering about with his hand to his head and groaning loudly. Ben yelled at him to phone for an ambulance. The kid froze at the sight of his girlfriend lying there, and the blood. Ben thought he was going to go into a state of paralytic shock – but then the young guy came to his senses and focused and whipped out his phone to dial up the emergency services.

The girl's hair had fallen away from her face. Her skin was pale under the floodlights and her breathing was shallow. Ben didn't know if she could hear him or understand, but he kept talking to her as he maintained pressure on the wound. The boyfriend was off the phone, and standing helplessly over them, slack-jawed with anguish. Ben said to him, 'What's her name?'

'Carla. I-Is she going to die?'

Ben shot him a fierce look that said to shut up. 'Carla,

you're going to be fine,' he said to the girl. 'You hear me? Hang on. You're doing great. Help is on its way. You're going to be fine.'

Help was on its way, but it seemed to take an eternity to get there. Ben's hands were slippery with blood as far as his wrists. He thought the flow had slackened. He kept up the pressure, and kept talking to her in the same reassuring voice the whole time. It was like Victor all over again. Except he was damned if he was going to let this one slip away from him. At one point she let out a rattly kind of gasp and her eyes seemed to glaze, and for a chilling instant he thought she was gone. He slapped her across the face, leaving a bloody streak, and she started breathing again. She tried to speak, but her words turned into a cough. Ben gently caressed her hair and said, 'Shh. Save your energy, Carla. Stay with me. You're doing fine. You're going to be okay.'

At last, the wail of sirens that had been growing steadily louder was here, and the lights of the ambulance spilled into the piazza. The minutes had seemed like hours, but their response time had actually been stellar. The ambulance driver was a hero. He mowed down a row of barriers so that he could drive into the square and get right up to the foot of the steps. The paramedics leaped out and swarmed up towards the monument. As they took over the scene, Ben stood up and backed off to let the professionals do their work. Carla was strong. She was a fighter. He believed that she was going to be all right. He knew she was.

The paramedics quickly got her on a stretcher, doing all they had to do with efficiency and concentration. All the while, the kid was babbling anxiously to them about how this crazy lunatic had appeared out of nowhere and attacked them, and how this guy here – pointing in Ben's direction – had saved her.

One of the paramedics glanced up from her work and said, 'What guy?'

The kid looked around to where the stranger had been standing a moment earlier, but there was nobody there.

Ben slipped quietly away from the scene while they were all intensely preoccupied with the girl. He wished he could have stayed with her, but the police would soon be crawling all over this place and it wouldn't be long before they found Albertu lying there down among the trees with his neck broken. Now was a good time to disappear.

He hurried from the monument in the direction he thought Petru must have gone. But hurrying seemed point- less, because his expectations of finding him were close to zero. So much time had gone by. Petru could be anywhere by now. Ben's carefully laid plan was in pieces and the trail had gone cold again.

Ben blamed himself for what had happened to Carla, because if only he'd taken the shot when he'd had the chance, none of this would have happened. The angrier Ben grew with himself, the faster he walked. He passed through more trees until he reached the far perimeter of the Place d'Austerlitz, and crossed over the wall to where Avenue Nicholas Pietri looped back around on itself to become Avenue de Verdun. He'd left the car just a couple of minutes' walk from here.

He wondered where Petru might have gone. Putting himself in the man's place wasn't easy, because it involved having to think like a psychopathic killer. But if Ben had been Petru, he might well have felt inclined to go straight from here to Rocco Vanucci's place, to kill him for his betrayal. Ben decided that was where he would go next. If that failed, he'd try the hospital. If he didn't find Petru at either of those places, then he'd have to admit that he was back to square one again.

He was deep in thought as he retraced his steps towards the car, and at first only absently registered the sound of more sirens. His initial thought was that it must be the ambulance speeding off from the scene with the injured girl. Or that it was the sound of police sirens incoming, as the cops rushed to the scene of the incident at Place d'Austerlitz. Then he realised that the two-tone ululating wail of the departing ambulance should be getting further away, and that the pee-paw screech of the approaching police response vehicles should be getting closer. But they weren't doing either of those things, because now it dawned on him that what he was hearing was happening *elsewhere* – the sound carrying from some distance away and remaining static, with neither the rise nor the fall in pitch created by the Doppler effect.

He slowed his walking place a little, listening more acutely. What he was hearing sounded as if it was taking place in different part of the city. Close enough to be clearly audible, but far enough away for it to be a separate incident happening. A fairly major incident, by the sound of it. Maybe accounting for the fact that the police were being delayed in responding to the stabbing.

It was as all these thoughts were swirling around in Ben's mind that the distant confusion of sirens was suddenly peppered with the staccato crackle of gunfire. A sound that he had heard enough times in his life for it to be pretty damned unmistakable.

He started racing more quickly towards the car.

Chapter 53

Whoever was the cunning, tricksy bastard who'd designed the cross back whenever in the day, Petru had to admit he'd invented a hell of a useful gadget. The girl's blood was still on the blade of the hidden dagger as he thrust it back into its gold scabbard, replaced the precious weapon in his ruck-sack and kept running.

Petru had no idea how the crippled guy could have found him. Just his luck; but right now there was no time to question it. He needed to get out of here, because for all he knew the crippled guy wasn't working alone. Petru thought of doubling back around the square to the van, but then remembered that Albertu had the keys. Anyway the fucking cops would soon be all over the Place d'Austerlitz, cutting off that means of escape.

What he needed was another vehicle. Beyond the trees at the edge of the piazza he vaulted a low wall and started running along the edge of Avenue Nicholas Pietri. Traffic flow was thin this time of night, but still steady. As the lights of a fast-moving car approached, Petru dashed out into the road with his gun pointing at the windscreen and braying at the top of his voice, 'STOP THE FUCKING CAR!' And had to leap out of the way to save himself when the car only accelerated straight towards him and then went roaring past.

Petru screamed at its disappearing taillights and was about to take a wild potshot at it, when the lights of another approaching car coming up behind made him turn. This one was moving much more slowly and hesitantly, and this time the driver screeched to a panicked halt at the sight of the gun-toting one-eared lunatic in the road. Petru ran around to the passenger side and wrenched open the door. The driver and lone occupant of the car was a beaky middle-aged guy who looked like a sales rep, in a cheap suit. His mouth was hanging open and he raised his hands off the wheel in supplication. 'Please don't hurt me!'

Petru dived into the empty passenger seat, poking the gun in the guy's face. 'Go! Move it, asshole!'

The driver shakily did as he was told, putting his hands back on the wheel and moving off at a snail's pace. He smelled of spirits. Probably returning home late via some bar, Petru thought. His night of fun was over. Petru jammed the gun against the side of his head and yelled, 'Come on! Step on it! Get me out of here!'

'Please don't hurt me,' the driver repeated in a mumble.

'I'll blow your fucking head off if you don't go any faster!'

The driver swallowed hard, pressed his foot down, and the city lights and traffic began to stream by more quickly. With the Avenue Nicholas Pietri behind them, now they were on Cours Général Leclerc, which led to the Avenue de Paris, a fast, arrow-straight tree-lined boulevard heading towards Place Foch and then the harbour. Petru's borrowed digs in Ajaccio belonged to an old buddy who was currently serving eight years in prison for armed robbery. His flat was a useful bolt-hole, but if the crippled guy was onto him, Petru worried about returning there. Hatching a new plan in his mind, he decided he would steal a boat. It was easy to do, especially this time of year when there were fewer people around the harbour. Petru could quickly slip off around the coast, where there were dozens of little coves and beaches where he could lie low until he could figure out his next moves. Which at some point would include paying a return visit to that treacherous little scumbag Rocco Vanucci. But not yet, not while the crippled guy was around. He was a problem Petru was going to have to deal with.

Petru still had the gun jammed up hard against the side of his terrified driver's head. The car was moving faster and faster, trees and parked vehicles and balconied apartment buildings and café terraces and shop awnings flashing by. The twinkling lights of the harbour were visible in the distance, at the bottom of the long straight. Now they were coming up to the intersection with Rue Rossi where the boulevard became Cours Grandval. Petru's thoughts were broken as a delivery truck suddenly appeared to their left and came shooting across their bows. His hijacked driver had plenty of time to brake and avoid a collision, but only now did Petru realise the beaky little guy was half drunk and barely in control of the vehicle at this speed. That was why he'd been driving so slowly before.

There was a squeal of brakes, a blare of horns, and the car went into a skid. The beaky guy recovered it, but only by sheer luck, and they shot through the intersection swerving and fishtailing all over the road. Petru screamed, 'Slow down, you fuck! You trying to get me killed?'

But the damage was done. The driver was pouring sweat and his nerves were so badly shredded that he no longer had any control. He gamely held on for another few hundred yards, but by then he couldn't keep it in a straight line. As they hurtled into Avenue de Paris with the Place de Gaulle on their right, he careered wildly across the road, narrowly avoided crushing a motorcyclist, ploughed into a metal railing, turned a complete three-sixty and came to a crunching halt against the trunk of a great fronded tree. With no seatbelt, Petru was launched violently into the dashboard and almost hit the windscreen. The whole front end of the car was crumpled up like an accordion. He managed to boot open the passenger door and staggered out clutching his precious rucksack.

Some late-night pedestrians had stopped to gawk and a couple of cars had stopped, their drivers getting out. Dazed and bloodied, Petru stormed around to the driver's side of the crashed car, ripped open the badly dented door, hauled the bleeding and injured beaky guy out of his seat and dumped him on the road, yelling, 'You drunken piece of shit! I'll kill you!' He was seeing red and nothing else in the world seemed to exist. He pointed his pistol and emptied five rounds into the guy's chest, just to teach him a lesson.

Panic and mayhem. Someone screamed. The small groups of onlookers scattered and ran, and the motorists who had been about to rush over to offer help dived back into their vehicles and fled. Standing over the dead body with the gun in his hand, blood spattered on his face and shirt and a look of animal hatred in his eyes, Petru screamed at them, 'Yeah, run and hide, you assholes!'

But Petru's unlucky streak had just taken a turn for the worse, because a police car containing two officers on their way to a stabbing incident at the Place d'Austerlitz just happened to be passing at that moment. The police car skidded to a halt by the kerbside and the two cops spilled out of it, guns drawn. One was an older sergeant, the other a youth fresh out of the police academy. The young officer spoke urgently on his radio while the sergeant yelled at Petru to drop the weapon and get down on the ground.

Petru laughed. He raised his pistol and fired two more shots. The sergeant took both bullets, one in the chest, one in the throat, and went down leaving a red smear against the side of the car. The rookie officer dived behind the cover of the front wing and returned fire, but his shots were rushed and wild. Petru stood planted where he was and blasted six more rounds at the police car, punching holes in the bodywork and fissuring the windscreen. The terrified young cop ducked down behind the car, then popped up to let off two quick shots. His first bullet shattered the large plate-glass window of a fashion boutique behind Petru, and the second passed through the sleeve of Petru's jacket.

At which point Petru decided things were getting too hot and fell back, firing as he went. He stumbled up the kerb to the smashed frontage of the boutique and scrambled into the window display, battered aside the semi-nude female mannequins that stood in his way and stormed deeper into the shop. The lone officer should have waited for backup, but made the plucky decision not to let the shooter escape, and pursued him inside.

And Petru was waiting for him there. As the young cop hunted through the darkness of the boutique, Petru came at him out of the shadows and thrust the long, slim stiletto blade of the golden cross dagger through his neck. The young cop was dead before he even started to fall. Petru wiped the blade on his uniform. He was liking this dagger more and more. When the time came, he planned on using it on the crippled guy as well. His gun was low on ammo. He tossed it away, ripped the police-issue automatic and spare mags from the young cop's belt, and lurched back outside into the night.

More sirens were wailing in the distance, but the police response to the developing incident was ragged and disorganised. A second police car had just rolled up on the scene. The two officers aboard piled out into the street, pistols at the ready, taking in the scene of death and destruction: the bullet-riddled police car, one officer sprawled dead on the road, the other missing, and the driver of the civilian vehicle inert in a gleaming pool of blood, bits of twisted railing and broken glass and spent cartridge cases littered across the ground. But the one thing they didn't notice, until it was too late, was the squat, bloodied figure of the one-eared man emerging from the shattered boutique window behind them like some kind of demonic troll. Petru strolled up to the officers with a manic grin, shot the first one in the back of the head and then shot the second one in the face as he turned around. They fell over one another in a heap, making a twisted X on the ground.

This was even more fun than shooting dogs.

The street was completely deserted. Any citizens in the vicinity had fled for their lives long since. Drunk on blood and feeling like an invulnerable gangster rock star Terminator master of the universe, Petru stood in the middle of the carnage, raised both arms high in the air and screamed to the world in general, 'ANYONE ELSE WANT TO FUCK WITH ME?' When there was no reply he screamed, 'NO? I DIDN'T THINK SO!'

Nobody except the rest of the Ajaccio police force, who would be rolling up to the scene any time soon. The incoming sirens were getting louder. As invulnerable as he felt, Petru decided he would be gone before they arrived.

Petru considered his transport opportunities. The first police car was Swiss cheese, but the second was undamaged and its motor was still running. He stepped over the bodies of the two dead cops, threw his rucksack onto the passenger seat and himself in behind the wheel. That was when he happened to glance in his mirror and saw the headlights speeding up Avenue de Paris behind him. No light bar or siren. It wasn't a police car. As it passed under a street lamp he saw it was a blue Beemer.

The same kind of blue Beemer that the crippled guy drove. That bastard Ben Hope was back, and Petru's plan to steal away up the coast in a boat had just gone up in smoke.

Petru almost stepped out of the police car to confront him, but at the point of doing it he felt his courage shrivel like a deflated balloon. Though he hated himself for admitting it, the crippled guy was even more dangerous than he was. The way he'd taken down Albertu proved that. Petru was afraid of an armed confrontation with him in the open street. Besides, the cops would be here any moment.

Petru gritted his teeth in rage, jammed the police car into gear and took off.

Chapter 54

As Ben came fast down Avenue de Paris he could see the scene, like something out of an urban war zone. Bodies on the ground, smashed cars and a blown-out shop frontage. And Petru Navarro, jumping into the police car whose occupants he'd just shot to death.

The police car accelerated hard away, and Ben chased. Petru Navarro wasn't just a murdering psychopath on the rampage, he was an idiot too. Only an idiot would make a stolen cop car his getaway vehicle, because even a third-rate, down-at-heel police force like Corsica's would have their whole fleet kitted out with GPS trackers that could monitor their location in real time at the flick of a keypad. At any moment, the amplifying chorus of sirens Ben could hear would be right on them. He wanted to get to Petru before the police did.

Ben wasn't much into cars but he knew that what he was chasing was a Renault Mégane GT with all the performance bits they added to police interceptors. Probably good for 230 kilometres an hour top speed, and this one had a lunatic at the wheel. Petru was using up the whole road, straightening the bends kerb to kerb like a racing driver at Monaco, piling through red lights and ripping by the scanty night-time traffic as he raced eastwards towards the harbour and then cut north, running parallel with the quayside.

Ben was right on his tail. But now his rear-view mirror was filled with flashing blue light as the police finally made their appearance en masse. It looked like half the cops in Ajaccio had joined the chase. Ben was all too aware that the other half would be waiting somewhere ahead, deployed to cut them off. Their undermanned and relatively disorganised force likely didn't stretch to helicopters, but they had the SWAT teams and everything else.

Now they were hurtling up the long straight of Boulevard Sampiero, a high wall streaking by on one side and glimpses of the dark ocean and jetties and boats flashing through the trees and buildings to their right. Petru was driving like a man possessed. The Alpina's engine note climbed to a rich howl as the revs soared and the speedometer crept closer to the 200 kmh mark. And then Petru's taillights flared red as he braked for what was ahead.

As Ben had anticipated, the police had blocked the road. Barriers and armed response vehicles lined the boulevard from kerb to kerb, and more had barricaded an adjacent street to the left. Petru had dropped speed, but not much. Now Ben saw him lean out of the driver's window with his pistol in his left hand, the high-speed wind tearing at his clothes and hair and the white-orange muzzle flash as he started firing in the direction of the roadblock as though he thought he could blow it aside with bullets.

Storm was perched in the back of the Alpina with his

head through the gap in the front seats, eyes fixed on the road. Ben shoved him back and commanded him to get down. The dog hunkered in the rear footwell. Ben's fists tightened on the steering wheel and he braced himself for what was about to happen next.

And then it did. Flashes erupted from the police roadblock and sparks flew from the bodywork of the stolen cop car as Petru raced straight into a wall of gunfire. His car was weaving all over the road. A bullet cracked into the Alpina's windscreen and Ben felt the little hammer blows as more of them punched into his bodywork. It was just a matter of time before one found its way through to the cab.

Up ahead, Petru had ducked back inside his car and was steering a crazy course towards the police barriers. Then his brake lights flared again, and suddenly he was bearing sharp left into the junction with the adjacent sidestreet. A couple of patrol cars and a van blocked his path but Petru hammered straight into them, knocking them violently aside and making armed cops dive for safety. One officer was too slow to get out of the way, and Petru ran him down and rolled over him with both left-side wheels. Flashes from inside the stolen car as he rattled more shots off at them. A van window smashed. More return gunfire raked the stolen Mégane.

Now it was accelerating hard away again, and all Ben could do was hang on tight and follow him through the remnants of the broken barricade. He had to swerve to avoid the body of the run-over cop. It didn't look as though much could be done for the poor man. A crack, and Ben's right rear window burst apart, showering Storm in the back with glass fragments. Ben yelled at him to stay down.

Bearing inland now, away from the quayside. The road was narrower and climbed steadily as they cut deeper into the maze-like warren of streets of the centuries-old town. Ben went on chasing, close on his enemy's tail as Petru darted left and right, taking turnings apparently at random so that they cut a wildly jagged line between the buildings and red-tiled houses that clustered willy-nilly over the tiered urban landscape. The police were right behind them, sirens howling, filling the canyons between the looming buildings with myriad blue lights. Caught like the meat in a sandwich between the fugitive and the law, Ben knew this couldn't go on.

It didn't. Seconds later, Petru was leading the speeding procession in the wrong direction down a narrow one-way residential street when the stolen police car abruptly skidded ninety degrees left, tyres pattering and sliding, flattened a parked motor scooter, mounted the kerb and plummeted through the tight gap between two old houses into an alleyway. Or that was what Ben thought it was, until he steered hard into its mouth after Petru and saw that it was a long flight of steps carving back down between the buildings to the street tier below. Weeds sprouted up through the cracks in the steps and the crumbling walls were barely far enough apart for a car to pass through.

Only a deranged person would even try it. The downward angle was as steep as a ladder and the Renault was in serious danger of flipping tail over nose as Petru went careening down the steps like a demented bobsleigh driver. The only way to stop was to crash. The Renault was veering left and right in a crazy slalom, grinding and scraping against the walls on each side.

Ben had thrown cars, trucks and motorcycles into some hair-raising descents in his time but his heart was in his mouth as the Alpina flew down the impossible slope with its front suspension hammering up and down against the stops and both front wings crumpled. All he could see through the fissured windscreen were the gyrating taillights of the Renault just ten feet in front of him.

Then Petru hit the bottom of the steps with a loud scraping crash and veered out into the street. An instant later, the Alpina was following right behind, hitting the level ground with an impact that sent Storm tumbling against the back of the front seats and would have put Ben through the windscreen if he hadn't been belted up. Not a moment too late, because the police car that had ventured down the suicidal slope in Ben's wake had panic-braked midway and flipped over forwards. The car hurtled end over end, an unstoppable missile destroying itself and threatening to crush anything in its path. It reached the bottom of the steps half a racing heartbeat after the Alpina's tail had cleared the gap and came to a halt there, completely blocking the mouth of the stairway. The police car behind it smashed into the crumpled wreckage. Then the one behind that. Then the one behind that, jamming the stairway solid with crumpled metal. And then Ben saw no more, because he was chasing Petru away up the street.

It was just the two of them again. Petru's car was virtually in pieces, one wing hanging off and sending up a shower of sparks from the road as he went on screeching like a maniac through the streets. It was all Ben could do to keep up with him. Seconds later he realised it was more than he could do to keep up with him, because one of the Alpina's front tyres had blown out on impact with the bottom of the steps and the car had suddenly become hard to steer. The blown tyre was thumping like a machine gun against the inside of the wheel arch, sounding as if the whole front end of the car was about to explode. Ben fought to keep it in a straight line and maintain his speed, but the distance between him and the taillights of the Renault was quickly widening.

Ben swore as Petru skidded around a bend up ahead and was then lost from sight. Floundering around the corner in pursuit, he swore again. The street layout ahead was split into a fork, and he had got there momentarily too late to see which way Petru had gone.

If in doubt, always turn left. It was a motto that hadn't always served him well, but it was a fifty-fifty choice either way. Ben stamped on the gas and sent the swerving, hammering, half-controllable car up the left-hand fork. Around the next corner, the road opened up into a longer straight and he saw with a sinking heart that it was empty. He'd taken the wrong turn.

He threw the car around in a screeching one-eighty and stamped on the gas again, retracing his steps to the fork in the road. This time he took the right turn and accelerated fast along it, but he'd lost too many precious seconds. A little way further up the street he saw the taillights of the Renault where it had mounted the kerb at an angle and buried its front end in the rubble of a collapsed house doorway.

Ben skidded the Alpina to a halt beside the crashed police car and jumped out, drawing his pistol. The police car's driver side door was hanging open. There was nobody inside. Ben scanned the street. It was empty. Alleys and sidestreets ran off in different directions, and Petru could have disappeared down any of them.

Ben turned back towards the house, to see a middle-aged overweight guy dressed in stripy pyjamas emerging from the ruin of his home's doorway. He was gazing at the wrecked police car and scratching his head in confusion. He saw Ben approaching and said, 'Wh-what happened?'

Ben asked, 'Did you see which way he went?'

'I was in the bathroom when I heard the crash,' the householder muttered. 'It shook the whole house. Look at this mess. Who's going to pay for this?'

'Sir, did you see him or not?'

'Through the bathroom window. I saw a man run off. Didn't look like a police officer.' The householder pointed across the street. 'He went that way, I think.'

Maybe not the world's most reliable witness. 'You think?'

'Pretty sure that's where he went. If he's not the police, then are you?'

Ben ignored the question and looked where the man was pointing, towards the entrance of a pedestrian alley with two thick iron bollards barring the way to traffic. If Petru had gone that way, Ben wouldn't be able to follow by car. The car had pretty much reached the end of its road, in any case.

He stepped quickly back over to it and wrenched open the dented, scuffed back door, and Storm hopped out. The householder said, 'Is that your police dog? Are you going to catch the man who did this?'

'You'd better get back indoors, sir,' Ben warned him. 'He's a dangerous armed criminal.'

'You catch him and make him pay for my house!'

But Ben was already running across the street towards the alley, with Storm at his heel.

Chapter 55

At the bottom of the alley Ben found himself in a dimly lit pedestrian market precinct with shuttered shop and café front-ages with names like Spaghetti 3 and Rundinella. No sign of Petru. He hurried onwards, and fifty yards further down the precinct opened up into a little square with a couple of restaurants and a large corner nail salon, all closed up for the night. He peered hard into the shadows of recessed doorways, but there was nobody around here either. More maze-like streets radiated in all directions off the square. Impossible to tell which way Petru might have gone – and that was assuming the guy in pyjamas had been right that Petru had come this way at all.

Ben had lost him again.

It wasn't often that he felt completely lost and helpless, but he was feeling that way now. As he stood there gazing around him and wondering what the hell he was going to do now, Storm sidled up. A wet, cold German shepherd nose nuzzled Ben's side and a warm tongue licked his hand. Ben petted him, thankful for the comfort of the dog's company. But then it hit him that Storm was trying to say something. *Hey, don't forget I'm here. Maybe I can help.*

And maybe he could.

Ben took out the ear, unwrapped it and offered it to Storm to sniff at again.

'Can you find him for me, boy?'

It only took a tiny whiff for the dog's scent memory to be rekindled. He instantly reprised the behaviours Ben had seen him perform at Rocco Vanucci's apartment, sniffing loudly with his nose to the ground to draw as many scent molecules into his hypersensitive olfactory system as possible, and isolate the particular ones that would earn him his reward. There were few creatures as intensely focused or as fiercely joyful as a German shepherd with a job to do. He scouted busily in one direction, then gave that up and scouted in another.

'Find him, boy! Find him!'

The dog seemed to hesitate, standing stock still with his muzzle touching the pavement. And then he was off. He'd picked up the trail, and it led down one of the sidestreets off the square. No human technology ever invented could have told Ben which way to go.

Storm was moving at a fast trot and Ben had to run to keep up. The sidestreet had a mixture of residential homes and shuttered shop windows. Graffiti sprayed on the walls. The dog kept onwards. Ben ran faster.

And then, the warning signs that he'd been ignoring all this time suddenly came back to bite him. He was thirty yards down the street when his left ankle folded over. Pain speared all up his leg to his knee and he stumbled and almost fell. The agony was so intense that he had to catch his breath for a moment before he forced himself to keep going. He was suddenly mindful of Sandrine's stark advice, the day he'd persuaded her to take the plaster off: *You start running around on that leg unsupported and there's a chance that you could cripple yourself for life.*

'I'll take that chance,' Ben had said. But his luck had failed him. Forced to run with a lurching gait to keep weight off his left foot, now he was falling behind. Storm was out of sight around a corner. Ben was afraid of losing him. He tried to move faster, but the pain was too bad and he worried that his ankle might give up completely.

Ben was hurrying as best he could to catch up when from around the corner he heard a frenzy of wild barking, and a man's hoarse angry yell, then the flat report of a gunshot followed by a high-pitched canine yowl of distress. With his heart in his mouth, forgetting his own pain, he reached the corner and ran for all he was worth.

And there was Storm. He was lying on the pavement some distance up ahead, under the light of a street lamp. There was blood on the ground, dark and glistening. He wasn't moving. Nobody else in sight.

Icy cold horror swamped Ben's whole body. He called out the dog's name and reached him at a stumbling sprint. Dropped to his knees beside him.

'Storm! Storm!'

The dog raised his head, whimpered and licked Ben's hand. Even at a moment like this, he was full of love for his master. Ben feverishly checked him for the source of the blood, and found the gunshot wound high up on the dog's right shoulder. Storm tried to struggle to his feet, but then fell back down. Ben caressed him and spoke close to his ear, fighting to keep his voice calm and reassuring. 'Stay, boy. Don't move. I'll come back for you. I promise.'

Ben clambered to his feet and looked around him. Petru was gone again, but he hadn't escaped unhurt. Storm had managed to inflict some damage, and not all the blood on the ground was his. Ben saw the first big red spot of it gleaming under the street light. Then the second, and the third. There was a trail to follow. And this time, Ben was going to follow it.

He hated leaving his fallen companion behind. But there was no choice. He rechecked his pistol and set off in the direction Petru had gone.

Chapter 56

Petru hated that damned dog almost as much as he hated its owner. He'd have killed it, but the bullet he'd managed to divert its attack with had been the last round in his gun and there'd been no time to grab the dagger from his backpack to stab the vicious brute to death, because he knew Ben Hope wouldn't be far behind. The man was relentless.

And so Petru had left the dog where it fell, and run. His left jacket sleeve was shredded into tatters where it had grabbed him, and his arm felt numb and wouldn't work properly. Without slowing his pace he used his right hand to stuff his left into his jeans pocket. It was pissing blood all over the place, but at least it didn't swing about when he ran. He'd check the damage later. The important thing was that his legs were still working fine, and he still had his precious gold cross.

He sprinted around another street corner and found himself in a wider, straighter avenue that offered nowhere to hide from his pursuer. Spotting a gap in the wall with a flimsy wooden gate he shoved through it, into a narrow lane running off perpendicular to the street and leading around the back of a residential building.

Petru closed the gate behind him and ran along the lane. To the rear of the dark building were some fenced back yards that he guessed belonged to the residents of the apartments. He threaded his way through the shadows until he came to a door. It wasn't much less flimsy than the gate, and yielded after a few kicks. It seemed to be a back entrance into the apartments. Inside the hall he found a fire escape stairway, and ran up it.

Petru emerged from the stairwell into a dingy corridor, and crept along it looking for a place to hide. An automatic light came on and he saw there were numbered apartment doors to both sides of the corridor. He was thinking that someone's apartment would be a good place to take refuge in, when a door opened up ahead and an old guy with a scraggy neck like a chicken and crazy white hair sticking up at all angles peered sleepily out. The sound of kicking in the back door must have woken him. The old guy saw Petru and said, 'Hey, what's all the commotion? Who the hell are you?'

Petru hated old people, as a rule. This one was no different from the rest, just another geriatric fuck who'd outlasted his useful purpose and needed to be culled. Without a word, he strode up to the doorway and shoved the old guy hard, making him stagger backwards into his apartment. Petru stepped in after him and slammed the door shut behind them. The old guy was protesting and struggling and yelling loudly, 'You can't come in here. What do you want with me? Help! Help!'

'Shut up, you stupid old shit.'

But the old guy wouldn't shut up. He was too scrawny

and frail to put up any kind of a fight, but Petru was scared he would wake the neighbours with all the yelling, and next thing there would be more cops. He grabbed the old guy by the neck and frogmarched him into a tiny, fusty-smelling lounge room. Petru thought that the apartment was even more of a shithole than Rocco Vanucci's place. How could people stand living like this? It would be doing the old guy a kindness to put him out of his misery.

Petru shoved him, hard, and the old guy fell back into the sofa with a squawk. Petru stood over him, reached into his rucksack and drew out the glittering cross. 'See this? Nice, isn't it?' He pressed the secret gemstone button that released the hidden dagger with a satisfying click. He couldn't use his left hand, so he gripped the shaft of the cross between his knees and drew out the long, slim blade, holding it up to let the old guy see what was coming to him. The blade was still tacky and stained from the blood of the girl and the cop he'd stabbed earlier.

The old guy was too rigid with terror to move or speak. He stared up at his assailant with bewildered eyes and his mouth hanging open. He had few teeth left. Petru thought the silly old fuck would probably starve to death before long anyway, left to his own devices.

Petru lunged downwards and pushed the sharp tip of the steel through the old guy's chest and deep into his heart. He'd have liked to clamp his other hand over his victim's mouth, in case he let out a shriek. But he needn't have worried, because the old guy died almost immediately.

Petru drew out the blade, wiped it on the sofa cushions, inspected it and then carefully replaced it in its jewelled scabbard. His appreciation for its beauty increased every time he used it. If not for the fact that he needed the cash, he'd have loved to keep it for himself.

He considered his victim for a moment, then left him sitting there dead on the sofa and went into the bathroom. His left arm had gone from being numb to tingly, and now it was starting to hurt like a son of a bitch. He gingerly removed his jacket, then rolled up his shirt sleeve. His forearm looked like raw steak where the dog had ripped him. Wincing and muttering curses, he washed the blood off down the old man's grubby bathroom sink. More blood kept oozing out. Damn thing was going to need stitches. But he'd worry about it later. He wrapped a towel around it, and dry-swallowed some painkillers he found in the old guy's medicine cabinet along with a bunch of other pills.

His plan was to hunker down here until morning. The cops would be everywhere hunting for him, but he was confident of being able to slip out of Ajaccio unnoticed. His last port of call would be to Rocco Vanucci, to repay him for his betrayal. Then he'd head for the hills, to hole up and heal up for a while before returning to Porto Vecchio to look for another fence he could pass the cross on to.

In the meantime, if Ben Hope was able to find him here, then Petru had a surprise for him. Come to that, Petru *wanted* Hope to find him. He left the apartment door deliberately unlocked, turned off all the lights, then returned to the lounge and sat on the sofa next to the dead man. He drew out the dagger blade once more, laid it across his lap and waited in the darkness.

Chapter 57

Ben couldn't think about his canine companion lying injured in the street back there. And he couldn't think about the agony that shot like fire through his ankle with every lurching step. He had to follow the blood trail. He must follow this through to the end.

He reached a straighter, wider avenue with more shops and houses and cafés, and found the trail come to an abrupt stop right next to where a smeared red handprint showed on a gate inset into the wall. With his pistol in his hand he carefully pushed the gate open, ready in case his enemy might be lurking right behind it. Instead, the telltale blood spots continued along a path around the side of a residential building, past a row of back yards, and then to a back door that had been very obviously, and recently, forced open.

Entering a hallway, Ben found another blood trace on the second step of a fire escape staircase. Another on the fifth step. Another on the first-floor landing, and a red smear on the handle of a door that opened into a murky passage with numbered apartment doors either side. The building was quiet, its sleeping residents blissfully unaware of the danger in their midst. As Ben crept along the passage he could feel Petru's presence close by. He could almost smell it.

The first floor of the building comprised apartments seven to fourteen, with odd numbers to his left and evens to his right. He traced the length of the passage, searching for blood spots. He found two of them near the second door on the right, number ten, and none beyond. Apartment ten it was, then.

Ben paused a long time outside the door, listening hard, but could hear nothing from inside. He contemplated the best play. Older apartment buildings in France were built with solid doors and enough heavy bolts and deadlocks to make them virtually impregnable. His own flat in Paris, seldom used these days, was in one of those grand old buildings where things had been made to last. But this wasn't one of them. Running his hand along the surface of the door and frame they felt thin and flimsy, and his intuition told him they were probably equipped with minimal security.

Whatever was behind that door, Ben wanted to find out. He could do it the long-winded stealthy way using his trusty little collection of lock picks. Or he could fall back on the time-honoured methods he'd employed many times before now, when bursting in on the lairs of terrorists and kidnappers, using the three deadly principles he'd learned in the SAS. Speed. Aggression. Surprise.

Kicking down a door with a half-busted ankle was going to hurt like hell. He thought, *Fuck it.* Took a step away from the door, ready to rock his weight backwards on his left heel and smash the sole of his right foot against the wood where the lock met the frame. But at the very last moment, some instinct or sixth sense made him hesitate. He crept back towards the door and very slowly, very cautiously, tried the handle.

The door wasn't even locked.

Ben pushed it open an inch. Listened hard, waited for a response, but there was none. Then another inch, and still nothing happened. He eased the door open wide enough to slip through, and stepped into the darkness of apartment ten.

Absolute stillness, utter silence and pitch darkness. Ben remained immobile for a long minute. He could sense death in here. But he could sense something else, too. A heaviness in the atmosphere, immeasurable, almost too subtle to detect, like a ripple in the aether. The presence of something watchful and malevolent that lurked here, darker than the darkness, waiting for him. Daring him to enter its domain. Willing him to.

Ben stalked deeper into the apartment. Making no sound. Finger on the trigger. Barely breathing, only peripherally aware of the jolting agony that each step fired through his left ankle. As his vision slowly adjusted to the pitch blackness, he could make out shapes and contours among the deep shadows.

When the attack came, it all happened in a wild rush. One of the contours detached itself from its background and moved towards him with blinding speed and uncanny silence. Ben spun towards the threat, raising his pistol. Then came the whistle of something long and thin slicing through the air. Ben felt the cold steel slash through his sleeve and split the flesh of his wrist, and the sudden visceral shock of the cut made his fingers involuntarily lose their grip on his weapon. The gun fell from his hand.

Unarmed and hurt in the darkness, facing a murderous psychopath with a razor-sharp dagger. Ben had been in better places. Only one of them would walk out of this one.

The black shadow closed in on him, bearing down with fury and rage. The stiletto blade hissed towards him again, carving a fast horizontal arc that would have split his throat wide open in a fatal gash if he hadn't stepped back quickly enough. Ben heard his attacker's grunt of effort as the weapon swung harmlessly past. He struck out hard towards the sound, and felt his knuckles connect solidly with flesh and bone.

For a moment they edged apart, circling one another in the darkness. Ben's eyes had adjusted and he could make out the expression of burning hatred on his enemy's face. Ben's punch had opened up a cut on his cheek.

'I was hoping you'd find me here,' said Petru Navarro. 'You shouldn't have come looking for me. Because now you're going to die.'

'One of us has to, Petru,' Ben said. 'That's how it has to be. It always was.'

Then the blade was coming at him again, point first instead of edgeways now, spearing towards his sternum and ready to skewer him right through. But its needle tip found only empty space, because Ben was no longer where he'd been quarter of a second ago. Petru felt the dagger go nowhere, and hesitated. Only for an instant, but that was long enough for Ben to move in. He flowed like water around his opponent, trapped the hand clutching the weapon, twisted it the way only a man schooled in the art of maximum damage can twist it.

All the way to its breaking point, and beyond.

And in the next instant, Petru Navarro's right wrist was snapped like a dead branch and the golden-handled dagger was in Ben's hand. Ben brought its heavy pommel down hard on Petru's head. It hit with a skull-cracking *thonk*. Ben hit him again. Savage. Uncompromising. Petru fell away from him and disappeared into the darkness. Ben heard the heavy thud of his enemy's body falling to the floor.

Petru was down, but he was still battling like a cornered tiger. Thrashing legs lashed out at Ben, trying to bring him down with a kick to the knee. Ben dodged, thrust the dagger out and Petru's foot impaled itself on its sharp point. Ben jerked the blade loose, thrust again, felt the steel sink into the flesh of a leg.

Then Ben was on him, down on the floor, grappling, striking, feeling the berserk, unbridled fury of the man under him. Petru fought with hardly a sound, though his right wrist was all but useless and Ben realised that his left forearm was badly damaged too, torn up by German shepherd teeth. Most men would have given up the fight at that point, but not Petru Navarro. The more you hurt the man, the more dangerous he seemed to become. He would claw and gouge and bite and head butt his way to victory if Ben let him.

Now the struggle reached its bloody climax. This was the moment when you kill it or it kills you, all or nothing, in a burst of pure primal energy that lasts only a few instants but seems to transcend all notion of time. Ben pounded the heavy gold pommel into Petru's face, his forehead, smashing and smashing again until he felt the man's energy begin to ebb, the fight leaking out of him like water from a perforated bucket.

After a few more blows, Petru was too weakened to resist any longer. He slumped back against the floor.

He was done. It was over.

Or, almost.

There was still one detail to take care of.

'Fucking kill me then, Hope,' Petru muttered through his bleeding lips and splintered teeth. 'Go on and do it.'

There had been so much Ben wanted to say to the man. But now that the moment had come at last, he no longer had the words, or the will to say them. He just wanted it to be done with. He said only, 'You had this coming, Petru. Tell me you understand why.'

Petru's bloody teeth snarled up at him from the shadows. He spat blood and muttered something obscene. No, of course he didn't understand. A man like him never could, never would. It was just in his nature to be the way he was, like a venomous snake or an infectious bacterium.

Ben knelt astride his defeated enemy. He knew what he had to do. The act of killing a fellow human being, up close like this, face to face, metal and meat, was the core *raison d'être* of the profession for which he had trained. That didn't mean he enjoyed doing it. But a world that contained Petru Navarro was one he couldn't live in himself.

'His name was Victor,' Ben said. 'He was a better man than any of us. I just wanted you to know that.'

Petru Navarro still said nothing.

And then Ben put the knife in.

EPILOGUE

Two weeks later

Somewhere in the flat, open, wintry countryside between Caen and Lisieux, the SNCF train rattled along the tracks towards its destination. Ben sat alone in a window seat, watching the world zip by without really seeing it, and slowly drinking railway coffee from a paper cup without really tasting it. Few people occupied his car. The guy sitting across the aisle was buried in a newspaper. Ben's green bag lay on the seat next to him and the two opposite him were empty, which allowed him to elevate his left foot.

The ankle was much less painful than it had been, but the new cast was a nuisance. He'd been wearing it for twelve days now, courtesy of Sandrine, who had given him the whole 'I-told-you-so' speech, a tongue-lashing as severe as anything a disgruntled army sergeant-major ever threw at a misbehaving squaddie. But even she'd had to admit that the damage could have been a lot worse. The ankle hadn't completely refractured, and as long as he promised to take it easy and didn't do anything really stupid for a couple more months, it would heal up as good as new. The knife laceration that ran six inches down his right wrist and forearm had needed thirty stitches, but would be a fading scar long before then.

As if he would ever do anything really stupid, he'd told her.

Though Ben didn't worry too much about such things, he'd been much more concerned about his wounded canine friend. If not for the intervention of an unlikely new ally, Titus Navarro, Storm probably wouldn't have made it.

The last two weeks had been a time of reflection. He'd replayed recent events so many times in his mind, but they were still as vivid to him as the moment they'd happened. Ben's first urgent action after leaving Apartment 10 had been to hurry back to where Storm was still lying there bleeding and half unconscious in the empty street. His second action had been to call the number he'd been given by the Corsican crime boss's men. Titus Navarro had sounded far more upset about the dog than he was about the news of his late nephew's demise. And he'd come through for Ben.

Within minutes of the phone call, a car had appeared and moments later he and Storm were being whisked across town for an emergency consultation with a vet whose surgical skills and discretion Titus assured him could be relied on completely. His name was Marcello, and before relocating his private practice from Porto Vecchio to Ajaccio, he'd been responsible for saving Titus's beloved Pomeranian, Mitzi, from a life-threatening illness none of the other vets could figure out.

By the time Ben and Marcello got Storm on the operating table, he was deeply unconscious and his vital signs were beginning to fade. It had been touch and go. The vet had worked hard to resuscitate him, and he'd had to go deep to pull out the bullet. For several hours that night, Ben had been frantic with worry that the dog might not make it. But Storm had fought like the hero that he was, and as dawn had broken next morning, he'd opened his eyes and given his first feeble bark.

From that moment on, he'd gone from strength to strength, to his master's intense relief. The pair of them had been flown home in luxury aboard a jet plane belonging to Ben's billionaire former client Auguste Kaprisky. Storm was currently convalescing at home at Le Val, regaled with fresh sirloin steaks to boost his strength. He'd soon be fighting fit again.

It was also thanks to Uncle Titus's reach and power that the various loose ends associated with Ben's visit to Corsica had been so neatly tied up. In the wake of the dramatic events in Ajaccio, the body of Petru Navarro would never be found. That was what Titus had meant by 'keeping it in the family'. His connections had seen to it that the remains of his disgraced nephew were magicked out of Ajaccio and transported in secret to the town of Lecci, north of Porto Vecchio, there to be entombed deep under the cement of a major construction project being overseen by someone who owed them a favour.

Ben had never been much in favour of corruption, but it certainly had its uses at times. At his own request and to avoid facing difficult questions, the bullet-riddled Alpina had similarly been erased as though it never existed. He hardly missed the car. He'd already lost count of how many he'd had trashed, crashed, blown up or sunk. It was a mistake to get sentimental about these things.

The old man Petru had murdered in the apartment building in Ajaccio was another, more delicate matter. Fortunately, once again, the Navarro family organisation had had considerable experience of such dealings, circumventing the need for the authorities to be involved, and Uncle Titus's men had quickly taken care of the situation. Petru's elderly victim had turned out to be one Alcide Brambilla, a lonely widower with a terminal illness and no surviving family. Titus, even more appalled and disgusted at his nephew's behaviour, had given his word that poor Alcide would be given a lavish funeral as a mark of respect.

Meanwhile, as far as the police were concerned, Ben and Storm had been the victims of a completely unrelated gun and knife attack at the hands of one or more unknown perpetrators, most certainly an attempted robbery. Hey, these things happened all the time in the lawless streets of Ajaccio. Another stabbing had taken place the very same night, this time involving a young girl, now recuperating in hospital. In any case the cops had bigger fish to fry than minor incidents like that, because they were still hunting for the unidentified killer who'd murdered several of their officers and led them a merry dance across the city.

And so, the waters had closed over Petru Navarro and his exploits, with barely a ripple to mark his passing. A tiny piece of good had been done for the world, by ensuring the safety of the man's future victims. But now that the deed was accomplished, all Ben could feel was a sense of melancholy emptiness. After hanging around at Le Val for a few days, helping as best he could with the repairs and rebuilding, caring for Storm and with thoughts of his lost friends increasingly on his mind, he'd asked Jeff Dekker to give him a lift to the railway station in Valognes.

And here he was, speeding towards Paris. Inside his bag on the empty seat next to him was the gold cross, cleaned and shiny and now on its way to its new home.

Later that afternoon, the train pulled into the Gare Saint Lazare. Drinking in the familiar sights and smells of Paris, Ben wandered out of the station and soon found the obligatory battered and grubby white Mercedes saloon at the taxi stand.

'Where to, buddy?'

'The Louvre Museum,' Ben replied.

The meeting had been arranged by phone the previous day. Ben was greeted at the museum by Victor's friend Jules Dampierre, whom he'd last seen at the funeral. The old, old man seemed to have aged ten years since then. Also present at the meeting was Henri Carbonneau, the museum curator, who shook Ben's hand with great solemnity and thanked him for coming. Nothing was said about the bruises on Ben's face, the dressing on his wrist or the fresh cast on his foot. They obviously sensed that retrieving the cross had required a certain degree of effort, but were far too discreet to probe for details.

Ben was led to a private room where, for the second time, the priceless gold cross that Queen Eleanor of Aquitaine had gifted to her loyal crusader and protector Gaspard la Roche nine centuries ago was taken out and laid in front of the admiring eyes of the experts.

'I understand that Jules has told you of its unique background, its inestimable historical importance, its iconic cultural significance?' Carbonneau asked Ben, unable to tear his gaze away from it. He was practically drooling.

Ben replied, 'I don't give a damn what it is. I wish I'd never laid eyes on it, and that it was still buried in the ground. It's caused nothing but pain. I brought it here to offer to the museum, because that's what Victor would have wanted. Otherwise, I'd happily have tossed it in the sea or had it melted down into a golden bowl to feed my dog out of. God knows he's earned it.'

Whether or not the speechless curator believed him, Ben would never know. But he meant every word.

'There is also the financial aspect,' Carbonneau said nervously after a beat. 'As you are the cross's de facto owner, on behalf of the museum I'm authorised to make you a generous offer, subject of course to the usual conditions . . .'

'Relax, Henri,' Ben said. 'I'm not interested in your money. The cross is yours now. Take it. Before I change my mind about the dog bowl.'

Carbonneau managed to contain his excitement to mutter some expressions of gratitude. 'Well, gentlemen, on such an occasion I believe our dear old friend would also have wanted us to celebrate,' Jules Dampierre said wistfully, producing a bottle of champagne and three crystal flutes. 'Let us drink to the recovery of the crusader's cross, and to our beloved Victor, who would have cherished this moment more than anything in the world.'

'I'll drink to Victor,' Ben said. He couldn't refuse to raise a glass, but he hadn't intended on staying any longer than he had to, and once the toast had been drunk it was time for him to go. They shook hands again, and he left the museum without another glance at the cultural icon of inestimable historic importance. He would never see it again, and that suited him just fine.

Rather than take another taxi straight back to the station, he decided to walk for a while. He was in no particular hurry. Moving slowly with his new walking stick and smoking a Gauloise, he made his way from the Louvre along the cobbled quay named after some famous French president. It was a cold, crisp day in a city that he used to love, and maybe one day would be able to love again. Right now, the Seine looked as steely and bleak under the winter sky as he felt inside. The arches of the Pont des Arts were visible in the distance, and further away behind that he could see the towers and flying buttresses of Notre Dame.

A little way up the street, right on the corner with the Quai du Louvre, was a café-bar that Ben had been to before. He paused outside. Some things change in this life. But others never will.

He thought, *Fuck it*. Tossed away his cigarette and went inside. Perched on a stool at the bar, he hung his stick on the rail and said, 'Give me a whisky. Single malt, double, as it comes, no ice.'

'Coming right up, monsieur,' the barman said with a smile.

THEY TOOK HIS FRIEND.

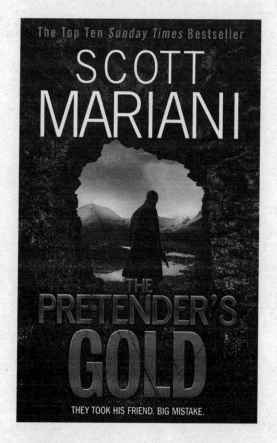

BIG MISTAKE.

EVIL NEVER RESTS.

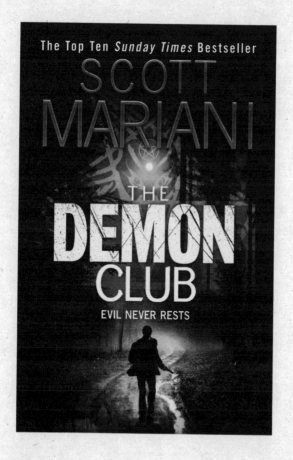

THE TRUTH HAS
BEEN BURIED . . .

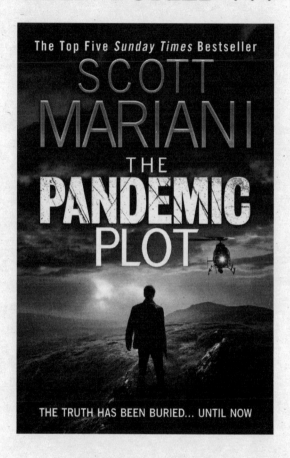

The Top Five *Sunday Times* Bestseller

SCOTT MARIANI

THE PANDEMIC PLOT

THE TRUTH HAS BEEN BURIED... UNTIL NOW

UNTIL NOW.

Ben Hope returns in a thrilling new book

May 2022

Available to pre-order now